THE

GOVERNOR'S

DAUGHTER

THE

GOVERNOR'S

DAUGHTER

DAUGHTERS *of the*
NEW AMERICAN REVOLUTION

★★★ BOOK ONE ★★★

MARIA ERENI DAMPMAN

The Governor's Daughter
Daughters of the New American Revolution
—Book One—

Copyright © 2021 by Maria Ereni Dampman

A Lickenpoodle Press Publication

Lickenpoodle Press
Attn: Permissions Coordinator
P.O. Box 255
Round Hill, VA 20142

ISBN: 978-1-7371770-0-5 (paperback)
ISBN: 978-1-7371770-1-2 (ebook)

Editorial development and creative design support by Ascent:
www.spreadyourfire.net

For my beloved husband.

When I had been silenced, you taught me to speak.
When I lost faith, you taught me to believe.
When I stumbled, you steadied me, and
When I fell, you taught me to fly.

1

July 2, 2045

Emma

The enormous dust bunny lurking in the corner of the room bares
its teeth and snarls, enraged that we dare disturb its slumber. The
gray beast, a mixture of multiple years' worth of over-teased hair,
sloughed skin cells and chunks of congealed makeup rumbles a low
growl of warning every time we invade its territory. We give the brute
a wide berth, understanding and accepting the boundaries it has set
for us. We aren't looking for a fight, none of us interested in starting
a war that history has already proved we are destined to lose.

I shiver in my embroidered corset and voluminous petticoats, the
temperature in this room far too cold for comfort in my current state
of undress. Even when I'm eventually fully clothed, the satin and tulle
won't alleviate my icy fingers and frozen toes. I wonder for whose
benefit it has to be sixty degrees in here. Certainly not ours.

I'm thankful when a torrid breeze created by an industrial-strength
blow dryer warms my arms until I realize it also sends the dust creature careening in my direction. At first I'm tempted to draw my feet
to my chest, not wanting to risk ruining my never-worn shoes, but I
change my mind. In a moment of uncharacteristic bravery, I leave my

feet planted on the floor and dare the savage organism to invade the space I have claimed as my own. I narrow my eyes in warning as I stare it down, the two of us standing off like two territorial cowboys in those cheesy old west movies they haven't shown on TV since the early 2030s.

I'm fairly certain no one has ever bit it as a result of death by dust bunny, but hey, I guess there's always a first. I know there are certainly worse ways to go, but just to be safe, I strike first when the dirt devil lunges. Mere seconds before the creature makes contact with my ankle, I lift my leg and stab my attacker in the heart with my jewel-encrusted stiletto. My victim disintegrates into a sloppy poof of particles that sticks haphazardly to my shoe.

I take a perverse pride in my handiwork. What took years of neglect to create is now dead, my dainty diamond-studded shoe apparently as deadly to dust fauna as any saw-toothed dagger. I don't feel remorse for what I've done. After all, it was a *dust bunny* for Christ's sake. There was not a living, breathing molecule anywhere in its sinister little body, the only thing giving it life being my freakishly overactive imagination.

Do I feel sorry for it? Hell, no.

I *envy* it.

I think about death a lot these days, often finding myself wondering what it would feel like to die. I don't mean what it would feel like to get shot, or starve, or drown, because I'm pretty sure that part has to suck. What piques my interest is what, if anything, you feel right *after* your heart takes that final beat.

I like to think that final moment is peaceful, a moment where you hover over yourself, omnipresent yet unfeeling. I imagine you aren't sad or angry or happy or *anything*, because, well, you're dead. After all, if you aren't breathing, you're probably more concerned with that particular problem than how you *feel* about no longer being alive.

I imagine that initial moment of death feels exactly how I feel right now. Despite the fear and anxiety crackling in the air like an unfurling bolt of lightning, I feel absolutely nothing. I care even less.

If this is what it feels like to die, then I've been dying for years.

I find these experiences of mind and body detachment both terrifying and comforting. Although I know this sensation cannot possibly be normal, I'm not afraid. This feeling of disunion has always been a friend to me, a soothing retreat during some of the worst periods of my life. It's a place where I can escape and no one can hurt me, a place for me to safely lick the too-frequent wounds that come with harboring a traitorous mind.

There is an electricity to the air as hairstylists and makeup artists put the final touches on their respective masterpieces. The woman next to me is contemplating just one more curl to her charge's already over-styled hair while another is second guessing the saccharine shade of bubble gum pink painted on her client's lips. She's looking for the color that represents just the right mix of child-like purity and ravish-able woman, the color guaranteed to make her the most sought after stylist for next year's ceremony. I wish I could tell her that the color she's looking for, that shade that straddles the fine line between Madonna and whore, does not exist.

"Move your fat ass over," a stylist hisses too loudly to the makeup artist blocking access to her client's hair, the hot curling iron in her hand brandished like a weapon.

"I've been working around you for the past hour. It's my turn now," the artist spits back.

A dirty look from the women at the table next to them does nothing to silence the bickering. I could stop their squabbling with one look, one word, but I just don't care enough to do so. It's not worth the energy.

I soothe my budding anxiety by studying my dingy surroundings. The clattering AC unit in the ceiling drips steadily into an overflowing bucket, the ceiling a Rorschach test of water stains giving away the inherent disease of the decaying roof. Faded floral wallpaper peels along the seams, the glue giving up its desire to hold things together in the same way I imagine many of tonight's tributes have already surrendered their will to live.

For being the evening's 'honored' guests, they sure as hell have done nothing to make us feel special. They couldn't even be bothered to vacuum the dressing room. Bastards.

I am getting colder by the minute. They do this, I think, to freeze our bodies into submission, not wanting us to sweat, perspire, or even glisten. Girls of our class are above having such bodily functions according to the powers that be, whoever they are. God help the girl that accidentally lets loose a fart at one of these events. I shudder at the thought of what sort of punishment would follow such an act of disrespect.

I'm not at all surprised that in this pivotal moment I'm having these sort of crazy thoughts. I've known forever that there's something seriously wrong with my brain, my ability to think the wrong thing at the worst possible time getting me into a few lifetime's worth of trouble. I remind myself what I've been told by my father so many times that I've lost count—that I am blessed and should be grateful, and that there are a million young ladies who would kill to be in my designer shoes.

Sure, I have spent the past nineteen years living in luxury as the pampered possession of wealthy parents. I live in what many would consider a palace, and unlike the majority of the nation, I have never once worried from where my next meal will come. I know I should be on my knees, thanking my parents, the Lord, and whoever else I'm forgetting at the moment for all the blessings in my life.

Yet, I just can't bring myself to do it.

If I was a *good girl, a dutiful daughter, a worthy woman,* I would have already said my prayers of thanksgiving and been looking forward to my upcoming rite of passage with pride and excitement.

Instead, I'm scoping out the exits and looking for some way out of tonight's festivities. I know very well I shouldn't think about the things I do, the times my thoughts leaked between my lips getting me into enough trouble to last a lifetime. I try to be good, I really do, but the more I try to muzzle my overactive brain the more defiant it becomes.

I don't know why obedience is so hard for me. The other girls in the room appear to be agreeably, even if not necessarily happily, doing their duty. Their eyes are modestly downcast as they remain silent unless spoken to and then only respond in the sweetest of whispers. As we've all been taught, their hands are folded gently in their laps, their right delicately draped over their left. *Always* right over left. I don't know why and I'm afraid to ask.

I check my own hands and find my left is over my right.

Get it together, Emma. You screw things up tonight and your father will kill you.

In theory, being a biddable daughter is not remotely difficult. Remain silent unless you are asked to speak, then open mouth, let the words they want to hear come out, close mouth. Smile. Do only what you are told and always behave like a lady. Follow the rules set by your father, the State, the Church and never, under the penalty of death, have an original thought. *Ever.*

Many years ago, my brother told me if unconditional obedience was really that easy, we wouldn't need to be threatened into compliance. He told me stories from before the Great War about rebellious teenagers who voiced original thoughts and were lauded for them. Back then, people encouraged acts and words of youthful idealism using words like *courageous* and *strong*. Those same actions and ideals are now vehemently condemned with shameful words like *perfidious* and *treason*. What once were acts of childish indiscretion punishable by having cell phones taken away are now grounds for beatings, imprisonment and even death.

My, how times have changed.

As I've gotten older, it's become a full-time job just remembering to keep my mouth shut. The watchers are always lurking, their word against yours all it takes to destroy a life. The one responsible for your death may be a stranger or a friend but often the danger comes from inside your own family. It is truly a sad state of affairs not to trust those who share your blood but the rewards for turning in a subversive are, for most, often too great to think twice. The New State Church tells us it's the Christian thing to do—to turn in your brothers and sisters for their misdeeds—so they can be brought to the light. It also doesn't matter if the accusations are true, all that matters is they are made.

An announcement that we have but a half hour left to prepare jolts me back to reality. The room erupts into renewed frenzy as stylists commence their last minute preparations. As if on cue, every one of them grabs a perfume, a hair spray, an over-powdered chunk of fluff and emits copious amounts of sneeze-inducing pollutants into the already over-saturated air. Everything in the near vicinity, including my bare shoulders, is already covered in a thick, sticky layer of hair spray, the fresh coating landing on my chilled shoulders just another layer of lacquer. I lick my lips, the bitter taste of aerosol products making me grimace. If this evening I am honored with a goodnight kiss, the gentleman's lips that meet mine will taste the acrid flavor.

I hope he doesn't get angry when I don't taste as sweet as my father has lied and promised I will be.

I glance at the other girls from under my thick, false lashes and wonder who my fellow tributes are and how they got to be so *blessed* to share this propitious occasion with me. When I catch the eye of the pretty, white-blonde girl seated at the table across from me, I can't help but roll my eyes to see how she responds. My annoyance is clear in the expression of tedium and contempt that I wonder if she also feels but doesn't feel safe enough to show. She gasps in horror at my irreverence, her mouth forming a ladylike O of shock as her hand flies up to cover her surprised expression. She breaks our tenuous bond with a self-righteous huff and turns away, no doubt disgusted by my lack of decorum.

There's always one in every crowd who's drunk just a little too much of the Committee's Kool-Aid.

I want to laugh at the ridiculousness of my current situation but I'm just too tired, too annoyed, too stinking *hungry* to bother. I haven't eaten in two days and I am uncharacteristically famished. It's amazing how much you want something you are told you can't have when otherwise you wouldn't care. All of us being "honored" tonight are suffering from forced food abstinence, the twenty-four hours before today's auspicious ceremony a mandatory fast dictated by The New State Church. My father felt that wasn't enough, that forty-eight hours of fasting were more appropriate for a girl of my status. I know he doesn't give a rat's ass about the religious significance of today. I think he only forces my adherence to the ridiculous edict in hopes I'll be too weak to misbehave.

Some of the girls' mothers and grandmothers are here, primping, priming, and smiling sadly at the fruit of their loins. Their hopeful dreams for their daughters to have a better future than theirs is etched in the lines around their eyes and mouths, every one of them careful to keep their true feelings about tonight behind tight-lipped masks of approval. Despite her promises to attend to me today, I'm not surprised my mother has failed to appear. Last time I saw her was before breakfast when she silently downed her customary handful of morning pills with three giant mimosas. With tears in her eyes, she wished me luck before claiming one of her daily migraines and stumbling back to her rooms. Although she tried to be stealthy, no one missed her swiping a new bottle of vodka from the bar for her day's consumption.

As for Mother Barbara? Well, she's too insulted at not being invited to the ceremony as a participant or honored guest to bother to attend. God knows that unless there's something in it for my selfish grandmother, she has no time for anyone.

Thanks, ladies. Nice to know you are every bit as helpful getting me through this ordeal as I thought.

I like to think my mother's heavy drinking is something new, a symptom of her difficulty dealing with my rite of passage. I would like to think that she cares, that she's worried for me. I wish to hear whispered words of solidarity, to hear her say my participation in tonight's event is as hard on her as it is on me, but I know it's not. My mother hasn't cared about anything except her latest fix in well over a decade. I have no idea why today of all days I'm having last-minute fantasies of her swooping in to save me or where this glimmer of hope is coming from. I haven't had a reason to hope in years.

The girl at the table next to me is being stuffed into her too-tight gown. I cringe as I watch the roll of excess flesh fold painfully over itself as she whines in protest. The corset laces snap under the excessive strain, sending her stylist stumbling backwards and crashing to the floor on her ass, the broken ties still clutched in her fists. Before I can stop myself, I snort out an unexpectedly loud laugh and the women nearly dislocate their necks as they spin angrily to face me. I quickly compose myself and look around the room accusingly, trying to act like the unladylike noise didn't come from me.

I feel my stylist's presence over my shoulder, the rustle of my gown in her arms giving away her arrival. "My grand-mama always said you can't fit ten pounds of shit in a five pound bag. Turns out the ol' bitch knew what she was talkin' about."

I burst into a loud peal of laughter that echoes in the otherwise mirthless room. Caitlin's whispered southern drawl is a balm to my tattered nerves, the naughty gleam in her cornflower-colored eyes the only sign of her involvement in my unladylike outburst.

Bless her heart. The all-purpose phrase she taught me earlier this year comes to mind, the words that range in meaning from a genuine desire to bless to a veiled, ladylike *fuck you.* I mean the words this time the first way. Caitlin is my guardian angel, my friend, my confidante who always knows just what to say to calm me. I don't know how I would get through this without her.

Caitlin kneels at my feet and looks up into my face that, despite my continued giggles, I know is as pale and frightened as those of my fellow honorees. I nod and smile as I blink back the tears that suddenly form in my eyes.

"You gonna be okay, sugar?" Caitlin's words of concern are the first and only ones I've heard today and they touch me more than she could ever imagine.

"I'm just nervous." I give her a quivering, implausible smile. "I'll be fine." I choke on my words, the lie catching in my throat. I look up to the water-stained ceiling, hoping the backward tilt of my head will somehow force the tears back to wherever they originated.

A girl across the room, who at most looks like she's twelve years old and has been sniffling for the past hour, finally loses her emotional battle and begins to cry. She's not leaking the occasional tear—oh no, she's crying like it's the end of the world. The tiny child's attendants try to quiet her, begging her to not ruin their handiwork. There are hours' worth of makeup on that child, all in an unsuccessful attempt to make her look older. The spackled-on cosmetics have failed their purpose. The tarantula-like false lashes and too-bright lipstick making the girl look like a baby prostitute. It's hard to tell if the sickening final result of her team's hard work is by mistake or purposeful design.

I have heard rumors that some of the more perverted attendees, ironically usually the higher-ranking members of The New State Church, actually request that type of look for the younger ones. I wonder if her parents slipped and told her what is about to happen, if she knows what her future holds and it's as awful as we all fear.

Buck up, Buttercup. As bad as things are, at least you aren't her.

I wish I could go over there and comfort her but I'm not allowed. There is nothing I can do except pray that somehow this poor child pulls herself together. I wonder if she's simply too young to understand that today is not the one to test the bars of her gilded cage. My heart aches for her, for me, and yes, even for the girls too stupid to realize that this event is not a to-die-for moment, and we are anything but lucky.

"Deep breaths, sweetie. It's all goin' to be okay."

Caitlin must see the bleary look in my eyes and can tell my vacant look is more than fear. My body has joined forces with my brain to bring me to my knees, the two days of hard fasting taking its toll on my ninety-four pound body. My hands shake as disorientation creeps into my sapphire eyes, Caitlin immediately putting the pieces together and realizing that if she doesn't do something quick she'll be picking my ass up off the floor.

She nods conspiratorially as she reaches for her purse and turns her back to the armed guard at the door. She discreetly peers around the room while pouring a few inches of some clear, fizzy liquid from a bottle into a plastic cup. Her eyes urge me to drink it quickly, the sweetness surprising me as I greedily gulp the contents before I'm caught. The bubbly sugar water buoys my body, the small act of dissension just what I need to calm my mind with its illusion of control.

"Better?"

I nod. It's moments like these when I realize I don't know what I would do without Caitlin. She's the closest I've ever come to having a girlfriend in my entire life even if she is a paid member of my father's staff.

The clock over the door chimes the quarter hour. Fifteen minutes to go. Caitlin helps me into my gown, the white satin gently hugging my body. The artful tailoring somehow even manages to give the illusion my lithe dancer's form possesses a few modest curves. Below the tightly cinched waist the yards of fabric fall to the floor in a stunning array of overlapping underskirts. She leads me to the full-length mirror and I take a long look at the end-product of over six months' worth of careful design and planning.

Unlike the other honorees, my gown is not flouncy or lacy, there are no large bows or childish frills. The silhouette is womanly, the only adornment a thick crust of pearls and diamonds across the bodice that makes my small breasts appear larger. The top half of the gown feels more like a piece of armor than a dress, hundreds of thousands of dollars of perfect diamonds and smooth pearls heavy enough to stop a close-range bullet.

The gown is obviously not meant for protection, but to show off my father's wealth and power. I may be an honored tribute but even I'm not stupid enough to think this ceremony is about me. I am his prop, nothing more than the proof of his virility, his abundant wealth and nearly limitless power. I am something of his to control, to barter and sell to suit his needs. Tonight he will act as if he cares for me even though I am, by far, the least favorite of his possessions.

I am stirred from my thoughts by the booming of someone tapping on a too-loud microphone, the announcer cheerily stating they are ready to begin. The girl that was so offended by my eye-roll looks at me expectantly, her fear-filled eyes now begging that I somehow stop the ensuing insanity.

I cock an eyebrow in surprise and wonder if maybe, *just maybe*, deep down inside more of these girls feel like I do than I thought. Maybe that's why they don't let us talk to one another. They don't want us finding strength in numbers.

My breath catches in my chest and I cannot breathe; I feel cold all over yet my face is flaming. My hands are trembling and my legs have turned to stone pillars rooting me to the ground. Knowing I have to walk down those stairs, that there's no way of stopping the show that will go on, has turned my body into a series of conflicting sensations.

I wonder if this is how Anne Boleyn felt when she walked towards her executioner's waiting blade?

A gut feeling tells me I'm walking into danger, my inner crystal ball warning me to watch every step. I know that tonight can only go one of two possible ways, that I'm either going to execute my destiny or be executed by it. Just like Anne Boleyn, there will be no reprieve, there will be no last second pardon. I will perform my duty.

I have no other choice.

After our attendants are ordered to leave, we tributes form a line behind the mahogany double doors, my position at the end of the line symbolic of my superior status. I am the grand finale of tonight's ceremony, everyone below waiting with baited breath, each person excited to tell their friends tomorrow they had been deemed worthy enough to be invited.

One at a time, we are announced by name and descend the stairs. With each name called my terror increases. I try to compose the serene face I practiced and, for the life of me, I can't. I need to clear my head and muster a mask of quiet resignation before that door opens as if my life depends on it. I like to think those words, *as if my life depends on it*, is an exaggeration even though I know that they're not.

> *Theirs not to make reply,*
> *Theirs not to reason why,*
> *Theirs but to do or die.*

Tennyson's poem that's been running through my head all damn day restarts its forbidden chant, bringing my anxiety to a fever pitch. Just like the soldiers of the Light Brigade, my brain is reminding me I do have a choice, not that one option is better than the other. I am either going to do what I am supposed to or they will kill me.

Easy-peasy. I wonder if this is my brain's way of attempting to pre-serve itself or trying to commit suicide.

I'm going to go insane thinking about this.

I turn back to look at the door and meet the icy stare of a white-uniformed patrolman, his gaze devoid of emotion as he appraises my current level of threat. Almost as if he can hear my thoughts, his trigger finger taps menacingly against the hard casing of the automatic weapon cradled in his arms. He nods at me, a silent jerking motion of his head that clearly warns me to turn around and behave. He places his finger on the trigger, the simple motion more than enough to make me face forward and accept my doom. I don't need to be warned twice.

I again try to compose my face as the door opens and the girl directly before me moves forward.

Mine is but to do or die.

I hear my name called and I close my eyes and pray for strength.

I must obey.

The door opens, this time for me to walk through. This is it. From this moment on, my life will never be the same.

2

MY FATHER, Governor Edward James Bellamy, stands tall at the top of the stairs, resplendent in his navy blue dress uniform, the left side of his chest covered in shiny medals earned over decades of service. Everything about him is polished to perfection, his white hair cropped short and not a trace of dark stubble on his cheek despite the hour. He is smiling, but the friendly tilt of his mouth does not match his threatening gaze. I don't doubt he senses my fear. Hell, he may even be able to smell it. I certainly wouldn't put it past him to have that sort of predatory ability.

I step forward, the blood rushing to my face as I enter into view of hundreds of rapt people seated below. I take my father's proffered arm and we pause at the top of the stairs so the press can snap a few million pictures of us. As practiced, I turn my head and look up into my father's dark brown eyes, our gazes meeting for a long, uncomfortable moment. He smiles again before dropping his proud chin and kissing me gently on the forehead.

Our well-rehearsed move gets the desired effect. There is a collective sigh from the crowd, a smattering of applause and a bit of sparked conversation—*how sweet, what a wonderful father, oh, why can't all daughters be so biddable*—before he tightens his already death-like grip on my arm. We gracefully descend the staircase, my wobbling ankles blessedly concealed by my swishing skirts.

My father and I proceed arm-in-arm between tables filled with the country's most prominent politicos, religious magnates, and high-ranking military and patrol personnel. He nods and smiles at the men he favors while blatantly ignoring those too eager or unworthy of his attention. Although this is supposed to be my moment in the spotlight, the eyes of every single person are glued to him. I can't blame them; the way my exceedingly-handsome father carries himself and the haughty air of confidence he exudes is awe inspiring. Next to his grandeur, I am inconsequential.

As we approach the stage, my stomach lurches. We stop the appropriate distance from the seated individuals and my father salutes as I drop into a deep, graceful curtsy. Because of my dance background, my father's advisers were adamant my veneration needed to be deeper, more elaborate and more graceful than one ever before executed. The fact this feat is required to be executed in four-inch heels while not being able to breathe or having eaten in two days is apparently my problem with which to deal.

I'd like to dress those old farts up in this getup and see them try this. Assholes.

I wipe the thought from my mind and pray that it hasn't seeped from my brain to my eyes. Somehow, despite the battle raging between my brain and body, I make it through my perilous reverence without falling flat on my face.

Up on a high dais perches the figure who presides over us all. He stares disinterestedly off into space, His vacant eyes unfocused, His mind anywhere but here. Our Beloved Supreme Archon is dressed in his usual white and gold military uniform with enough unearned gemstone-encrusted medals pinned to His chest to feed half the country for a year. Loops of real gold braid cascade from His shoulder, enough rope there for them to hang me by when I inevitably screw up tonight.

This once in a lifetime moment for me to be in the same room with who I've been told is the "greatest Leader our nation has ever seen" should be an awe-inspiring sight, but it's not. Even though His clothing alone costs more than all the presentation gowns in this room, something about His appearance is off. Unlike the precise tailoring of my father's uniform, our Supreme Leader's attire is strangely misshapen. I have heard he has always been a sloppy man, but what I am seeing before me is much worse than even I could imagine.

A thin thread of drool drips from His drooping lip, His attendants too caught up in the pageantry to remember they are there to wipe it away. Looking closely, I see the rumors of His imminent demise are likely true. I'm not sure if I'm happy about that or not, as there is much speculation about what will happen to our fledgling country once he dies. As bad as things are now, I'm not stupid enough to think things can't get worse.

The spotlights are focused on Him, the extra bright lights accentuating the telltale signs of His advanced age. His trademark sparse blonde hair combed over a balding pate is riddled with discolored, probably cancerous, growths; the unnatural orange-ish color to His skin that has always been a source of whispered laughs even brighter up close. I can't decide if the freakish hue is either trying to hide or a symptom of some terrible disease. Maybe it's both.

There is no amount of makeup that can hide the unfocused eyes of advanced dementia, no corset strong enough to tighten the body gone flaccid from decades of abuse and disuse. I try to banish my thoughts, doing my best to clear my mind and my face that I know the man I am supposedly honoring will soon be fertilizing daisies.

Okay, Emma, cut it out. You have been blessed with the opportunity to revere Our Beloved Supreme Leader. Be grateful. Honor Him and, oh yeah, stop thinking about the old man dropping dead. Remember—it's treasonous to think of the possible, although inevitable, death of the Supreme Archon.

As my father escorts me closer to the aged leader, a horrific odor wafts from the stage that everyone is doing their best to ignore. I believe the old man has soiled himself, but I cannot, *I dare not*, let on. The organic stench of fresh fecal matter combined with the sharp ammonia tang of a piss-filled diaper assaults my nose.

My eyes water and my body involuntarily recoils. I step back only to slam into the solid wall of my father's broad chest, trapped between him and the stink of impending death. The odor is so strong I imagine it must have been weeks since the last time someone changed the pudgy, man-sized baby's diaper.

Chin up, sweetheart. As much as your life sucks, you could be the poor soul who has to wipe His ass tonight.

A rueful smile tugs the corner of my mouth just as my father sneaks a quick glance at me. I can tell he doesn't like what he sees when his hand tightens painfully around my upper arm and my hand goes numb.

I look up on the stage at the woman sitting next to the Supreme Archon, an aged trophy wife dressed in a fitted, long black gown. I can't remember her name or if she's wife number six or seven. There's not a speck of life in her eyes as she gently lifts and supports His flaccid hand so my father and I can both kiss His ring. She doesn't look at us, but keeps her solemn gaze pinned to some far off spot on the wall. I can't tell which of them looks more dead inside, but if I had to put money on it, I would say her. I've been instructed to ignore her, the Supreme Archon's consort having ceased to have importance many years ago.

After waiting another second, my father pulls me back from the stage, my cue to again drop into another death-defying curtsy. I wait, head bowed, eyes lowered. The entire room is plunged in suspenseful silence, the tension palpable as we all await the grand finale. Within the next few minutes we will all know in whose hands my father has placed my life. For better or for worse, I am obligated to the man who will help me rise, my consent to our upcoming union as unnecessary as binoculars to a blind man.

The clip of leather shoes on the hardwood move quickly and sound eager in tone. Great cheers erupt from the audience and there are progressively louder calls of congratulations as individuals clamor to be heard above the din. They wish him good fortune, telling him he has made a fine choice, that he is blessed. I listen carefully for a clue, something that will give me some idea who he is, but there is nothing. It takes every ounce of willpower for me to not peek.

My future husband stands next to me, salutes the Supreme Archon and reverently kisses His ring. He enthusiastically shakes hands with my father, his voice familiar. His other duties complete, he finally turns towards me. He gently takes my trembling hands in his strong, warm grip, his careful attention to support my rise ensuring my graceful ascent. My head remains submissively bowed until he takes one hand off mine and places it gently under my chin. He raises my gaze until our eyes meet.

I startle for a moment before composing myself, his shockingly pale blue, nearly colorless eyes taking me by surprise. I cannot read his expression; his eyes betraying nothing behind their veil of thick blonde lashes, his tanned face neither smiling nor displeased. He is a full head taller than me, his shoulders broad, his body fit without being bulky. He's a man that takes pride in his appearance, the formal way he comports himself denoting his own perceived level of extreme self-importance.

I gasp when I realize who the man is standing before me. Archon Ryan Gregory is a decorated war hero, well-respected politician and regarded by most to be the man most likely to ascend to the Supremacy. It's hardly a secret that he has been doing the job since the old man had that near-fatal stroke a number of years ago. When the Constitution was destroyed and The Articles of Incorporation took their place, the men drafting the document hadn't accounted for what to do in case of the mental incapacity of the Supreme Archon. Without a plan in place and a leader so disabled he couldn't wipe his own ass, Ryan took over, the rest of the Committee too busy leading the good life to stop him. All he needs now is for the old man to flat-line to officially sit on the Supreme Archon's golden throne.

Ryan is at least in his early forties, making him, at a minimum, twenty years my senior. I realize I am lucky, as this is really not that big of an age gap, as past presentations joined together brides and grooms with upwards of fifty years between them. He is most certainly handsome, well-built, wealthy and powerful. I should be thankful. I should feel blessed. I should get down on my knees and thank my father for bestowing upon me the honor of such an auspicious marriage.

So why do I feel like vomiting?

Ryan drops to his knee, kisses my hand and takes a ring with a diamond the size of an egg out of his jacket pocket. He places it on my left hand while reciting a well-practiced oath promising to love, cherish and honor me and then asking if I will take him to be my husband, to love, honor, and obey.

I want to run screaming from the room but I don't dare. Saying no is not an option. I panic, the entire room silent as they wait for me to do something, *anything*, to release us from this moment that has now stretched on for far too long. My choking fear only worsens once I realize the entire room has registered my reluctance, that feeling escalating to one of terror as a flush of rage colors Ryan's face.

It's so silent you could hear a mouse fart. Despite the tension, or maybe because of it, the thought of mouse flatulence brings a burbling giggle to my throat. Before it can erupt from my mouth, Ryan's furious eyes narrow in warning. To my horror, I realize my protective mask has slipped and every single thing I'm thinking and feeling is visible to every person in the room. The thought of the consequences makes me lightheaded.

If I pass out, my father will kill me.

Ryan narrows his eyes further as I start to sway. He squeezes my hand hard, almost as if he means to fuse my fingers together, the edges of the giant ring painfully digging into my fingers.

I might not need to worry about my father killing me. The way Ryan looks, he's going to beat him to it.

I remember where we are in the ceremony and open my mouth to speak the only word I'm allowed but I am rendered mute. I force myself to smile and nod my assent as tears cloud my eyes. The anger dissipates from Ryan's eyes only to be replaced with promises of retaliation.

He rises and plants an emotionless kiss on my mouth, the taste of stale tobacco and expensive scotch making my stomach flip. A single tear escapes my eye that Ryan reaches over and wipes quickly from my cheek. The blaze in his eyes and the tightness of his pressed lips are the only evidence that this drop of leaked emotion is the final nail in my coffin. After receiving the grunted approval from Our Beloved Supreme Archon the deed is done, and I am well and truly screwed.

At dinner, I sit between my father and Ryan in probably the most uncomfortable seat for a woman in the history of dinner parties. They both shoot glares at me as we wait for our meal to be served, their displeasure over my less-than-stellar performance obvious to the other men at our table. None of them say a word as they are too polite—well, more likely too *afraid*—to let on.

The waiters set tiny plates of salad before us, everyone waiting to get the blessing from the Supreme Pontiff before digging in. The benediction goes on forever, the heavyset leader of The New State Church feeling his importance as he drones on. My father's so irritated he starts eating despite the benediction not being complete while Ryan sits next to me with his eyes closed and hands reverently folded. The rest of our table pretends they don't see the zealotry to my left and the blasphemy on my right that is so damned ridiculous I'm forced to disguise my giggles as coughs into my napkin.

When it's finally safe to eat, I pick up my fork and toy with the wilted lettuce and overripe tomato. Even though I was ravenous a mere hour ago, the anxiety knotting my stomach has robbed me of my appetite. I tune out the mind-numbing conversation, the men at our table petitioning Ryan and my father with their wants and needs. Occasionally someone forgets and addresses a question to me that my father steps in to answer when Ryan proves too disinterested to respond.

Yes, there will be a lavish New State Church wedding ceremony next September.

No, Emma will not be moving in with him right away. Archon Gregory is a pious man. He does not believe in cohabitation before marriage.

Yes, she is dancing with the National Ballet this year and will be staying at the dorms near the theater.

Oh yes, we are all very proud of her.

I look up from the anemic bean sprout I am toying with in hopeful surprise only to see the lie in my father's eyes. For a brief second, I had hoped that maybe this time his words are true, but there is not an ounce of affection or pride in his gaze. His look of dissatisfaction is exactly the same as every other time he has looked at me over the past nineteen years.

Tears well up in my eyes. I hate that I am a constant disappointment, that I never do anything right, that no matter how hard I try I am never good enough. Considering my failure of a performance tonight, I have no right to think he should be proud. I have disgraced myself. I am unworthy. I wonder if this is the reason my brain is always so quick to rebel; that if I am to be a chronic letdown, I might as well be terrible enough to make loathing me worth his effort.

The conversation turns back to politics and I tune out most of the discussion. The usual dinner topics of increased food rationing and outbreaks of virulent disease in the CAFOs are nothing new. One of the men at our table turns the conversation to the continued acts of domestic terrorism in the eastern coastal territories and my interest perks.

Continued?

It had been years since the Great War, the redistribution of the cities and the culling of the undesirables. The National Registration Act keeps those of us living in the cities safe, the wall watchers and the Purity Police ever-vigilant. For as long as I can remember, there have been no acts of domestic terrorism.

So why did he say continued?

I have so many questions, the excitement of overhearing these dangerous truths carbonating my blood. I keep waiting for someone to point out these are not topics fit for discussion with someone of the lesser sex in attendance, but no one does. The men speak openly and candidly, my presence ignored. As the night goes on and the drinks are refilled, the men discuss even more sensitive topics without censure. New missile designs and how we will never be able to pay the looming debt we owe an increasingly irate Chinese Imperial Power are discussed at length. These are just a few of the many secrets I hoard with none of them being any wiser.

I assume they believe I lack the ability to understand the complexities of politics, that my womanhood somehow makes me less intelligent. Well, if they think I'm stupid they are sorely mistaken. I focus intently, committing every word spoken, every snide comment, and every roll of the eye to memory. My eidetic memory and finely honed skills of observation are assets I hide at all costs. Abilities like mine are extremely dangerous for women, especially for ones of my social standing.

My brother warned me from a very early age to keep my talent under wraps. Growing up in the Governor's household, I saw and heard many things I never should. If anyone knew the extent of the information I can recall without error, I would be in grave danger. By now, I have dirt on nearly every official in this room, and that information, should it become public, would threaten too many people. So I swore to my brother that my perfect recall would remain our secret, one that I am prepared to take to the grave.

I gently place my hand on Ryan's arm and whisper for his permission to go to the ladies' room. He nods his disinterested assent, not even bothering to look at me. I teeter into the safety of the woman-only sanctuary and sink to my knees in one of the stalls, resting my cheek against the cool porcelain bowl. I wonder if there is some sort of deadly germ that I can catch from this obviously unsanitary act, but the smell of bleach and the still intact sanitary strip across the seat squashes any hope of imminent viral demise. As I have done for years, I force myself to vomit up the two bites of dinner I managed to choke down.

I don't care that what I'm doing is unhealthy. I don't care if it kills me. In fact, I hope that it will.

I rise from the floor and open the stall door to find Ryan standing directly in front of me. I gasp and take a shocked step back, bumping into the toilet. He grabs my arm painfully, his nails digging into my skin as he drags me out into the lounge and shoves me against the rose-stenciled wall. My head cracks against the plaster, my heavily teased hair no cushion against the blow.

His hand is tight around my throat. I claw at his hands and wrists, trying to loosen his hold but only manage to break off a few fake nails in the process.

"What the hell is wrong with you? You made me look like a fucking idiot!"

Angry spittle hits my cheeks as he speaks and I stare in shock.

My silence exacerbates his anger the way a hurricane gains strength over tropical water.

"Answer me!"

I don't know what to say, no words springing easily to mind. I am at his mercy and he is fresh out of clemency. When his arm coils back and his palm slams full force into my cheek my knees buckle and I fall. My hand rises to my cheek to comfort the wound, but the pain is overwhelming. My fingers return covered in blood.

"Get up."

When I don't rise immediately, he reaches over and fists my hair, the pins keeping the perfect curls in place digging ferociously into my scalp. He throws me onto the plush maroon ottoman in the center of the lounge, the caress of the velvet against the nape of my neck juxtaposing the sweaty palm that takes vicious hold of my windpipe. He straddles me, pinning my arms against my sides with his knees, his grip threatening to choke me to death with every passing second.

He raises his other hand to me and I involuntarily flinch. I close my eyes, expecting the sting of another vicious slap, but instead his fingers land lightly against my cheek. He caresses the unscathed side, running his fingers lightly, tenderly, across my forehead, and brow. His other hand remains menacingly around my throat.

"I know what you're thinking." He leans closer to me, our lips mere millimeters apart. My eyes flash up to him in terror and he smiles. "I bet you think that if you misbehave, if you perform poorly, that I will call off the engagement."

His fingers trail down my throat and across my collarbone to the jeweled bodice of my gown. He toys absently with one of the many baubles before his eyes again meet mine, his stare intensifying as his hand rests heavily over my breast.

"There's nothing you can do to prevent this wedding. *Nothing*. There is no way out of this union now that the Supreme Archon has given his blessing. So you are going to have to make the best of this. You are going to learn to behave, to obey my commands, and you are going to like it. Because, God help me, I will not tolerate bad behavior, Emma. I refuse to have you embarrass me. You will honor and respect me, and if you do not, there will be grave consequences."

His fingers tighten against my throat, an obvious precursor to the kinds of punishment I am doomed to receive. His fingers travel lightly to the slight dip between my breasts, slipping one thick digit under the silky fabric and tracing the inner swell of my cleavage.

"I had a feeling you would prove to be a spoiled child, that your parents have spared the rod far too often in your upbringing. Your father seems to have forgotten Proverbs 23:13-14. *Do not withhold discipline from a child; if you strike him with a rod, he will not die. If you strike him with a rod, you will save his soul.* Tell me, Emma, how many strikes will it take for me to save your soul?"

I'm unable to suppress the look of horror blazing in my eyes, terrified that it will restart the beating. But my fear soothes his rage, a strange, small smile curling his lip as he continues to speak in crooning tones.

"Is that what you need, my pet? Do you need me to save your soul? I think you do. I think you *want* me to save you."

He loosens his hold on my throat just enough for me to nod but I'm too terrified to move. I think he wants me to agree with him, but I'm not sure. I don't know what the right answer is and I'm positive the wrong one will get me killed. Considering the question he just posed, it's likely the right one might too.

Ryan smiles almost kindly as he brings his lips down to meet mine. He takes my mouth in a lingering kiss, his tongue finding the seam of my lips and forcing its way inside. The invasive wet thrusts gag me with their force, his teeth biting at my lips when I try to close my mouth. His palm slams across my cheek again as he hisses for me to open my mouth and kiss him properly.

I do as he says, tasting my blood and tears mix with the tobacco and alcohol flavors of his mouth and want to retch. The metallic tinge to our kiss has the exact opposite effect on my attacker who is now licking the blood from my lip like it's a delicacy.

"I think that with some proper discipline you may yet be saved, and luckily for you, I am always up for the task. *For the moment all discipline seems painful rather than pleasant, but later it yields the peaceful fruit of righteousness to those who have been trained.* Hebrews 12:11. One of my favorite verses, and one that I think will soon become one of yours."

My body stiffens, the implied threat not lost upon me. He whispers for me to kiss him goodnight, that my curfew is near. He advises me to think carefully about our discussion, to study up on my *New State Church Text* and the *Purity Protocols for Unmarried Women*. His hand closes around my throat as he stands, lifting me with him from the ottoman. I catch my reflection in the full length mirror, my dress askew, my hair disheveled. My cheek has dripped blood onto the bodice of my gown, the fine fabric ruined.

He leans into me and I cringe. His eyes are murderous, the sting of his slap making my eye feel like it explodes into my brain. I cry out in pain which only spurs on his hateful assault. When he finally lets go I fall to the floor, a sobbing, bruised and bloody mess. I hear the quick cadence of his shoes as he walks over to the mirrors to fix his hair and straighten his jacket.

"Proverbs 8:36. *Heed my warning: the one who goes against me will only hurt himself, for all who despise me are playing with fire and courting death.* For your own sake, take these words as gospel. Next time, I will not be so lenient with my punishment." He strides regally from the room, leaving me in a puddle of blood and tears on the floor.

3

A SHRILL RING pierces the silence of my room, the blaring summons echoing in my throbbing head. It takes a moment for me to realize I'm in my bed in the dorms and the incessant trill is not an air raid siren but my phone.

Duty calls.

I have no memory of how I got home last night or how I got out of that jeweled monstrosity of a gown alone. The phone continues to blare and I am loath to answer it. There's no one I either want or need to talk to, but I answer, knowing it otherwise won't stop its endless subpoena.

"Emma, honey, you up? Your papa wants to see you and he doesn't sound happy, so we need to git a move on. I'm on my way."

Great. Just what I need right now.

Outside my window, heat rises from the asphalt in thick, wavy lines. It's going to be another blisteringly hot and humid day, the type of day for sundresses and sandals for everyone but me. That type of attire would show off every bruise, cut and abrasion—the absolute last thing I want my father to see. Even with Caitlin's makeup I know there's no way to hide what happened.

I am still in bed when Caitlin lets herself in. She strides purposefully into my rooms balancing two coffee cups in her hand, her heavy bag of makeup over her shoulder. Her high-heeled shoe kicks the door closed behind her with a thump, her cheery voice and chirpy "Good morning!" making me feel even worse.

"So, I saw the paper and I want to hear all about it. Every detail, girl, dontcha dare leave one out! What's he like? Is he as handsome in person as he is on. . . ."

I know she's finally seen me when the coffee cups slip from her hands and our creamy lattes spill all over the pristine white carpet. I stare at the growing stain on the floor, unable to meet her eyes. I'm beyond embarrassed.

"Jesus Christ, Emma, what did he do to you?" She drops her bag and climbs onto my bed and takes me in her arms. I start to sob, each breathless cry sending bolts of pain through my swollen face.

"My sweet, sweet, girl, *shh*. It's okay, I'm here."

I hear the tears in her voice and part of me wants to comfort her as much as I know she wants to console me. I babble out the story, and by the time I'm done, both Caitlin and I are drenched in tears and I've ruined her new silk blouse.

"Sweetie, let me take a look at you, okay?" I see the alarm she's unable to mask, the realization that there is no makeup in the world able to cover the damage. "Your father can't possibly expect you to marry Ryan now, not after this. Can he?"

I shake my head woefully. "I don't know, but something makes me think he won't care. I'm going to beg him to get me out of this. There's something very, very wrong with Ryan. I honestly thought he was going to kill me. His eyes, Cate, his eyes have no soul. I just know it's only a matter of time before he's going to kill me. What he did, he's going to do again. . ."

My words break off into sobs as she again takes me in her arms and gently rubs my back.

"I have to get out of here," I whisper into her ear. "Please, Cate, you have to help me. He's going to kill me if I stay."

Caitlin's body goes rigid and her breath stops at the words even I can't believe breached my lips. She pulls out of my embrace and places her hands firmly on my bruised upper arms and sternly shakes me. Her words are a cold, hard whisper, her eyes steely.

"Don't you ever say that again, Emma. Do you hear me? Don't you *ever* let anyone hear you say that. I'm gonna pretend I never heard you speak that. . . that *treason*. You are a woman born into the most elite Provenance. You've been born and bred to live *here*. I've been outside these walls, and sweetheart, you don't stand a snowball's chance in Hell of survivin' out there. The people that live outside the city won't take you in. In fact, as soon as word got out you were missin', those savages would hunt you down to rape, torture and kill you. Dontcha watch the news, sweetheart? It's not safe for a girl like you outside of the city."

My heart plummets. I know she's right, that the area outside of the city is filled with dangerous people unfit to live within our walls. After all, that's why the barriers were built—to protect those of us with pure, unmingled blood.

So why do I feel like I'm trapped?

"Honey, even if you made it past the wall you would never outrun the patrols. They would search until they found you and they would bring you back. You know this, Emma. Even thinkin' about leavin' your designated territory is treason. You better pray a watcher doesn't catch on and turn you in. I guarantee if you end up in an interrogation center they will beat you until you pray for death. I know you don't want to marry Ryan and I certainly don't blame you, but isn't stayin' alive more important than a few bruises now and then?"

Her words are as sharp and painful as one of Ryan's slaps. She makes it clear the conversation is over when she starts rummaging through my closet, handing me a high-neck long sleeve dress to cover as much of my neck and forearms as possible. The bit of concealer she dabs over the worst of the cuts stings and does nothing to make my injuries less noticeable. In a last ditch effort, she hands me a large black floppy hat and a pair of oversized sunglasses. She shakes her head and lets out a sigh.

"I'm sorry I was so firm with you, sweetie. But speakin' like you did could get both of us in terrible trouble. I love you like a sister, Emma, and I only want the best for you. But you've got to be more careful."

We drive in silence to my father's estate. Caitlin holds my hand for support as I await our arrival like an impending execution. My parents live in a large gated community about fifteen minutes from the Executive Mansion in a home that could easily be mistaken for a palace. It is overly grand and disgustingly ornate with gold gilt mirrors and tacky signs of excess like gold toilets and heavy velvet curtains. It was last redecorated shortly after the Supreme Archon ascended, all his men eager to garner favor by adopting his flair for the perversely extravagant. As a result, my childhood home is cold and false, more of a museum than a house. It's a place designed to be admired and strike awe and absolutely not to be lived in.

I have always hated that house.

The compound is surrounded by sharp glass-topped stone walls and a staff of armed guards line the perimeter at precise intervals to prevent "visitors." As a child, my brother half-heartedly joked the wall wasn't there to keep people out but to keep us, our father's unwilling subjects, in.

Caitlin is escorted to her appointed waiting area as another guard steers me into my father's office. I wait for him to appear, fiddling with the hat, trying again to pull the neck of the dress just a trifle higher to hopefully cover more of the bruises. I sit in silence for a surprisingly long time before I hear his shoes stomping along the marble corridor.

I sit up straighter, knowing I'm in enough trouble and I don't need an additional reprimand for sloppy posture. I can tell by the cadence and volume of his steps he is in a particularly foul mood. Through the years, I've had a lot of practice learning how to correlate his moods with his stride as either my brother or I awaited punishment. I've only heard steps like these one other time and they preceded the worst beating my brother ever received.

"You took long enough getting here," he says gruffly as he slams the door behind him. Even the lock sounds angry as it clicks in place.

"I'm sorry to keep you waiting, father. It took a while to make myself presentable this morning." My reply is quiet and submissive, my eyes averted and hands folded carefully, right over left.

"Hat and glasses off. You know the rules." He seats himself behind the intricately carved wood desk, every inch of him a king. I swallow hard to dislodge the lump in my throat as I remove the offending items. I keep my eyes downcast, too afraid to see his reaction.

His chair creaks as he leans back and peers at me wordlessly for several long minutes. I can feel his penetrating gaze cataloging the angry bruises, the swollen nose and the cuts on my lip and cheek. I pray that his silence is a sign of his outrage, that he is furious Ryan treated me this way.

I know that I shouldn't, but I feel a glimmer of hope.

Despite what Ryan said, I honestly believe that if anyone can loop-hole me out of this marriage, it's my father. Edward James Bellamy is an extremely important man, a man that has given his entire life to the service of his country. He had been an Admiral back when that rank still existed, and even though he's no longer active duty, he is still one of our nation's top military minds.

When the country's wealth and power was redistributed after the war, he had been highly compensated for his many years of service. But when the new hierarchy of power was announced, my father's name, surprisingly, was not among those elevated to the rank of Archon. No one knows the real reason why, but rumor has it that the Supreme Archon and my father had some sort of falling out. Others whisper my father has dark, sinister secrets that make him ineligible for further promotion. I have no idea if either or both of these are true, but I do know one thing: The fact my father has yet to become an Archon pisses him off to no end.

As my father formulates his thoughts I summon every ounce of my courage and force myself to look up. I stop breathing when I meet my father's furious glare. I have never before looked him in the eye without permission and it takes every ounce of my willpower to not cower before him.

"I can't marry him, father." I startle at the sound of my own voice, the words that come out as clear as if I were to say *the sky is blue* or *the grass is green*. He doesn't speak for a few more uncomfortable minutes; he just sits there, silently appraising me, taking in my frozen stature and the fact I have yet to break eye contact. His eyes dare me to keep staring and with every second I do not look away, his face hardens further.

By the time he speaks his entire body is rigid. "Are you in pain?"

I blink in surprise, stunned that the first questions my father is asking is how I feel. I nod before remembering my father always requires a verbal response.

"Yes, sir. I am." I tilt my head downward in shame.

"Good. Perhaps you will remember this the next time you decide to anger him."

I look up, my mouth dropping open in shock and anger. "Father, I did nothing wrong! I swear to you, this was undeserved."

"Judging by what he did to you, I disagree. Only a severely provoked man would feel the need for this level of premarital punishment, especially on the sacred night of Presentation. Think, Emma. What did you do that made him so angry? You must have done *something*."

My voice is a plea for mercy. "I did nothing wrong, I swear to you. I followed my training, I did everything I had been taught. I was sweet and quiet and willing. . . ."

"That's not what he said."

"And you believe him over your own daughter?" I cry out in incredulity.

"It doesn't matter what I believe." There is not a drop of emotion or concern in his voice. "Emma, your marriage contract has been signed, sealed and approved by the Supreme Archon. If you came here hoping I will get you out of it, you are sorely mistaken. What has final approval from the Supreme Archon cannot be undone by anyone. You will marry Ryan. End of discussion."

"Father, please...."

"Emma, let me give you a little advice. First of all, I want to remind you that when Ryan ascends, and with my help he most certainly will, he will be our next Supreme Archon. When that happens, he will be above the law. The happier you make him now, the better things will go for you in the future. I suggest that you follow his orders no matter how distasteful you find them. You are contracted to him, you will marry him, and you have a duty to bear him an heir. Your sole purpose in life is to serve him. If you are smart, you will do everything he tells you with a smile on your face and a song in your heart."

He pauses for a moment to carefully choose his words, but when he speaks again, the stern tone of his voice does not change. "I am aware that he can be a difficult man, but you must learn to make this marriage work. I cannot stress enough how important this union is for our family, our Provenance and our Country. Am I clear?"

Tears spill down my cheeks. I rise from my chair and race to his side and dive to my knees in supplication. My lip quivers and words pour like vomit from my mouth. "Please, please, Father. Please don't make me marry him. I'm begging you, please. He's horrible and cruel and a monster. He's going to kill me, I know it. I...." Before I can utter another word, my father's palm slams across my face and I fall to the floor.

"I won't say it again, Emma. You will marry him even if I have to lock you in a closet and keep you under guard for the next year. I can take away everything I have given you and make your life a living hell if you choose to continue this ill-fated path. It has also been reported to me that you are thinking of running away, of thumbing your nose at the gifts I have bestowed upon you during your entire ungrateful life. What do you have to say about that?"

I stare in horror. How could he possibly know what I've been thinking?

"You have no idea what lies behind the walls of our city, of the mobs of violent criminals that would just love to get their hands on you. Do you really think you can survive in those lawless territories? Tell me Emma, do you really want to take your chances with the savages, the murderers and rapists that live beyond our walls? I'll tell you right now, they won't help you. They *hate* you. They see you as nothing more than the spoiled, privileged brat you are. They would rip you to shreds."

How the hell does he know what I was thinking?

"W-what?" I stammer.

"Emma, there is nothing you do, say, or even *think* that doesn't get back to me. You have been bred and raised for one job and one job only. It's not a difficult one and yet you insist on making it harder than it needs be. Your job is to keep Ryan happy. Period. Do not argue, do not fight. You won't win. The only rule for Ryan is he cannot take your virginity until your wedding night. Everything else of yours he is allowed to have with both my permission and blessing."

I'm not certain if I am more shocked, embarrassed or insulted that my father has a contract somewhere that spells out all the ways Ryan can violate me within the next year.

He looks at me carefully, his features softening, his voice slightly less harsh. "I see in your eyes that you think I'm cruel for putting you in this situation. But honestly, Emma, I'm entering into this agreement to save you. You need to understand that for people of our status, marriages are arranged to help protect certain interests. I normally don't like to discuss things of a political nature with you, but this one time I will make an exception."

He walks over to the window and looks out over his pristine garden. "I'm sure you have heard the hateful rumors spread by those who are envious of my good fortune, the ones that claim my heritage is tainted, that my blood isn't pure enough for the highest stations of the Committee. The rumors come up once a decade or so and every time I have been able to squash them."

He pauses for a few moments, the only movement in the room the slight tic of his jaw. "This time I can't. This time there is proof."

The embarrassment is clear in his sharp features, in his dark eyes and drawn black brows. This isn't the first time I'm hearing about the rumors, but it is the first time my father has admitted to their truth. To say I am shocked is an understatement, the shame of being of mixed blood sending a shiver down my spine. Should this become public knowledge, everything we have and the life that I know would be over. For hiding such a secret, my whole family could be put to death.

"To save you, your mother, and everything I have worked for all these years, I had no choice but to enter into an alliance with Ryan. To cement our treaty, to make our family safe, you must marry him and bear him a son. That's the only way we can assure ourselves he will never come out against us. Your marriage will link our families and force his silence. I will achieve the rank of Archon despite our smudged heritage and he will become the next Supreme Archon. Your sons will be Archons and your firstborn will ascend to the Supremacy at the time of his father's passing. You will be the consort of the most powerful man in the nation, thus making you the most powerful woman in America. Our families will be an impenetrable political dynasty. What more could you want?"

What more could I want? *Seriously?* Maybe to not live the rest of my life in fear? Maybe to be allowed to choose something, anything, for myself without having to worry about what would best serve my father, the Committee, or our Nation?

"I don't doubt that he will be a difficult man to live with. You will need to be a grateful, obedient and attentive wife. If you do what he says there is no need for him to punish you like this again. Am I clear?"

I frantically think of something else I can say or do to change his mind, but with this new knowledge, I know there isn't. All I can do is whisper a desultory, "Yes, sir," as I choke on a fresh torrent of tears I'm too terrified to shed.

"Good. I do not want to hear anything more about you not wanting to marry him or running away. I'm warning you, if you do anything to ruin this treaty, you won't have to worry about what Ryan will do because I will kill you, myself. Do you understand me?"

The sharp edge to his voice reminds me his threats are never idle. I look at him with a mixture of sadness, shock and loathing. "Yes, sir."

"You are dismissed." I slowly rise and head for the door.

"Emma, one more thing," he adds as he sits down at his desk, already shuffling through the papers. "Put some makeup on before you go to class tomorrow. You look like hell."

* * *

Back in my rooms, I pace wildly as I try to figure out how my father knew of my thoughts to escape. I ransack my rooms, pulling books off the shelves, searching inside cabinets and even checking inside my alarm clock for any planted device that could be tattling my secrets. I go so far as to open up the seams on my tattered, childhood stuffed bunny, wondering if a recorder is stuffed inside.

There is nothing.

Although my rooms are hardly large, it still takes most of the night before I give up. I finally fall asleep snuggled up tight in my flowered comforter. I get no respite from my unease, even my dreams filled with the terror of being watched.

My alarm doesn't go off the next morning, probably because I broke it taking it apart. I curse my own stupidity as I realize I'm going to be late for my first company class. The day promises to be bright and sunny, a beautiful breezy day giving our overcrowded city respite from the scorching heat. I feel betrayed by the weather that dares to be so freakishly chipper while my life disintegrates.

Despite knowing I'm going to sweat to death, I choose a long-sleeve, high neck black leotard to help cover the bruising that's getting darker with each passing day. I put my hair up in a well secured bun, and slather nearly a half-bottle of foundation on my face to help cover the bruises and cuts, all to no avail. I still look like shit.

I moved into the dorms last week and have yet to meet any of my fellow dancers. I am housed on a separate floor strictly for the female principals, our accommodations more spacious with a gorgeous river view glittering from every floor to ceiling window. My rooms are professionally decorated, the furniture luxurious and the bedding a dreamy pile of snuggly goodness perfect to lounge in with a good book. This is my first time living alone, my first real taste of freedom and I plan to relish every moment. I try not to think about how this is all temporary, that in one year, the bars of my cage of servitude will be welded shut.

I know I'm getting preferential treatment by the company's leadership, my immediate elevation to principal dancer as well as my gorgeous rooms not based on skill but in deference to my father's rank. Despite the fact my promotion will certainly cause resentment from my fellow company members, I've been enjoying the freedom way too much to think about the consequences until now.

As I hurry down the halls to the main studio, I peek into the smaller rooms along the way where small groups are already in session. A familiar calm washes over me as a piano accompanies a graceful couple practicing their *pas de deux*, just as another room full of preteen girls line up studiously at the barre, eagerly waiting to be told the next series of combinations to perform. This is my life, what I live for, and the only bright point in my otherwise bleak existence.

As I near the main practice hall, I overhear a heated discussion coming from inside. It's hard to make out the man's words, his lightly accented voice soothing and quiet in comparison to the venomous tone of the irate woman. There is a sharpness to her words, a thick Russian accent she isn't even attempting to hide. Her words are as piercing as shards of shattered glass.

"Jeremy, this is ridiculous. I am to give up all best roles again this year to spoiled brat because daddy is some big, important government man? Do you remember what happened last time you do this? The twat could not dance! You even make choreography so simple my one-legged grandmother in nursing home could dance better and still she was horrible!"

Oh, Sweet Jesus, she's talking about me.

I can hear the others laughing in the background. They haven't even met me yet and I am already the punchline of their jokes.

"Anna, sweetheart, I know this is unfair, but Emma will be here just one year and then you will be right back at the top where you belong." Jeremy is trying desperately to soothe the angry prima donna and it isn't working.

"Yes, until another big money daddy wants *his* daughter to be Swan Queen and I am booted back to chorus like a doe-eyed idiot. No, I will not do it. I quit."

"And where exactly will you go? Where else is there a company of this level in this country? Nowhere. If you want to dance, this is it, my dear."

"I'll go back to Russia. If I constantly get shit roles, I might as well go back to Bolshoi and dance their shit roles. At least there we dance the parts as they are supposed to be danced, not this bullshit we do here since the war." She stomps her foot to emphasize her point.

The room silences in the blink of an eye, a telltale sign that Anna's dangerous tirade has finally gone too far. She's broken one of the most basic of the Fundamental Laws, the one that states if you want to stay alive, you *never* talk about *anything* from before the war.

Before I can potentially hear anything worse, I enter the studio, stopping just inside the doorway. Everyone stares at me in that terrible, fearful way that can only mean they are afraid of what I may have overheard. The one who must be Anna slowly turns around, her hands fisted on her hips, a mixture of hate and fear on her face.

I'm sure she thinks I'm going to snitch, something part of me says I should tell her I would never, ever do. But the wicked side of me wins out, and I don't bother to put her at ease. If she's already decided to hate me there's nothing I can say or do that's going to change her mind. I decide, spitefully, to let her suffer.

I take my bag to the corner and pull out my pointe shoes and prepare for class. I avoid looking in the mirrors, the swelling of my face worse today than yesterday. The cuts have barely scabbed and threaten to ooze at any moment. I catch words here and there as my fellow company members gawk and gossip about my battered face.

When we are called to the barre I find a space in the back row and do my best to hide. Jeremy steps forward and introduces himself as our dance master before introducing the rest of the large staff. He spots me in the back of the room and drags me forward. I hiss that I am more than happy to stay where I am, but he ignores me. He introduces me to the staff and fellow students and, to my horror, moves me to a prominent spot at the front of the class, right next to Anna. She looks like she's ready to spit on me.

Within minutes, I am in absolute agony. As my heart rate rises, the pressure in my bruised and swollen head intensifies. After fifteen minutes, the throbbing is incessant, a violent steady beat threatening to explode out my ears. I try my best, but it isn't long before tears of pain and frustration well up behind my eyes.

I don't dare cry, knowing if I start to bawl I won't stop; the embarrassment of that thought alone enough to provoke fresh tears. I futilely try to blink them back, my hand swiping clumsily at my face as one tear breaches my lash line the exact second the studio door swings opens and catches me by surprise. I stumble and nearly fall on top of Anna. The room erupts in laughter when Anna pushes me away with a foreign-sounding curse.

"Silence!" Jeremy shouts angrily and the tittering ceases. He glares at the man standing in the doorway who's casually munching on an apple as he leans against the frame. He's completely unconcerned by the disturbance he caused, his black eyes lazily roaming the room, giving each of us an appraising glance. When his eyes meet mine they darken, his gaze menacing. He takes a fierce bite from the apple, a warning if I ever saw one.

"Declan, so nice of you to join us." Jeremy addresses him with no shortage of sarcasm as he looks up at the wall clock. "Relatively on time for you, too. Only fifteen minutes late."

"Ya' know," he says between another mouthful of apple, "I just love how you state the obvious with such a sense of discovery." He throws the core in the trash can and wipes his hands on his cheap khaki pants. "If you're waiting for me to give a shit, I hope you packed a lunch because we're going to be here a looong time, brother."

There's a moment of strained silence and then the men laugh, their years of friendship evident in their easy banter and the way they bump fists in greeting. Yet despite Jeremy's ease with him, there is something about this arrogant man I find unnerving. There's an air of superiority about him, a level of authority and presumption rare to find in one so obviously low of rank. His calm demeanor and lazy stare appraise each person carefully, I'm certain noting everything in great detail for later use.

OK, Emma. Not everyone is a watcher. Now you're being paranoid.

Another staff member takes over the class as Jeremy and whoever this Declan guy is stand by the mirrors and watch. I overhear bits and pieces of their conversation as they discuss specific dancer's past injuries and potential future concerns, and I deduce he must be a doctor or therapist of some sort. Declan gets excited when he talks about his work, and when I sneak a look his way, the gleam in his eye makes it obvious he thoroughly enjoys what he does.

When they discuss Anna's most recent knee surgery, I can almost feel her preening under his gaze. Her posture becomes just a touch straighter, her every move more graceful and lovely when his eyes rest on her. Anna's movements take on a slightly sexy swagger that makes his lip curl into a smile and when they lock eyes, he winks. She giggles like a schoolgirl until Jeremy reprimands her lack of attention. Annoyed, Anna sticks her tongue out at him and laughs that Jeremy is only jealous that Declan prefers her to him.

I look around the room in concern but no one seems at all upset. In fact almost everyone is laughing. Doesn't Anna realize that she just jokingly made an accusation that could get the man killed? Even if he's not a sexual deviant, even if her words aren't true, doesn't she know how dangerous they are? A watcher could spin them into any number of meanings that could easily end with all three of them in front of a firing squad. As the accused, I wonder if Jeremy and Declan are as unbothered by her careless quip?

When I glance his way again, I find Declan's eyes trained on my face. His unapologetic stare catalogs every bruise, cut and pronounced swelling that contorts my face. He wipes his hand under his eye and my hand flies up to my own to find it has again begun to bleed.

He steps towards me, pulling a crumpled wad of tissues out of his pocket and stuffs them into my hand. "You're bleeding on the floor," he says gruffly with narrowed eyes before walking away. Anna shoots me a hateful glare, obviously angry that Declan addressed me, if only for all the wrong reasons.

Great. Yet another reason for her to hate me.

I struggle through the rest of the class, now making sure to keep track of my dripping cheek. The second we are dismissed I sigh in relief, thankful I can return to my sanctuary. Jeremy smiles at me as I leave, my heart leaping into my throat when he places his hand on my arm to catch my attention. I flinch at his touch and he recoils as if my skin burned him. I'm not sure which of us is more freaked out.

"Are you alright, my dear?" Jeremy moves us away from the door, his voice barely above a whisper. He points towards my face. "Is there anything I can do to help?"

"I'm fine, really. This looks worse than it is. I just tripped and fell down the stairs yesterday." My tone is much too cheery to be truthful, and the way he cocks his head and rolls his eyes couldn't possibly be clearer that he knows I am lying.

"Since when do stairs have hands?" He points to where my high-neck leotard had ridden down and Ryan's handprints are visible. Even though it's way too late, I grip the material and try to cover my neck.

He thinks for a bit before speaking again, this time in a low, conspiratorial whisper. "Emma, I like to think of all of my dancers as my flock and I as your shepherd. I am here not just to teach you, but also to keep you from the mouths of the wolves. If you ever need anything, please come to me. If I cannot help you, I will find someone who can. Here we are a family. An odd one, yes, but we look out for each other."

He takes his hand and pinches my chin gently with his fingers and turns my head so he can get a better look at the cut on my cheek. He makes a noise of concern in his throat before releasing me. I head towards the exit, surprised when some of the members give little waves goodbye as I pass. I feel lighter with each smile I return despite the fact my cheek throbs from the effort.

When I pass the last rehearsal room I peek through the window and see Anna and Declan having some sort of argument. I stop for a second to watch them yell and wildly gesticulate even though I can't make out their words. I nearly yelp when Declan turns his black granite eyes towards me, his face etched with lines of fury. The rage radiating from him is practically palpable when he narrows his eyes in recognition, and I instinctively know that his wrath somehow has something to do with me.

I just have no idea what.

4

WE WORK six days a week, each session harder and longer than the one before. Jeremy's demanding tone is crisp and harsh when warranted but also kind and complementary when earned. I rarely leave the studio before seven or eight at night, often putting in a few extra hours to work by myself.

Each night, I fall into bed exhausted but happy despite the aches and pains that come with a full day of working my body until it can give no more. Tonight, my lower back is sore from the intricate lifts and combinations my partner and I practiced for hours and my feet are raw and swollen from the pair of too-stiff pointe shoes I should have prepared better before class.

So far, my pride has suffered the only real injury as I realize how much I still need to perfect. Anna makes certain I am painfully aware of my imperfections with her continual stream of barbed comments and dirty looks. Jeremy rolls his eyes whenever she decides to interject, careful to not let her see him. He tells me after each class how pleased he is with my progress, praising me for how hard I'm working. The first time he does this it's such a novel experience, I nearly cry.

Anna never fails to keep my ego in check, always finding something to critique within seconds of Jeremy's approving comments.

No doubt, her snarky words are to remind me of my place in the company, and that it's most definitely not as her equal. In the grand scheme of things, if Anna's venomous mouth is my biggest problem, I'm doing pretty well. After a while I'm able to tune her out, and she tires of baiting me when I no longer respond to her taunts.

In the strict schedule of rehearsals and classes I take six days a week, I soon lose track of the days. Two weeks pass in the blink of an eye. It's not until the morning of my engagement party that I remember I must once again enter the lion's den.

The party will be held in the grand ballroom of the famous historic post office where Ryan lives on the top floor. The building had once been a famous hotel and remodeled after the supreme Archon's Ascension into luxurious apartments for the Committee's highest ranking members. I expect it to be another tacky, glitzy monstrosity, but the building is surprisingly understated for something associated with our Supreme Leader. The Romanesque architecture is stunning both inside and out, its air of opulent wealth not coming from a spectacular show of excess, but from its lack thereof. I enjoy taking in the details of the building, delighting in the many antique features of the post office left in place that only add to its charm.

I don't have long to explore before I am whisked up to my own suite to get ready. Caitlin opens the door when I arrive, shooing me into the room and quickly closing the door before enveloping me in a tight hug.

"I've missed ya, girl," she whispers. "How've you been?" She takes my face in her ice-cold hands and I shiver as she surveys the healed damage to my face. Only a tiny pink scar is left to remind us of Ryan's violence, not that what he did is something either of us will ever forget. She sets to work on my hair, her normal happy chatter absent, her hands unusually rough as she pins my hair into place.

"Caitlin, what's wrong? You aren't acting like yourself."

She gives me a strained smile. "Nothing, sugar. I'm fine, really. I guess I'm just extra focused on my work, today, that's all."

I let it drop, my mind preoccupying itself with all the ways things can go horribly wrong tonight. Although our preparations take hours, the time passes in a blur and it's soon time for me to dress. I peer in the full length mirror and hardly recognize the girl looking back. My skin is so pale you can hardly tell where my flesh ends and the snow-white gown begins. Diamonds drip from my ears and my neck, a few million dollars' worth of gaudy jewels a heavy, proprietary collar around my throat. My hair is piled on top of my head in curls, a diamond studded tiara-like band digging into my skull. The party has yet to begin and already my head aches.

"Don't forget this." Caitlin presents me with my final shackle, the enormous diamond engagement ring I have come to loathe. I huff as I slide it into place, giving it the dirty look I wish I could give to the man who demands I wear it.

There's a knock at the door and Caitlin looks at me expectantly. "That's probably him, sugar. Stay safe tonight, you hear me?" She leaves with one last squeeze of my hand.

Caitlin's sweet quiet drawl pours into the room like honey as she greets Ryan. Feeling a stab of dread, I realize I forgot to remind her to curtsy. It's not often she gets to meet people of his status, and Christ Almighty, for her sake, I sure as hell hope she remembers.

I hear his growling voice and break into a cold sweat. "She better be ready. I don't want to be late." When I walk into the room I find Caitlin has not only remembered, but has yet to be released from her reverence. Ryan stares down her v-neck blouse, practically drooling into her ample cleavage I'm sure he wishes I possessed.

I clear my throat and drop into my own reverence, doing my best to divert his attention from a thoroughly-uncomfortable looking Caitlin. I barely hear my own whispered, "Good evening, sir," over the thumping of my heart. My cheeks redden when I feel his gaze swing from her to me.

"Is it? That has yet to be seen. Stand up and let me look at you." He stalks towards me and it takes every ounce of my will to not shudder at his nearness. "Yes, you will do." His voice is dismissive and completely devoid of emotion. He slips a loose hair behind my ear and I flinch despite his gentle touch. "Let's go."

His fingers dig into my upper arm and I pretend he isn't hurting me. We walk too quickly for me to safely negotiate the four-inch stiletto sandals that strangle my ankles with ligature-like straps. Coupled with the long gown and overabundant underskirts on the slick marble floor, I am an accident waiting to happen. I'm actually thankful for the tight purchase he has on my arm when we hit the over-polished hallway and my feet slide out from under me.

"You are such a damn klutz," Ryan spits, dragging me into the elevator. "Get your shit together and don't you dare embarrass me tonight, do you hear me?" He backs me into the corner and I nod fearfully as he towers over me.

I can do this, I repeat over and over in my head. I am fully capable of making it through the night without pissing him off. If I am perfect, he will have no reason to hurt me. I must make him proud. I must not make any mistakes tonight. I must be flawless. I must not anger him.

I must not stab him in the eye with a fork during dinner.

I wonder if he senses that last thought when his eyes narrow. "Okay, Emma. I'm going to make this simple for you since you are obviously not that bright. Tonight, I want you to keep your mouth shut. Don't speak unless spoken to and stay at my side at all times. And for the love of God stop looking at me like you are terrified. Although I appreciate that look in the bedroom it's not appropriate for a party."

Grabbing me from the corner, he pulls me into his broad chest. His lips smash onto mine and his arms wrap around me just as the elevator door opens. Flash bulbs burst and my eyes squint against the blinding light. He pulls away, a bashful grin on his face as he pretends that kiss actually means something to either of us. I follow behind him, more confused than ever.

The night is long and tedious and I do exactly what I'm told. I nod and smile. I am polite. My etiquette is beyond reproach and I comport myself with utmost dignity and grace. I force myself to not cringe at Ryan's touch, recoil at the feel of his lips on mine, or to otherwise react negatively when he whispers threats in my ear.

He eventually releases me to use the ladies room and I am swarmed by the wives and escorts of the other attendees. The ladies say the sweetest things to my face, telling me how beautiful I look and wishing me a lifetime of happiness, only to whisper loudly that I am an undeserving whore the second I turn around. A few women whisper *traitor* as I pass through the crowds, others making snide remarks about my mother and grandmother I don't understand. What is it about them they know that I don't?

By the time I make it to the restroom I'm in tears, their hatefulness too awful for me to bear on top of Ryan's abuse. I lock myself into one of the stalls and immediately throw up the four bites of dinner I managed to swallow. When I'm done, I sink against the tastefully floral-papered wall and sob silently.

If only the New State Press was here to capture this moment. I wonder how they would caption this.

The irreverent thought makes me laugh through my tears.

If this isn't how insanity starts...

I stay in the stall for as long as I dare before stepping out to fix my makeup in the lounge. I get a wide variety of looks when the other women see my tear-stained face; some beam triumphantly, some look cowed. One or two stare with sadness and dismay obvious in their dark eyes and knit brows. Not one asks me if I'm alright—just one look at my face answers any questions they could possibly have.

I've somehow managed to lose track of time, but instinct tells me

I've been gone too long. I hurry back to the ballroom, hoping that my lengthy absence hasn't been noticed. Rounding the corner, I find Ryan and my father in a heated argument, both looking mere seconds from tackling each other. Backing away, I pray I haven't been spotted when Ryan's head turns and sees my shocked look. He sways slightly on his feet and downs the remains of his drink, shoving the empty glass into my father's hand and pushing him aside.

He barrels towards me, grabbing my arm and dragging me towards a private elevator. I look over my shoulder at my father who stares after me with a mix of rage, shock and relief. When the elevator doors ding open, Ryan shoves me inside, punching the buttons as if they have somehow personally offended him. He doesn't even look at me, his grip on my wrist bruising and sweaty. When the door opens, we are outside Ryan's personal residence.

Oh, no.

He gives me no choice but to teeter quickly behind him or fall on my face and get dragged. He opens the door with a shove forceful enough to send it slamming against the wall before pushing me into the apartment. A few seconds later, I hear the unmistakable tell-tale click that's as loud as a gunshot in the otherwise silent room.

I am locked in.

I don't know what is about to transpire, I just know that it's wrong. We aren't married yet and shouldn't be alone. I know Ryan knows this. For Christ's sake, he's one of the men who wrote the freaking *Purity Protocols for Unmarried Women*! I have no idea what to do. Should I risk angering Ryan further by voicing my concerns or risk my father's anger tomorrow if he finds out where Ryan brought me and I didn't protect my virtue?

Ryan stalks over to the generously stocked bar and pours himself another hefty drink. He doesn't look at me as I glance around my surroundings from the safety of the doorway.

"Don't just stand there. Come in." It's a command not a request.

I tiptoe into the luxury apartment outfitted in a mixture of rich leather, dark wood, metal and granite. Not a single piece of furniture looks remotely comfortable, the hard surfaces and sharp edges coolly sterile. There's not a single chair or sofa that looks like one I could curl up in comfortably with a book and a blanket and pass a rainy afternoon. The walls are floor-to-ceiling glass in the open-style living room, offering what I'm sure is an amazing view of the city during the day.

I peer through the darkness and catch my first glimpse of the terrifying world outside the razor-wire tipped walls of my Provenance. In the dark, the sharp edges of exposed metal beams, crumbling rock and plaster jut up from over the wall in sinister, spiky teeth. As far as the eye can see, the buildings are in ruin, some bombed to their foundations, others hanging on to shreds of their former height by a whisper and a prayer. One more hurricane and most of what remains upright will be blown to the ground.

An icy chill runs through my body, the sort of physical premonition those being stalked say they felt shortly before an attack. I turn in alarm to find Ryan staring at me, the look much the same as how a tiger eyeballs its next meal.

"Follow me," he demands, his voice thick and low and completely unlike how he sounds on television. I do as he commands, not because he asks me to, but because I'm afraid what will happen if I don't.

When he turns into a dimly-lit bedroom I stop in the doorway, knowing there is no way in hell I should be walking into his sleeping quarters. Ryan continues into the room, unbuttoning his heavy wool uniform jacket and tossing it towards a corner chair. The jacket misses its mark and falls to the floor, the medals clanking heavily together. He doesn't care that the expensive garment lies on the ground, his attention focused solely on polishing off the drink in his hand. I have a suspicion this sense of entitled disregard is not new but has been carefully honed during a lifetime of over-privilege. As I am his newest possession, this type of behavior doesn't bode well for my longevity.

"Close the door and come in," he says through gritted teeth. "Don't make me tell you twice."

His tone is so cold, so firm, I don't dare argue. I walk over to the windows and look out through the heavy drapes at yet another view of the destruction. One of the buildings has #RISEUP spray painted in bold red letters across its bullet riddled facade, the color brighter than the other graffiti. I wonder if it is new and, if so, what type of person would risk their life to write it. I wonder if they knew when they painted it Ryan would see it every day from his window. I have a feeling if I were to ever meet that person, I would like them a great deal.

I'm broken out of my reverie by Ryan coming up behind me and wrapping his arms around my waist. He removed his shirt at some point, revealing the sculpted muscles of his forearms and hands that now rove across my body. I feel his breath hot and moist against the back of my neck, the fumes of excessive amounts of expensive alcohol exuding from his pores nearly thick enough to make me drunk.

He turns me around and presses his mouth to mine, his hands digging into my shoulders so I can't back away. I know I'm supposed to kiss him back with feeling, to pretend I enjoy his wet, fumbling atten-tion, but I just can't. His tongue invades my mouth, the force of his actions bruising my lips. His touch is not passionate—it's possessive. I'm horrified to realize there's little difference between this intrusive kiss and the act of forcing myself to throw up. Both are invasive acts of penetrating violence; the only difference being I feel better after I puke.

Ryan's kisses become vicious, painful bites on my neck while his hands roughly knead my breasts. I try to remove his grasping hands but he pushes them away. His fingers dig in, making me want to claw at his naked chest, but I do nothing. I don't dare invoke his wrath. If he's this rough when he isn't angry, I don't want to find out what he's capable of when he is.

I hope that if I stay passive he will get bored and let me go. He presses himself against me, and I feel his erection jam against my stomach. He begins to lift my skirts. "Ryan, no," I whisper, trying to pull the bunched material from his hands.

"You know you want this," he growls. "Why else would you agree to come up here with me? It's too late for you to change your mind now."

Among the feral human reactions of fight, flight, or freeze, I try to figure which is my best option only to realize they all suck. I try to think of a fourth. When his hand reaches his destination over my most private of places, I take a step back but find myself pressed against the wall. I have just enough room left to let my hand swing back and slap him across the face. Hard.

"I said no!" My voice comes out forceful and commanding, surprising even myself. Ryan lets go of me, the shock on his face as he rubs his reddening cheek almost comical. But his next look—one of pure hate—makes me shake.

"You frigid bitch," he hisses. "What are you, a fucking lesbian? Do you need to spend a few months in a reeducation facility? Trust me, you don't want me recommending you for treatment. A little thing like you wouldn't survive twenty-four hours."

For a moment, I swear to God, my heart stops. What he's threatening is no treatment—it's a slow, eventual death sentence. I know enough about those facilities to understand I never want to step foot in one. The whispered stories of tortured human remains found in the dumpsters behind the local center are enough to sicken even the most intolerant people.

Ryan steps forward, and I back away until I hit the wall. I look up into his cruel eyes in fear, knowing this man can destroy me in so many ways right now. He places his hand firmly against my throat and presses hard enough to make me lightheaded. My gasps for air produce the most sinister grin I've ever seen bloom on Ryan's face.

"Maybe you're not gay. Maybe you're deviant in other ways. Maybe you just like it rough. I had assumed you were raised to be an old-fashioned, missionary-style whore like your mother. You must get your kink from your father."

His sneering tone and glassy eyes terrify me. The tension in his body, his hands that clench and unclench into tight fists, are all the proof I need that he intends to hurt me. Badly. "Come on, whore. You want to fight? Let's see just how much fight you have in you." Grabbing my wrist, he drags me towards the bed.

"I said, no!"

"The wife shall give to her husband her conjugal rights for the wife does not have authority over her own body, but the husband does. What is written in Corinthians in the *Text* is law. Refusing to obey your husband, failing to provide for his needs, is against the teachings of the New State Church. Are you willing to risk prison to deny me?"

"I am not yet your wife," I hiss while trying to twist my wrist out of his grasp. "It's in the contract, I am to be a virgin on our wedding night. They are going to want proof. My father will kill you if you disgrace me!"

Ryan laughs so hard he lets go. I bolt for the door, my heart pounding against my corset. I hear him mutter curses as he chases after me, overtaking me in the hallway. Before I can register what is happening he flings me up against the wall, my head smacking loudly against the dark walnut paneling. My head spins. Gripping my arm painfully, he pulls my dizzy, weakened body from where I cower and slaps me so hard my knees buckle, his thick gold ring of office reopening the thin skin over my barely-healed cheekbone. He is in a blind rage, each slap harder than the last. When I stumble and start to fall, he wraps his hand around my throat and pulls me back up, choking me. The edges of his short, sharp fingernails draw blood as they dig into the back of my neck.

For just a moment the violence stops. He leans into me, his lips a breath away from mine, his thick finger tracing a tender line from my temple to my jaw.

His lip curls into an evil smirk. "You think your father gives a shit about your virtue? He was the one who told me to bring you up here and take you for a test drive. Would you like to call and ask him? I'll even dial the fucking number for you."

No, no, no. This cannot be happening. I'm having a nightmare and any second I'm going to wake up.

Ryan moves closer, his lips grazing mine. The hostile glint in his eyes makes it clear he would be just as happy to snap my neck as he is to defile me. I honestly cannot decide which option is worse. He drags me back into the bedroom and throws me to the ground, my palms shredding against the deep-pile rug. I lie there, stunned and motionless, struggling for each breath; the feel of his fingers wrapped around my neck lingering on my throat. I gasp, coughing and sputtering for air, a fine spray of blood flying with every wheezing exhalation. My lower lip has split open and is dripping a slow stream of blood onto the bodice of my gown. I'm not sure when I started crying, but my face is soaked with tears.

As I struggle to pull myself together, Ryan walks calmly over to his discarded jacket and pulls out a pack of cigarettes. He lights one as he sits heavily on the silk upholstered chair. He stares disdainfully at me, his hateful glare intensifying with each deep drag.

"You think you are something special, don't you? You've pranced around like you are some sort of princess all these years, your father parading you around like some sort of fabulous prize. You probably even believe the bullshit that your virginity is something special, a tremendous gift for you to bestow upon your loving, grateful husband on your magical wedding night. That's what they've told you, isn't it?"

I hope this is a rhetorical question because I can't answer him, my muteness again rearing its ugly head. We are locked in a staring contest, yet another battle I'm not going to win.

"Just so we're crystal clear, I don't want you as a wife. I never wanted you. I want a wife with blood as pure as her untouched cunt. Your lineage doesn't even remotely compare with mine, and I have no desire of breeding with someone as tainted, as *foul*, as you."

Tears stream down my face and drip from my chin, the ones that leak into the open cut on my cheekbone stinging sharply. When I wipe at them my hand comes back covered in watered-down blood.

"But your father insisted that in exchange for him to twist a few arms, to get those last old fucks who are holding out to finally give me their allegiance, I have to marry you. It's actually quite ingenious of him—if you're my wife, if you are the mother of my children, there's no way I'd ruin my own future by spilling the truth of your disgusting lineage. He sees this as a win-win, not that I do, and judging by those hateful glances you keep giving me, neither do you.

"But there's nothing that can be done to stop this. *Nothing.* Our union has been sanctioned, and what the Supreme Archon rules no man can put asunder. We are going to have to find a way to make this marriage work because at this point, the only way out of this marriage is death."

Ryan rises from his chair and walks over to the fireplace mantle. In a place of pride and prominence propped on a small stand is a large bone-handled knife, the kind I think that's used for gutting deer and other gruesome acts. This knife is far from just being a utilitarian tool, the handle intricately carved with scrolling symbols of a sort I have never seen. Ryan pulls the blade from the leather scabbard and runs his finger down the serrated edge before pointing it in my direction. He holds it lovingly—clearly, it's one of his prized possessions.

I hold my breath, having no idea what the sinister gleam in his eyes means as he looks at the blade and then at me. He crouches down, the knife just inches from my face. I freeze as he traces a gentle path down my cheek and jaw with the point, stopping at my throat. He presses the blade against my pulsing jugular.

"I wonder if I can bleed the impurity from you? In time, would shedding enough of your blood drain you of your diseased heritage?" A vicious smirk spreads into a wide smile across his face. I flinch and cry out as he flicks the ultra-sharp point against my throat and punctures my flesh.

"Wives, submit to your own husbands, as to the Lord. For the husband is the head of the wife. Ephesians 5:22-33." He stands and re-sheathes the blade, placing it reverently back on his mantle. I exhale weakly in relief once the knife is out of his hands. Ryan beckons to me, a sly grin forming on his lips. I am shaking so hard I can't stand. Annoyed, Ryan stalks over and grabs me by my hair and pushes me to my knees. He unzips his pants, pulls out his engorged cock and begins to stroke it.

"Tonight, you are going to submit. From here on, I am your Lord and I expect you to obey me as one." His hate and lust-filled eyes harden into chips of ice.

My throat is sore and my voice raspy, but my single word is crystal clear. Despite my fear, I look him squarely in the eye and enunciate the one word I know will get me killed. "No."

For a split-second my single syllable jars him into incredulous immobility, his hand frozen in mid-stroke. I know this is my last chance for flight and I scramble to my feet and make a run for the door. My tight corset and thick underskirts make rising difficult and I lose precious time untangling myself from the fabric wrapped around my legs. I underestimate his speed, as even as drunk as he is, he is quick. He grabs me fiercely by the upper arm and spins me painfully towards him, agonizingly twisting my ankle as my narrow heel catches in the thick carpet. He pulls me towards him and grabs a handful of my hair, shoving me back down to the floor.

"Get on your knees, your filthy whore, and do your job. I want you to wrap those pretty lips around my cock and suck me off. I'm not going to ask again."

I look up at him, all the fire and fury of a thousand suns in my eyes, his own every bit as hateful and determined as mine. We both know I'm not strong enough to successfully fight him but I have to try.

I know I'm baiting the bear when I quietly but firmly respond, "I said no."

"So be it."

Ryan stands motionless. For the briefest of moments I wonder if I have won, if my show of strength has maybe earned his respect. When his lip curls back into a lecherous sneer, I know I misread him. He's not impressed with me.

He's going to *kill* me.

He grabs me roughly by both arms and stares into my eyes, not a single spark of humanity evident in their colorless depth. I scream for help and try to pull free as he laughs like a demented demon. He grabs me by my hair and drags me to the bed as I kick and claw, and despite my efforts to tear him apart, he easily picks me up and throws me on top of the covers. My legs tangle between the layers of petticoats, disabling me further. With little effort, Ryan straddles my thrashing body and, in less than a minute, I am pinned helplessly beneath him.

He leans forward to whisper into my ear. "You will never say no to me again once I'm through with you."

I am so petrified with fear that, at first, I don't even register the pain of his fist smashing into my stomach, his other hand clenched around my throat holding me in place. I beg him to stop, which only fuels him to hit me harder. I claw at him with outstretched fingers, feeling his skin collecting under my pink-painted nails. Nothing I do even slows him down as he's too big, too strong, too enraged for me to stop.

He straddles my face, placing a knee on each of my forearms, pinning my wrists together and holding them over my head with just one of his large hands. The pain of his body weight balanced on the thin bones is excruciating; every time his weight shifts they threaten to shatter.

I have no more fight left—all I can do is sob. I am a prisoner of his body and the voluminous gown that has betrayed me. He grabs my hair and pulls my head back until I scream again. After a moment of fumbling with his pants he shoves his rock-hard penis in my mouth.

I try not to choke as he pumps himself in and out, yanking my head further and further back to get deeper and deeper down my throat. I gag and spit and try to bite, but the way he fists my hair makes it impossible. As he gets closer to climax he rides my face rougher and faster, not looking at me, but with closed eyes and a look of utter satisfaction. His dick cuts off my air, and I gag and sputter as saliva and blood leak out of the sides of my mouth. The first taste of his seed on my tongue makes me want to puke, the pungent odors of alcohol, sweat and his musky arousal mixed with the first drops of his cum too much to bear.

My mind finally takes pity on my abused body and broken spirit and offers me a way out. I'm no stranger to this phenomenon, having experienced it during traumatic times too often to fear its arrival. I grasp for the opportunity disassociation provides to check out of my hellish reality, giving up my futile attempts to fight and choosing instead to preserve what's left of my sanity.

I feel myself slowly rising, floating above my body like some form of ephemeral, perverse spectator. I no longer feel the pain, the mortification, the terror. I have a reprieve, if only temporarily. I welcome the darkness that promises protection with open arms. I will deal with the consequences later.

Ryan has no idea I'm no longer in my body but watching from afar. I witness as he tears at my hair, my near unconsciousness having tipped the scales of his arousal. He groans loudly as he bucks a few more times, his body stiffening in preparation for the final phase of my humiliation. Thick streams of hot, viscous seed shoot down my battered throat as his entire body shudders with release.

I'm close to passing out when he extracts his shriveling cock from my mouth, my throat so abused it feels like I swallowed razor blades. Ryan places his hand around my throat and sadistically instructs me to swallow every drop of the cum that's running out of my mouth.

I do what he commands, not a single ounce of defiance left in my body, and he smiles as he sweetly runs his fingers across my tear and blood-soaked cheeks. His touch under any other circumstances would be considered loving but in this moment, the cruelty of his gentleness is what breaks me. I lose all track of time as he caresses each of the cuts, the bruises, and the marks of ownership he bestowed upon me. I watch as my body lies there, broken and used, as he contemplates attempting a second round.

Sweet Jesus, please, please, no. I can't go through this a second time.

My lack of response bores him, his face twisting back into a mocking grimace before he rises from the bed. I hear him enter the bathroom, the shower turning on and the door closing behind him. Something in me finally snaps and I break into wracking sobs. I try a few times before I successfully manage to sit up with a gasp, my ribs stabbing me into breathlessness as broken bones shift painfully under my corset.

As I fight to regain my composure, I catch a glimpse of myself in the silver gilt mirror across from the bed. My hair hangs in limp disheveled curls, my mascara bleeding down my cheeks and blending with the bruises that have already begun to bloom. Bloody cuts drip from above my eye and over my cheekbones where Ryan's ring sliced my skin. Fresh blood seeps from my split lip, staining my teeth and dripping down the bodice of my gown. I close my eyes, no longer able to face the unrecognizable woman in the mirror.

I would rather die than be his wife.

Behind my closed eyes a picture takes shape. I'm in a gown similar to the torn, blood-stained one I now wear, a lacy veil draped over my long blonde hair. I'm looking in a mirror at myself.

I am a bride.

A single tear drips down my pale cheek as I look down at the bouquet in my hand. I peek through the blooms, searching intently for something and smile when I pull out the straight razor hidden among the white roses and baby's breath. I can almost feel the cool weight in my hand, my heart pounding not in fear, but relief.

In my dream, I take a deep breath and do what I must. I drag the blade up both arms, slicing into the lengths of blue vein, biting my lip to contain my screams. In a matter of minutes, my agony is over as I die amid twin pools of bridal white and crimson death, a dramatic tableau for my father to find when it's time to escort me down the aisle.

It's a simple yet oddly comforting plan, the tool easy enough to procure, the strength to use it a harder commodity to muster. It's easy to say you would rather kill yourself than do something. We've all said it, almost always facetiously, but when you are facing a lifetime of something this awful, when you truly mean every word, is the impetus easier to find?

Somehow, I don't think so.

I know better than to pray for a miracle, to hope God might deliver me from evil like that old prayer says. If I am looking for salvation, I know I'm going to have to find it myself.

I only wish I knew where to look.

5

Ryan

I wake up the next morning naked in my bed with a throbbing headache and a mouth that tastes like I spent last night licking the bottom of an ashtray. My hand is covered in blood, my knuckles split, swollen and raw.

Who the Hell did I brawl with last night?

I sit up with a groan as the room swims around me. I grab the bottle of water and the three pain relievers left for me by some God-send of a servant. I wince as I fall back into the pillows, the soft, feather-filled cushions causing fresh waves of agony to shoot through my head. With the pain comes the memories, and the happenings of last night return in a sudden rush. I don't want to think about it. I don't want to think about *her*.

Shit, I drank way too much last night.

I reach for my cigarettes and pull one out, lighting it and taking a long thoughtful drag. My mind keeps wandering back to her and I don't have the energy to stop it. I open my phone to the news and groan when I see the picture of the two of us kissing in the elevator. Apparently, we are the top story of the day in *The New State Press*. There are countless pictures, all with my arm around her, touching her, kissing her, most of them with a fake, shit-eating grin on my face.

They make my skin crawl.

For decades before the Great War people spoke of white privilege, how we Caucasian men have it so easy, how everything is ours, all we have to do is reach out and take it.

Easy, my ass.

The perception that white men live simple, perfect lives compared to the crap everyone else goes through is complete shit. We have our own trials and tribulations, if anything, those of us at the top of the food chain have greater issues because we have more at stake. Most people of the lower ninety-eighth percentile don't realize that. They're too busy looking for government handouts to think of what we in leadership go through.

There's nothing easy about being in the top one percent. Under the microscope of the public's eye you have to be perfect twenty-four-fucking-seven. Appearances are everything. A righteous man must not only be strong, smart and clever, but also pious and brave. We must be successful, provide for our loved ones and be potent in the bedroom. Above all, a man must never, ever appear weak, especially not in the eyes of an enemy.

Taking Emma as a wife is proving to be nearly as bad as if I were to shack up with her father. I know everything I do will be reported back to him, that she's been groomed to be his little spy. With the blackmail I'm holding over his head he's desperate to find something on me. No doubt he's already looked everywhere to find my hidden skeletons and is going crazy because he can't find them. Little does he know how deep I had to bury the bodies so they will never be found.

I flex my hand and cringe as the skin reopens and blood trickles from my knuckles. If my hands are anything to go by, last night got out of hand, but from what I can remember, Emma hadn't given me much choice. I have a reputation to uphold. If she tells her father she refused me and I did nothing about it, he will tell everyone. I will be a laughingstock. If I do not uphold the laws, if I fail to correct my own wife's errant ways, who will ever respect me?

Through the years I've realized that, in regards to women, respect and fear go hand-in-hand. A man that can't control his woman shouldn't call himself a man. A bruised woman is a disciplined woman, her spilled blood proving the strength of her husband's belief in the New State Church. Last night I sent a clear message to Emma, her father and the rest of the Archons. Step in my way, tell me no, and I will destroy you. If beating a girl that weighs 100 pounds less than me to a bloody pulp is how I have to show my dominance, then so be it.

My queasy stomach flips in protest as flashes of what Emma looked like when she left my bed pop into my mind. If she has any sense she will stop fighting me now. Doesn't she realize that short of one of us dying before the wedding there is nothing to be done? Even killing her and making it look like an accident won't help, the provisions Edward insisted upon in the contract for her "accidental" death made crystal clear. He will make sure any attempts on her life will absolutely come back to bite me in the ass. As much as it pains me, I'm stuck with the bitch. I sold my soul and turned my back on my deepest beliefs for her father's backing. Now, I must live with my decision.

All those years ago I made a vow on my sister's grave that I would get my revenge, never once dreaming that singular purpose would lead me to where I am now. I worked my way up from nothing to become the second most powerful man in the nation. I never thought it would lead to marrying a girl with tainted blood, but it's a sacrifice I'm willing to make if it guarantees me the Supremacy.

Looking again at the pictures, I have to admit Emma does have a few redeeming qualities. Her vibrant blue eyes and what appears to be unbleached blonde hair fit the ideal criteria for my consort, her slight build making her easy to physically control. Her skin is free of blemish and about as shockingly white as white can be before it begins to glow in the dark. You would never know that nineteen percent of the blood running through her veins is tainted and vile, a dark stain only visible on the Ancestry DNA test her mother had been stupid enough to run way back in the day. I remember that trend, when everyone wanted to know where they came from, wondering if there were deep, dark secrets in their roots. Little did they know while swabbing their cheeks that their DNA profiles were being kept on government servers—a ticking time-bomb just waiting for future use.

I wonder how many of those people looking for a little entertainment ended up deported or dead?

I really shouldn't berate Edward's wife for her stupidity. After all, if she never sent in her brat's DNA, if the proof hadn't been there for me to find, I wouldn't be where I am now. It's that single sheet of paper, that shred of proof, that led to my appointment as an Archon and will enable my ascent. Just as I think it would be nice of me to send her a lovely thank you note I always remember the catch; it also means I have to marry her contemptible daughter.

I look back at the picture of us kissing in the elevator. Yeah, Emma is pretty in a pixie-like way. She looks younger than her nineteen years, the only curves on that girl created by foam pads and artful tailoring. I tried to find some semblance of tits in that gown last night and found nothing. She was as flat as a ten-year-old boy.

Well, there's always implants.

As disappointed as I am in her frail, child-like body I know it's not her looks that are giving me third and fourth thoughts this morning. I'm embarrassed to admit that even with her dirty blood, she is certainly fuckable. As much as I wish I wasn't turned on by her, my traitorous dick had zero problem performing *his* duty last night. My life would be easier if I didn't want to fuck her. I can't bear the thought of breeding with her, of knowingly creating another life tainted with dark blood. This is one of the few instances where birth control *should* be legal but since the Articles of Incorporation went into effect nearly fifteen years ago, there has not been a pill or condom to be found. Of the ones the government hadn't confiscated, the rest, I'm sure, were used long ago.

Even if I could get my hands on birth control there's still the problem of those additional clauses her father insisted upon. He wants Emma to have a child within the first year of our marriage. *Why* he wants that is the question I haven't yet been able to answer. I know he wants to tie our families together to keep the blackmail tight, but I know there has to be another motive, something I'm missing. Judging by how he treats his offspring, I know he's not dying to become a grandpa. Aside from me, a less paternal man would be hard to find.

I slam my phone down on the nightstand, my stomach's visceral response to even the thought of breeding with Emma enough to make me gag.

I bet my sister's laughing her ass off in her grave.

I close my eyes and snippets of last night flash through my brain. I cringe slightly, knowing my hands should not have fisted when I hit Emma and my grip on her wrists had been too strong. If she hadn't been so belligerent, so haughty, I never would have gotten that angry. I know I'm not at fault, that I have nothing to feel guilty about. Her lack of submission is what caused me to lose my temper, and I was well within my rights to discipline her. The *New State Church Text* is crystal clear on the ways a husband should handle an errant wife. Last night, I was doing God's work by bringing her to heel. She has only herself to blame for whatever little bruises she's dealing with today.

She better watch her step before she ends up like Janey.

I want to gouge my brains out with a spoon for daring to even think that. My twin sister, God rest her soul, had been as pure as the driven snow until he came around and corrupted her. She was as sweet as a newborn fawn until he wormed his way into her body, into her blood, and tainted her with his poison. When she was gone no one was surprised when our father took his own life just a few weeks later. I hate him for that. I hate him for being weak and leaving me and my mother behind. I hate knowing that if I had been the one to die, his life would have gone on, business as usual.

My head is pounding in rhythm with my heart, the pills I took doing nothing to ease my pain. I pick up the copy of the *Text* I keep at my bedside and flip through the ear-marked pages. I reread my favorite verses, looking for comfort for my oddly conflicted mind.

Wives, submit to your own husbands, as to the Lord. Ephesians 5:22-24. I take another drag of my cigarette and exhale another long breath of smoke. Yeah, she most certainly needs to work on her submission. Hopefully after last night she will have gotten the hint. I feel better, knowing the New State Church may not condone the extent of my discipline but certainly backs my right to teach my wife the ways of the Lord.

Titus 2:9. Slaves are to be submissive to their own masters in everything; they are to be well-pleasing and not argumentative. I most certainly was not *well-pleased* with Emma's behavior last night and I'm not any happier today. Anger swells inside my chest, the same hate that overwhelmed me last night rearing its head once again. No half-breed bitch is going to tell me what to do. The rules are right here in black in white, the laws of both God and State firmly in my corner.

I close the *Text* reverently, my soul buoyed with the knowledge that what I did is justified by the Highest Authority. Last night, I performed my duty to the Church by addressing Emma's shortcomings. Yes, the only person she can blame for last night is herself.

1 Peter 3:5-6. *For this is the way the holy women of the past who put their hope in God used to adorn themselves. They submitted themselves to their own husbands, like Sarah who obeyed Abraham and called him her Lord.*

Emma should be on her knees *thanking* me for last night, my actions the route to the redemption of her immortal soul. If she read her *Text* as she should, she would know how to behave, how to please me. She *made* me beat her, it was *her* hand that compelled me to make her submit.

I suddenly have no idea why I feel even remotely guilty about last night. *I* was the one without choice, her lack of respect, her inability to honor *me* forcing my hand. She deserved everything she got last night and probably more.

I know Edward has some sort of sinister plan up his sleeve, some trump card he plans to pull out to bring me to heel, but he underestimates me. He thinks I'm unaware that he's up to something but my eyes are open and I'm waiting for him to make a mistake. Meanwhile, I'm enacting my own schemes in this twisted game where we are both the thickest of allies and the gravest of enemies.

So for now, I will let him continue to think I am unaware. I will go along with his plan. And when the time is right, I will strike hard and fast.

I will bring him down, and I will use his daughter to crush him.

6

Emma

I wake the next morning in my own bed and for one sleepy moment everything seems normal. Then I make the mistake of moving and the stabbing pain in my ribs reminds me that my life right now is anything but.

I manage to limp to the bathroom and look in the mirror at a reflection that can't possibly be mine. My face is bruised beyond recognition, my left eye swollen shut and my throat covered in purple and blue imprints of Ryan's grasp. My split lip is held together by a thin coating of dried blood that threatens to give way at any moment. I try to flex my grossly swollen ankle and find that although it's too tumescent to function it's more than happy to hurt. Sharp pain shoots up my leg with the few degrees of motion I manage to produce.

How am I going to face the world after receiving a beating like this on the night of my supposedly blissful engagement party?

Out of the corner of my eye, I see the pile of cloth that had once been my lavish gown lying mutilated and bloody on the floor. I had been too exhausted and traumatized to undo the laces and double-tied knots that would have preserved the priceless garment. Instead of taking the time to calm my shaking hands, I had cut it off using a knife

I found in the kitchen. It had been a frenzied and vicious mutilation of months of detailed work, but I didn't care. I had screamed and sobbed like a crazy woman, stabbing and tearing the fabric. In some perverse way, I had tried to get some satisfaction out of destroying this symbol of my future, but all it did was remind me that I had been as desecrated and defiled as the scraps of satin and lace at my feet.

I take a long hot shower, letting the water massage my battered body, every drop of water pelting like a needle of scalding hail. I had hoped to receive some relief, some comfort from boiling my skin and scrubbing away the lingering traces of Ryan's touch, but by the time the hot water runs out, I just feel drained, burned and raw.

I spend the rest of the day curled up in my bed, the covers over my head as I stare unseeingly at my shroud. My phone doesn't ring, no one calling to check on me, no one caring enough to see if I'm still alive. Every breath I take stabs like a knife, my ankle throbbing and my throat so sore I can't even take sips of water. I wonder if my ankle is broken, if my one year of dancing is already over. I look at the kitchen knife that still lies on the floor by the discarded scraps of fabric.

If it's broken, then there's no reason to wait.

7

I GET NO REPRIEVE from the pain in my body and mind from either the light or the dark. I refuse to close my eyes, Ryan's snarling face flashing before me forcing my eyelids open with the force of a once tightly-wound spring. The next morning, I remain in the sanctuary of my bed until the very last minute. There is no point in attempting makeup to hide what happened, no way to style my hair to cover my inconcealable shame.

I'm in tears when I stagger into the studio camouflaged in dark glasses and a loose sweatshirt with the hood pulled over my head. The wrap around my grotesquely swollen ankle gives little support and only succeeds in making the throbbing worse. I sink into my customary corner and prepare myself for class as the other dancers chatter gaily around me. I keep myself as hidden as possible with my eyes down, unable to face the floor to ceiling mirrors that mock me from every angle. I am so ashamed I can hardly breathe.

Jeremy enters the room and claps his hands twice, our cue to take our places at the barre. I take a deep breath. Rehearsal is three-and-a-half hours today.

I can do it. I will do it. I must do it.

I rise on unsteady legs, peel the hoodie from my body and take my place at the barre, hearing the muffled gasps of my fellow company members. All speech ceases. I don't even have to look at them to know they are gawking at the gory sight before them. My partner, Michael, reaches out to steady me as I stumble and I flinch away from his fingers. He withdraws his hand as if my shame has tainted him, his eyes wide and afraid.

I line up next to Anna, who gapes at me intently with those all-seeing, insightful green eyes. I try to decipher the look she gives me, but all I can figure is it's a mix of hate, surprise and pity. I had expected her to be smug and gloating. I hadn't expected her to look angry.

Jeremy strides towards me and I shake my head to not come closer. He sees it all, he knows it's bad, and I can tell by his expression he wants to help me so badly, but he's also afraid. Hell, we're all afraid. We've all learned at some point that it's not safe to stick your nose where it doesn't belong, and that Good Samaritans often come to grisley ends. The safest thing to do when faced with someone else's tragedy is to offer up your worthless thoughts and prayers and be thankful that, this time, it's not you.

Yup, schadenfreude at its best.

I try my damnedest to perform the complicated combinations but within minutes, I am in agony. The other dancers sneak concerned looks at me and with each other, and I can almost feel some of them willing me the strength to continue. Their kindness makes me want to push through and pretend everything is fine, but the pain is excruciating. My tears are brimming and threaten to fall as I try to do the impossible and blink them back. I swipe clumsily at my face just as the first one escapes, and without my hand on the barre my ankle gives out. I land on my ass with a sickening thud.

The rehearsal pianist stops, the silence beyond deafening. Every dancer stands frozen and stares as they watch their greatest fear come to life. Watching a company member fall and not get up is one of the most terrifying things a dancer can see in their always-too-short careers. Your heart breaks for them, knowing they must be overcome with terror as they face a potential future outside of the spotlight.

I'm too tired, too broken both physically and mentally to hold it all together and I burst into frustrated, unapologetic tears. I give up. They win. My shame is complete and total. I have no more pride to wound.

Someone, just hand me a fucking knife. I'm ready right now. I can't do this anymore.

Jeremy hurries over to where I am trying my best to become one with the hardwood. I clutch my ankle, the pain so intense I know it must be broken.

Jeremy's face is pale and anxious as he asks me a million questions. *Where does it hurt? Did you hear a pop? No? That is good. Okay. Here's a tissue. Blow your nose, you will be okay. Will someone please call for a transport to medical?*

He's trying to catch my eye, trying to make me look at him but I can't. I don't want to see the pity in his gaze, the deep sorrow wrinkling his forehead, the turned-down edges of his usually smiling mouth. He puts his hand under my chin and lifts my face. His eyes are so warm, so caring, their deep brown depths so empathetic my heart warms as my tears begin to slow. He gently picks me up and carries me out into the hallway as another staff member takes over the class. My last glance before the door shuts behind me is Anna's angry glare, her eyes glittering with hostility.

Bitch.

Once Jeremy gets me seated in the hall, he asks if he can take a look under my leg warmer and I nod. He only lifts the thick knitted fabric an inch before he sees the gross swelling. He swears in some foreign language, then blanches, knowing he has just broken the third of the Ten Fundamental Laws, the one that states we all must only ever speak American.

I give him a tired look that I hope conveys I don't care about his slip. I think he understands. He remains silent for a few minutes, taking in my blood crusted lip, the cut over my eye, the terrible bruising and swelling that disfigures the entire right side of my face.

"This injury to your leg—it did not just happen now, in class, did it?"

My lack of answer is enough of a response for him to understand. He pats my shoulder, calls me a brave girl and waits with me silently until my ride arrives. As the members of the medical staff help me out to the waiting van, Jeremy looks at me sadly, the pity I so didn't want to see evident in his eyes. I'm sure he thinks he will never see me again, and I'm terrified he's right.

It's a short drive to the emergency room where I am whisked into a wheelchair and taken directly to a private room despite the packed waiting area. There are people with all sorts of injuries and illnesses, the metallic scent of blood heavy in the air, the thick coughs of the chronically ill too loud in the over-occupied room. One man sits in a chair holding a blood-saturated rag to his hand, his severed finger propped up on the table before him in a clear plastic cup filled with ice.

Of all the people in here, I'm probably the least injured. I have no right to feel wretched, no right to preferential treatment when there are sicker, more injured people waiting for God only knows how long to be seen. I get a few nasty glances at being taken back right away, a few people whispering and staring as if they recognize me.

I only realize just how big a mistake it was to come here when the nurse asks to scan my state issue ID we're required to have on us at all times. If the wrong people find out I'm here, if the extent of my injuries become public, my father and Ryan will be furious. Already too many people have seen my battered face, too many people have witnessed the shame I've brought on myself and my family. Once my card is scanned there will be proof that the woman they saw rolled in doesn't just *look* like Emma Bellamy, she *is* Emma Bellamy.

Shit. I have to get out of here.

I tell the nurse I made a mistake and I want to go home, but the second my feet hit the floor, I nearly fall over from the pain. The short, stocky woman looks at me with the bored superiority of one used to getting her way as she helps me back up on the table and tosses a hospital gown in my lap. She tells me if I want to someday get discharged I *will* get changed and *will* be examined, and to be quick about it because they are swamped with patients and she doesn't have time to "dick around." She leaves without scanning my card, not that I point out her mistake. Despite her detailed, officious manner, I get the feeling she's forgotten on purpose, that she somehow knows the sort of punishment I'll receive for daring to come here.

Within a few minutes an older gentleman with salt-and-pepper hair and wearing a long white coat enters the room. He smiles as he extends his hand to me even though he shouldn't. There's no way we are of the same class as someone of my status would never stoop so low as to work in a public hospital. I still shake his hand, albeit tentatively, not wanting to seem rude.

"Hello, Miss Bellamy, I'm Dr. Andrews. I understand you hurt your ankle in class today?"

I nod.

"May I take a look?" Again, I nod.

He gently pokes and prods, asking me what hurts and apologizing profusely whenever I hiss or gasp in pain. He types some notes on his laptop when the exam is finally over, and I'm thankful I made it through with only two nods of my head. But instead of leaving, he puts down the computer and pulls up a small stool and sits down in front of me.

He has warm, dark blue eyes that wrinkle at the edges when he smiles, his mouth also showing the grooved lines of laughter of someone having lived at least half a century. He has the look of a kind man, a man that jokes with his wife on a regular basis and good-heartedly teases his children during dinner. His hands are large and gentle, the hands of a man that would never dream of using them for violence, only to heal.

"Would you like to tell me what really happened?" He gestures in the general direction of my face and neck.

When I don't respond, he continues, sounding a bit exasperated, but at least not angry. "Emma, I can't help you if you don't tell me. Different types of injuries can do different types of damage. If you don't tell me truthfully what happened, I could miss something serious, maybe even life threatening."

There is no way in hell I'm telling him the truth. Public hospitals aren't places to divulge private information, the cameras in the waiting rooms, the computerized records, the low-paid employees just waiting for an opportunity to spill information and make a few bucks. Even though Dr. Andrews seems sincere enough, if he doesn't report me, there's a good chance someone else will.

A person can go insane thinking about this stuff. Who to trust, who to confide in, who's really on your side and who's out to get you. Since there's no way of knowing, the smart thing, the rational thing, is to trust no one.

"I fell," I whisper, averting my gaze to the floor.

"I see." His noncommittal tone is still somehow full of disbelief. He nods to himself before placing his fingers under my jaw and tipping my head so my eyes are forced to meet his. "Emma, I'm not a stupid man. I know that's not true."

What does this man want from me? I sit frozen, my panic cresting again. I fight it down, turning my head away and looking down at my hands as I pick at a piece of loose skin next to my thumbnail.

"Emma, I would like to fully check you out to make sure you are alright, but I need your permission. I promise I will not take any notes or tell anyone what I see. I understand yours is a very delicate situation and the last thing I want is to make things worse for you. I just have this gut feeling that there is more hurting you than a very angry ankle and a banged up face. I will never be able to forgive myself if I turn a blind eye and something terrible, something I could have prevented, happens. There are too many people out there I'm unable to help but you aren't one of them. Please, let me help you, Emma."

I remain as still as the proverbial deer in headlights. I continue to pick at that loose piece of skin until the first drop of blood surfaces.

"Look at me, Emma." He takes my hand and holds it carefully between his, preventing any further self-inflicted violence. "I will not judge you and I won't tell anyone what you say, I swear on my life. I know you are afraid, but you are safe here. I promise."

A single tear slides down my cheek and he wipes it away with a swipe of his thumb. I nod my assent. He pats my arm lightly, a comforting gesture I hadn't realized I really need right now. His hands are gentle and clinical, starting at my temples and pressing over the bones around my eyes. As his hands move systematically over my body, he tells me exactly what he is doing so he doesn't take me by surprise. When he gets to my ribs, his light palpation through the hospital gown causes me to yelp. His sharp, shocked inhalation as he peeks beneath the gown and discovers the extensive areas of twilight colors ends with a muttered curse.

When he's finished, he faces me, and against my better judgment, I look up into his steely blue eyes. He's angry, his lips pressed together in a thin white line, his brow drawn and his breath coming fast. My entire body stiffens, my eyes widening in alarm.

He chooses his next words carefully. "I know you won't tell me what actually happened, or who did this to you, but I have a fairly good idea. I know I am supposed to ignore these types of injuries in women. I know that by law, a woman's body is the property of either her father or husband, and she can be disciplined as they see fit. But right now, I want you to forget all of that and listen to me.

"I don't care what anyone says, there is no justification in the world for what happened to you. None. Beating women is not God's work. No matter what he said to justify this, you did not deserve it. If you were my daughter I would kill whoever did this to you."

I suddenly realize he's not outraged *at* me. He's outraged *for* me.

"I know my thoughts are unorthodox and against the *New State Church Text* and I'm taking one hell of a risk saying this to you, of all people. I know you can turn me in, and right now, I don't even care, because I cannot stay quiet. What was done to you is wrong."

"Thank you," I whisper. Tears spill from my eyes as he takes my hands in his.

"Listen to me carefully, Emma. I am very concerned by what I'm seeing. I know that at a minimum, you have multiple bruised ribs, but more than likely they are broken. I would like to take some films and also get a CT of your abdomen—there could be internal bleeding based on your pain and extensive bruising. May I do that?"

I try to quell the paranoia that rises again. I don't know what to do. My trust in men in positions of authority is so wrecked I don't know what to do when one is being nice. If he wants to protect his own neck he should send me home with painkillers and pretend he never saw me. That's what he *should* do.

Instead, he is putting himself out there, choosing to trust *me* when, based on my last name alone, he certainly shouldn't. I wonder what possible reason could prompt him to say what he did. From past experience, when someone is being nice there's always a selfish motive, yet he seems so sincere. I sigh resignedly. I know I shouldn't, but if he's willing to trust me, I'm willing to trust him.

I just hope I don't live to regret this.

"Promise me no one will know," I whisper. He smiles sadly as he nods. He tells me to not worry, he will only use his most trustworthy technicians and will make sure all the records disappear. I have a strong suspicion this isn't the first time he has done this and that makes me like him even more.

"You are not alone, Emma. We want to help you," he says before slipping from the room like the white-jacketed angel I suspect he is.

* * *

Once the tests are done, I wait in silence for a long while, my eyes scanning the nearly bare room in boredom. I inventory the scuffs and stains on the faded tan walls wondering what they were made by and how long they've been there. The broken cabinet door hangs by its remaining loose screw; much like my brain, it appears one slam shy of losing its grip completely.

There's a tentative knock at the door that breaks the silence and makes my heart lurch into my mouth. Before I can say "enter" the door opens to reveal Anna standing in the dingy hallway with my dance bag slung over her shoulder, my sneakers dangling from her opposite hand.

"I thought you might want these," she says, dropping the bag and shoes on the floor. Her Russian accent sounds thicker within the confines of the room. "Cranky nurse-lady say is okay for me to come in."

She's almost sheepish as she leans against the door frame, but her eyes study me carefully. I search her face for clues to her unexpected appearance, but she hides whatever she's thinking behind an emotionless mask. The only sign of her feelings is the fire in her eyes.

Not caring if my actions are rude I stare back at her. Under close scrutiny, I'm surprised how much Anna and I look alike—close enough, in fact, we could be mistaken for sisters. We are both slight of build although Anna is a few inches taller than me and slightly curvier. Instead of having blue eyes, hers are a dark emerald green;

her hair dyed whereas mine is naturally blonde. The lines around her eyes give away she's a good ten years my senior; the slightly pouty expression on her full lips one I can't tell if is by nature or attitude.

I can't help but wonder why she's here. She's the last person I'd expect to bring me my things, and I can only imagine she came because she feels guilty for being cruel to me the past few weeks. Is she now offering the proverbial olive branch with this uncharacteristically thoughtful gesture? The bitter side of me thinks that's giving her way too much credit. She's probably here to ask if she can move into my rooms when I'm sent home for good.

"I'm sorry about your ankle." Her voice takes on a slightly different tone—one that's mildly predatory and puts me on edge. "Did they tell you how bad it is? How long until you dance again?"

I stare at her in shock, stunned speechless as anger floods my veins. I have always hated the c-word and have never once said it in my life, but Anna has not only crossed the line from *bitch* to *cunt* but has continued to run a full mile past it. Something in me snaps, nineteen-years worth of unexpressed rage boiling over and pouring out of me.

"Wow, you are a real piece of work, you know that?" I growl. "You aren't here because you give a shit about me. You just want to know how long I'm going to be out of commission. You're hoping I'm out for the season, aren't you? Aren't you?"

My bitter words startle her, her face drawing tight and her eyes widening. I take a strange satisfaction from her surprise, my voice growing louder and more venomous as I continue. "What kind of fucked-up asshole makes a special trip to gloat at someone when they're down? I always thought you were a bitch, but damn, you've completely outdone yourself, today. I tried my hardest to be nice to you from day one, knowing how hard it must be for you to constantly get demoted, especially when you probably only have a few years left in those knees. When I got here, I felt guilty for taking one away, so

I did my best to overlook your bitchy behavior, but I just can't do it anymore."

Judging by the look on her face, I successfully shocked her. "No, that's not. . .Look. I am sorry. I just. . ." She fumbles for words, pausing for a moment as she decides what to say next. But whatever she originally thought, she changes her mind.

"You know what?" She takes a menacing step towards me, her finger pointed at my face like she's ready to deliver a lecture to an ill-behaved child. "You think you know me? You think you know why I am here? You think I'm a bad person? Let me tell you something. You know nothing," she hisses, eyes narrowing. "You know *nichto* about me, but I know you. I come here today because I see you have great pain and it makes me sad. I come to see if you need help, knowing you have no one in your life who cares about you. But you decide to put words in my mouth before I even ask what it is I can do.

"How can you think I am happy to see you like this? As a dancer, I am scared for you, for your career. As a woman, I have outrage that Ryan do this to you. Do not try to lie to me and say it was not him. I know it was him. You act as if I am monster, like I am happy seeing another woman hurt, and I take this as insult. I will not stand here and let you say such ugly things to me. So, here, take your shit. Have a nice life." With a final dramatic glare, she strides gracefully from the room, flipping me the finger on her way out.

I immediately feel sorry for my outburst. I just can't get a read on her, and her broken English doesn't make her any easier to understand. But what Anna can't possibly understand is how much I envy her. She's traveled the world. She's the master of her own life, a rare unmarried woman with no living father or brother to rule her universe. She must follow the Purity Protocols for Women, sure, but as long as she takes no husband, she can continue to perform. The Commission for Women's Purity deemed years ago that it's not respectable for married women to perform on stage so that leaves me one lousy year to dance. One. As privileged as I've been from birth, I would give it all up for the freedom she has. I know that makes me sound ungrateful. Maybe I am. But is it really so awful for me to want to have some say in my own future?

Dr. Andrews reappears with a brown paper bag filled with something that smells absolutely amazing. He unwraps a large sandwich from its tinfoil cocoon, filling the room with the hearty aromas of seasoned steak, onions, peppers, and some form of sharp, pungent cheese. My mouth waters and my stomach rumbles as he hands me half. I try to refuse, telling him I'm not hungry, but he doesn't take no for an answer. As we stand off over the proffered food, my traitorous stomach demands to be fed with a loud gurgle.

Resignedly, I take the half and stare at it like it may bite before gently nibbling at one end. Sweet St. Sebastian, it's the most delicious thing I have ever tasted. I ask him what it's called and he confesses that he doesn't dare say, as the cheese steak's namesake city is a place we are no longer allowed to mention by law.

He changes the subject by diving into the results of my tests: Grade 2 ankle sprain, three cracked ribs and a few more that are deeply bruised. Films of my orbital ridge are inconclusive with something that could be a minor fracture of my cheekbone or possibly just a shadow. The abdominal CT was clear, but for safety's sake, he begs me to refrain from "falling" again anytime soon. His voice is light, but his eyes implore me to take caution.

"I think, with some luck, we can have you back on your feet in two months. I have our best PT guy coming down to look at you in a few minutes. He can start with you this afternoon, if you have an extra hour or two to spend with us."

"I have no plans." I take a bigger bite of the sandwich and chew happily. I am beyond relieved that the ankle isn't broken, that my dreams of dancing are not yet over. We finish our sandwiches as the kind doctor asks me questions about ballet, his easy manner so comfortable I finally drop my guard. Before he leaves, Dr. Andrews takes my hand gently and clasps it between his. "If you ever need me again you know where to find me."

My eyes fill with tears. "Thank you, Doctor. Your kindness means the world to me."

Little does he know that his benevolence has tipped my mental scales in favor of giving life another chance. He smiles sadly as he backs away, placing his hand over his heart in silent admission that my words have touched him, as well.

After Dr. Andrews departs I sit alone, again victim to the cruel workings of my mind. I feel horrific guilt for eating that sandwich knowing very well that not being able to dance or work out for a few months means no caloric splurging. Luckily, there's an adjoining private bathroom in my room and I limp over to the toilet to take care of business. I'm on my knees in front of the toilet with my fingers down my throat, the bathroom door only partially closed when I hear the main door swing open without notice.

Crap.

The last thing I need is whoever's coming in reporting what I'm doing to Dr. Andrews as he may never let me out of here. I shuffle over to the bathroom door and slam it shut with my uninjured foot. I flush and wash my hands and rinse my mouth before limping back into the exam room to face the music.

The man in the room and I just stare at each other for a moment. He has to be the physical therapist, the long sleeve black t-shirt with the embroidered Sports Medicine logo suggesting his identity. The low-slung khaki pants, the thick black belt and scuffed combat boots make him look more like a thug than a member of the medical staff. His black hair is untamed, almost as if he had just woken up, his dark eyes wide with surprise. He looks familiar.

"Jesus H. Christ on a cracker." The guy recognizes me, his pale skin blanching further, his mouth opening in incredulity before catching himself and closing it forcefully. His brown eyes darken, becoming almost as black as his tousled curls. His face hardens in fury, his wrath evident in the taut way he holds himself, each of his well-toned muscles bunched for either fight or flight. As much as I try not to, I flinch back a step, his eyes widening in response to the fear he sees in mine.

Without another word, he turns on his heel and flees the room, slamming the door behind him.

8

Declan

I had a feeling today was going to suck balls way before I even got paged to the ER.

I've been working in Sports Medicine for the past four years and although it isn't the department I want to be in, it's at least a job in medicine. If I've learned nothing else in life, it's that beggars can't be choosers and, trust me, I'm well aware of the fact I'm in no position to choose anything. Hell, a few years ago I never would have dreamed even this job would be possible. So I do my best to remind myself to behave and remain grateful. I try my damnedest not to be too big an asshole and be a model employee, to fly below the radar and keep my head low. Some days I succeed better than others.

Today is most certainly not one of my better days.

Knowing I'm always only one step away from being tossed out on my ass, I come in at the crack of dawn and do all the stupid shit the people I work with feel is beneath them. I make coffee, tidy the waiting room and restock supplies before getting the day's files in order. I hate doing all these bullshit jobs but they help keep me employed when I do blow a gasket and flip out on someone. So, in the long run I guess it's worth it.

I started working in physical therapy as an aide and over the years I've worked my ass off to become one of the best full-time therapists this shitty hospital ever had. I know my job better than most of the guys here who have fancy University degrees and legitimate licenses. I study more, I read more and I have more experience putting people back together than the rest of the morons I work with combined. I never talk to them about how or where I got my education. It's none of their goddamn business. In all honesty, most days I do my best to not talk to anyone at all.

Everyone in my department knows I commute in from outside the wall, the color of my state-issued ID card, much like the color of my hair and eyes, giving me away. I get asked to show ID so often I've resorted to wearing the damned thing around my neck so I don't have to waste time yanking out my wallet whenever someone wants to fuck with me.

Every morning starts with a long-ass hike into work. As I near the checkpoint, I always pray this isn't the day the wall watchers remind me that every day they let me pass through without a rifle shoved in my face is a gift. I then work a twelve hour shift with a forced grin, and a whole bunch of *yes sirs, no ma'ams* and a fuck ton of *my pleasures* that, trust me, are never pleasurable.

It sucks, but it sure as shit beats prison.

I get all the patients nobody else wants, the miserable ones that are now doubly pissed off because they've got a half-blood touching them. Most of them act like I've got cooties they're going to catch from me, some so paranoid they demand I wear gloves when I touch them. Others treat me like I'm an exotic and dangerous zoo animal that's going to maul them and steal their wallet at any moment.

So far today, I dealt with a skank of a Director's wife who wanted me to rub the non-existent knots out of her shoulders while she moaned like a whore and kept trying to grab my dick. Then there was the racist fuck recovering from a stroke that kept calling me a lazy spic. This last one was recovering from shoulder surgery, a skin-head beyond pissed off the operating doctor fucked up his detailed swastika tattoos. By the time I was done with him, I was ready to slit my fucking wrists.

This all happened before 11 am.

Yeah, good times.

In the grand scheme of things this is a typical day in my life. But right now, I'm so aggravated I don't even care that I'm already running late and I've got another patient waiting. I sneak out of the office to grab a cup of free coffee from the hallway cart, because, you know, a nice boost of caffeine is always helpful when you're already borderline murderous. Just as I'm almost feeling sorry for the fuckers that have to deal with me this afternoon, my pager goes off with a STAT summon to the ER.

I know it's most likely John. Sometimes he brings bagels for the department for breakfast and if there are leftovers, he lets me take them instead of tossing them. I walk a little quicker when I think that maybe, just maybe, this is one of those lucky days when his wife has been thoughtful enough to pack an extra lunch for me. The days that happen are like winning the lottery. She knows I don't eat during the day unless she packs something extra in John's brown bag.

Nobody with my kind of ID gets paid well enough to afford to eat out during our shifts, that is, if I can even find a place willing to serve me. Even though I'm the one in my department who handles the lion's share of everything, because of my mixed blood, I get paid less. I'm the one left starving unless someone gives me a handout, and I fucking hate taking people's pity food. Depending on who's offering, I'd rather starve.

My stomach growls at the mere thought of food. I haven't eaten in about twenty-four hours and I swear to Christ, I can actually feel stomach acid burning a hole through my guts. With all the time I spend at work I have little time for luxuries like waiting in long lines at the grocery store that's always already picked clean. I can't afford much more than a dozen eggs, a jar of peanut butter and a loaf of stale bread each week, and I ration that shit carefully to make sure I can at least eat something every day. Sometimes no matter how careful I am, I can't make it stretch. This is one of those times.

John is busy with another patient when I get there, so his nurse directs me to where I'm needed. I head down the long corridor, noting the lights that burned out a month ago still haven't been replaced, the bathroom set aside specifically for the D-class, people like me, is still out of order. I know my kind is never a priority, but for Christ's sake, it's been six months, already. How much longer is it going to take for them to find someone to fix the shitter down here?

In the hallway, I catch a whiff of what is obviously one of Marta's signature Philly cheese steaks. My mouth waters at the delicious scent of perfectly spiced steak, peppers and onions. I can practically taste the bite of the hot peppers and the creamy sharp provolone that smooths away the sting. I lick my lips in anticipation, my excitement for this sandwich so overwhelming I'm surprised I haven't sprung wood.

Marta knows her cheese steaks are my absolute favorite and always packs extra for me when she's able. I hope when I'm done with this patient I can take my half back to my treatment room and devour it while reading the most recent medical journal I "borrowed" from the hospital library. It drives my coworkers nuts when I do occasionally bring food back to eat but I don't care. Bringing the spicy ethnic specialties back to my cramped office and stinking up the place is one of the few ways I get my kicks anymore.

I am lost in my nearly pornographic food fantasy when I open the door and walk into a scene that stops me dead in my tracks. A wisp of a girl someone had very recently beaten the shit out of is on her knees in front of the toilet, her fingers down her throat. Her other arm is wrapped around her ribs like she's trying to hold them in as she pukes with practiced silence.

The look of agony on her face has me wincing in sympathy knowing too well how God-awful a beating like that hurts. The tell-tale bitter, acidic odor of bile hangs in the air, the look of guilt on her face making it obvious she doesn't have the stomach flu. Always one to put a puzzle together pretty quickly, I surmise she just hurled up my half of John's lunch just as my stomach takes that exact moment to gurgle embarrassingly loud.

I mentally swear at my protesting stomach to shut the fuck up as it continues to growl in dissatisfaction. I glare at the girl, wanting to shake some sense into her. I want to shout that if you are going to agree to eat someone's food, for fuck's sake, at least have the decency to digest it.

I know I sound like a real prick, but I can't help it. Judging by her shiny hair and expensive clothes, this girl has money to spare. She could have afforded to buy lunch, she sure as shit didn't need a handout. The girl narrows her eyes at me and leans over, using her foot to slam the bathroom door in my face like somehow she's the aggrieved party here.

Oh, I so don't have the patience for this right now.

Apparently, little Miss Princess has a metric fuck-ton of problems in which I have no intention of getting involved. In my five-second assessment of this train wreck's issues, my advice is to stop getting the shit kicked out of her and learn how to both eat *and* digest her food. She needs to lock down those two life lessons prior to dealing with me. Hell, if she can't handle the stress of digestion, there is no way she's strong enough to deal with me, especially when I'm hungry. I wonder evilly how long it would take me to make her cry.

Wow. My level of enmity right now is surprising to even myself. I only get this nasty when my blood sugar drops too low. I can be a real asshole when I go too long without eating.

As I wait for her to reappear I realize there's something familiar about the girl that I just can't place. Blonde, big blue eyes, petite but with legs for miles. I can't tell if she's pretty as the swelling and bruises are too extensive to figure out what's underneath.

When she exits the bathroom, I recognize her immediately. It takes me about ten seconds of gawking before I realize I'm staring like a fool with my mouth half open.

Jesus selling junk bonds, I'm going to fucking kill John. It's a good goddamn thing he works in the ER, because by the time I'm through with him he's going to need a doctor.

Of an entire department's worth of people, I have no idea why he called me. Well, no, that's not true. I know *exactly* why he called me, but it sure as shit doesn't mean I'm gonna do it. Accepting Emma Bellamy into my service is a surefire way for me to end up swinging from a noose.

Nope. No way. Someone else is going to have to tackle this one. Seeing her here once is bad enough, but having to see her multiple times a week for the foreseeable future? I'm no Gandalf, but I also don't need a crystal ball to tell me getting involved in this girl's life will end badly.

By the time I track John down, I am beyond pissed. I get pretty nasty with him, something I haven't done in a long time. When that gets me nowhere, I appeal to his better sense and try to point out how dangerous assigning me this case is for us all. I do everything but get on my fucking knees and beg him to assign her to someone else. I'm even seriously thinking of crossing that line and letting my kneecaps hit the floor for the first time in my life and I'm not the kind of guy to get on my knees and beg for anything from anyone.

Ever.

That's when the fucker pulls out his high-and-mighty card and makes me feel I don't have a choice professionally, ethically or morally to do anything but agree to take care of the girl. When he asks me if judging her by her privilege, her name, and who her fucking father is isn't as bad as the snap judgments people make about me every goddamn day, we both know he's got me. He may be my boss and be able to twist my arm until it fucking breaks, but it doesn't mean I'm going to like it.

Asshole.

I head back to the room, not bothering to clear the angry scowl off my face as I bark at Emma to follow me. For a while I don't care that she's hobbling painfully behind me, still too pissed that she recycled my lunch to give a fuck about her comfort. After a few loud, painful gasps and several agonized grunts, I feel like a complete douche for making her walk. I find a wheelchair along the way and motion for her to sit as I push her quickly through the halls. Her tiny hands white-knuckle the torn, padded arms like she's afraid I'm going to bank the next turn and toss her ass out of the seat.

When we get back to my treatment room, I motion for her to get on the table. While I pull her scans and x-rays up on the wall screens, I ignore her clumsy attempts to hop up. It's not until I see the films of her busted ribs that I realize she's got a lot more going on than a badly sprained ankle and a banged up face. I turn to offer her a hand, but she gives me a firm glare and somehow manages to pull herself up with a sharp inhale and a pained wince. She stares at me with those deep, sapphire eyes, angling her chin defiantly as she looks me over.

I can only imagine what she sees. My dark, unruly hair and eyes so dark brown they're nearly black against my painfully pale skin. My mixed heritage is evident, my dirty blood obvious at a glance. I'm waiting for her to tell me she wants another therapist, that I'm too foul to touch someone like her. It wouldn't be the first time that's happened, that's for sure. Her eyes take in the cheap fabric of my clothes, the scuffed and worn boots that need to be replaced. Finally, her gaze lingers over my damaged hand, the brace I wear that covers the worst of the poorly-healed injury and shields my patients' sensitive eyes from the gruesome view.

As I do my examination, I find myself angry. Angry at whoever beat the shit out of this scrap of a girl, angry at John for making me treat her, but mostly angry at myself for being such a prick to her yet somehow not being able to stop. I poke and prod harshly at tender places, waiting for her to complain and demand another person, but she remains silent except for a few gasps and a couple hisses. Her glare gets sharper with each touch, her eyes hardening as she gets angrier. Finally, she breaks.

"Are you enjoying this?" she spits.

I look at her with a mix of boredom and contempt. "Not particularly."

"Do you have to be so rough?"

"I'm not being rough."

"Do you have to be so rude?"

"I'm not being rude. I'm just doing my job." I pause for a brief second and look up into her disbelieving face. "Is that okay with you, Your Highness?" I add nastily under my breath.

She recoils from the snide remark that even I can't believe slipped through my lips. "What did you just say?"

"You heard me."

What the hell am I doing?

"Why are you being so nasty to me? Have I done something to you I don't know about?"

I place her injured ankle gently back on the table and look up at the ceiling while composing my thoughts. I take a predatory step towards her and lean in until she flinches back. "You shouldn't have come here."

I'm barely containing my rage, my unblinking stare and sneering lips doing their job and frightening this girl silent. I suddenly realize if I play my cards right, I won't have to kick her ass off my service. If I'm enough of a bastard to her, and if she decides to continue treatment, she couldn't possibly want it to be with me. I just have to somehow make it her idea without somehow getting reported and ending back in the clink, if not somewhere worse.

I adopt a more conversational tone, tilting my head as I stare at her until she squirms. "Why didn't you have daddy dearest get someone to fix you up? Why did you come here?"

"I-I didn't have a choice," she stammers in a voice hardly louder than a whisper.

I laugh like that's the funniest thing I've heard all day, which in all honesty it is, before resuming my former cold hatefulness. "Sweetheart, for people like *you* there's always a choice. *You* could have said no but *you* didn't. *You* became John's problem and now *you* are *my* problem. See where I'm headed with this? If something goes wrong, it will be John's and my ass in front of the firing squad, not yours."

I sit on the edge of the table, causing her to scoot back another inch to put more distance between us. "You see, I worked my ass off to get this job. Despite working nearly sixty hours a week, I can still barely afford to eat. Now, I don't give a crap about working hard or that I live in a shithole, but I do care when someone puts my life and the life of my friends in jeopardy. You've put *all* of us here at risk, princess, simply by putting us on the Committee's radar."

I pause my angry tirade for a moment to let that information sink in. She's trying to act like I'm not upsetting her, but she's frightened and she knows I know it. I lean in a little further, my lips so close she can feel my breath on her cheek. I toy with her the way a cat plays with its cornered prey.

"So to answer your question—no, little girl, I don't hate you and I'm not trying to be *mean* to you. I'm just trying to do my job and keep my head attached to my neck. If you want me to treat your injuries, you are going to do as I say and not bitch and complain about everything I do.

"Oh, and just so we're perfectly clear, I don't want to be your friend, or chit chat, or hear your life story and I promise I won't bore you with mine. I'm sorry if I'm not appropriately grateful for the honor of your attention. I understand you are used to a certain level of ass kissing and boot licking and I'm telling you right now, if you need that from me, you aren't going to get it. I don't beg and scrape to no one."

She's so scared, she's barely breathing. Her eyes are so wide they look like they're going to bug out of her head any minute as I close in for the kill. "And if what I'm saying offends you, then please, do forgive me, My Lady, but I just don't give a fuck."

I step back and bow lavishly in front of her like the way chivalrous knights used to, only the look on my face is one of loathing mockery. Emma is stunned silent, her hands trembling. She looks terribly conflicted, like she has so many things to say but can't decide what, if anything, to verbalize.

She remains silent for a long beat before nodding her head and whispering a choked, "Fine. I promise I'll do whatever you tell me to. Just please, I need you to fix me so I can dance again. That's all I want. Please."

I rear back from her words, beyond surprised not only that she still wants me to treat her, but that she said please. Twice. Now I'm the one shaken and confused, muttering something about getting supplies before racing from the room. When I reach the supply closet I flip on the light and shut the door behind me, my back against the smooth fiberglass. I bang the back of my head against it a few times in frustration, staring up at the ceiling as I try to figure out what the hell to do now.

This is all fucked up and none of it should be happening. John must realize this is too much for me to handle, that what he's asking of me is too stupid, not to mention too dangerous, for us all. Now that Emma has decided to continue treatment, I'm fucked. I have to treat her. Bailing out now would raise too many questions that would end with my body rotting in an unmarked mass grave somewhere.

I reach for a few rolls of athletic tape and gauze, my hands shaking as I gather bandage scissors and a splint. I take a deep breath and try to calm my pounding heart, my mind coming up with all sorts of retaliatory demands I'm going to make on John for forcing me into this mess. And when his grand plan falls spectacularly apart and we all end up in front of the firing squad, I damn well know one thing for certain.

I absolutely plan to tell him *I fucking told you so* before they put a bullet in each of our heads.

9

Emma

The next two weeks are filled with daily, hours-long appointments with this strange, moody man. I spend much of my copious spare time trying to figure him out, but the key to his temper proves as elusive as the location of the Holy Grail. Most days, I can count on one hand the number of words he speaks to me and precious few are congenial.

I don't take his nasty attitude to heart as I have a feeling Declan doesn't like anyone. Most of his coworkers give him a wide berth, some of them acting as if they actually fear him. Is he more than a little unhinged? Probably. Do I think he would intentionally hurt me? No.

I'm so bored reading the same outdated copy of *The Committee* magazine during each long appointment that I make up ways to entertain myself. I create a mental game where I try to get Declan to speak a certain number of non-PT related words each day. So far, I have yet to win a round. It isn't until my fifth appointment before I realize he's never even introduced himself.

"So, I know you don't like to talk, but you never even introduced yourself to me."

"You know my name," he responds with disinterest from behind his computer. "No reason to introduce myself if you already know who I am."

"Declan's an unusual name. Is it a family name?" I press, trying to turn his response into a dialogue.

He finally looks up and stares at me blankly. "Yes."

"It suits you. I like it," I say with a smile as he stares at me like I'm insane.

I only need four more words. . . .

"I'm glad you approve," he retorts in a bored tone as his eyes return to his screen.

YES!

I am actually smiling, my body lighter, my heart swelling with excitement and pride.

So this is what it feels like to win.

"I'm going to have Andrews write a script for a MRI on that ankle, I'm not happy with how it's progressing. I'll be back in a few."

I am attached to an electric stim machine and have a thick ice pack on my ankle, so I'm stuck while he's gone. I lay back on the pillows and close my eyes, trying to relax on the hard padded table. I'm still not sleeping well, nightmares of the engagement party waking me multiple times a night. Often it's not just difficult but impossible, to fall back asleep, leaving me exceptionally exhausted and weak, like how I feel today.

The quiet classical music playing in the background and the lowered lights must have lulled me to sleep because I awake with a start some time later. The room is dark, the overhead lights shut off, only a single dim light shining on Declan's workstation. There's a scratchy blanket thrown over me and I have no idea what time it is. I stretch out languidly, my joints popping and cracking like firecrackers.

"You were sleeping so peacefully, I didn't want to wake you." Declan's quiet voice drifts out from where he sits slouched behind his computer.

"Christ Almighty, you scared me," I yip.

Our eyes meet and, for once, neither of us look away. For just a split-second, I see a glimpse of Declan for who he really is and not who he wants me to see. No longer fending off his angry, aggressive nature, I study him carefully.

Declan's pale skin almost glows, his tousled raven's wing hair blue-black in the low light radiating from the computer. His eyes are large, the color of delicious dark chocolate, and framed by thick, silky black lashes that any woman would kill for. His face is thin but not gaunt, his cheekbones prominent, most likely by genetics, but no-doubt aided by a lifetime of too little to eat. My eyes drink in his lush pink lips that are full and firm, his slightly chapped lower lip bearing the marks where he has been chewing it. It's an unconscious habit of his when he's deep in thought, one I find especially adorable when it triggers the dimple in his cheek. I don't know how I never noticed it before, but in that moment, in the harsh glare of his laptop, he is devastatingly and heartbreakingly beautiful.

I know I'm staring and I can't help it. There is something in those eyes that lures me to him, something darkly intoxicating that makes me want things I shouldn't. He swallows thickly as his eyes hold mine in an intense gaze that makes heat bloom in my body in places good girls don't discuss.

The spell his eyes hold me under breaks when he looks away uncomfortably and reaches for the lights. The room returns to its usual glaring fluorescence and I blink hard to help my eyes adjust. Before I can say another word, Declan slips from the room, the only clue he was here the door slowly closing behind him.

* * *

It takes a full month before I can go back to class and even then, it is just stretching and a heavily modified barre. Declan teaches me how to tape my ribs to give them support but not constrict my breathing too badly, pneumonia always a concern when you can't take regular deep breaths. The bruises and cuts on my face and neck have healed into mostly invisible scars that, to me, are still as obvious as the day I received them.

A handful of times I catch him staring at me, the strangest look on his face that I am unable to decipher. In the seconds our eyes lock, he's usually the first to look away, but sometimes he surprises me by staring back. I can't tell if he's simply daring me to break our gaze first or if the look in his eyes is saying something I lack the skills to decrypt. These are the times I look away first, my cheeks flaming.

While I heal, I have four weeks of blissful reprieve from Ryan as he travels the country holding large rallies and garnering accolades from a concerned, starving populous. Word somehow leaked that Our Beloved Supreme Archon is once again spiraling the drain and the outlying areas beyond the District walls are again demanding a return to democracy. Every night on the news we see footage of Ryan shaking hands and kissing babies as he pretends to listen to the plights of the residents within the other walled cities. Not once does he say anything of value, but his presence manages to soothe the protests and riots that have begun again.

But all good things eventually come to an end. Nearly two months to the day of my presentation, I receive an early morning call from Ryan's social secretary telling me I'm scheduled to appear the following evening at Ryan's birthday celebration. She urges me to be ready promptly at six, to wear the dress that will be delivered later today and to not forget my engagement ring. I wonder if Ryan somehow knows the gaudy bauble has done nothing but gather dust in its box since he gave it to me. I can't stand the sight of the thing.

The outfit is delivered just as I am going to class and I am not at all surprised to find a pair of four-inch heels to go with the short, pale blue and silver dress. I know my ankle's nowhere near ready to safely wear these shoes, at the same time knowing if they were sent, they must be worn. I shove the shoes in my bag, hoping Declan will have some way of getting me through tomorrow night without breaking an ankle. When I get to his office after class, I pull the shoes out of the bag and plunk them wordlessly down on the table.

"Thanks, but I don't think they will fit me."

As lame as his joke is, I'm touched that he's finally attempting something close to humor with me. He picks up one of the shoes and examines the jewels with his fingertips, no doubt wondering if they are real. The shoe looks disproportionately small, almost childish, in his large, masculine hands.

"You have freakishly tiny feet, you know that?"

"Yeah, yeah, I know. No, my question is how I'm going to get through a night of wearing these without making my ankle worse."

"It's simple. Don't wear them." He taps the side of his head and looks at me like I should have come up with that myself.

"Sorry, not an option. The boss requires them." The mere mention of Ryan makes Declan's entire body stiffen, the light dimming from his eyes until they are the deep black that signals the presence of his worst moods.

"That ankle isn't ready for this type of torture yet. Honestly, with the strain on your knees and ankles from those crazy pointe shoes, you shouldn't wear heels at all if you value your ability to walk in your old age."

"I have to *get* to old age first, but thanks for the advice. Seriously, can we tape the ankle? Something discreet? Come on, help me. There has to be something you can do. Please?"

He stops and looks at me and chews his lip for a second before letting it go with a sigh.

"Fine, I'll tape it up for you tomorrow, but I really don't know how much it's going to help. I'm telling you, one wrong move and your dancing days are over. Understand me? Be careful. I'm not going to have you ruin all my hard work because some asshole wants you to be four inches taller for the night. I want to see you Monday morning before you go to class to make sure it's okay to dance on."

I let out the breath I'd been holding and smile. Without thinking, I reach forward and take him into a grateful hug. The minute my arms wrap around his wide shoulders and I feel the hard, tight muscles of his back tense under my hands I realize my mistake. If I was smart, I'd let go and quickly back away but my body refuses to budge. I feel the warmth of his chest through his thin shirt, the thick muscles of his chest like cables against my breasts and it just feels too good to cut short. I close my eyes and inhale his unique male scent and whisper, "Thanks, Declan. I mean it."

Flustered, he backs out of my embrace like I assaulted him, his cheeks flushed and eyes wide. He looks around quickly, making certain we weren't seen. "No thanks needed. Just doing my job." He shrugs as he walks away, his usually languid pace clipped and quick as he flees the scene of my crime.

10

Ryan

I hate my fucking birthday.

It's the one day of the year I wish I could lock myself in my bed-room with a bottle of scotch and get so drunk I sleep through the whole fucking thing; that one day I'm powerless to control the waking nightmare that lasts a full twenty-four hours. Every "Happy Birth-day" is like a knife in my chest knowing that another year's passed where I have aged and my twin sister remains eighteen.

I have no idea what I'm going to do when I ascend to the Suprem-acy and my birthday becomes a national holiday. Fuck, is that going to suck. I don't talk about my sister because losing her is still too painful to even think about; in fact, few people even know I had a twin because I never talk about my family. *Ever.*

Thinking back, I can't help but imagine all the ways things could have been different. The *if onlys* and *should haves,* the 20/20 hindsight, the ability to redo that day, that hour, that minute where if only one thing had been different she might still be alive.

I would give my left nut for a do-over. I really would.

My sister had been the quintessential Abel to my Cain. The golden child. The sort of daughter every father would love to call his as she was perfect in every way. She was devoted to our family, to our community and to the church. She loved all of God's creatures and couldn't imagine a day of her life being spent away from the cattle farm where we grew up. She was always the first one up in the morning and the last to go to bed, the one who volunteered to stay awake all night with sick calves or expecting mares. No matter how tired, she never missed her long morning rides with the staff to go check on the cows in the furthest pastures and make sure the mamas and calves were all happy and healthy.

I still remember the last time I saw her head out with the men on a ride. Damn, she had been beautiful. She was willowy and tall, almost as tall as me, with a body gorgeous and curvy enough to put any catwalk model to shame. Her hair was the color of sun-bleached corn silk, her eyes as blue as the deepest pond on our farm. She had a smile that lit up a room and a laugh that made even the dumbest jokes funny.

I couldn't have been more different than my sister. I was the family screw-up, a lousy student that hated our country life and only gave a shit about a cow when it was presented to me rare on a plate. My only redeeming quality was I was super athletic, the stereotypical popular high school quarterback, the cliched good-looking, All-American jock. If it hadn't been for that, I bet my dad would have drowned me in the pond like an unwanted kitten long ago.

I have always been quick-tempered—I get that trait from my dad. He'd never been one to spare the rod and spoil the child, the scars on my back proof of his violent nature. Although I never would have admitted this when I was a teenager, I deserved the beatings I got back then. Over the years my father bailed my ass out of more shit than I care to remember, each time he picked me up from the hospital or jail ending with him whipping me until I passed out. He was convinced I was cursed, the Devil in me too ingrained to be driven out with the sacrament of confession and sprinkles of holy water. He told me every time he scourged me the beatings were for my own good, that the only way the evil could be dispelled was through the shedding of my blood.

It took me a while to figure out how to be stealthy, how to still do everything I wanted and not get caught. My sister had perfected the art in grade school, some of the shit she got into was considerably worse than what I did, but even when she did get caught, I never once remember my father even punishing her with going to bed without supper. It was like she was perfect in his eyes. He never even raised his voice to her and he most certainly never hit her.

Maybe if he had she would still be alive.

A knock at my door reminds me it's time to head off to the celebration. I down the rest of my scotch and recheck my tie before heading to my car. I school my face to look happy and hope my eyes aren't as glassy from drink as I suspect they are. Fucking Bellamy is on my case about how much I'm drinking at events and the last thing I want is for him to realize I've premedicated to get through tonight. I'm getting really tired of his unsolicited advice about my behavior when he should be more focused on his daughter's errant ways. All I know is Emma better be on her fucking A game tonight. I'm not in the mood to deal with her shit.

11

Emma

"Nice bruises," Declan mutters sarcastically as he ambles into the tiny exam room early Monday morning. I see the tension escalating in his already rigid frame as he studies the mottled purple-black after-effects of Ryan's hands that once again decorate my face and neck.

"You think so? Thanks," I snap. "They were a gift."

I have no idea where those words come from or how they manage to slip through my lips. Declan looks up in surprise, my uncharacteristic snarky comeback taking him off guard. He doesn't say a word as he steps up to the table I'm sitting on and looks carefully into my bloodshot eyes. I am in a particularly rotten mood, my body sore, my head aching and my period choosing this of all mornings to grace me with its irregular presence. Of all the days for Declan to be in a snit, this is not it.

I already decided today is *my* day.

He gestures for me to swing my feet over the side of the exam table and steps between my legs. My breath catches as he nears, my body flinching involuntarily. He raises his hands in the air as if I just put a gun to his head, the little color in his cheeks draining away as he backs off. I can't decipher the look in his eyes, the mix of fear, rage and sadness too mingled to decide which emotion to give precedence.

"Hey, hey, easy, there, tiger. I'm not going to hurt you. I just want to check your eye, okay?" His tone is low and soothing, the sort of voice one would use to talk a crazy person off a ledge. I take a deep breath and close my eyes for a second before nodding my assent. When I open them I see a new expression on his face. Pity.

Good God, I hate that look.

He steps in between my knees slowly this time, his eyes never leaving mine as I feel his scratchy pants brush the inside of my calves. He raises his hand slowly, his fingers reaching cautiously for my cheek as his other hand slides to hold the back of my head steady. As strong and calloused as his hands are, they are so gentle the examination barely hurts. He speaks to me slowly in deep reassuring tones, always telling me what he's going to do before he does it. His touch is so calming, so tender, that when his fingertips brush against my swollen lip I close my eyes and wonder what it would be like to have him as a lover.

Oh, Emma. Don't you even think about going there.

I wonder if it's just my imagination or if the air in the room has just been charged with a violent jolt of electricity. My entire body is on edge, my breath shallow, my lips opening ever so slightly as I exhale a gentle sigh. Even though I know I shouldn't, I lean my head into his hand, enjoying the rough sensation of his palm on my cheek. For the first time since before my brother's death, I don't fear a man's touch.

He steps away abruptly, my head dropping from the loss of his supportive hand. He's agitated to the point he's vibrating, his jaw twitching under the strain of keeping his mouth shut. I've made him angry.

Great. Not him, too.

"You know that real men don't hit little girls, right?"

When he speaks his voice is low and steady, a rumble of thunder that threatens with vicious intent. I stare at him, partly thankful he's not angry with me after all, partly wanting to smack the look of pity off his face. Why don't people understand that when they look at you with obvious pathos it only makes you feel worse?

Tired of feeling sad and miserable, I choose to get angry. "Yeah? In which fairy tale did you find that piece of wisdom?"

He looks at me in surprise. "What he's doing isn't right, Emma. I know the law and the church say he can, but *I'm* telling you, it's not right. Fucking none of this is right."

His words have a venomous bite I haven't heard from him in quite a while. He stares at me a minute longer before speaking again in a quieter yet equally direct tone. "Does he force himself on you?"

Whoa, there buddy. This is getting too real.

I immediately break eye contact and look down at my hands that are, for once, situated correctly. "He takes his premarital rights as our contract allows-"

"That's not what I asked." His tone is as hard and rough as his strong calloused hand that cups my chin and forces me to look into his eyes. Our faces are only inches apart.

I try to make light of the situation with a little laugh that comes out strangled and hoarse. "Declan, according to the Law and the New State Church, Ryan is within his rights to both discipline and take certain liberties-"

Two fingers from his damaged hand press against my lips, silencing me. He leans in closer, speaking slowly and with great restraint. "Listen to me, Emma. If you remember nothing else of what I say to you today, remember this: what he's doing isn't *taking a liberty* or *exercising his premarital rights*. The words you are looking for are *assault* and *rape*."

I'm trembling at the nearness of him, his fingers still on my lips, his breath warm against my cheek. Tears spill from my eyes and land on his hand. My words come out as a cracked whisper. "I thought the law determined there's no such thing as rape."

"Yeah, well, they're wrong." He steps away from me and places his hands against the closed door and hangs his head as he composes himself. "Did he hurt you anywhere else?"

"No," I say, with a decisive shake of my head, a reply that even I know is too quick and vehement to sound truthful.

He turns back to me, searching my eyes for the truth. "Don't lie to me, Emma."

His voice is hard, his words coming out as a command. I feel guilty for lying, knowing he's only trying to help.

"I'm a little sore," I confess as his eyes darken further. "He hit me a few times, but nothing like last time, I swear. I'm okay."

He isn't having it. He leans in to me, slowly and quietly enunciating each word. "It. Is. *Not*. Okay." He speaks through clenched jaws as if he's depending on his tight facial muscles to hold back a torrent of unwise words and poorly-concealed emotion. There is a look in his eyes that I can't describe except to say that suddenly, I feel I could trust him with my life.

I am so confused. Declan has so much to lose by speaking what he thinks instead of what we are told to believe and yet he does it anyway. He's older than me, probably by a good ten years or so. I wonder if that's what prevents his abject obedience of the law. Maybe people that remember the time before the war are just naturally more rebellious. Maybe despite the potential consequences, righteously-felt insubordination simply cannot be taken from a person's soul. After all, just because it's illegal to discuss the time before the war doesn't mean you forget it.

As angry and moody as Declan can be, there's a rare goodness inside of him. He does his damnedest to hide his old-school morality just as much as I try to smother the mutinous voice in my head. In our world, I wonder which is more dangerous, a woman with a rebellious streak or an ethical man that speaks what he believes no matter the consequences?

Does it really matter? As soon a watcher catches wind they would be equally dead.

I wake from my reflection to realize we've been staring wordlessly at each other for quite some time. Declan's eyes probe mine for answers to questions he has yet to ask. Under his gaze my chest tightens, my heartbeat gallops and a strange flutter develops in my belly. I want to reach out and touch his face, to feel the prickle of his dark stubble on my palm. I want to run my thumb over those full lips and determine for myself if they are as lush as they look.

Before I can do anything stupid, Declan breaks our trance and steps away. He grabs a roll of athletic tape from the drawer and starts wrapping my ankle, looking as if he suddenly realized he's very late for something important.

"You should be fine for class. I'll see you again afterward for our regular session and we can discuss you advancing back on pointe at that time."

As he prepares to leave, his cheeks are flushed and his pulse pounds visibly in his neck. He reaches for the bandage scissors next to my thigh but the handles slip from his shaking grasp and clatter to the floor. His cheeks redden further as he grabs them with a muttered oath before stealing from the room like a thief in the night.

Even after it's clear Declan's not coming back, I sit for a few minutes longer to think. I have no idea what just happened, what sort of energy flowed through us that bound us ever so briefly together. I know that good girls don't have these needful feelings and wanton daydreams about caressing strange men. Proper young women do not fantasize about any man, no matter how kind or handsome, and especially not a man that lives outside their provenance and social class. I know my thoughts are exceedingly dangerous. I know I have to stop these desires before I give in to them and do something stupid.

I also know how desperately I long to feel this connection again.

12

WITHIN THE NEXT few weeks, my ankle heals enough that Declan discharges me from his care. At the end of our last session together he stops for a moment at the door, his head down, his eyes staring at his gloved hand on the handle for a lengthy moment. He exhales softly, obviously thinking better of his next actions before slipping silently from the room with not even a hint of farewell. As disappointed as I feel by his easy dismissal, I know our lives are safer this way.

The weeks pass quickly now that I am strong enough to take a full day's worth of classes. I am exhausted in both body and mind as I ready myself for my first professional performance. My time in the studio is some of the happiest of my life as I commit myself heart and soul to my art.

Events are scheduled a few times a week for me to accompany Ryan where I dutifully play my part and nod, smile and look happy while secretly wishing there's some way to kill him and get away with it. After almost every event there is always something additional he wants of me that I've learned to not refuse. The less I balk and the more I willingly stroke his ego, among his other parts, the less physical pain I am dealt.

Every time I'm with Ryan, I feel a bit more of my soul slip away. Every time I force myself to touch him, to say something sweet, or apologize for my misdeeds that are nonexistent and therefore unrepentant, I feel myself die a little more. It takes every ounce of my willpower to not shudder at the sight of his dick and do the things he demands, and despite my whole-hearted attempts at good behavior, the beatings continue. I am getting better at hiding the evidence of my transgressions under the thick foundation and countless tubes of cover-up Caitlin brings each week, but just because no one can see the bruises doesn't change the deep shame I feel for having them.

Even when I do go to class with split lips and inconcealable swollen eyes no one says a word. No one is stupid enough to mention it; no one willing to get involved. Even Jeremy is more careful with his words and actions, as raids on ballet companies and other artistic outlets are on a steady rise. Those of us in the arts are always nervous when the Purity Patrols are unleashed, their frothing desire to rid the nation of sexual deviants and those who dare to associate with them wiping out entire companies in the blink of an eye.

I have already almost forgotten Declan's vehement argument that the things Ryan forces me to do are wrong. My father's and Ryan's weekly verbal and physical rebukes remind me just how disappointing a woman I have grown to be. When someone tells you the same thing day after day after day, their truth eventually becomes your own. I wonder if *The New State Text* is actually correct stating that willful women are inherently evil and must be culled if they can't be corrected. If that is so, after nineteen years of constant admonition, I'm living on borrowed time.

I wish with all my heart I was like other young women my age. I wish I could be content following orders and executing my husband's whim. I hate that I want to be the master of my fate and am neither eager or willing to follow my father's and Ryan's every dictate. My life would be so much easier if I could just be happy with the things

I have and not yearn for those that I don't. Of the things I could ever want, it's the one I will never, ever be granted that I long for the most.

My freedom.

As much as I've tried, I simply cannot force myself to give up the dream that somehow, someday, I will find a way out of my gilded cage. It's this last tidbit of hope that prevents me from accepting my fate and bending to their will. To be passive, especially if that is not your innate, God-given personality, is a choice. But I have not been given a choice—my submission is demanded by cruel men in a broken system. Maybe if they didn't force my subservience I would find submission to be less distasteful, but I don't think so. I'm starting to think the need for rebellion is one so deeply buried inside me I'm only beginning to uncover the surface. I worry what will happen when I exhume the full treasure, and to what extremes I'll be willing to go when I'm finally forced to live my life kneeling at the feet of another.

As my wedding day looms closer, my vow to not marry Ryan swirls in my mind. Some days, as I soak in a scalding tub of water, I scrutinize the veins in my arms and wonder if I will be able to open them when the time comes. I trace my fingers along their delicate blue lengths, unemotionally imagining splaying them wide with the whisper-thin edge of a razor I've already procured. If practice truly makes perfect, I hope these mental rehearsals help me on my big day.

I have no one to confide in, no one to break down and cry to. The few times I try to talk to Caitlin she snaps that I need to stop whining and be thankful for my many blessings. The day she tells me she's tired of my complaining, that I am a spoiled brat that deserves Ryan's violence for being ungrateful, her words nearly destroy me. She apologized shortly after that, but the damage was done. I vow to never confide in her again.

Most nights I sob myself to sleep. Crying into a pillow may make you feel a little better immediately after but it does absolutely nothing to solve your problems. Every morning I wake up in exactly the same circumstances as the day before with no more hope, no new prospects and no miraculous way out.

When my brother died all those years ago I stopped eating. For the first week it hadn't been intentional, anything I ate came back right back up on its own accord within minutes. Countless doctors and tests later, I was diagnosed with a case of Female Hysteria and given a prescription of pills. After the first one I took I never took another. I may have been inconsolable, but I didn't want to be a drug-addled zombie like my mother, either.

Over time, I learned to cope with the lack of control in my life by micro-managing every bite that went into my mouth. It started off innocently enough with intermittent fasts of varying lengths and sending back nearly untouched plates of food because *I'm not hungry* or *I don't like it*. Now my refusal to eat takes on a new purpose. Every time I skip a meal, or force myself to throw up, I take a little of my power back. When my ankle is strong enough, I take long jogs on empty stomachs in an effort to run my body faster into failure. I start throwing up everything I eat, a way to weaken my esophagus more quickly in hopes it will rupture and put me out of my misery.

I know everything I'm doing is wrong. I know not revering my body is against the teachings of the New State Church, that what I'm doing is a sin and a crime. I just don't care enough to let any of that stop me. Death by eating disorder may be a coward's suicide but it's the only way I know I am brave enough to get the job done. Starving yourself to death doesn't require the courage of grander forms of suicide, like leaping from a tall building or throwing yourself in front of a train. I am not brave, I wasn't bred or raised to be, but this path to the grave doesn't require strength.

All it needs is persistence and time.

13

I QUICKLY EARN the respect of my fellow dancers with my insane work ethic and drive for perfection. I work painfully hard, throwing my heart into every step, every turn; every movement of my hands telling a piece of the story. I agonize over every gesture, even pacing my breath to make sure my body only ever creates the most exquisite motion. I practice each day until I've bled through my toe shoes, the pain so intense I have no choice but stop. It is only in these moments, as I pull off my sodden shoes and stare at my bloody and disfigured feet that I feel anything at all.

My ankle heals quickly enough that I am able to perform in the early October performances of Giselle, one of my favorite ballets. It's about a young country girl who falls in love with a Duke disguised as a peasant. As Giselle is flitting around, hopelessly in love and thinking she and her handsome suitor will soon be blissfully wed, she runs into a group of noble folk who are out on a hunting party. A beautiful princess comes forward and asks the young girl why she is so happy. When Giselle says because she is soon to be wed, the noble lady smiles and says, what a coincidence, so am I. They laugh and smile together until the Duke shows up and Giselle realizes *he* is the princess' intended. The poor girl comes to the grim resolution that she has been lied to and goes mad. She dies of a broken heart at the Duke's feet.

The second act is set in the woods by Giselle's grave. She has become a restless spirit, led by a ghostly Queen who seeks revenge on unfaithful men. As part of her initiation into this harem of vengeful women, Giselle is instructed to kill the Duke by forcing him to dance to his death. But when she sees him prostrate and grief-stricken at her grave, she's unable to follow the Queen's order. She loves him so much she protects him until the dawn when she and the other spirits vanish, their power obliterated by the rising sun. By saving the Duke, Giselle's spirit is free to move on to the next world, able to be at peace at last.

Because of my injury, I had been cast to dance the part of the Queen as Jeremy was afraid my newly-healed ankle wouldn't hold up to the punishment of the more demanding title role. But as we inch closer to performance and my ankle grows stronger, I regret agreeing to the smaller part.

With less than two weeks to opening night, Anna suddenly stops rehearsal in mid-step of the second act with a loud stomp of her foot and angry wave of arms. "This is not working for me!"

We are rehearsing the scene where Anna's Giselle confronts my Queen, so I know what she's really saying is I am somehow mucking things up. Again. Just like every other time Anna has thrown a tantrum, everyone stops and stares. Jeremy runs up to her, ready with cajoling words, but she raises her hand and stops him before he can open his mouth.

"This is not believable," she states with more wild waves in my direction, her Russian accent more pronounced than usual because she's agitated. "How can she be Queen of Wilis when she looks half my age? She is a little girl, a baby pussy, no is not a pussy, is *kitten*. She has no claws. She has no bite, no venom to be evil Queen. She should be Giselle."

I spin on my heel, shocked. What the hell is Anna doing?

"Emma, *koshechka*, do as I say. We trade places. You know the steps, yes? Good. Jeremy, watch her. You will see, I am right."

The thing is, she is right. Despite everything going so horribly wrong in my life, I simply don't have the venom to be the Queen. Although it's too late to save the fabled Giselle, deep in my heart I am still tragically hopeful that my life won't follow her script. Dare I hope that the Giselle in my personal production doesn't die, but lives a long life in the loving arms of the Duke?

After rehearsing the scene a few times, Jeremy and the director agree to the casting change and when we finish rehearsing for the day, the company members swarm me with heartfelt congratulations. I look through the crowd at Anna who stands alone by the wall sipping from her water bottle, staring at me with a raised eyebrow and a smirk.

I know I need to thank her, that what she has done is unimaginable and I am incredibly grateful for her uncharacteristically selfless act. We've barely spoken since that afternoon in the hospital, both of us choosing to keep our distance in an attempt to not provoke the other, making what I'm about to do even more brutally awkward.

After packing up my belongings, I walk up to her sheepishly and ask to speak with her alone. We walk out to the hallway, our bags over our shoulders and I ask her if she would like to go for a cup of coffee.

"No, not really," she says with an emotionless face and my heart plummets at her dismissive tone. Then she lifts one side of her lip in a cheeky grin and adds, "But I would love a nice glass of wine. Yes? Come with me."

Anna laughs heartily as she threads her arm through mine. We exit the studio surrounded by countless shocked faces that stare at us like we each grew a second head. Anna acts like we have been best friends forever and that it's no big deal for her to have given up a title role. As much as I know I shouldn't look a gift horse in the mouth, I can't help but feel there's some sort of ulterior motive behind her generosity. Prima Ballerinas don't give up leading roles. *Ever.*

Anna is up to something. I just don't know what.

* * *

"I am now going to tell you about me. Yes? Good. I was nine when I move to Moscow from London, and fourteen when I dance my first role with Bolshoi," Anna starts after we are comfortably seated in dried-out leather club chairs in a nearby basement cafe. We face each other across a low dusty coffee table stained by hundreds of glass rings, the smells of musty basement and cat piss strong in the air.

I'm sure this is hardly Anna's top choice of locale, but most places won't serve alcohol to unescorted females, and this dark, dirty establishment does. An old jukebox plays a song I've never heard before, the singer repeatedly crooning *you can't always get what you want.*

Damn. Ain't that the truth.

Anna cradles a giant glass of red wine in one hand, her feet propped up on the coffee table. She already slammed two shots of vodka while we waited for our wine and seems none the worse for it. I, on the other hand, feel tipsy just sniffing my glass.

"I move to Moscow because I want to be the best, and the best ballerinas are always trained in Russia. So my family send me there, all alone, but I don't care. I have opportunity. I have drive. So I dance, and dance, and dance and I bleed and I cry and I starve, and for what? To make art. To make beautiful dance. I am best in class, better than even older girls, but all I get is shit roles. I ask why is that? And they say because I am not *born* in Russia, that make me less than other girls.

I say my parents are both Russian-born, but that is not good enough. I get angry and ask what must I do? They say, you must do *more* to get good roles. I need man, or woman, with money and power to demand I get good role. I ask them, what do I give them in return? People love ballet so much they give money to me with nothing in return?"

She laughs loudly, a sarcastic jolt that makes the few others in the filthy space turn our way momentarily. The new attention doesn't bother her one bit. She makes eye contact with a man at the bar, wiggling her eyebrows at him as she speaks. "What they want in return, I find out, is me. I think is okay, is better than giving money I do not have, so I make deal. I fuck them, they buy me roles I want." Not tearing her eyes from the man, she takes a long swallow from her glass, making a show to lick her lips before running her wine-stained tongue lewdly around the rim of the glass. When he gets up to come near us, she turns her back on him and focuses her attention back to me.

"Sometimes it work, sometimes not. Everyone say I am the best, but still, I do not always get best roles. Then, my friend tells me about American ballet. She says you go there, you be huge star. So, right before war, I come here even though everyone tells me no, Anna, don't go! War is coming! But I am silly girl with stars in eyes wanting American dream.

"So, I come here. I make good money. By Russian standards, I am very rich. I have big apartment in New York, more clothes than I can wear. Men and women want me because I am beautiful, famous, new. I am in all magazines, even make few movies. Then we have war and I lose everything.

"I try to go to England, their government says no. I think, okay, Anna, go back to Russia, but they also say no. They now think I am spy or something ridiculous. So, now I am stuck here, I think for good."

She sips from her glass, her dark red lipstick staining the rim with a blood-like grin. Her eyes slide back to the man at the bar, the two of them exchanging a glance as she once again licks the rim. "You know, I take classes to make accent less noticeable, so I sound more American," she explains. "I think I sound American now. Yes? You think?"

I stare at her, afraid what will happen if I say no. She watches me carefully for a few seconds before taking another long drink from her quickly emptying glass. "I guess I should not complain. I have many good years, but I get pissed when I must give up roles when I am better dancer. I feel like all my sacrifice is for nothing. Now, I lose roles to rich girls with bad feet all the time. They all have important daddies to buy their way. Had I known American dream would die I would have stayed in Russia."

Her voice is bitter, as if somehow she really should have known better. She laughs dramatically to herself and then sets her narrowed, cat-like eyes on me. "You, yes, you could make it in Russia, I think. You are very pretty and very good dancer," she nearly sings as she winks at me. "If you fuck as good as you dance, you may even get lead."

I nearly spit my wine out across the room. *What?*

"I think you and me, we are much alike. Dancing is in our blood, is in our soul. If someone tell me I can no longer dance, I would die. I think you feel the same. I live for it. It gives me joy no orgasm ever could. Yes?"

I haven't recovered from my first near-choking reaction and now I'm trying to keep the same mouthful of wine from getting spewed across the room a second time. She pauses like she's waiting for a reply from me while I continue to sputter.

What the hell am I supposed to say? Thanks for what I assume is a compliment? I'm glad you get off from dancing? Good Lord, I must be drunk.

"I am not stupid. I know you are not happy with your life." She stumbles a bit as she searches for the right words. I open my mouth, ready to object, to lie and tell her I love my life, but she raises her hand and stops me.

"Do not lie, Emma. You are not happy. You do not eat, you do not drink. You are engaged to very bad man who beats you. What? You think I do not see? I am not blind. We all see, but we respect you enough to not shower you in platypus. There is nothing we can say to help, but there are things we can do."

I look at her in shock. What is she trying to say?

Anna snuggles back into her chair with a deep stretch, like a cat that just drank an entire saucer of cream and is ready to take a long nap in a sunbeam. "All you do is work, work, work, with no time for play," she says between sips. "You need to learn to play."

I sip my wine. I still have no clue what to say and this is absolutely not the time to correct Anna's malapropism. Anna looks like she's going to say something else, but then minutely shrugs her shoulders, changing her mind and the topic as she gives me a wide smile.

"Now, you dance the perfect piece for you. You are not evil Queen, you are sweet little girl. Production will be better this way, you see. But you must do one thing for me."

Oh boy, here it comes. She must need a kidney or something.

"You now are Prima Ballerina in major production. Many, many people count on you to put on stunning performance. I do not say this to frighten but to inspire you. See? Now, you have purpose to live. Eat. Be strong. Have fun. Do not worry so much about tomorrow. Enjoy today. Who knows? The tomorrow you so afraid of may not come. There is hope." She takes my free hand and squeezes it.

"You are not alone, Emma," she mouths in a voice barely above a whisper. I'm not sure how drunk she is, but this certainly is a side of her I've never seen before. Before I can even register her heartfelt words and expression, they are gone.

"After last night of show, we will have fun. European style fun.

You will see, it will be a very good night," she grins as she drains the remains of her wine.

"Two more glasses!" she hollers as she dashes her empty glass on the floor, shattering it into a thousand pieces as she laughs. I'm not sure if I was more afraid of her when I thought she hated me or now that we are apparently best friends, but I do know she is right about one thing.

I need to live while I still can.

14

Opening Night

I have never wanted to throw up so badly in my entire life.

My entire body is on high alert, my body ready to jump out of my skin at the slightest noise. I recoil when someone touches me in passing and flinch whenever someone calls my name. I am sweating so badly I'm constantly mopping at myself with a towel, my hands so wet and clammy I'm terrified I'll have no grip when it's time for Michael to lift me.

Oh my God, I need to get my nerves under control or this ballet is going to be a complete disaster.

My father and Ryan are thrilled at the casting changes and determine to make my triumph theirs. They somehow commandeer all of tonight's tickets and give them out to their most influential contacts. My father has managed to turn my premiere into the most anticipated political and social event of the season.

I'm glad my debut at The National is working out so well for you, father.

The good news is I can fall flat on my face and no one will notice. The hand-picked audience will be too busy watching the Supreme Archon's box where my father, Ryan and their chosen sycophants will sip champagne and figure out ways to make themselves richer. After all, who would dream of watching a world-class ballet when you can watch middle-aged men drink and conspire to take over the world?

I manage to hold onto the few complimentary tickets I am allowed and send two to Dr. Andrews for himself and his wife and one to Declan. Although I'm pretty sure he isn't one to spend a Friday night at the ballet, I still want him to know how much I appreciate his help over the past months. The few available opening night tickets are going for upwards of $2,500 a piece on the open market and even those sell out in record time. I figure if Declan doesn't want to attend he can at least sell the ticket and make a few bucks.

"You will be brilliant," Anna says as she hugs and kisses me on both cheeks as I wait on stage to begin. "Break a leg," she whispers as she straightens the bow on the bodice of my costume and walks off into the darkened wings. Jeremy has a few last minute notes for me and Michael, and then we are given the five minute warning to curtain.

Oh, God, please help me.

One of the girls from the corps takes a quick glance from the side of the curtain and gleefully squeals there are so many people in attendance, they are standing three deep in the back of every level. My stomach lurches.

"If you are going to be sick, do it now, honey," Michael whispers to me while pointing to a strategically placed bucket in the wings. I run for it, retching, but nothing comes up except some clear, foamy saliva. I know better than to eat before an important performance.

"Another one bites the dust!" Michael sings and laughs. I glare at him as I spit into the bucket. "Oh, honey, we all toss our cookies on our debut! It's a good sign, you will see. I would be more concerned if you didn't hurl. Puking means you're nervous, and you're nervous because you care." He gently rubs my back and hands me a bottle of water. "Now rinse and spit, they are calling places."

I do as I'm instructed and turn to face him. He kisses me gently on both cheeks for luck. "Don't worry, I will make you look brilliant." Then he's gone as he prepares himself for his entrance from the other side of the stage.

I wish I could say that I was the best Giselle that ever existed, but I really can't because I have no memory of dancing the ballet at all. I am so in character I am no longer Emma Bellamy, the Governor's daughter, but Giselle, the naive country girl doomed to die of heartbreak. I feel the overwhelming heart-bursting joy in the beginning sequences, the dreamy, doe-eyed idealism of first love, the searing pain of betrayal and the complete loss of control as madness ensues.

I die with a fluid grace, welcoming death with wild eyes, fluttering steps and a sickening collapse to the floor before the curtain closes. I don't know if I hit my head when I fall, I only remember darkness before Michael's hands on my shoulders rouse me with a shake. I hear him calling my name from a distance and I'm confused.

"Emma? Emma, darling, you can get up now. The curtain's closed. Emma? Are you alright?"

My mind feels fuzzy. Had I been so in character I actually died on stage? That would solve a lot of problems, I think wryly as I shake the cobwebs from my brain and slowly stand, swaying slightly.

"I'm alright, I think. What happened? Did I pass out? Oh, my God, did I screw up?" Shocked back to reality, I'm terrified I somehow botched everything up.

"Sweetie, are you kidding me? That was the best mad scene I have ever seen! You were amazing, even better than Anna, but don't you dare tell her I said that!" Michael smiles, kissing me gently on the forehead.

"Now come on, let's get something in your system before you pass out, again. Maybe a little port to get some sugar in your blood? I'm sure Anna has something stashed in her dressing room that will help."

He marches me toward her dressing room where Anna is putting on the last touches of her ghostly makeup, something I should be doing right now, too. She takes one look at my white face and orders me to sit. She hands me a sleeve of salty crackers and a bottle of port and tells me to take "big drinks." She begins to remove my makeup, redoing it like hers for act two.

"I watch you from the wings and you were beautiful. Simply beautiful," she murmurs as she applies the heavy white foundation. "I could not dance it better and I am brilliant, so do take complement and calm the fuck down. Act two, you always dance better. Do not make me look like amateur, okay?" Anna smiles and winks.

"Anna, I...."

She cuts me off by shoving another cracker in my mouth. "Just take complement. Say thank you, Anna."

I laugh as I chew the cracker. "Thank you, Anna."

"Stop laughing, or I will mess up your makeup, silly girl," she reprimands, her self-satisfied grin never leaving her face.

In the second act I feel even better. Stronger. I don't know if it's the port or if I'm working off the energy from the audience, but for the first time in my life, I feel powerful. When I stand up to Anna's vengeful Queen and vow to save the penitent prince there is not a sound to be heard from the audience. Anna's eyes widen a bit more than usual as even she can detect the change in me from rehearsal to performance. It is a moment of magic I wish I could tap into in reality.

When the curtain descends, the entire company crowds around me in the wings as the audience erupts in thunderous applause. I take sixteen curtain calls as flowers rain down from the audience and a huge bouquet is placed in my arms. I am blinded not only by the lights but by tears that fill my eyes, as I mouth *thank you* over and over to the clamoring crowd.

It is absolutely the happiest moment of my life.

* * *

The opening night Gala is being called the grandest event to ever be held at the National. No sooner than I am safely behind the curtain, I am whisked out of the congratulating arms of my fellow dancers and herded towards my dressing room. Caitlin and a team of professionals are ready to transform me from ballet dancer to super-glamorous future consort, complete with yet another white designer gown and enough diamonds to choke a horse.

I am so lost in the glow of a great performance I barely speak as they work, the huge dreamy smile on my face one of many clues to my overwhelming happiness. Caitlin gives me a few disapproving looks before finally scolding me, reminding me that *a good woman is a humble woman.* For the first time in my life I want to slap her.

I am ready in record time with Caitlin damn near shoving me out my dressing room door with a warning that I have just a few minutes left to race to the front entrance before I'll be late. I am escorted into the huge lobby by our director to a roar of resounding applause. By now, my face is starting to hurt from smiling so much, but I don't care. I take a quick demi-curtsy as I'm not capable of much else in my tall, crystal-studded heels. The sleek fitted gown encrusted with pearls and diamonds is a work of both art and genius engineering. The gown is so heavy it took two people to help me get into it and three to do up the complicated system of hidden stays and hooks that hold it up.

Our director, Daniel, takes the microphone and asks for quiet as waiters buzz through the crowd handing out champagne. He looks at me fondly, the pride he's taking in my performance emboldening me further. He thanks everyone for their attendance, complements the cast on their excellent performance and introduces me as the newest Principal Dancer of the National Ballet Company.

I was told ahead of time how to act—to look a bit embarrassed at the attention, to flutter my eyelashes and appear modest, to look at the floor while everyone toasts in support of my long career. Everyone here knows my time on stage has a predetermined terminus, but tonight we all pretend I have a future.

In the blink of an eye, my exhilaration shatters.

No wonder I dance the mad scene so well. I *am* Giselle. Right at this moment, I am the happiest I have ever been in my life, but in a short period of time, the only thing I love about my life will be taken away. Giselle lost her mind when she thought the prince didn't love her. Am I doomed to go insane when I am no longer allowed to dance?

As this alarming comparison sinks in, Ryan strides towards me. With a huge fake smile, he kisses my hand gallantly, whispering loudly enough for the press to easily hear.

"You were amazing tonight," he says before kissing me passionately on the lips. There are hoots of encouragement as everyone applauds, voyeurs to the biggest romantic lie in history. Tears fill my eyes and my throat closes. I am scripted to say something, but for the life of me, I can't remember what.

Ryan covers my foible well. "How sweet is she? I think she is overcome, aren't you, my pet?" I nod, smiling, trying to will my mutinous body into following the script. I take a deep breath as Ryan is handed a glass of champagne and raises it in salute.

"To Emma, the most talented ballerina, the most beautiful woman alive, my future wife and someday soon, God willing, the mother of my children. To Emma!"

Luckily, I have next to nothing in my stomach because that toast is enough to make me vomit. Leave it to Ryan to make my moment all about him. As angry and upset as I am, I'm still too afraid of him to do more than give him a quick glare. All I can think is today I dance, tomorrow, I'll be nothing more than his imprisoned broodmare.

I don't want to live like that.

Now that I've tasted the glory of a huge adoring audience, it will be impossible for me to live the cloistered life he has planned. I hate him so much I'm shaking, my eyes burning into his. I finally remember my next choreographed move, which is to lean forward and kiss him on the cheek and recite some nonsense that I'll be damned before I say in front of this crowd.

The moment drags on uncomfortably long. I know what I'm doing is stupid and will most certainly end up in a beating, but I don't give a damn. I'm sick and tired of playing a part I never wanted, and in this moment, I cannot, I *will not,* pretend to love a man I loathe. The anger in Ryan's eyes is unmistakable, but he covers it quickly. He mutters something about me being adorably overwhelmed before pulling me to him for another bruising kiss.

"You will pay for this," he whispers into my ear as he pulls away, his fake politician's mask unable to cover the threat in his eyes.

15

THE INVITATION-ONLY opening night party is being held in a waterfront ballroom a few minutes' walk from the theater. Like the rest of the wealthy too good to do anything as pedestrian as walk, we get into a limo for the thirty second drive. As I am escorted out through the congratulatory crowd, I catch the eye of Dr. Andrews and am dumbfounded to see Declan standing awkwardly next to him. Our eyes lock for just a moment before I am swept by the momentum of the crowd into the waiting vehicle. I feel my cheeks redden as I smile, knowing that he cares enough about me to see me perform.

The car door slams shut behind me and I flinch. My father sits next to me as a seething Ryan glowers from the seat across from us.

"You made me look like a fool up there you dumb bitch! What, are you so stupid you can't remember a simple phrase? You can remember all those silly steps to that idiotic dance, but you can't remember one stupid phrase that is important to my career? To my future?"

I cringe back into the seat when he raises his hand to strike me and I close my eyes, steeling myself for the stinging slap. When it fails to arrive, I open my eyes just enough to see my father's hand wrapped around Ryan's wrist, stopping my punishment in mid-flight.

"No," my father commands as he pushes Ryan back into his seat. "Not tonight."

Ryan is furious. "How dare you—"

My father cuts him off, his eyes blazing and his tone cold as ice. "Emma is not yet your wife. You are not yet the Supreme Archon. People are talking about your temper and that you may not be suited for the Supremacy. If you don't cut this shit out even I won't be able to get you the support you need. Until you are married you are not to touch her again. Am I clear?"

I am too stunned to even breathe. Is my father actually protecting me? Does this mean that from now until my wedding day I no longer have to worry about Ryan hurting me? I almost want to ask my father to clarify, but one look at Ryan's face makes it obvious my father's words are not going to protect me for long. The next time we are alone, I'm going to pay dearly for tonight's impudent display.

It's stifling inside the tension-filled confines of the car. My lungs seize up and I feel like I can't breath. Just as I realize Ryan has no intention of taking the rebuke lying down, he lunges for my father.

To say my father is taken by surprise would be the understatement of the century. The look of shock in his eyes is all the proof I need that even he underestimated his future son-in-law's capability for violence. The realization that my usually precognitive father has been caught off-guard scares me much more than the fact my future husband is currently trying to choke my father to death with his bare hands.

I look between the two grappling men like I'm watching a blistering tennis volley. I'm not sure who actually wins the standoff; Ryan eventually releases my father from where he's pinned, but my father is the first to look away. Ryan's visibly flustered and unsure of what to do next as my father faces him and stares him into submission. I can almost see the wheels of my father's brain plotting Ryan's demise. No one threatens my father and gets away with it. No one.

We arrive at the ballroom not a minute too soon. Ryan exits the car, that fake smile again plastered on his face as he heads towards the venue. If Ryan thinks this is over, he is sorely mistaken. One glance at my father's pissed off face proves the battle between the men is far from finished.

No, it has only just begun.

16

THE NEXT TWO WEEKS are a blur of performances, galas, fake laughing, forced smiling and even more appearances wearing enough high-heeled, painful shoes to last me a lifetime. I am featured on the covers of *The National* and *Committee News* magazine. Ryan and I are even interviewed together for an evening news and entertainment telecast. We both deserve awards for our performances as the sweet couple in love. Watching the broadcast I gag when I see how we almost pull it off. *Almost.*

Anna and I spend a great deal of our free time together, talking, relaxing, drinking, sometimes even going for long runs in neighborhoods that I never before dared visit. She lets down her facade and we speak candidly of the problems we face in our lives. I confide in her about my overwhelming fear of Ryan, detailing how he attacked my father in the car before the gala. Anna holds me as I break down and sob when I tell her the truth behind the injuries sustained the night of the engagement party. It feels so good when she gently strokes my hair and lets me cry, allowing me to expel some of the fear and pain I've kept bottled up for so long.

"Have you ever thought of running, Emma? If you could leave, would you go?" The gravity of what we discuss automatically makes us drop our voices, even the remotest chance of someone hearing us enough to send us to the gallows.

"There is no way out. They will never let me go."

"No, they will not let you go, but there are people who can make you disappear."

I pull back from her embrace, puzzled.

"Emma, I trust you, I do, but I can tell you no more. All I can say is there is a way, but is very dangerous. If they catch you, they will kill you. My question for you is this: when the time comes, would you do whatever needs to be done to be free?"

Her eyes focus on mine, searching for her own answer. She nods once, her face becoming more determined, "Yes, *koshechka*, I believe you would."

17

AFTER CLOSING night's performance the company is given a week off. I relish the down time, most of my vacation spent curled up on my bed drinking hot tea and losing myself in my favorite books. There are few things I am willing to risk punishment for and the pleasure of reading a great book is certainly one of them.

Today's selection is one I found in my brother's room shortly after his death. Adam often lent me books from his precious clandestine library; from where he got the banned books I never did find out. Even as a child I devoured the ones he selected for me, many nights sneaking into his room and asking him questions about what I read. The worlds on paper were so different from ours. How did the authors think these things up? These books were once our world, he had explained. I hadn't believed him at the time. Stories about women who made their own choices and fought in wars were just as bizarre to me as books about people living on Mars being eaten by aliens.

Adam told me if anything ever happened to him, I must protect these books at all cost. Once the last generation of prewar people die and the written word is gone, there would be no chance of returning to those freer times. If there's no record of how things were, people will lose sight of what we had once been, and you can't covet something you don't know exists.

I lovingly run my fingers over the faded red cover, the dark gold title and the plastic-covered jacket that protects the banned words from coffee spills and mouse bites. The content is dog eared and underlined, highlighted and stained; the tome read so many times the pages are nearly transparent. There are notes in Adam's handwriting in the margins, the last tangible proof my brother once existed.

There are few things of mine that I consider precious, and this worn paperback novel tops that list by far. Adam stole this particular book from a library shortly before the book raids and *The Catcher in the Rye* had been his favorite. Just holding the book in my hands helps me to feel close to him. I miss him every day. I know my life would have turned out so different if he had only survived.

A knock at my door jolts me out of my reverie. It's nine pm. I open the door to see Anna standing there with a mischievous smile on her face, a bag over her arm and a bottle of vodka in her hand.

"Grab your coat, we are going out." She opens the bottle and takes a drink before holding it out to me.

"No thanks."

She huffs and rolls her eyes before jamming the bottle into my hand. "Drink, you pussy, and yes, you are coming with me. It is time you have some fun."

We leave the building a few minutes later, the armed guard at the entrance not even looking at us. Anna said he's a friend of hers and with him at the door tonight, we can come and go as we please. An hour later, we are still walking and I am getting annoyed. Any time I ask a question, Anna shoves the bottle at me and tells me to shut up and drink.

It's cold and windy and I am starting to get drunk as we march along sections of town I've never been in before. I know we shouldn't be out here, we shouldn't be doing this, but I remain quiet until we come up to one of the few remaining chain-link sections of the wall. Anna pulls a pair of wire cutters from her bag and heads into the tall weeds by the fence.

Now I'm certain she's lost her mind. I grab her arm. "That fence is electrified! You will be killed!"

"Lies, all lies," she replies with a dismissive wave of her wrist. She snips a few strategic sections and a small panel of loose wire gives way. She holds it open and motions for me to crawl through.

"This is insane. What if we get caught?"

"We won't. I do this all the time. Go! We don't have all night."

I have a bad feeling about this as I watch her zip-tie the panel back together and kick the fallen leaves back in place. When she's done, it looks like the fence hasn't been touched in years. She grabs my hand and we duck into a crumbling apartment building. She opens the door to one of the apartments, pulls out a small flashlight and looks around before locking the door behind us.

"This isn't much of a party," I comment dryly.

Anna drops the bag she had been carrying at my feet. "Get dressed. You cannot go dressed like that," she says pointing to my baggy jeans and old t-shirt. "Here, let me help you."

In less than a half hour, Anna has me fully disguised. I'm wearing a short black wig with thick, heavy straight bangs and straight hair that curls slightly to hit just above my jawline. She glues false eyelashes on me and lines my eyes with kohl, which she then tops with a vibrant green glittering paste that sweeps up to my eyebrows. She darkens my eyebrows, and puts a sticky, dark purple stain on my lips. I stare at my reflection in the cracked wall mirror, unsure if I'm horrified or fascinated.

"Put these on and let's go," she instructs while handing me a tiny pile of clothes and then continues to fumble around in her bag. "Here's your ID for tonight—remember the details and put in your bra in case you must show. No one can know is you or we are both dead. Yes?"

I look at the green-rimmed Government Issued ID card. Emilia Rosa Rodriguez. Age 22. God damn, there is my face, in this wig, my blue eyes staring out at me.

"Anna, what the—"

"Do not ask questions, *Emilia*, and do not talk if we get stopped. I will handle things. Got it? Now, get dressed and let's go."

I do as I'm told. I tuck the ID in my bra before putting on a cropped skin-tight red leather top that barely covers my breasts and has a thick industrial-style zipper that runs up the front before shim-mying into torn fishnet stockings and a minuscule leather skirt. A pair of thick-buckled leather boots that reach half way up my thighs finishes off my whorish costume.

"I feel ridiculous, Anna. I cannot be seen in this."

"You may not go out in this, but Emilia would," she grins naugh-tily. "Tonight, you are Emilia, not Emma. No one will recognize you, I bet on my life. Now, let us go."

Anna takes off her heavy coat, revealing a low cut skin-tight black dress that barely covers her ass. She has a similar pair of thick-heeled tall boots covered in thin chains that make a faint musical clinking as she walks. She adds some flourishes to her makeup and the same dark purple stain to her lips before grabbing the vodka bottle and dragging me from the building.

"There are rules to these parties that you must obey or you will find yourself in trouble," Anna confides as we walk. "These parties have a rough crowd. Do not drink anything unless you see bartender make. If you put down drink, do not drink from it again. Do not go into tunnels. Do not look anyone in the eye. Men here think seeing eyes from woman is invitation to fuck." She pauses for a second. "Unless, of course, you want to fuck," she adds with a questioning shrug.

She turns and sees my terrified face. "Look, I would not bring you if I think you would not have fun. Relax. You will be in chains in less than a year. You need to live now while you still can."

A note of seriousness tinges her last words and she pauses for another second. "Have you thought more about getting out?"

"All the time," I answer quietly. "It's impossible."

"Nothing is impossible. Nothing. You just need to know the right people."

What does she mean by that? Does she know someone who can help me? I have little time to ponder my scattered thoughts when we reach a section of road that had been badly bombed. It takes all my concentration to pick through the rubble without turning an ankle in my more than slightly inebriated state and highly inappropriate footwear. If I ever write a tell-all memoir, it will have to be titled something about my inability to ever have appropriate shoes for any occasion. The thought makes me giggle.

"Emma, are you drunk?"

"No. Yes. Maybe a little." I giggle again. We stop outside what looks like it once was a huge fancy hotel the size of an enormous warehouse where we can just barely hear loud, throbbing music. Anna knocks on the door of a basement entrance partially hidden by the collapsed roof. Three raps, two, then four, and as if by magic, the door opens. There are two huge dark-skinned men inside who greet Anna by name and lean over to kiss her cheek. They turn their gazes to me as I pretend to belong here.

"She is with me." Anna's words are oddly possessively as she threads her fingers through mine. She lifts our laced hands to her lips and seductively licks my palm. She winks at the guards while I stare at her like she's lost her mind.

"Go ahead," he says with a dirty smile. He looks me over appraisingly before giving me a frown. "I dunno, Anna. This one seems too innocent for your taste. If she doesn't satisfy you, I'd be happy to join you ladies and pick up her slack. Maybe even teach the new girl here a few tricks." He winks at her before bursting into hearty laughter at my shocked face. He slaps me on the ass playfully just as Anna jerks on my hand and drags me away.

"What was that all about?"

"He knows I like women and assumes you are my kitty of the night. He thinks it would be great fun to fuck us together. Both at same time." She wiggles her eyebrows at me as I stare at her in shock. I had been told sexual deviants were extinct in our city, the ones that lived here before the Purity Protocols were enacted having either fled or been exterminated. Apparently they missed a couple.

"Oh, my innocent little flower, you will learn so much tonight," Anna teases as she pats my stunned cheek with her hand. "Tonight, you will see a free world, a world as it should be, a world as it was before the war," she whispers dramatically. She laughs as she pulls me into a dimly lit room the size of three ballrooms and drags me up to a makeshift bar.

"Bastien, two large vodkas. The good stuff, not the donkey piss you serve everyone else."

"Anna, darling, where have you been? We haven't seen you in weeks. I've been worried!" The male voice is thickly accented, maybe French, and I look to find the source. An extremely handsome shirt-less young man wearing tight leather pants leans across the bar. He plants a lingering kiss on Anna's mouth as she runs her hand through the short inky spikes of his hair. His eyes are rimmed in koh, his lashes unnaturally long—Is he wearing mascara?

"Ah, you know when I'm on stage, I have no time for fun," Anna pouts playfully. "Bastien, this is Emilia. She is with me tonight. This is her first time here."

He takes my hand and kisses it reverently. "Enchante, mademoiselle," he purrs seductively before letting go and putting an ice cold glass of vodka into my hand. "It is always nice to meet a virgin."

I nearly choke. *What* did he just say?

"Za nashu druzjbu!" Anna hollers as she lifts her glass and a number of other people at the bar lift theirs in return. She downs the glass in two gulps, whereas I can barely manage a sip without sputtering. I nearly put the glass down before remembering Anna's warning and instead clutch the sweating glass protectively against my chest.

"Take care of her tonight," Anna says to Bastien with a knowing look before dragging me onto the crowded dance floor.

"What did he mean by that—me being a virgin? Is the fact I've never been with a man somehow tattooed on my forehead?"

Anna laughs. "He means no harm, just that this is the first time here for you, but yes, you reek of being virgin, too, you poor sheltered girl." She takes the now half-empty glass out of my hand and takes a large sip before handing it back to me.

"Finish that," she orders, pointing to my drink. "I think you need much liquid courage tonight."

The thickening crowd is made up of people of all ages and skin colors, most dressed like Anna and me, ready to party, while others are considerably more subdued. A number of people are looking strategically around the room; for what or whom I have no idea. Everyone looks like a potential watcher, and it would take the word of only one person for all of us to hang. I try to not think about it and instead focus on enjoying myself, but my thoughts keep drifting to dark places.

"Stop staring like watcher and dance with me." Anna tries to drag me onto the dance floor but I anchor my feet and refuse to move. "Anna, please, I can't do this!"

She rolls her eyes. "Go get another drink and pull yourself together. Relax. When you are ready, find me." She's distracted by a beautiful woman with long ebony hair, her body covered in colorful tattoos. She sidles up behind Anna and starts licking the nape of her neck. She whispers something into Anna's ear that makes her blush, and in less than a second, Anna takes her hand, winks at me and vanishes into the crowd.

I walk back to the bar and order another drink. I have to admit, this place is fascinating. Here there are no rules, you just do whatever you want. I wonder what it's like to live with such freedom all the time. What would I do if I could live my life as I choose? I realize that aside from dance, I have no idea. I've been told what to do for so long I realize I don't know how or even what to choose for myself. Tonight very well may be my only chance to give it a try.

"Hey there, pretty lady." A handsome young man with short blonde hair and baby blue eyes approaches me. "We haven't seen you here before," he drawls as he gives me an obvious looking over. Another man joins him in leering at me.

"I've never been here before. I came with a friend." My tone is crisp, my intention clear that I am not interested in whatever they're offering.

"Really? I don't see anyone here with you. Do you Marcus?"

"No, I can't say that I do," the dark-haired, brown-eyed sidekick responds as they move in closer.

"I just needed a drink and now I'm headed back out to dance." I pound the remains of my nearly full glass as I plot my escape. I don't know what is up with these two but they make me nervous.

"Oh, no, don't run away, little rabbit," the blonde says with a sultry voice as he reaches forward and toys with the zipper on the front of my shirt. We were hoping to get to know you a little better, weren't we, Marcus?"

"Hmm, hopefully, much better," he purrs as he moves close enough that I feel his breath on my neck. Every muscle in my body is tense and I'm ready to run, but I've been strategically boxed-in against the bar.

"I'm Brian," Marcus' buddy whispers seductively. He's so close to me his lips brush the shell of my ear when he speaks. "What's your name?"

"Emilia," I answer hesitantly.

"Emilia." He looks knowingly at Marcus who nods nearly imperceptibly. "How funny, Marcus. Didn't I just tell you I thought she looks like an Emilia?"

Okay, these two are creeping me out. I look for Anna but she is nowhere to be found and Bastien is busy pouring drinks for a rowdy group that just walked in. Great.

"You know, you are very, very pretty, Emilia," Brian whispers as he presses closer. He sensually runs his finger along my exposed collarbones, his fingertips lightly traveling up the side of my neck before he places his index finger lightly against my closed mouth. He presses his finger firmly against my lower lip forcing my mouth to open slightly as he presses his fingertip into the sticky purple stain.

I back up a step and slam right into the rail of the bar as the men laugh. I run my tongue over my lips to relieve them of the feel of his touch. My lips taste strangely bitter, almost like someone placed a wet aspirin on them.

"Here's to new friendships, Emilia." Brian smiles as he lifts his glass. A scuffle breaks out before me as a frighteningly large guy pushes his way through the crowd and violently grabs Brian by the arm.

"Get away from her, asshole," the guy growls as he pulls Brian away.

"Fuck off," Brian retorts angrily as he yanks himself free. "We saw her first."

"Really, *you* are telling *me* to fuck off?" The burly stranger reaches forward and wraps his hand around Brian's throat. A few seconds later, a few equally large guys back him up, grabbing both Marcus and Brian and dragging them forcibly from the bar.

"I'm so sorry about that. Are you okay?"

I nod, positively speechless. The man in front of me is huge with muscles protruding from every part of him. His tight, short sleeve t-shirt leaves nothing to the imagination, his abs as toned and tight as any soldier's. Yet as stunning as he is, my eyes are glued to the series of numbers burned into his left forearm.

I have never met a marked man before, as they aren't allowed within the walls of the Premier city. *Ever.* I wonder what he did to earn those numbers and if he's as dangerous as I've been told these people are.

Of course he is, Emma. He didn't become a marked man delivering meals to the elderly.

The giant is blocking my path and I am too afraid to try to push past him, so I just stand there, trembling.

"Hey, are you alright?" He sees my wide-eyed stare that I can't seem to move from his arm. He follows my gaze, understanding the cause of my fear.

"I swear, I won't hurt you. You are safe now, I promise, but those two guys are bad news. The past few times someone left with them they disappeared for good. I don't know who they are or what they're up to but I just didn't like how they were looking at you like you were gonna be their next meal."

He stops for a second, squinting at me almost as if he recognizes me, but then shakes his head. "Look, I'm sorry if I scared you, but I would never forgive myself if I didn't say something and I found out later something horrible happened."

He bends down to look into my eyes when I still don't respond. "Hey, are you alright? Yo, Bast—get her a glass of water, will ya? She doesn't look so good."

I'm starting to feel fuzzy and warm, almost like one does when woken unexpectedly from a sound sleep. My body relaxes as another guy brings over a stool for me to sit on. I slowly sip the glass of water Bastien hands to me.

"I think she's in shock," I hear him say. "She didn't take a drink from him, did she?" Even though the big guy is still standing next to me his voice sounds very far away.

"No, I didn't drink out of his glass," a quiet voice pipes up.

Wait, did I say that?

"What's your name?" I ask him, feeling braver and warmer with each passing second. It feels like someone turned up the thermostat twenty degrees. I pull the zipper down on my shirt a few inches to get more air, but all that happens is the eyes on the guy in front of me start to bug out of his skull.

"Randall."

"Thanks, Randall. I owe you one." I stand up slowly and raise my hand to pat his cheek. "I would kiss you if I could reach you."

I laugh in a way that does not sound like me at all. My other hand reaches forward of its own accord and grabs him firmly between his legs, awkwardly stroking the bulge in his pants. He groans aloud in obvious pleasure and I giggle. I am surprisingly proud of myself for doing something so uncharacteristically bold. I feel absolutely amazing, positively superhuman, like I can do anything.

And tonight, I want to do *everything*.

The music beats in time with the growing cock pulsing in my hand. Randall closes his eyes and leans against the bar, obviously enjoying my unorthodox massage. I laugh again when I pull my hand away and his eyes pop open comically. Suddenly, I have an overwhelming need to dance, the music pulling me towards the crowd like a siren's call. I skip away from the bar, turning once to blow a confused and disappointed Randall a kiss as I squeeze my way through the crowd.

The music takes over my body and mind, the steady, electronic beat feeding my desire to be in the center of the throng. There are bodies everywhere, their movement snakelike and writhing as they couple, and uncouple, their eager hands grasping, their needy fingers stroking, all to a rhythm that allows the freedom to explore our own bodies as well as those crushed against us. I lose myself in the movement, in the unfamiliar music, in the glory of a night that screams of danger and desire. I am completely free for the first time in my life, the intoxicating effect of that reality making me dizzy.

Sweat drips from my brow and between my breasts as I raise my hands above my head and move my body in the most un-ballerina-like ways. The music mesmerizes me with its hypnotic bass, the people surrounding me glassy-eyed and in similar trance-like states. I'm blasted with colored lights that strobe wildly as the crowd screams and cheers in delight, many of the people here using this strange altered reality as an excuse to drop the last of their inhibitions.

At first, the hands that touch my body surprise and startle me, but I soon understand these aren't hands that want to harm. No. These are curious hands attached to curious arms attached to curious bodies that want nothing more than to feel good and to make me feel good.

The room is sweltering and people are removing clothing as they dance, stamping the discarded items into the spilled alcohol and broken glass littering the floor. Around the room people are kissing, groping and a few, I think are even screwing, all in the guise of illicit, passionate dance. The asking of names or the normally required conversation before taking a partner ceases. Here, words are unnecessary. A stranger laying possessive hands on you doesn't want to talk—they want a few minutes of you and your body alone.

I don't know how many men I touch or even if all of the bodies I stroke are male. I fondle bodies in places I would have otherwise never dreamed, my fellow anonymous souls likewise caressing, petting, and groping me in delicious, forbidden ways. Each person that chooses to worship my body with their touch makes me feel beautiful and desired, like some form of scantily-clad goddess.

Oh, God, I don't want this night to ever end.

I feel yet another pair of large, strong hands wrap around my waist and pull me into a set of magnificent, muscular arms. I easily find the rhythm of his movement and rock along, pushing my shoulders and upper back into his firm chest and grinding my ass against what feels to be a generously endowed groin.

His hands are covered in the fitted, thin leather gloves that many men wear in here to protect their anonymity yet allow them to still fully enjoy the night's activities. His fingers move smoothly and gracefully over my body, never rushing, never harsh or grasping, as they expertly explore every inch of me. These are experienced hands—hands belonging to a man that has unapologetically known countless women. I can tell by his firm touch that he is secure in his ability to please a woman in a wide variety of decadent ways. I feel privileged to be the woman in his capable hands—to be the body who holds his attention—if only for a few brief minutes just this one evening.

He tenderly kisses the back and side of my neck as he reaches for my breasts. I hold my breath as his fingers find the zipper on my top and slowly lower it, tooth by tooth, until he can slide his hand under the thick leather and thin lace of my bra. He caresses my breast and I gasp loudly when his adroit fingertips graze my nipple. When he pinches it between his thumb and fingers, the mix of pain and pleasure brings me to the edge of ecstasy. I moan aloud, wishing it were his lips bringing me to this divine sensation.

I push my ass harder into his groin and feel his erection jerk in response. He takes his free hand and places it flat on my pelvic bone, pressing me harder to him as he grinds the most private part of himself more roughly against my ass. The bulge in his pants grows larger and harder in response.

The stranger alternates between fondling my breasts and playing with my nipples while slowly sliding his teeth up my neck to take my earlobe into his mouth. He bites down and gives it a quick, rough tug, chuckling darkly when I squeak out a shocked gasp. He immediately releases my ear from between his teeth, soothing the sting with sweet licks of his tongue.

He clearly understands the very fine line between pleasure and pain and I find that strangely arousing. Despite having no idea who this man is or what he looks like, I feel safe with him. I know he won't hurt me, at least not in the ways I'm used to.

I slide my hands to the sides of his legs, rubbing them with my palms, before snaking my arm around him and grabbing his ass. Jesus Christ, there is not a single part of this man, aside from his talented lips, that isn't hard as a rock.

I want him so badly I ache.

He spins me around and pulls me roughly to him, his hands firm on my ass, pressing my body into him, my cheek pressed against his chest. His shirt is made of a tight, rough mesh that shows off his finely sculpted body that I investigate with pleasure. I touch every plane, dip and bulge as I run my hands over his finely muscled chest, feeling them lengthen and flex with the rhythm of his rapid breath.

I take his nipple in my hand and pinch gently at first, and then getting only a little response, I twist the nub harder between my thumb and forefinger. He tilts his head back and moans loudly and I reward him by taking his other fully erect nipple into my mouth, tasting both salty skin and cool metal through the thin fabric. My tongue plays roughly with the small bar pierced through the tender flesh and he gasps when I take the rod between my teeth and give a quick tug. He cries out, I'm not sure if either in pain or enjoyment, as I am pressed so firmly against him, I can't see his face.

I release my hold, now licking and sucking lustily at his breast, greedily lapping up his delicious, salty taste. He threads one hand into my hair and places the other one on my lower back and holds me to him as he grinds against me.

My God, I would do anything to see this man naked.

As if he can hear my body chanting for more, more, more, he slides his hands under my ass and picks me up off the floor. Instinctually, I wrap my legs around him, trying to find some way, any way, of getting closer to this man who is setting my body on fire. I loop my arms around his neck, holding on for dear life as I savor this intensely erotic moment. He slips one hand between my legs, gently rubbing me through the thin layer of cotton and lace separating us. I am so incredibly aroused I have soaked through my panties, the movement of his slow stroking fingers igniting something feral inside me. I am desperate to throw caution to the wind and beg him to take me with reckless abandon. I plant lingering kisses on his throat, sucking the sensitive skin of the juncture between neck and collarbone into my mouth.

"Come home with me tonight," he whispers breathlessly between moans as his leather-clad finger finally displaces the damp cotton and traces a line down the drenched slit between my legs. His voice is deep and thick with lust, his mouth now only centimeters from mine. I want nothing more than to suck on his luscious full lips, to feel his tongue explore the inside of my mouth as we undress each other with groping, needy fingers. Only when I am so lost in him I cannot remember my own name will I beg him to put me out of my misery by making love to me with every ounce of energy he can muster. I pull my head back a few inches so I can look into his eyes.

Yes, yes, take me, whoever you are, take me, make me yours, and never, ever, let me go.

His eyes hypnotize me with their dark beauty. Unquenched lust burns within the black tempest of his all-consuming gaze, scalding my skin with its intensity. Long, thick, butterfly-soft lashes frame his piercing eyes, lending a softness to the intimidating, glittering beauty within. His heated stare gives away his arousal, his need to be touched with desirous hands burning hotter than the sun. There is an aura about him that is fiendishly and proudly savage and yet aches to be tamed and loved, to be humanized, to be saved.

As I remember that I have seen those eyes before, that I know those eyes, I loosen my hold around his neck and reach out to trace the peaks of his perfect, panting lips. My fingertips just barely brush them when he suddenly lets go, breaking the enchantment which binds us.

His look of lust is now one of shock, his suddenly fully-sober face telling me what I feared the most has happened. I've been recognized. He backs away from me, his hands held up like a man at gunpoint, the grim realization that he has just broken so many laws he could be shot on the spot coloring his face with an ashen pall.

We stare at one another, both shocked to find not only that each of us is here, but that out of all the people crowded together, we found ourselves the object of each other's passion. I don't know how to say I still crave him, that knowing his identity only makes me want him more. But before I can say a single word, the power goes out and we are plunged into total and terrifying darkness.

18

Declan

What the ever-loving fuck is Emma doing *here?* And of the hundreds of women here tonight, how did I manage to end up with *her?*

Motherfucker. I knew from the first time I saw her in that hospital exam room that somehow Emma Bellamy was going to be the death of me, but I sure as shit never thought it would be at a black market rave on the wrong side of the wall.

What makes this all so much worse is I'm not even supposed to be here. Unlike these other imprudent fools, I didn't initially come here to dance and get drunk, I'm here for the illegal trade that happens in the tunnels. Only because my contact didn't show did I decide to join the festivities, throwing caution to the wind on what's apparently becoming the worst possible night to decide to cut loose.

I swear to Christ, if it weren't for having the sort of shit luck I do, I'd say it doesn't exist. But nobody can be this genuinely and regularly fucked without some cosmic undercurrent that only rears its head when it's in riptide mode and looking for someone to drown.

I got here a few hours ago, the walk quicker than usual for some reason. I was early for my meeting, so I figured, what the hell, I'll grab a drink. Surveying the room for possible risks, my eyes instead scope out the most beautiful young woman I've ever seen standing at the bar surrounded by men clamoring for her attention. It's obvious she's in disguise, my desire to find out who she is and who she's hiding from piqued.

As I knock down another shot of cheap vodka, I can't help but feel a tingle of familiarity, that there's something about her movement I've seen before. I chalk it up to probably having seen her here some other night, or maybe she's a hooker I treated at the ghetto clinic at some point. Not giving her a second thought, I wander back to the bar for another drink. I remind my dick we're not here to get laid. Tonight we're here on business.

I down another shot before heading to the designated defunct tunnel to meet my contact. I wait for almost an hour and he never shows. I know this happens, that black market trade is notoriously unpredictable, but I'm still annoyed at the colossal waste of my time.

I head back to the bar and grab another drink, thinking I might as well get hammered and see if I can find a cute girl with a bit of a kinky streak that's up for some fun. My dick jumps in my pants, clearly agreeing that this sounds like a fan-fucking-tastic plan. I look around for the pretty girl in the black wig but she's nowhere to be found. Probably out on the dance floor.

I reach into my pocket and take out the pill I stashed for just this possible occasion. I look at it sitting innocently in my palm, the devil on my left shoulder telling me to take it while the angel on the right says I'm too old to be doing this shit. For some reason that pisses me off and I dry swallow the pill without a second thought.

On an empty stomach, it doesn't take long for the drugs and alcohol to put me in a partying mood. I hadn't eaten anything since before I went to work today which was probably not a smart thing before loading my body with drugs and alcohol. I shrug off the thought, my body having been through so much over the years that a little liver damage shouldn't take too much more time off my lifespan.

As I work my way onto the dance floor the smells of alcohol, sweat and sexual arousal overwhelm me. Just being in this gyrating crowd, getting touched, touching others, all of us here with one purpose—to live tonight like tomorrow may not come—gets my blood pumping. For most of us, living to see tomorrow is not a given. We cherish every day, every hour, most of us having learned the hard way to never take our right to life for granted.

I must have drunk more than I thought, or the drugs I took were stronger than usual, because the tenuous grasp I have on my last strand of self control slips. Joining the undulating crowd, I let my mind go blank, for once refusing to think of the millions of things I'm responsible for or the countless things that can go wrong. I let myself get wrapped up in the moment, my life's purpose right now to find that hot girl and fuck her until I pass out.

My mom once told me a true gentleman only ever thinks with the brain in his head, not the one between his legs. The way I feel right now, I have no plans to be a gentleman.

Sorry, mom. I'll make sure to add tonight to my list of sins for my next confession.

It takes a while before I find her, and when I do, I can't tear my eyes off of her. She's dancing with complete abandon yet with a sultry grace that's intoxicating to watch. She's perfection personified, even if she's too skinny, her lithe body glistening with thin rivulets of moisture that drip slowly down her neck, staining her red leather top. The need to lick the salty dampness from between her breasts, to fist my hands in her thick, black hair, and to feel her naked body writhing under mine, is overwhelming. I'm enjoying watching her so much I almost don't want to approach her. I fear that once I have her in my arms, I won't want to let her go.

Fuck, I must be high. Of course I will let her go.

It isn't long before my body demands to touch this stunning creature, the throbbing in my pants now calling my moves. I find my way through the crowd to her, almost as if pulled by some invisible force. When she's finally in front of me I reach for her, my hands skimming the sides of her waist before I snake my arms possessively around her. I pull her firmly against me, her tiny frame flush against mine.

When she feels my hard cock pressed against her lower back, her first reaction is to freeze, but it takes only a few seconds before she accepts my rhythm, pressing her small, hard body into mine. The two neurons in my brain not bewitched by her think she has to be an athlete of some sort, as damn, she's strong with sculpted muscles and what has to be a freakishly low body fat percentage. Her breasts are small in my grasp, not much more than a handful, but perfect in their feel and incredible sensitivity. I bet if I were to take one in my mouth she would make the most amazing sounds as I lash it with my tongue and suck on it until she comes.

I have to have her. Tonight.

Just as she's getting ready to respond yes to my whispered invitation, I'm jolted back to reality with the realization of just who I'm asking to come home with me so I can fuck her until we bleed. Of all the people in all the world, I hold in my hands the most dangerous and unattainable prize a man like me could dream of.

Emma-fucking-Bellamy.

I don't mean to drop her, I really don't, but in that split second, my brain demands I get my hands off of her *immediately*. In my shock, they react like I just laid my hands on a live wire and they dump the poor girl onto the sticky floor.

Touching any woman, even your wife, in public the way I did is strictly forbidden by the Purity Protocols. Touching a woman of Emma's status at all without the consent of her father or her asshole fiance is grounds for the death penalty, and what I'd been doing to her was *a lot* more than just touching. I cringe when I think how I stroked between those creamy thighs, feeling how her slick arousal dampened my gloves. Yeah, that's the kind of action that leads to the noose, for sure.

As I back away, looking down into Emma's shocked and wounded eyes, I'm torn. My brain tells me to get *my* ass out of there now but my heart wants me to get *her* out of here before anyone else figures out who she is.

When the power goes out I know we are all eyeball-deep in shit. Panic sets in as people scream and rush the exit. Bright spotlights flood the room as armed guards punch and kick their way through the crowd. The sound of people being beaten and the sickening, coppery smell of blood pierce the air. There's just enough light for me to spot Emma sitting in a pile of broken glass on the floor with her arms protectively crossed over her head. I reach out and drag her to her feet.

"Stay quiet and come with me. Don't let go of my hand. Understand?" I fiercely grip her sweaty hand, no doubt crushing her fingers as I scan the room for the nearest unguarded tunnel. I'm probably hurting her, but I'm more concerned about losing her in the panic than her comfort.

Over the years, I learned the old train and Metro stations and service tunnels well. Some are blocked from cave-ins while others are still passable. They are all dangerous due to the nature of the people that seek their refuge, but right now, they are our only option. I've been jumped a few times so I always come armed with at least a knife when I have to use them. Tonight is no exception.

"Declan!" Emma yells as she suddenly slams on the brakes. "I can't leave without Anna!" She turns to go back into the crowd but I refuse to let go of her hand.

"No, it's too late. Emma, you can't get caught. Anna will be okay, she's resourceful. She would want you to get out now while you still can."

We both know I'm lying. If Anna gets caught, things will be anything but okay for her.

We run as fast as we can through a few long straight expanses of track. By the time we finally get to an ancient station escalator that climbs into the void above, my lungs are raw and there's a stabbing cramp in my side. No matter how bad my lungs burn or how much I feel I'm gonna puke I know we have to keep moving.

God, if you are listening, if you can please help us get out of here I swear I'll cut back on the drinking, drugs, whores and using your name in vain. I also promise to work on my cardiovascular fitness. Amen.

Emma and I run up the stairs hand in hand. About halfway up I realize she's starting to falter and she's only keeping up to avoid being dragged. I'm sure she needs to stop as much as I do, but we can't. Not yet. The heavy-soled boots of the patrolmen behind us are gaining ground.

"I need a moment," she gasps.

"We don't have a moment. We're being followed."

When we finally reach the top we duck into a doorway. I flatten Emma against the wall with my outstretched arm across her chest and place my other hand over her mouth. With my eyes I enforce the notion that right now, silence is golden. She nods that she understands and I remove my hand from her lips.

I don't know how long we stand there, panting heavily, the smell of our fear strong in the air. The beams of high-powered flashlights are visible before we hear the voices. We freeze when the lights shine up the escalator and land within inches of our boots.

"That way's blocked, nobody can get out. No point in climbin' the stairs, Bruce. Set up the standard check points and just wait 'em out. They have to come down sooner or later and we'll grab 'em then."

Emma turns her head sharply towards me, her eyes panicked. I shake my head a few millimeters, just enough to let her know I have a plan. After what seems like an eternity, the patrolmen move on. I motion for Emma to walk to the iron grate in the floor and take the side opposite me. Together we lift, revealing a cobwebbed service tunnel below. I jump noiselessly into the hole and motion for Emma to jump down into my outstretched arms. I catch her well before her feet hit the ground, her slender frame sliding along the length of my body to slow her descent. She lands silently, her hands on my chest and her face tilted up towards mine.

With the force of a baseball bat to the face, I'm hit with the sudden urge to kiss her, just the touch of her body against mine enough to start some seriously pornographic thoughts rolling through my brain. I pull away, disgusted with myself as I remind my hardening cock that I'm in this perilous predicament because of him. This is not the time or place for his bullshit—after all, this is all *his* fault. I'm sure as shit not going to *reward* him for this.

I will my dick back into neutral as I take Emma's hand in mine. Even though the blackness of the service tunnels is absolute, I've taken this route so many times I know exactly where we are. With my free hand, I feel along the familiar walls for the markers that will eventually lead us to an unlocked door and out in the damp evening air.

Normally this is the point when I start breathing a little easier, when I start thinking I just may keep my head attached to my shoulders for another day. Not this time. I still have to figure out what the hell to do with the stowaway in my custody. Because as long as she's with me, I am anything but safe.

19

Emma

"Keep quiet and follow me," Declan instructs as we pick our way through the rutted roads.

The rain is coming down in torrents and without coats, we are soaked through in minutes. More patrol vehicles fly past us, my entire body flinching every time I hear shots fired. We walk quickly and silently, sometimes seeing glimpses of other people who were lucky enough to find a way out. Declan doesn't speak again until we reach a rusty metal fire escape on the side of a crumbling apartment building and even then his only words are "fourth floor."

He ascends the rickety ladder without even a hint of trepidation so I follow. We scramble into the building through a shattered window and follow a hallway past a few apartments before coming to a door locked with a heavy chain. Declan pulls a key out of his pocket and lets us in, motioning for me to go through first. Once inside, he resets the basic security system, locking me into the tiny apartment with him.

"Where are we?"

He walks quickly around the small room and lights a few candles, relieving us of the darkness and illuminating ominous shadows in the corners of the room. In the low light he looks even more dangerous, his eyes taking on a sinister gleam.

"Home sweet home," he replies with a blank expression and even emptier tone.

"You live *here*?"

"Yeah, I do," he replies defensively. "Not all of us can live in the Taj Mahal."

I look around. The floors are uneven and judging by the need for candles, there's no electricity. The glass doors that lead to a small balcony are spider-cracked and covered in a layer of thick, clear plastic to keep out the weather. The balcony is a crumbling mass of concrete without a rail, the quickest exit from the apartment a terrifying four-story drop to the macadam.

His furnishings, if you can call them that, are few. There's an old, torn-up sofa covered with a threadbare sheet and a small plywood coffee table covered in deep scratches. Several thick textbooks and a few legal pads and pens litter the coffee table where he had been reading and taking notes. I flip through one of the pads and try to make sense of his atrocious handwriting. A small metal kitchen table with two mismatched chairs and a half-dead plant in a chipped terra cotta pot occupy the kitchen. A thin mattress on the floor covered with a number of blankets that are all tucked in with military precision serves as Declan's bed, his closet a few cardboard boxes holding his carefully folded meager wardrobe. Although nothing matches and most of what he owns is ancient and worn, his home is tidy and well-cared for. He's proud of what little he has.

I rub my bare arms for warmth. "I guess if there's no power, there's also no heat? Do you have a working bathroom? Why don't you live in the villages with the others of your registration class? At least they have power there."

Declan glares at me with unveiled agitation that's quickly morphing into unbridled anger. I'm asking too many questions and probably coming across as terribly rude, but I'm strangely unable to stop the deluge of questions pouring from my mouth.

"You know something, sweetheart? If you don't like it, you can leave," he growls, pointing towards the door.

Yup, I offended him. I really am sorry and I'm just about to apologize, but he doesn't give me a chance before he stalks towards me, an ugly sneer on his face.

"Oh, wait, where the hell are you going to go? It's past curfew. Do you want to risk getting shot for being out this time of night? Wait—did you even know that after midnight the residents of our *villages*, as you so quaintly call them, can be shot on sight? Do you even know where you are or how to get home?" He pauses for a second for emphasis before adding nastily, "No, you don't."

I just stare at him. As much as I hate to admit it, he is right. I don't know what to do or say so I stand awkwardly dripping in the middle of his tiny home.

"I'm in no mood to hear your thoughts on how I should live my life. But you know, if you do feel the absolute need to keep yammering on, a 'Thank you for saving my sorry ass' would be nice. You know, I could have left you there to fend for yourself, but I didn't. A little gratitude would go a long way right now."

His snide remarks unleash something hateful in me. "Oh, Declan, thank you so much for saving poor little me," I spit with wide-eyed sarcasm. "I'm so sorry I ruined your night, but I didn't ask you to rescue me."

I realize that is the wrong thing to say when he grabs me by the upper arms and gives me a hard shake. "This isn't some game, you stupid little girl. A lot of people *died* tonight, do you understand that?"

His eyes are black and hard as he stares furiously into mine. "No, you had no idea," he answers for me. "You know nothing about this world, *my* world, or about the people in it and furthermore you don't care, do you?"

I feel his accusation like a slap across the face.

"Tonight you were just out to have some fun and it didn't go as you planned. Boo-fucking-hoo. So now I'm stuck with figuring out how to get you back to your perfect little world without getting a bullet in my brain in the process. So, once again, thank you for putting my ass on the line."

He lets go of my arms and shoots me another look of disgust. He takes no more than two steps from me when I pounce. I grab his arm and forcefully spin him back to face me. I laugh bitterly. "You really think I have it that good, do you?"

Something inside of me snaps, nineteen years of repressed anger, fear and sadness welling into hysteria. Everything in my life that has ever made me feel helpless and hopeless rises to the surface as hot tears well in my eyes.

"I get to spend the rest of my life married to a monster. Every single day until the day he eventually kills me, he can hurt me, beat me, and torture me however he wants, whenever he wants. Sounds great, doesn't it?"

Now it's Declan's turn to stare. I am shaking with a cold rage, my teeth chattering, a burning flush creeping over me. "Let me tell you a little about *my* life. My mom's a drunk and my dad is a power-hungry bastard that knowingly sold me in marriage to an insane, violent alcoholic for his own gains. My only real friend in the world, my brother, is dead. So when Anna practically kidnapped me and dragged me to the club, I went. You want to know why? One, no one ever says no to Anna, and two, I was lonely."

I confess angrily, surprising even myself with the vehemence behind my painful revelation. I pause for a moment, registering Declan's silence and the softening of his features that are no longer rigidly irate. I choke back my tears, unsuccessfully restraining them as a few slide through my ridiculous false eyelashes.

When I speak again, my words are but a whisper. "After I get married, did you know that I will never dance again? It's not "seemly" for a married woman to make a spectacle of herself on the stage. Dancing is the only good thing I have in my life, the only reason I bother to stay alive. Tell me, Declan, does this sound like a great life to you?"

His face is blank, but his eyes are empathetic.

"You don't know me at all and yet you constantly judge me because of my family. I am not my father, or my mother, or Ryan or the Committee. I am their pawn, their tool, and so the world sees me as an extension of them. Explain to me, how is that fair?"

Tears slide down my flushed cheeks. Now that I have finally found my voice, the words won't stop forming. I am completely out of control.

My God, it is suddenly so damned hot in here.

"So yeah, I may have heat and running water in my house, and if that makes me a princess, then so be it. But you have something I never will. You have at least *some* choices in life."

I am breathless from emotion and my body is shaking like a leaf in a hurricane. I'm sweating heavily, the cheap wig sticking to my salty cheeks, beads of sweat rolling unchecked down my back. The dizziness is getting worse and my stomach is cramping like someone is trying to tie my intestines into a bow. I cry out as I double over in pain and look imploringly at Declan for help. The walls of the room are sliding in to crush us, the room getting darker with every passing second, yet he doesn't seem at all concerned.

He doesn't care what happens to you. If you die, that will make his life simpler. You can't trust him. You have to get out of here.

My mind is in overdrive as I search for a way out. I run to the balcony door and rip it open. Declan scrambles to stop me, but he's too late. I stumble out onto the balcony, the night air cold against my damp skin. A bright flash of lightning illuminates the sky, the following clap of thunder making me jump. I laugh hysterically as I tear the rain and sweat-soaked wig off my head and watch it fly over the edge.

I wildly yank out the pins that kept my hair neatly tucked under my wig, freeing the waves to cascade down my back.

"Blow, winds, and crack your cheeks! Rage! Blow!
You cataracts and hurricanoes, spout
Till you have drenched our steeples, drowned the cocks!"

I laugh again, finding it hysterical that the girl that barely over a week ago embodied Giselle is now playing the part of mad King Lear in the middle of a violent storm. What tragic character will I be next week? Ophelia? Desdamona? Why must my life imitate art only in the tragic sense?

My heart pounds in my chest and when I look down, I see it beating much too quickly and much too hard through translucent skin. I turn to Declan who stands like a statue in the doorway. His hand is outstretched to me, but I do not take it. It's too late for him to save me. I am too far gone.

"O! Let me not be mad, not mad, sweet heaven; keep me in temper;
I would not be mad!"

I pray for death to come quickly, before the monsters lurking in the corners come for me or the balcony caves in and I fall. I stumble over to the edge and kick a few of the tiny loose pieces of concrete to the ground below.

How easy it would be for me to just take one more step, lean just a
little too far forward. . .

"Emma, step away from the edge. Please. I'm sorry. I didn't mean what I said." I turn to see Declan now out on the deck with me. He is as white as a ghost, obviously afraid as his eyes scan the crumbling concrete as he reaches for me.

"Come on, my boy: how dost, my boy? Art cold?
I am cold myself. Where is this straw my fellow?
The art of our necessities is strange,
That can make vile things precious. Come, your hovel,

Poor fool and knave, I have one part in my heart that's sorry yet for thee."

I beckon to him, to this man who has nothing. Surely he would like to end his misery with me? But he only looks at me with horror. His voice is cajoling as he tries to soothe my fraying mind.

"You aren't yourself right now, Emma. Please, come inside and we can talk."

The wind picks up along with the rain that lashes against me, cooling my flaming skin as it violently fans out my hair behind me. I laugh quietly, my tears continuing to spill down my cheeks, but my voice now remains steady.

"Don't you see, Declan? This *is* the real me. This is the first time I have ever told anyone what I really think and feel because what I want has never mattered before. *Tragic,* isn't it?"

He stares mutely, his hand still reaching for me as he continues to eye the concrete cracking beneath my feet. His wide, beautiful eyes beg me to take his hand and step away from the edge and I take a strange satisfaction from the terror in their depths. Is he afraid I will fall? Jump? This is the first time anyone has ever looked at me like I have any power and I am drunk with the feeling.

Let's play a game. If he begs, I come in. If he doesn't, I jump.

I giggle at the thought.

Yes, let's play.

To push the envelope a little further, I go up onto my toes, the change in balance over the drop making me sway before I catch my balance. I perform a dozen perfect changements on the edge of the balcony as more concrete crumbles from the edge and I laugh. I turn my head and smile wickedly at Declan who stares in breathless horror. He stands firmly rooted to the deck as waves of fear radiate from him.

"Emma, please. You're scaring me."

Nope. Not good enough.

I turn back to the ledge, flinging my arms out wide and scream into the night.

"Things that love night
Love not such nights as these; the wrathful skies
Gallow the very wanderers of the dark,
And make them keep their caves."

"Emma, please. . ."

I ignore Declan's plea. My mind wanders off like an untended puppy, transporting me back in time, watching myself as a young child, on my knees, deep in tearful prayer.

"Do you want to know what I wished for on my eighth birthday? I wished with all my heart that God would let me grow wings. I wanted to be able to fly," I reminisce with a small, tight smile. "I didn't want them for myself. No, I wanted to be able to swoop in and save my brother from my father's beatings. I wanted to be able to fly us to some remote island where we would both be safe. I offered God a deal, that if I could have that, I would never ask for anything from him ever again."

I take a graceful demi-plie and set up for a triple pirouette. One wrong move and I go over the edge. I spin beautifully, perfectly, landing lightly and going up into an arabesque. I reach into the night sky, feeling the rain envelop me as the wind changes direction, blowing a gust of water around me.

"As you can see, no one heard my prayers, or if they did, they didn't care enough to grant them."

My voice is barely above a whisper. I come back down onto the balls of my feet, my toes ever so slightly over the edge of the balcony. I lean forward, my arms outstretched, my head tilted towards the sky. I close my eyes as another wave of dizziness washes over me.

When I speak again my tone is hard. "I won't marry him, Declan, I won't. I'll kill myself first." I pause for just a second, opening my eyes, looking up into the starless night sky. "It's so easy to say that. *I'll kill myself first.* Have you ever said that? Do you think that if that time came, you would be able to do it?"

The tears flow faster now, my heart so full of sorrow I think it may burst. "I am so afraid that when the time comes I won't be able to do it," I confess. "Do you think I could do it, Declan? Do you?" My voice sounds far away as my words carry off on the wind. That odd feeling of watching myself, of being out of my body returns.

"Emma, please, come inside, you are terrifying me. Please, I'm *begging* you."

Even though I lost the game I don't want to step away. I don't turn around, knowing that if I see concern in his eyes I won't be able to do what needs to be done. I have the perfect opportunity to make the pain go away right here and now. All I have to do is jump.

How poetic. The ballerina diving to her death a la Swan Lake.

I shiver as my burning skin freezes under the icy caress of early winter wind. I hear the night calling me home, the darkness enveloping me, promising me respite from a world gone terribly wrong. The storm has blown through and tiny stars begin to punctuate the sky.

It's the perfect night to die.

Just as I close my eyes and give myself to the darkness, Declan lurches forward and wraps his arms around my waist. He yanks me roughly backwards, the pull of my forward momentum no match for his strength. We tumble together as Declan loses his footing and we fall gracelessly in a heap onto the damp concrete. He curses quietly under his breath as I land on top of him, knocking his head into the ground. Seconds later, the section of concrete I had been dancing on gives way and breaks off in a large chunk. That's the last thing I remember before losing myself to the overwhelming blackness of unconsciousness.

20

Declan

I should have fucking stayed home tonight.

I lie on the wet concrete, my head throbbing and my heart pounding like a jackhammer with Emma's limp body tight in my arms. I check her neck for a pulse and thankfully find it thumping away. It's too fast and beyond erratic, but at least she's still alive. I manage to gently dislodge her from me and slowly stand, feeling my body already objecting to the dive it just took. I gingerly touch the itch at the back of my head and my fingers return covered in blood.

Great.

I pick Emma up with little effort and carry her to my bed. After I've laid her down, I check her vitals and gently open her eyes, her enormous pupils a sure sign that somehow drugs are involved in tonight's theatrics.

Damn it, what did she take? Or worse, what did someone slip her when she wasn't looking? She's so naive, she would have been an easy target for any creep in there. I'm unsure if the anger I'm feeling is directed more at her child-like trust or at the bastards that were more than happy to use it against her.

Her body is shivering and she's sweating profusely. I pour some water from the bathroom sink into a large bowl and grab a clean washcloth and towel and carry them to the bed. I remove her muddy boots before drying her off as best I can with the towel and placing her under the covers. I hope the extra blankets I tuck snugly around her will control her involuntary tremors, but if this is all part of the withdrawal, only time will help.

I start to gently wash the makeup from her face. Her skin is a ghastly shade of pale blue-gray and I think, not for the first time, that this girl needs to be in a hospital. I notice something odd about her lower lip. Looking closer, I brush my finger over her mouth and a piece of thin plastic flips up into my hand. No doubt it's coated in some sort of vile synthetic drug. Women had gotten smarter about not accepting drinks from strangers, so now criminals are resorting to more creative ways to lure prey into their lairs.

Assholes.

The question of the drugs now answered, I dry her face after I remove the last of the makeup and take the bowl back to the bathroom where I empty and refill it. I splash water on my face, removing the sweat and dirt of the evening and dry it on the same towel I used on Emma. It smells faintly of her flowery scent and I inhale deeply, momentarily soothed by her fragrance. Peering at myself in the cracked mirror above the sink I again ask myself the million dollar question.

What the fuck do I do now?

I know it's going to be a long night so I change into a faded long sleeve t-shirt and loose pants, ready to sit a hopefully uneventful vigil. Knowing I should do something about ridding the pollution in my own system, I grab a pint glass and fill it with the water from the bathroom sink and drink thirstily. I refill it before going back to bed.

I check Emma's vitals which are still all over the place. She's still shivering but is now also murmuring unintelligible words, her face full of pain. Whatever is happening in her unconscious state, it isn't good. I want to comfort her, but I don't know how. She's in the middle of a very bad trip and I am powerless to help her.

It's not long before she's dripping with sweat and clawing at the covers to get free. I fill another bowl with cool water and tenderly wipe her face. Her entire body is drenched. I slowly work my way down her neck and arms, watching her body relax under my touch.

I grab a clean cotton shirt from a box on the floor and head back to bed. Emma might be pissed about this when she wakes up, but I'll deal with that later. I remove the rough leather shirt, noticing how the cheaply-dyed hide has bled a deep burgundy over her pale skin and what had once been a demure pale pink bra. After washing the sweat from her skin I dress her limp body in my shirt.

As I lay her head gently onto my pillow, my eye catches the laminated State ID card that had fallen from her clothes. I toss it onto the coffee table where it slides under *Grey's Anatomy* and out of sight.

I sit back on the lumpy mattress and just stare at Emma. She's an enigma, that's for sure. The press has made her out to be nothing more than a piece of brainless arm candy, but I'm realizing she's so much more than the beautiful dumb blonde they want us to see. The girl's smart, and not regular smart, but *freakishly* smart. For Christ's sake, she was spouting off Shakespeare as she was dancing on the ledge tonight. Fucking Shakespeare!

I reach forward and check the pulse in her neck, and when I'm done, I can't seem to pull my hand away from her face. I let my fingers graze her silky cheek, gently tucking a few loose golden hairs behind her ear. My fingertips dare to touch the lips I had been so close to tasting, boldly testing their plumpness against the calloused pads of my fingers. They are every bit as soft and yielding as I dreamed. My mouth waters at the thought of them doing all sorts of delicious, forbidden things as my mind tries to convince me that just one taste wouldn't be wrong.

I pull my hand away, disgusted with myself, but I can't stop staring at the beautiful woman in my bed. I wish the world could see her how I see her right now. She doesn't need the makeup, the gowns, the heavy jewels and the high heels. Right here, clad in little more than my worn out T-shirt, she is by far the most stunning woman I have ever seen. Although I had meanly gotten in the habit of calling her a little girl, tonight I'm realizing that I couldn't have been more wrong. Emma is one hundred percent all woman.

When she starts to shiver harder, I pull the blankets up to her chin, tucking her in like you would a small child. It doesn't help. Her face is contorted in what looks like fear and pain and she starts thrashing, gasping and tearing at the covers with her nails as if she's trying to rip someone apart. I place my hands gently on her shoulders in an attempt to calm her but it only makes things worse. From bits and pieces of her words and reaction to my touch I conclude that not only has the abuse she endured at Ryan's hands been both verbal and physical, but sexual.

The anger coursing through me is blinding, my desire to kill the man that tortures Emma filling my muscles with the kind of strength only years of unrequited rage can give. I've wanted to murder that son of a bitch with every fiber of my being for the past sixteen years. Watching Emma endure his punishments over the past months has only exemplified that need to the point that I no longer want to kill him—I want to fucking *destroy* him.

When she starts to scream, I know I have to get her to calm down before a late night patrol swings by and hears her. Although it's rare to have a patrolman venture out this far, the troops will be out in force after the raid. I grasp Emma's wrists in my hands and even in her altered mindset, she fights me shockingly hard. Surprised by her strength, she breaks my grasp and slices my cheek with a ragged fingernail, drawing blood and leaving a painful welt.

That's going to be a tough one to explain at work on Monday, if I live that long.

I recapture her hand, this time lacing my fingers through hers as I lay down on the mattress next to her. Wrapping my arms around her, I keep up a steady stream of words, murmuring soothingly for her to be still, to please hush, breathe, relax. I hope my calm, quiet tone will somehow penetrate her unconsciousness but she continues to struggle against me. I have my hands full restraining her before she either slips further into the darkness or merely gives up fighting, I'm not sure which.

Unlacing my fingers from her limp grasp, I use them to check the pulse in her neck which feels steadier, but is still too quick for my comfort. As I move around a little to relieve my stiff muscles, I look over to find her trembling again. I realize when she's pressed against me she shivers less, and that reminds me of a study I once read. The researchers proved that sick newborn babies healed quicker when they had skin-to-skin contact with another person, receiving something from prolonged human contact that medicine alone couldn't give.

I figure it's worth a shot. I pull my arm gently from under Emma's sleeping body and yank my shirt over my head. I don't care that my burns, tattoos and scars are visible, I just want to help her so damn badly I'm willing to risk her waking up and seeing who I really am. At this point, if she decides to report me I'm a dead man, anyway.

I dive under the blankets and pull them up around us as I press my bare chest against her back and wrap my arms carefully around her. The shivering slows but doesn't stop. I say a quick prayer before pulling her shirt up in the back so my chest presses against her knobby spine. I slide my arms under the cotton fabric around her tiny waist, feeling her damp skin under my forearms and fingertips as I try to contact as much of her bare skin with mine. I think about taking the shirt off of her altogether, but as much as my dick thinks that's a fabulous idea, my brain vetoes it.

I better be getting brownie points for good behavior here, God. Or is this just another of your sick and twisted ways to teach me good guys always finish last?

Emma sighs, pressing her perfect little ass into my again rock-hard groin. I close my eyes and take a deep breath. I mentally demand my cock to cut it the fuck out, that she's *unconscious* for Christ's sake. It doesn't work. I spend the rest of the night suffering from a raging case of blue balls while Emma sleeps in my arms, oblivious to the torture she's inflicting.

As the first rays of morning break across the horizon, Emma's vitals are steady enough that I allow my eyes to close. I'm strangely soothed by her steady, soft breathing, the rise and fall of her chest calming my heart and relaxing my muscles. Somehow, having Emma in my arms feels so right even if everything about this night has been so incredibly wrong.

I pull her tight against my chest, the back of her neck millimeters from my mouth. I gently press my lips behind her ear, knowing that once she wakes, my opportunity to do this ever again will be gone. I commit every detail of this moment to memory, every one of my senses overwhelmed as my weary eyes flutter closed. And for the first time in my life, I fall asleep with a woman in my arms and a smile playing at my lips.

21

Emma

I wake with a start in a strange room in an unknown man's arms with no clue how I got here. I start to sit up, but the dizziness and nausea are so severe I immediately abandon my plan to rise.

Where am I? Why can't I remember last night? Most importantly, who the hell am I in bed with?

Oh, you've really done it this time, Emma.

I feel the man next to me stir, but his breathing remains soft and regular. He's still asleep. His arms pull me back against his bare chest as he cuddles me to him. I am warm and comfortable and although I know this is a really dangerous situation to be in, I still somehow feel perfectly safe. I close my eyes and snuggle against his bare chest, enjoying the feel of his hard muscles against my back and his arms wrapped around my waist. I succumb to the comfort and warmth he provides and fall back to sleep.

When I wake again I am alone. I prop myself up on my elbow and take a look around the sunlit room. Bits and pieces of the previous night come back to me as I run my fingers through my messy hair, trying to make some sense of my confusion.

"You're awake."

The deep male voice startles me and I turn quickly to see Declan sitting stretched out on the sofa wrapped up in a thin blanket. He's dressed in faded loose sweatpants and a long sleeve t-shirt with a textbook draped across his lap, a notebook open and a pen in his hand. He closes the book and extricates himself from the covers and comes towards me. Kneeling down, he takes my wrist in his hand and feels my pulse for a few seconds, then checks the one in my neck.

"Better, much better." He pauses for a minute as he peers into my eyes. "Think you can keep some food down?"

I nod, suddenly ravenous. He gets to work making eggs and toast over a small propane camping stove, the finished product, coupled with a glass of discolored tap water, surprisingly delicious. After a few bites, I realize I'm queasier than I initially thought, and I push the plate away. I feel terrible not finishing the food, knowing he doesn't get paid much and yet is willing to share what little he has. I think this simple meal just might be the nicest thing anyone has ever given me.

Declan takes one look at my nauseated expression and wordlessly takes my plate and scrapes the remains of my breakfast onto his, tucking into the extra food with gusto.

"Drink the water. All of it. You need to flush the drugs out of your system."

I have no idea what he's talking about and I'm defensive that he thinks I'm stupid enough to take drugs. "I didn't take any drugs."

"Emma, someone drugged you last night. Between that and the alcohol you were a fucking mess. I don't know how much you remember, but you nearly launched yourself off my deck while reciting Shakespeare. I may be wrong, but I doubt that's how you usually spend your Friday nights."

The memories are cloudy but snippets of me laughing and crying while dancing on a ledge spring to the forefront of my mind. I wonder what other reckless and stupid things I did last night aside from sleeping in the same bed with Declan. As words are often more damning than actions, I'm also terrified of what I may have said.

I watch Declan silently as he washes the dishes, dries them and puts them away. When he comes back to the mattress and shimmies under the covers facing me my entire body stiffens.

"I'm not going to touch you, and I promise I won't hurt you. It's just cold in here and I didn't get much sleep last night. I just want to warm up. Okay?"

He's keeping a safe distance between us and I nod as I snuggle under the covers, my pounding head resting on his pillow, a pile of tattered sweatshirts under his head. He has dark circles under his eyes that match the black stubble of his cheek. He looks exhausted.

"How much of last night do you remember?"

"Bits and pieces," I admit. "It all seems like a dream."

He's silent for a while, forming his next question carefully while he chews on his chapped lower lip. "You scared the piss out of me last night. I thought you were going to die."

"From the drugs?"

"No."

I suddenly remember reaching for the stars, feeling the rain on my face and leaning forward inch by inch until Declan pulled me from the ledge. He saved me from myself.

"I know things are bad for you, but killing yourself isn't the answer. I know you think that's easy for me to say, but trust me, I know what hopelessness feels like. You're a strong woman, Emma, you'll find some way to get through this. You just have to believe in yourself."

I have no response. He's read me all wrong. I'm not strong. If I can't even speak up for myself, how the hell can I change my destiny? I'm too big of a coward to even kill myself, for Christ's sake.

We stare into each other's eyes for a long while, both of us trying to decide what to say next. His face is open, for once his thoughts evident. I'm sure my expression is similar to his, both of us wondering if we can trust the other. There's something about him I want to trust so badly but my rational side keeps reminding me of the rewards he could reap by turning me in.

"Emma, don't let them win. You need to fight."

I stare into his chocolate brown eyes and wonder how I ever thought them hard and menacing. He's been so kind and understanding, so unlike the person I dealt with over the past months, that I again wonder about his motives. I swallow hard, both the eggs and my heart in my mouth. I'm terrified he's setting me up for a dangerous fall.

I sit up and wince, my head pounding. I don't want to go in conversation where I am being led. I look around for my clothes. "I need to go home."

Declan reaches across the covers and gently grasps my hand. "You can't go anywhere until it's dark, it's not safe. There's going to be patrols everywhere after last night. Get some rest, we can talk more later."

Like hell I'm saying anything else.

He squeezes my fingers and to my surprised disappointment, lets go of my hand. He closes his eyes and within a few seconds, falls fast asleep.

* * *

It's dark when I wake. Despite the few lit candles it's too dim to clearly focus, and yet Declan is right back on the sofa, trying to read. He looks up when he hears me stir and closes the textbook on his lap. He stares at me for a moment, the hard glare of his eyes making me feel naked before him. When he reaches over to the coffee table and picks up a small card and flicks it over to me I flinch like he threw a grenade in my lap.

"Where did you get that?"

I don't say a word. If Anna is still alive I don't want to get her involved. My silence pisses him off, his features even more threatening in the shadows.

"Emma, I asked you a question." His voice is clipped and angry.

Declan rises from the sofa and stands over me, his hands in fists. I cringe involuntarily, suddenly afraid. He's really mad, and when men get angry they start swinging. It's bad enough I have no idea how I'm going to explain my twenty-four hour absence if anyone asks, but if I come back bloody I'm going to be in even worse trouble.

I stand up but keep my gaze lowered, not wanting to provoke him. "I see I've outstayed my welcome. Give me my things and some directions and I'll go." I look around the room for my clothes.

He grabs my arm and swings me around roughly to face him. "You aren't going anywhere until you answer me."

I flinch from his grasp and squeeze my eyes tight as I brace myself for the slap I know must be coming.

"Did Anna give this to you? Huh? Did she?" He pauses the interrogation for a second before grabbing my face and forcing me to look in his eyes. "Goddamn it, Emma, fucking answer me!"

I nod. He must see the terror in my eyes because he lets go and backs away. His grasp had been rough but he didn't hurt me, and now he's looking at me with a mixture of fear and sadness that I don't understand. Part of me wants to ask him what is going on and yet somehow I know I really don't want to.

22

Declan

I have to get her out of here. Now.

Things just escalated to a whole new level of crazy and I'm not getting involved. No fucking way. I'm going to just pretend this night never happened, that I never saw Emma, I didn't dance with her, or touch her, or bring her home with me, or sleep in the same bed with her, or anything else.

She knows where I live now. Damn it, I'm going to have to move.

I root through the box of folded clothes until I find an ancient pair of ratty jeans. I throw them at her along with an old canvas belt. "Put these on, I'm taking you home."

"Declan, what's going on? I don't understand."

She looks so tiny and afraid, standing there, holding up the jeans she dutifully put on but are about eighteen sizes too big. I take the strap from her other hand and run it through the belt loops before tying it in a knot around her waist. She looks ridiculous, like a child playing dress-up in her father's clothes. I grab the boots she wore last night and toss them at her before handing over my only decent winter coat. As much as I'd like to bring my Glock with me I don't need Emma knowing I illegally possess that sort of firepower. I check to make sure my knife is still in my pocket.

After securing the apartment, I take her hand as we work our way out of the building. The metal railings are especially cold and I am again pissed about getting jumped last winter and having my only decent pair of heavy gloves stolen. I walk fast, purposely making it hard for Emma to keep up so she will stop begging me to respond to her questions. I simply don't have the heart to answer them.

We duck into another tunnel entrance, Emma smacking her head on the low ceiling. *Shit, I should have warned her.* I use these tunnels almost daily, so I know them like the back of my hand. I forgot that she doesn't. I pull out a small flashlight from my jacket, mentally weighing the pros and cons of the light bringing unwanted attention against Emma knocking herself senseless in the dark. I opt for the light.

We don't have that far to go, as the metro tunnels are fairly direct. Although our lives are a world apart, we don't actually live that far from one another. I open a small side door and before entering, I place my finger to my lips, warning her to be silent. This tunnel is darker and much tighter, the twists and turns no doubt filling Emma's head with all sorts of questions I will never answer. After this, I fully intend to never see her again.

We scramble up a rickety ladder and through a trapdoor. The basement we're in smells damp and musty and my nose itches from the mold that coats the walls like a sneeze-inducing blanket.

"You're in the storage lockers in the basement of your building. Take the stairs to your room, do *not* take the elevator. Tomorrow, take all the stuff you are wearing and throw it away somewhere where no one will find it. Burn it. Dump it in the river, I don't give a shit, but get rid of it. Especially this. Do not get caught with this." I hand the ID card back to her.

She looks up at me with those beautiful blue eyes and I suddenly want to take her in my arms and kiss her the way I know she should be, the way she *needs* to be kissed. I stand there awkwardly for a second, like a teenager at the end of his first date unsure what to do next.

Declan, you dumb fuck, you are 31 years-old. This wasn't a date and you are never going to see her again. You need to go now before you do something else to earn the bullet you're obviously begging for.

I know I'm acting like a cagey asshole and I'm positive Emma had a million questions that all deserve to be answered. You better believe I have a fuck ton of questions, too, but I can't ask mine any more than I'm going to answer hers. Even though I see something in her eyes that tells me I can trust her with the truth, my lips remain sealed. The less she knows the better for us all.

Without another word, I start down the ladder, closing the trap door over my head with a muffled *thunk*. When my feet hit the floor, I pocket the flashlight, waiting a few seconds for my eyes to adjust. I lean against the damp wall, scrubbing my hands over my eyes and running my hands up into my hair and pulling on it like I always do when I'm frustrated.

I tell myself again that I'm doing the right thing, that it's much better for Emma to think I'm an asshole than to tell her the truth. The truth would kill her. And if I'm reading her wrong and she turns me in?

It will kill me, too.

23

Emma

The seemingly endless flights of stairs have left me breathless by the time I get to the floor Anna and I share. Thankfully, there are no cameras inside the building except in the lobby and in the elevators, a fact I'm surprised Declan knows. My father wanted internal cameras installed for safety purposes when I first moved in, but Ryan had refused to pay for the additional security. With all the lower windows barred and the exits patrolled 24/7, he had deemed it unnecessary. Whereas his decision had come across as cold and uncaring at the time, I'm thankful now that he's a cheap bastard.

I run into my room, slamming the door behind me. Thankfully, Anna suggested leaving the door unlocked and not bringing my keys because all of the stuff I had left with is still in that dingy apartment outside the wall.

My rooms are dark and silent. I lean up against the door and take my first deep breath since I left Declan's apartment. I'm back where I belong. I'm safe. There are no missed messages blinking on my answering machine, no one that noticed I had been AWOL over twenty-four hours.

I got away with it.

A delicious little shiver crawls up my spine, a smile blooming on my face. I had the craziest adventure that nearly went wrong a million different ways and yet I'm back in one piece. God must be smiling on me. I walk through the darkness of my rooms to my bedroom and flip on the lights.

"Just where the hell have you been, missy? I've been waitin' on you for hours."

I shriek when my eyes focus on a pissed-off Caitlin camped out on my bed waiting for me. She takes in my crazy attire with narrowed eyes that demand answers.

"Start talkin', sister. You've got a lot of explainin' to do."

24

I MAKE UP an inane story that doesn't make any sense even to my own ears. Caitlin's leary eyes and pursed lips give away the fact she doesn't believe me but she doesn't push. I tell her I'm tired and want to get a shower and ask if we can hang out tomorrow after class. She mumbles that she's got work tomorrow, her eyes suddenly downcast and glassy with disappointment.

"I was really hopin' we could talk. I know that you're goin' through a rough time, and well, I am, too. I'm so sorry I've been such a bitch lately, but I've got a lot of pressure on me to find a new client now that you're gonna be usin' Ryan's stylist. I know it's not fair of me that I've been takin' it out on you. I just want to say I'm sorry I haven't been there for you, sugar."

She reaches out to grasp my hand. A single tear breaches her lashes and spills down her cheek. I feel like a jerk knowing that my normally stoic Cate must really be hurting if she's crying.

"Of course I have time for you. Just let me get a quick shower and I'll be right back, okay?" I grab a set of flowery cotton pajamas and head for the bathroom. I leave the clothes in a heap on the floor with plans to drop them in a dumpster on the way to class tomorrow.

We spend the rest of the night curled up together on my bed talking the way we used to. As much as I want to confess the truth of last night, I'm afraid. My delicious taste of the wild side could not only land me in hot water, but get Declan and Anna boiled alive. I feel guilty not confiding in my best friend, but for now I decide it's better to keep the last twenty-four hours locked away in the Pandora's box of my brain.

I'm exhausted and cranky the next morning, two nights of little sleep doing nothing for my attitude. Everything about today seems wrong as I get ready for class, a weird sense of foreboding coloring my world in shades of distrust. Caitlin was gone when I woke up, not leaving so much as a note to say goodbye.

The second I walk into the theater I feel something's off. The normal chatter and laughter in the hallways is replaced by tense silence broken only by harsh male voices and the occasional screech of staticky radios. The second my feet breach the threshold of our rehearsal room, I'm grabbed roughly by a huge patrolman and walked to the center of the floor and commanded to sit. The ashen faces and terrified eyes of my fellow dancers implore me to do something. I shake my head sadly. This is one fight where I have absolutely no jurisdiction and whatever is going to happen, I am powerless to stop.

Nicknamed the "Purity Police" both due to their pristine white uniforms and their focus on ridding our country of deviant culture, these brutal forces remain a continual threat to artistic communities. It's well known that once you are determined to be deviant and taken into their custody you are never seen again. The lead white-coat nods to his underlings who lurch towards our huddled mass. They snatch up three male and two female dancers from the floor and place them in restraints. Our chosen friends face us bravely, a few of them shedding quiet tears while others glare defiantly. One of the older dancers starts reciting a prayer about a shepherd until one of the guards clubs her in the back of the head with his rifle and tells her to shut up. Blood drips from where she was hit but she doesn't stop praying. Her lips continue to move, albeit silently, until she finishes by mouthing Amen.

When Jeremy walks in the patrolmen seize him, dragging him inside and slamming the door shut. Unlike the others, Jeremy fights valiantly, but he is outnumbered. One of the guards cracks him on the skull with the butt of his rifle and he falls to the floor with a sickening thud. The lead officer pulls out a handgun and shoots him in the back of the head, killing him instantly.

I scream.

The handcuffed dancers are all forced to their knees, a patrolman behind each one, the muzzles of their weapons pressed against the back of their heads. The squadron leader reads aloud the charges. They are all pronounced guilty of Deviant Behavior and Acts of Treason. There is nothing that can be done to save them.

The squadron leader keeps his unblinking stare sharply on the convicted. He speaks slowly, making sure his words register in their terrified minds. "There is one more deviant we are looking for. Anyone who has information about the whereabouts of Anna Vasiliev will receive leniency. The first person to tell us information that leads to her capture will be spared the corporal punishment of family and loved ones."

My God, not only are they going to kill my friends but also their families.

There have always been whispered stories of the brutality of the Purity Patrols, but I had been told by my father they were lies—the work of the underground press that was well known for making a big deal out of nothing. Most of the fake news organizations had been culled years ago, the few stories that come out each year from rogue journalists quickly discredited, the authors found and drowned in the brackish water of the reflecting pool in National Square.

Ryan started his illustrious career as a squadron leader in the Purity Police. He claimed in past interviews that the stories of brutality were 'overwhelmingly false,' that patrolmen only use as much force as is warranted. I can't imagine anyone believing those statements, as the torture and dismemberment of those he arrested certainly spoke otherwise. Of all the purity patrols, his squad had the highest detainee mortality rates, a record of which he still boasts. His cult-like followers love him all the more for his unwavering brutality, chanting *"Cut them up!"* at his rallies.

"If any of you know anything, you need to speak up now. I can assure you, once we leave here, I will not be asking as nicely." His raptor-like eyes scan the faces of those of us trembling on the floor. His eyes fall on me and he arches a brow in question.

He thinks I know something.

His lip curls in a small smirk and his eyes never leave mine as he raises his hand and makes a slight gesture. A thunderous boom explodes in the room, our screams and sobs adding to the cacophony. Our lifeless friends fall to the floor before us in a grotesque pile of blood, brains and limp bodies. We are all too stunned to move. We sit in horror as the blood seeps towards us, a dark red tide coming for us all.

Less than an hour later, I'm sitting in a tiny room inside an Interrogation Center that smells of a toxic mix of blood, urine and bleach. I feel nothing. I'm so far out of body, my mind so detached, that the day's details are already fuzzy as my brain tries to block the horror. I have no idea how I am going to survive my upcoming interrogation when I couldn't even tell you my name right now.

When the door opens, a woman's tortured scream floods the room until the door of our soundproof unit slams closed. I break into a cold sweat as I wonder which of my friends emitted that terrible sound.

"Emma, I'm Director Graham," the tall, thin white-uniformed man says as if we have just met at a garden party and he's not getting ready to torture me. "I need you to answer some questions."

"I don't know anything," I blurt. "I swear."

"How can you say that when I haven't asked you a single question yet?"

I remain silent.

"Are you and Anna friends?"

"Yes."

"Close friends?"

I'm shaking so hard my fingers are drumming on the table. I flatten my palms against the scratched surface to steady them. *Pull it together, Emma.*

"Yes."

"How close?"

I have one possible chance of getting out of this and I decide now's the time to try. I feign a haughty tone, hoping to intimidate the officer. "What are you insinuating, Director? Do I need to remind you who my father is?"

"That does not make you above the law. No one except He is above the law. Answer the question."

Well, so much for that plan.

I gulp in fear. "We are good friends, yes."

"Did you know she participates in activities that are considered Deviant and Treasonous?"

"Of course not," I snap. "She never did anything that made me think she is, or was *different.*"

"The work you are looking for is *subversive,*" he corrects. "Did she ever ask you to participate in any deviant or treasonous acts?"

Would dragging me to an underground club where I got drunk, was drugged, ended up fleeing from patrol and spent the night in the arms of a man that is not my husband count?

I look him straight in the eye and lie. "No."

We stare at each other for what seems like an eternity before he pulls a picture out of a folder and slides it across the table to me. It's a picture taken from a security camera of Anna and me as we left the building the other night.

"Is that you?"

I say nothing.

"Is that you?" he repeats more forcefully.

"Yes."

"Where were you going."

"We went for a walk. We do that a lot together."

"At nine in the evening you went for a 'walk' with a bottle of vodka," he scoffs. "What did you have planned?"

"Nothing."

"Don't lie to me."

"I'm not lying."

The fast paced questions are starting to rattle me and I'm terrified that at some point I'm going to make a mistake. Even if I make it through this portion of the interrogation, there's no guarantee that I will make it through the review.

A knock interrupts us and the Director rises to open the door. He stumbles backwards as Ryan pushes past him. As much as I hope here's here to save me, the look on his face assures me that's not the case.

"Leave us."

Ryan stares down at me as the Director scurries from the room. When the door closes behind him, Ryan grips the back of my chair with one hand while pointing to the ceiling-mounted camera with his other. He leans in to whisper in my ear, his voice menacing and deathly serious. "You have a very large audience right now, Emma, and for your sake, they better not catch you in a lie. Do you understand?"

"Yes."

"Where's Anna?"

"I don't know. I swear, Ryan, I have no idea."

He walks slowly to the other side of the table as he contemplates my answer. "Emma, I'm telling you now, I have neither the time nor the patience for your shit. Tell me where she is."

My eyes fill with tears. "I swear to you on my life, Ryan, I don't know."

He strolls back across the room, standing in front of me and nodding his head. I never see the slap coming, and in my unprepared state, the force behind his palm is hard enough to knock me to the floor. Ryan descends upon me with such fury I'm helpless to protect myself.

I don't know how long we're in that interrogation room or how many times he hits me, but by the time Ryan is convinced I know nothing, I am shattered. Sobbing in a corner of the room, my clothes torn, my nose running copious amounts of blood and snot, I look up at Ryan with unchecked loathing. All I can think of is how I wish I jumped from Declan's balcony when I had the chance.

A thin trickle of blood runs from somewhere deep inside my ear and drips onto my shoulder, the back of my head throbbing from Ryan's repeated slams into the floor. I must have slipped up on a response or been caught in a lie to deserve this type of punishment. It's just a matter of time before they shoot me. I wish they would hurry the hell up and get it over with.

The Director visibly pales when he reenters the room but says nothing. He hands a clean handkerchief to Ryan so he can wipe my blood off his knuckles but does nothing to help me. They speak in low tones before they leave the room without a second glance, their certainty that I'm unable to go anywhere right now so absolute they leave the door open.

A few minutes later I hear the unmistakable cadence of my father's steps. I can't even look at him as he swears under his breath as he registers the scene. He crouches down and slowly reaches out to touch my cheek, his nearness causing me to scramble and thrash in an attempt to back myself further into the corner. There's a moment when I think he looks hurt by my fear, but he quickly replaces his look of concern with his customary aloof and emotionless mask.

"Governor Bellamy, how good of you to come," the Director intones almost cheerily as he reenters the room.

"Explain to me what happened here, Paul."

"Well, we are searching for a missing subversive -"

"I was briefed on the situation on the way here, Director," my father interrupts testily. "What I want you to explain is why my daughter was beaten half to death in your custody."

"Sir, we had to determine if she was breaking the Laws of Purity and committing Treasonous Acts. I was pursuing a much less *active* interrogation of your daughter, but then Archon Gregory took over shortly after I started. He was concerned I was giving her preferential treatment. He reminded me that my job requires me to be impartial in my interrogations and that no one except He is above the law, Sir."

My father glares at the visibly rattled Director. "You know god-damn well the law doesn't apply to members of ranking families."

"I'm sorry, sir. I truly am. I am well aware of the benefits of your status. This, I swear, was none of my doing. I never laid a hand on her."

My father takes in the Director's words carefully, reading between the lines. He utters another curse before raking his hand over his eyes. "I see. And the results of the interrogation? Are you going to tell me my only daughter is a deviant? Has she been found guilty of subversion?"

"No, sir," the Director gulps. "The Committee on Purity has found her innocent."

"Good. Then, I am taking my daughter home, if that is deemed acceptable by the Purity Committee."

My father doesn't wait for an answer as he crouches down and extends his hand. "Come on Emma, let's get you home." He helps me to my feet and I continue to shake. Thinking erroneously that I'm cold, he takes his overcoat off and places it gently over my shoulders, leaving his hand wrapped around my upper arm for support.

When we exit the building, the press swarms us like a horde of angry hornets. They shout questions and snap photos, the lights flashing in my face making me want to vomit. I raise my hand to block them, but my father whispers for me to lower it. He wants them to see me. He wants them to take pictures of him escorting his badly beaten daughter to his waiting car.

I have always disliked my father but this moment changes everything. He's using me and this incident somehow for his own benefit. He wants this on record for some reason and I am again nothing more than a prop to be used for his own devices.

I used to think I disliked my father, but right now, I know that's no longer true.

I don't dislike him.

I fucking *hate* him.

* * *

My father gives a brief statement to the press stating I was only here to give testimony against the guilty and that I was not here under interrogation. They all nod in agreement, believing his lies even when I'm the walking evidence of his falsehoods. No one dares to ask about my battered face or the fact I am sobbing hysterically.

No sooner than we get in the car my father turns on me. Gone are the concerned looks and quiet murmurs. He's furious. "What the hell, Emma? Are you trying to get yourself killed?"

I say nothing, knowing there's nothing I can say or do to remedy this situation.

"Where were you yesterday?"

"Home."

"Don't lie to me, Emma. Where. Were. You?"

"What, are you going to hit me if I don't answer you? Bring it on, father. What's a few more blows at this point?"

I can't believe the words coming from my mouth, my mental filter an obvious casualty of Ryan's heavy-handed blows. I don't bother to stuff them back in with an insincere apology as I can't possibly get in more trouble at this point. My father looks at me in stunned silence before he pulls a small card from his wallet and places it on my thigh.

Oh, shit.

"Where did you get this?"

My face on the fake, State-issued ID card stares back accusingly. What I really want to do is ask him where *he* got this.

"That's not mine."

"Emma, for Christ's sake, don't lie. I may have gotten you out of there for now, but this isn't over, not by a long shot. I need to know where you were this weekend, who you saw, who gave this to you and where you were planning to go. Your life may still depend on it."

I refuse to look at him knowing I can't, I *won't* tell him the truth. There's no way I'm turning in Anna and Declan. I wouldn't be able to live with myself. I look at the ID card and wonder who turned *me* in.

"Emma, I need to know everyone who knows about this so I can protect you. Those people must be silenced or you will end up swinging. I can help you, but you have to trust me."

My head is spinning. I'm incapable of rational thought, of trying to decipher the web of lies cocooning me like a fly in a spider's thrall. I try to piece together the raid at the underground and the culling in the studio with my father somehow getting his hands on this card and realize I'm missing some very important link.

My mind ping pongs between Anna, Declan, my father, and Ryan. Could this have all been a trap by one or more of them to get rid of me? Had Anna led me to that wild party like a lamb to the slaughter, the ID on me enough to get me out of her hair permanently? Had Declan thought better of his rescue and turned on me? How the hell did my father get the ID card that I was certain was in the bag of clothes I tossed in the building's incinerator on my way to class this morning?

It's all too much. My field of vision narrows as my father continues to alternately plead and yell. I'm only faintly aware of him grabbing me by the arms and shaking me hard. I hear him say something like *this is your last chance* before the sound cuts out on the picture before me like a faulty television. A few seconds later my body involuntarily goes limp and I'm plunged into darkness.

25

Declan

When I get to work the next morning I grab a cup of coffee and a copy of the *New State News* that's required in every hospital waiting room. Alone in the Sports Medicine wing as it's still freakishly early, I contemplate if I'd rather blow off some steam in the weight room or relax with a long, hot shower. I pull the rubber band off the curled up paper and drop it on the table, the brutal picture catching my eye.

Holy Mother of God. It's Emma. Or I should say, what's left of her.

I snatch up the paper and stare at the picture, my heart in my throat. She looks like she went ten rounds with a pro fighter, the article directly under her picture detailing the latest Purity Patrol massacre. Six members of the National Ballet Company have been found guilty and "dispatched" for a variety of supposedly treasonous crimes.

Jesus James Earl Jones Christ.

Scanning the names of the dead, I know them all. Over the years I treated every one of them at some point. None of them were remotely dangerous. Sure, at least a few of them were guilty of violating the

Anti-Homosexuality laws, but how does not being straight equate to treason?

I put down the paper, feeling sick to my stomach, the smell of burnt coffee making it worse. I log onto my computer and check hospital files for Emma's name. Just as I thought, she had been beaten so badly they had to admit her. I lock the door to the wing and stalk over to Emergency Medicine to find John. The minute he sees my pissed off expression he drags me into the safety of the mostly soundproof suture room.

"Did you treat her?"

"Yeah," he nods. "It looks bad, but she's going to be alright. . ."

"Really, she's going to be *alright*? This girl gets the living shit kicked out of her at least once a month and you think she's going to be *alright*? What the FUCK, John!" I see the warning in his eyes but at the moment, I'm too worked up to care.

"Lower your voice," he hisses. "Things are no longer safe down here. Be careful what you say and to whom. We are being watched. You keep talking like this and we'll be the next ones on the front page."

I glare at him. I am so tired of being careful, of slinking around. "Do you know what room she's in?"

"Why? Are you going to visit her? Bring her flowers?" John scoffs. "I'm sure Ryan would be just thrilled to know you are there to comfort his soon-to-be wife."

"Fuck you, John." He sees the look in my eyes, that mix of fear and rage and the deep-seated need to rescue Emma that's as much a part of me as my black hair and dark eyes.

"Do you have some sort of a death wish, Declan? Seriously, son, stay out of this."

I stalk off angrily, flipping him off as I walk away. Dammit, I know he's right. But being wrong has never stopped me before, and it isn't going to stop me now.

* * *

A little before 6:00 a.m. I find myself in the hall outside Emma's room. I'm surprised there's no guard stationed at her door until I see him flirting with one of the nurses at the station down the hall. I lock eyes with her, motioning for her to keep him busy and she blinks once in affirmation. She's a friend that sometimes hooks me up with drugs to be delivered to the ghetto clinic, so I know she's got my back.

My original plan of getting a quick glimpse of Emma as I walk by shits the bed when I amble past and see she's awake. She's staring out the window into the darkness, her shoulders shaking. She's crying. She looks up to brush the tears from her cheeks and our eyes meet in the window's wavy reflection. Even in the dark, I am horrified by what I see when she turns to face me. I can't contain my shock, causing her to cry fresh tears as she quickly turns away.

Fuck. Me. I can't walk away now.

Before my brain can remind me how stupid this is, I'm sitting in the chair next to her bed. I take her hand gently in mine and she pulls it from me fiercely.

"Please, Emma, look at me."

She shakes her head, sobbing harder. Before I can think through the potential consequences of my actions, I rise from the chair and sit on the edge of the narrow bed. I gently place two fingers of my right hand on the only unmarked section of her jawline and turn her battered face towards me.

"Why did you do it, Declan? Why did you turn me in?" Her voice is so quiet I almost miss her words but the look of hurt, distrust and fear on her face makes them unnecessary.

"What are you talking about?"

"It had to be you. No one else except you and Anna knew about the ID, and Anna hasn't been seen since Saturday."

"Emma, I didn't turn you in, I swear to Christ. Why would I do that after risking my life for you?"

I don't know what is happening, but my chest is tight and my words come out breathy like I just finished a ten-mile run. I'm desperate to have her believe me. "Emma, do you think I'd be here if I turned you in?"

She mulls the words over in her head. "Why are you here, Declan?"

I look into those huge, impossibly blue eyes and want to blurt out the words running through my head but my throat is suddenly too dry and tight to speak. If this was some stupid chick flick from decades ago I would explain my presence by taking her in my arms and kissing her senseless. As my life tends to take direction more from the likes of Quentin Tarantino, I decide against taking the chance when Conan the Patrolman could walk by at any moment.

As prudent as it would be to keep this strictly professional, my eyes give me away. I reach forward and take Emma's hand in mine and this time she lets me. I squeeze her hand reassuringly, trying to impart some of my strength to her. My gesture backfires spectacularly when she begins to sob in earnest.

"Shh, it's okay. I'm here, I've got you," I whisper. I'm not sure how it happens, but we find our way into each other's arms. I hold her as she sobs against my shoulder, her entire body shaking with the effort of her emotion. I stroke her hair, murmuring the same reassurances as just a few days before when I had her in my bed. I close my eyes and groan inwardly at the thought. I would give anything to have her in my bed again.

At the most I'm there for five minutes. The sun is rising and the seven am shift will be arriving soon. I need to leave before someone sees me, but God help me, I don't want to leave. Emma clings to my shirt, taking fistfuls of the fabric into her tiny hands and holding on for dear life.

I hear the elevator doors chime and the laughing voices of the changing staff coming towards us.

"Emma, I have to go." I feel her nod, but she doesn't release me. I slowly pull myself away from her, every movement a silent torture as our bodies part.

"Thank you," she whispers. She places her hand on my knee, stopping me briefly from rising. "Thank you for everything."

All I can do is nod as I don't trust my voice, not that I have any idea what I would say. I slip from the room and am just a few steps from her door when the elevator doors ding open and Ryan Gregory steps out.

26

Ryan

The dark-haired man ducks his head as he nears, a common reaction for those of lesser status wishing to remain unseen in my presence. But this guy is particularly fidgety as he averts his gaze, his body tensing up in the way only guilty people tend to do. After he passes, I turn and watch him as he takes his left hand and nervously runs it through his hair, the brace he wears to hide his scars giving away his identity.

I can't believe my fucking eyes. He's supposed to be *dead*.

Oh, someone's going to pay for this.

I'm seething by the time I walk into Emma's room, my hand wrapped so tightly around the long stem roses my PR adviser told me to bring their stems cut into my palm. If he's touched Emma, if he's defiled her, I'm going to break his fucking neck and make her watch me do it. I will not be disrespected by him. I *abso-fucking-lutely* will not be cuckolded by her. I will not have them make me a laughingstock.

Emma sees the fury in my eyes the second I step foot in her room. She scrambles out of bed, trying to put as much distance between us as possible. She's tethered by a short cord of IV line attached to a bag of clear fluids that prevents her escape, not that there's anywhere she can hide in the twelve-by-twelve room.

"Stop being so fucking dramatic and sit down." I drop the roses on the bed and sit in the seat next to her. I smell the scent of poverty that lingers in here, his cheap soap and generic shaving cream soiling the air. There's no question in my mind. He had been here.

I'm fucking ballistic. I wonder if he fucked her. Has he caressed her breasts with that wretched crippled hand? Did he take what's mine with his diseased cock and fill it with his filthy seed?

I want to kill her. Fuck the contract, fuck her father and fuck our agreement. I am *justified* to kill her. Hell, if he's had her, I can press charges against them both. *Thou shall not commit adultery. Thou shall not covet thy neighbor's wife.* The law and the church are on my side. I can have her stoned if I want. I can watch as he swings from the gallows. If I really want, I can have both executions happen at the same time and watch with a bucket of popcorn in my very own macabre Saturday double feature. But to do this, I need her to confess.

"I see you had a visitor." My voice is surprisingly calm even to my own ears. When she blanches further and then turns red I know I'm onto something.

"Yes, my physical therapist from the last time I landed in the hospital stopped by to see if there was anything he could do to help."

I see the lies in her eyes, but I don't let on. I sit tight as I let out a few inches of rope for her at a time, positive it's only a matter of time before she will have enough to hang herself.

"Really? That was kind of him. What sort of help was he offering?"

She looks confused, her cheeks getting redder by the second.

"Is he the one that promised to get you out of the country? Is he the one that gave you this?" I pull a sheet of paper from my breast pocket and hand it to her. She unfolds it and takes one look at her face on the false ID and gasps. It's too late for her to deny it, her guilty expression and terrified eyes as much a confession as yelling *I did it!* in a packed courtroom.

"So what did that man want from you in return for getting you out of the country? Did you get down on your knees and give him one of your half-hearted blow jobs? Did you fuck him? Come on Emma, tell me the truth for once. Don't make me beat it out of you. I'm growing bored with your constant need for discipline. I'm starting to think you enjoy it."

She says nothing. Her eyes, even the one nearly swollen shut, are huge with fear. I watch her eyes flick back and forth to the bathroom and I know she's going to make a break for it. I lunge across the bed for her as she bolts for the bathroom, the IV yanking out of her hand as she races across the tile floor. I grab her wrist and swing her around to face me and shake her hard.

"You are going to tell me everything, Emma, or so help me God, I'm going to kill you right here, right now. I refuse to be disrespected any longer. Did you let him fuck you?"

She's so scared she can only whisper. "Please, he's just a friend. There's nothing between us, I swear."

"Liar," I sneer. "I see it in your eyes. You fucking want him, don't you? You're hot for that spic motherfucker aren't you? Aren't you?" I'm screaming as I continue to shake her. "Did you fuck him? Tell me, Emma, did you bleed for him? Did you give him what's lawfully mine?"

"No! Ryan, I swear to you, we are just friends."

I drag her over to the bed and throw her on top of it. Blood is streaming from her hand and splattering us both as she thrashes in my grasp. "Then you should have no problem with me checking for myself."

She stares for just a second before screaming bloody fucking murder as I grab her behind the knees and drag her ass to the edge of the bed. I order her to spread her legs for me but she only clamps them tighter together.

Two horrified female nurses are at the door demanding to be let in, begging me to stop, but my guard refuses them entry. They watch as I pin Emma's hands in one of mine as I use my knees to force her legs apart. I pull up the thin hospital gown she's wearing and tear off her panties while she continues to shriek. My captivated audience gasps as I jam two fingers into her snatch and probe roughly until my fingertips jam against her barrier.

Emma begs for me to stop amid frantic sobs, my fingers scraping against her dry walls and my dick so hard it throbs to the beat of my pounding heart. I'm beyond aroused by her frantic screams and terrified eyes. It takes every ounce of willpower to not whip out my dick and fuck her, to not take what's rightfully mine regardless of who sees.

Stop it, Ryan. You're digging a hole from which even your genius PR men won't be able to extricate you.

I release my grip on her hands and pull my fingers from her. She curls into a ball sobbing loudly. I step away to wash my hands, disgusted by her tainted, splattered blood from the hole in her hand that now decorates my bespoke suit. The stink of her cunt on my fingers remains even after multiple washes with the hospital's industrial strength liquid soap.

She's hysterical, like she's the aggrieved party here when *I'm* the one who has been wronged. Just because her hymen is intact doesn't mean that he hasn't defiled her in other ways. She refuses to look at me when I return to her bed so I grab her chin in my hand and force her to face me.

"Shh, Emma, you are making quite a scene," I whisper in her ear. "I understand you want to protect your *friend*, but you are doing both yourself and him a disservice. If you don't want to tell me the truth, that's fine. I have other ways of finding out what happened.

Just remember, my pet, that if Declan ends up dead you will have only yourself to blame."

She stares at me. Even though hearing his name from my lips scares the shit out of her, she sticks to her story that he's never touched her. I know she's protecting him. I question her again and again about the ID card and all I get are denials. Emma has the same shifty look in her eyes as my sister used to when she lied to me all those years ago. I did not tolerate lies from my own flesh and blood and I'm certainly not going to tolerate them from Emma.

Ephesians 5:6. Let no one deceive you with empty words, for because of such things, God's wrath comes on those who are disobedient.

Few things rattle my chain more than someone that dares lie to me. To have a lesser being, a *woman*, spew falsehoods thinking she can outmaneuver me infuriates me like little else. Even though Ephesians warns us of God's wrath, while she's still on Earth, Emma should be more afraid of mine.

Before I release her I lean forward and kiss her lips roughly. "I'm very concerned about your mental health, my dearest. You seem hell-bent on a path of destruction that will only lead to ruin. I think you need better supervision, a second pair of eyes to help you make better decisions. After all, isn't everyone better behaved when they are being watched?"

I know she doesn't like this by the look on her face but a naughty child cannot be left to their own devices. It's only a matter of time before an unattended child will burn a house to the ground and I refuse to be the one to hand her the matches. I lean in closer, my lips now grazing the shell of her ear, my voice but a menacing breath.

"From here on, you will be guarded by my own security. They will follow you everywhere, watch everyone you come in contact with and listen to everything you say. They will report directly to me. You aren't going to be able to take a piss without me knowing. My watchers are loyal, and unlike you, they will not lie to me. You have proved I cannot trust you, so now I must place my trust in others. You made a huge mistake trying to run from me. Now you will spend the rest of your life paying for it."

She trembles before me. I've finally gotten through to her. "I'm going to give you one last chance, Emma. Start talking or I swear on all that is holy, I will make you wish you had never been born."

27

I LEAVE EMMA'S ROOM covered in her blood and storm down the hallway. I haven't been this pissed off in decades. I have no idea what is up with the fucking women in my life that drives them to be filthy spic-loving whores. She's protecting that bastard. I just know it.

She's protecting him just like Janey did with that motherfucker Dante.

I'm so furious I can't hold back any longer. With a roar, I punch a hole through the drywall as I wait for the slow-as-fuck elevator to arrive. The other people waiting scatter and I end up descending alone. When I'm back in the car, I pour myself a double despite the early hour. The memories of my sister, the ghosts of my past rearing their ugly heads.

So how does it feel to have yet another woman prefer a filthy spic over you?

In a renewed fit of pique, I throw the crystal tumbler at the divider between me and the driver. I do not want to think about the past or the present or my fucking future. I want to get so damned drunk I forget my own fucking name. I pour another tumbler to the rim and drink thirstily, not even tasting the expensive amber fluid. All I can think about is my sister and that last night on our farm.

* * *

From the minute I got home from military school that summer, I noticed something was up with Janey. She and I have always been inseparable, our bond as twins every bit as strong as while we shared a womb.

But now she was distant. Guarded. She was spending a lot of time with Dante, one of the caretaker's sons and whenever I saw them together, she was jumpy as hell.

I knew they were up to no good.

Dante was a quiet guy, a few years older than Janey and me. He was home from college for the summer to help his dad manage our farm. I thought it was weird when my sister dragged him to dinner one night and even weirder when my parents seemed unphased by his presence. My father politely asked him about his studies while my mother kept trying to feed him the best pieces of steak off the grill and offering him yet another slice of pie, perks she normally gave *me* as the firstborn son.

Dante told my dad in his soft, lightly-accented voice that his goal was to get into vet school, that since he was a boy he had always wanted to help animals. He told us that's why he was working so hard, that without a full academic scholarship he would never be able to pay the costly tuition. My father lauded his hard work as my mother smiled and my sister practically swooned at his feet. My father turned to me and told me there was a lot I could learn from a man with Dante's drive to succeed. I was so embarrassed I didn't know who I wanted to kill more.

I could feel in my bones Dante was evil, but I was the only one who saw the predator sitting at our table that night. I sat directly across the table glowering at him, hoping he would be so uncomfortable that he would get the hint and leave. But no matter what I said or did, night after night, he returned.

I tried to tell them. I warned them, and not one of them believed me. The more I pushed my parents, the more they fell in love with him. At dinner one night my father announced that when Dante got into vet school he would pay his tuition if he agreed to work at our farm for a few years afterward. Dante looked so shocked I thought he was going to fall off his chair. He refused at first until my father put his hand up and said there would be no discussion, that he had already put the money into a joint account and had a contract drafted for Dante to sign. He was even going to give him spending money so he wouldn't need to get a side job and could focus solely on his studies.

I was incapable of doing anything except stare at my father in shock. Was this really the same bastard that when I totaled my car he said he didn't have the money to buy another one for me? Did he really hate me so much he would rather give away my inheritance to some filthy spic instead of his own flesh and blood?

Yeah. Yeah, he did.

After my father's announcement my mother cried tears of joy. Janey squealed and jumped from her seat directly into Dante's lap and hugged him in such a way I knew that if they weren't already fucking they would be soon. My father beamed at him with a look of pride that I had never once seen in his eyes when he looked at me. I felt so alone that night, almost as if I was outside the dining room and peering in through the window. They were all laughing and hugging and smiling and I just sat there wondering how they could all be so fucking stupid.

That was the moment I realized I didn't dislike Dante. I *hated* him. I hated watching him weasel his way into our family. I hated how my mother doted on him. I hated how my father constantly compared me to him and always found me lacking. I hated how my sister looked at him like he was the second coming of Christ.

It was everything the guys at boarding school had said about these fucking spics and then some. He was infiltrating my life, my family, my country, a dangerous invasive species that was going to choke me right out of my own family. I didn't care what my stupid family thought. Dante was going to destroy us, and I had to get rid of him before it was too late.

For weeks, all I thought about was Dante's complete and utter destruction. I wanted him to pay for seducing my loved ones into thinking he was the perfect son, for thinking he could usurp me and have what was mine. I wanted him to spend the rest of his miserable life knowing he ruined his own future by reaching for the brass ring when he had no right to even ride the carousel. I never once thought about who else would get hurt. Furthermore, I didn't care.

I spent every moment of every day and most of each night plotting his demise. If it hadn't been for my sleepless mind being in overdrive that night, I would have missed the creaking of the uneven floor-boards and the quiet rattle of the loose handrail on the stairs. My sister was sneaking out and something in me told me to follow her.

The full moon enabled me to see and yet keep my distance as I followed her past the barns. I had been right, she wasn't out here for a late-night check. She was out here for some other purpose. When a shadow emerged from the dark she ran to the male form that seemed to materialize out of thin air. She threw herself into his arms and he caught her gracefully, swinging her around and around before setting her down. His mouth descended upon hers, devouring her lips, his large hands all over her. He touched her with such confidence it was obvious this wasn't their first tryst.

I wanted to break this up, to grab her by the neck and tell her to get her ass back in bed. At the same time, she and I were now adults in the eyes of the law and she had every bit as much right to screw around as I did. I couldn't see who the man was and figured it was some guy from her school who would be rightfully pissed if I cock-blocked him.

I was just getting ready to leave them to their own devices when his mouth slid down and began to kiss and suck at her neck. She moaned quietly as her hands moved to squeeze his ass as she murmured, "Yes, Dante, oh, baby, yes. *Te amo, Dante. Te amo.*"

In that second, I stopped breathing. I couldn't believe what was happening, my worst fears coming to life right in front of my face. My sweet sister, the good child, the one who always did as she was told, the one who sang in the church choir each Sunday, was whoring around with the fucking *help*.

I stayed in the shadows and watched as she wrapped those long legs around his waist and he carried her into the barn. I waited a few minutes before sneaking over and peeking through the doors to find them tearing at each other's clothes like wild animals. They landed on the straw-covered aisle in a heap of naked limbs, their lust building to a fever pitch.

My eyes were glued to them, the moonlight through the windows illuminating her flaxen hair, the curve of her perfect ass, the swell of her breasts that Dante fondled and suckled with porn star-level skill. I was the strangest mix of horrified and titillated, my cock hardening uncomfortably in my jeans as I watched in the same way it's impossible to turn away from a fatal car wreck. When Janey pushed him to the floor and mounted him, thin bubbling saliva began to pool in the back of my mouth. I bolted from the door, running as fast as I could before the urge to vomit overwhelmed me.

I spent the night waiting for Janey on the front steps of the house, every second that passed making me more furious. I wanted to kill him. I wanted to kill her. I was so fucking incensed that motherfucker dared defile my sister that I wanted to chop off his filthy dick and shove it down his throat until he choked.

As the sun began to rise, Janey moseyed towards the house, a dreamy smile on her lips that were puffy and bruised from kissing. Her clothes were a mess, enough hay in her tangled hair to feed a fluffle of rabbits for a week. She was so lost in thought she didn't even see me at first, but when she finally registered the look on my face she knew I was pissed.

I told her I was going to tell our father what she had been up to, that daddy's little princess was nothing more than a filthy, spic-loving whore. I spewed such rage and hate that I honestly don't even remember most of what I said. Fearful that my ranting would wake our parents, Janey dragged me away from the house, ducking into the same gabled barn where she had just fucked Dante. The smell of sex filled the air, the smell of him on her making my stomach churn.

Janey told me I had it all wrong, that she loved Dante and he loved her. He had asked her to marry him and she said yes, that she was only waiting to wear the ring he gave her until he asked our father's permission tonight. When the clock struck midnight we had turned eighteen, and she was certain that he would consent considering how he had told Dante just last night that he loved the boy *like a son*.

I was dizzy and sick. I turned away from her to gather my composure, and when I looked back, she was gently caressing the tiny swell of her belly that I hadn't before noticed.

Oh, fuck no.

I slapped her. Hard.

Hitting her made me feel better so I did it again. Then again.

I stormed off and left her sprawled on the hay-covered floor, thinking she would have the sense to stay away from me while I was out of control, but she didn't. She kept grabbing at me, begging me to listen and I kept pushing her away. I climbed into the loft knowing she was afraid of the spindly ladder. I needed time to clear my head, to think.

I really thought she would get the hint and head back to the house. When I felt her trembling hand on my shoulder and realized she had followed me up into the third-story loft I was beyond surprised. We argued. I slapped her again and yelled at her, calling her all sorts of filthy names. She started hitting back, but her feeble swipes were nothing compared to mine. I screamed for her to get away from me before I killed her. I told her I would kill him if he ever touched her again.

Janey stopped striking at me, my threats finally having the effect I desired. I knew she wasn't just scared, she was terrified, just like I wanted her to be. I wanted her so afraid she would never let him near her again. I told her she was going to have an abortion and get rid of that abomination she carried within her. She stared at me with such horror as she backed away, her hands in front of her a flimsy barrier against my rage. Her face was bruised, her lip bleeding as tears streamed down her face.

"Who are you? I don't even know who you are anymore, Ryan. The brother I love would never behave in such a despicable manner."

Her words shook me out of the haze I'd been in and now I couldn't believe what I had done. Dad always thought I was possessed by the Devil and at that moment, I knew he was right. The fog lifted from my mind, the light of day burning off the mist that still clung to my thoughts.

"Janey," I whispered her name like a prayer, hoping even in the low light of the loft she could see the remorse in my eyes. As I approached, her eyes grew wider and never left mine as she continued to back away. She didn't dare take her eyes from my advancing form, treating me the same way as one who happens upon a hungry mountain lion in the woods.

Neither of us saw the pitchfork lying in the hay until it was too late.

If only she had never met him.

I reached for her as she careened backwards, the lip of the loft now inches from her heels.

If it only had been anyone, fucking anyone, other than him.

My hand grazed her fingertips as I screamed her name. I lunged for her, doing everything in my power to prevent the inevitable, but she continued to stumble. When her foot stepped back and no longer met the floor, her eyes grew impossibly wide as the realization of what was about to happen registered. With her hair swirling around her face, her mouth open in a blood-curdling scream, she fell.

There's a lot that I don't remember after that, but what I do recall haunts me. I remember screaming her name over and over as I raced down the ladder. I remember the anguished howl that slipped from my lips and shattered the dawn when I realized her neck was broken. I remember sitting and cradling her bloody, broken body in my arms as I sobbed and begged God to please, please not take her from me. I remember the look of horrified shock when Dante walked in just minutes later to find me stony faced and silent as I stroked my sister's unseeing eyes closed with shaking fingers.

He came towards me, tears pouring from his eyes as he asked me over and over, "Dios mio, what have you done?"

Me? *Me?* He thinks this is my fault? How fucking dare he. The rage I felt earlier returned tenfold.

Dante fell to his knees and tore Janey from my arms and sobbed over her lifeless body. He turned to me, his devastation etched deep in his dark brown eyes. "You murdered her," he gasped between sobs. "You murdered your own sister. Your *twin*. Why? Why did you do this? Why?"

I stood up quickly, not wanting to be near him, not wanting to see his weeping, grief-stricken face. I realized how this looked, and now I was terrified that somehow this would get blamed on me. This was all *his* fault, and now he's trying to pass the blame.

He should have stayed with his own kind.

He was so lost in sorrow, he never saw it coming.

Although I've repressed much of what happened that day, there are some things I do remember clearly. I remember finding the piece of discarded baling twine on the floor and picking it up. I remember what it felt like to sneak up behind him and strangle him with the thin orange strand that cut into his neck; how easy it had been to fashion a quick noose from a few lengths of twine and make his death look like suicide. I remember sitting back down and retaking my sister in my arms as I forced myself to shed more tears.

It all ended up being surprisingly easy. The lies had come to me almost as if angels whispered them in my ear. I spun a story of a trusting family that was destroyed by an unstable, murderous young man unhappy about becoming a papa. When she told him she was pregnant, Dante had been furious and demanded she abort the child. When she said no, he attacked her. I said that's when Janey came to me, telling me Dante had gone crazy. She'd been afraid for her life.

I told my rapt audience of questioning policemen and devastated parents how, against my advice, she refused to go to the police. She had been too embarrassed to tell our parents what was going on, especially considering how my father thought of Dante *like a son*. When I told her I would talk to him, she refused, swearing that once he calmed down, she was sure everything would be fine. I assumed they worked things out, as Janey never brought it up again.

I looked at my listeners for a long moment, taking a dramatic pause as I summoned fresh tears before continuing. I told them how I found her body, beaten, broken and sprawled on the floor, Dante's body just a few feet away hanging from a rafter. My story of their tragic murder-suicide was never once questioned, the tale confirmed when the autopsy proved she was nearly three months pregnant.

Over the years I've asked myself the same question—If I could magically turn back the clock and do everything that morning differently, would I?

My answer is always yes.

Because I would have liked to watch Dante suffer more before he died.

* * *

I put my glass down as the wheels in my mind begin to turn. I lower the window between myself and the driver and change my route. A sense of calm washes over me. And just like that morning so many years ago, I know what I must do.

I put the still-full glass back in the cabinet. For what I have planned I want to be fully sober.

28

Declan

I'm a miserable fucking bastard all goddamn day.

I can't get Emma's tear-stained face or the sound of Ryan's self-important stride out of my head. That had been a really close call. Too close. I don't even want to think about what could have happened if he had walked in a minute earlier and seen Emma in my arms. But my concern, for once, isn't about what would happen to me—I'd be shot on the spot. My fear manifests itself solely for Emma and the many ways he could make her pay for my lapse in judgment.

I spend the rest of the day thinking about what Emma said. *Thank you for everything.* I don't know what she meant by that and I'm worried she's planning something; well, planning something even worse than what she already confessed. After this latest brutal beating she may decide to move up the date of her suicide, and in all honesty, I can't blame her. But I also can't help thinking there has to be something I can do to help her.

The mark of an immature man is that he wants to die nobly for a cause, while the mark of a mature man is that he wants to live humbly for one.

Thanks, J.D, for those wonderful words of wisdom. Why is it I always remembered these words from *The Catcher in the Rye* when I'm getting ready to do something that sounds like a great idea but later turns out to be colossally stupid?

By the end of the day I'm in a really shitty mood. I'm itchy and agitated and if I stick around much longer there's a good chance I'm gonna beat the shit out of someone. I leave the second I'm done with my last patient, realizing a better use of my excess energy would be to go for a run once I get home. A very, very long run.

I scan my red ID card as I walk through the crossing checkpoint, head bowed, eyes down and careful to not make eye contact. The wall watchers are a particularly twitchy group of fucks that have been known to go Battle Bots just for someone looking at them the wrong way. Just when I think I'm in the clear, I'm stopped by the muzzle of an automatic weapon shoved in my face.

Seriously. Can this goddamn day get any worse?

I go through the usual bullshit routine. Name, address, ID type and number. Where are you coming from? Where are you headed? These guys have seen me twice a day, five days a week, going back and forth to work for years. After all this time, they should know the answers to these questions as well as I do.

"Remove your jacket, hand it to me and stand over there with your hands up against the wall."

Luckily, I'm not smuggling any hospital goods in my pockets. I silently thank the powers above for being so preoccupied that I forgot the vials of drugs in my locker that I was supposed to bring to the clinic tonight.

One guard roots through my coat while the other frisks me, all under the watchful gaze of a third guy pointing a rifle at my head. I try to act like nothing's wrong, but I'm starting to get scared. Had someone turned me in?

Did Emma *turn me in?*

"Turn around and remove your shirt."

Shit. This is it. The lights are on, the cage is locked. It's dying time!

I find it strangely bizarre that I'm thinking of that ancient robot-fighting TV show right before I die. If this shirt comes off, it's game over, do not pass go, do not collect your fucking money. If they see what I'm hiding, my time playing the game of Life will be well and truly over.

I try to play it cool, knowing these guys aren't going to take any lip. "Come on, man, can you give me a break? I'm coming home from a really long day at work and it's cold enough to freeze the tits off a witch. Do we really have to do this?"

A line starts to form at the gate and I realize my death will now be performed before a live studio audience. I start to sweat. I could try to run, but I won't get far. The guy behind the rifle looks like he has a pretty good idea how to use it and is more than happy to partake in some moving target practice. I take a deep breath and pull my shirt over my head.

A few people in the crowd gasp when they see the numbers branded into my arm. The interrogating officer grabs my arm and straightens it, reading the numbers to yet another guard who types them into the computer and checks them against my ID. When he lets my arm go, I snatch it back. I'm just waiting for them to realize none of the information matches.

My audience is getting larger, about thirty people now waiting in line to cross. Most of them are men but a few women and children are all going to win the grand prize of watching my brains get splattered across the wall. Knowing I'm minutes from death, I start whispering the Old Faith prayers in hope that God may someday even think about forgiving my transgressions.

Someone turned me in, the million dollar question being *who*.

It had to be Emma, dimwit. They gave her a choice and she chose herself. Apparently she's not as suicidal as you thought.

No, that can't possibly be it. She wouldn't do that to me. Would she?

The next thing I know I'm sucker-punched by a guard and on the ground. Two of them grab my arms and cuff my hands in front of me. They drag me over to the wall and hook me up to a short length of chain just as another guard kicks me viciously in the back of my calf, causing my legs to buckle. With no way to break my fall, I land painfully on my knees.

"I don't know who you pissed off, boy, but they want you to pay for what you've done before you die," the guard hisses as he's handed a particularly nasty looking baton studded with small metal bolts.

I'd like to say I'm not scared, that I accept my punishment with a hateful glare and silent stoicism. I've had everything taken from me throughout the years, but damn it, I still have my pride and I intend to keep it. Although I know I'm fucked with a capital F, when they ask me if I have anything to say for myself I say nothing. I know this is when I'm supposed to beg for mercy, to make excuses or try to make a deal, but I stay silent. I refuse to give them the satisfaction of being on my knees and begging for mercy, especially knowing it's useless. There's no clemency for people like me.

Compared to most people I've seen in my situation, I probably seem like I'm handling my punishment fairly well, at least in the beginning. But after the first few minutes of their rapid-fire assault, the pain is unbearable. By the time they are finished, I'm screaming just like the other poor souls I've seen being beaten half to death in this very same spot. I do learn a very important lesson while having the shit kicked out of me. No matter how important your pride may be, when you are in this much pain, you don't give a shit who hears you scream.

All in all, the entire process takes about fifteen minutes, but it feels like I've been chained to that wall for days. When the guards are done with me, they unclip the cuffs from the chain and I fall to the ground. My face is splattered with the mud created by the blood, urine and filth from their other recent detainees. It had apparently been a busy day at Checkpoint 17.

The lead patrolman commands me to get up. When I don't immediately comply, he delivers a swift kick to my ribs that does nothing to make me rise any faster. The unmistakable click of a safety being removed and a gun readied to fire is my final warning before I'm yanked to my feet. The muzzle of a handgun presses against my head as I'm dragged away from my horrified audience.

I start my fervent prayers again knowing this is my last chance to beg God to forgive me. As the blood-splattered wall behind the firing squad looms before me, my chest tightens. As much as I would love to go out fighting, I'm too weak to even argue.

The guards take a quick left and drag me into the station. A wave of relief washes through me at the last-minute reprieve. Even though I'm not foolish enough to think this means I'm going to survive past the next five minutes, this at least gives me a few more minutes to make my peace with God.

But if they've dragged my ass in here, there's gotta be something they want, something they don't want to discuss in front of an audience. I know that something precipitated today's traffic stop, and honestly, there could be any number of reasons why I'm now in double, if not triple, jeopardy. And if I had to venture a guess to the answer: *The person responsible for your current situation,* I would bet my dwindling life to answer, *Alex, Who is Emma Bellamy?*

29

THE WALL WATCHERS drag me into an interrogation room and force me to my knees. They attach short chains to my cuffs that are bolted into the concrete floor, restraining me like I'm some sort of dog. After they leave I lose track of time, the sound of the ticking clock on the wall behind me the only distraction from my agony. I don't know how long I stay motionless in the windowless room, but it's long enough that my legs and shoulders cramp and my knees scream from the unyielding pressure.

The door behind me opens on squeaky hinges. I don't turn my head to look, not wanting to give them the satisfaction of my curiosity.

"Leave us."

Fuck. Me.

I would know his voice anywhere. I yank at the heavy chains and I don't have enough play in them to even stand. I'm on my knees like a recalcitrant slave and completely at his mercy. Considering he has none, I know right now, I am well and truly fucked.

"Mr. Byrne, so nice to see you again," Ryan Gregory states with a voice redolent of anything but pleasure. "May I call you Declan? After all, my future wife calls you by your given name. I feel I should be afforded the same courtesy, don't you?"

What do I win for guessing correctly, Alex?

Judging by the crazy game show thoughts going through my head, I've either had my brains scrambled from the beating or I've finally lost my mind. Either way, I'm not going to say a word until I figure out exactly what he knows. My jaw aches from the pressure of keeping my trap shut, the snarky comments and nasty quips that come so easily banging against the back of my teeth. It takes all my effort to not let them loose, the Herculean undertaking at least taking my mind off the stabbing pain in my knees and the itch of oozing blood as it trails down my bare back.

"So, you aren't going to speak to me?" He tsks at me like I've been a naughty schoolboy. "That's very rude of you. I thought maybe we could get to know each other a little better. After all, your mother and I were, how should I put it? *Very* well acquainted."

I know better than to take the bait. I clench my jaw so tightly my teeth vibrate. Ryan paces behind me, my unwillingness to engage pissing him off. He turns to face me but I still refuse to look at him. I don't need to see his face to picture his sanctimonious sneer just as I doubt he needs to look in my eyes to see my unchecked loathing.

As much as I hate to admit it, Ryan Gregory and I have one thing in common; we're both cold-blooded predators. I am well aware there is something seriously mentally wrong with both of us. I can't say what his damage is for sure, but I suspect he was born with a screw loose. To be the monster he is, he must have been born without a soul.

Not me. I had a soul once. I became the person I am because *he* made me this way.

I'll be the first to tell anyone that I'm not a good person. I've done things over the years that are wrong on so many levels that I can hardly stand to remember them. The memories of the brutal things I've done to survive make me hate myself whereas I firmly believe Ryan Gregory relives his with enjoyment.

Ryan stands directly in front of me, his dick just inches from my face. I can tell he's getting off trying to terrify me by the size of the growing bulge in his pants.

If he thinks I'll suck his cock to save my life, he has another thing coming. He puts that thing anywhere near me and I'll bite it clean the fuck off.

"You know, Declan, all these years I thought you were dead. After I heard about your *accident* in prison, I had just assumed you succumbed to your wounds. Imagine my surprise when I stepped out of the elevator today and came face to face with a ghost. It brought up such colorful memories of my youth, things I haven't thought about in decades. Now, I'm sure that's not the case for you. I don't doubt in the least you have thought about me every single day of your pathetic life."

Yeah, I have to give him that one. I've fantasized about killing him every day for the past sixteen years. I bite the side of my cheek until I taste blood, forcing myself to remain silent.

"I was quite disappointed you didn't stop to say hello. You were in such a hurry and you looked terribly guilty. That look piqued my interest, so I started to ask some questions, and well, I was able to get most of them answered. I do still have a few that I want to hear answered straight from your lips. Do you think you can help me with those?"

Not moving my head, I flick my eyes up at him and stare just long enough to tell him to go fuck himself before returning my gaze to the wall. I can almost hear his muscles stiffen in anger.

"What I want to know is what you thought gave you the right to touch my future wife?"

In the ensuing silence, the ticking of the clock sounds like a bomb clicking down to detonation.

"I asked the staff about you, had Emma's past medical records pulled, and found out that of all the people in this city, *you* had treated her after the unfortunate accident she had a few months ago. Of course, the name on the signed reports was Declan Brown, but I knew it had to be you. Let me tell you, Declan, how surprised I was to find out you have been a hospital employee for the past four years. How you managed to go from a maximum security prison to working in one of our finest hospitals is quite a mystery. Would you like to fill me in? Did our prison system rehabilitate you that well? Please, Declan, tell me. The curiosity is killing me."

His mocking voice drips with scorn. My mouth fills with blood as I continue to bite the inside of my cheek. The tension my jaw is putting on my teeth is enough to crack the molars into jagged shards.

Ryan's increased respiration tells me he is losing patience. "You know, if you cooperate with me and tell me what I want to know, I can make things easier for you. Now, I'm not the good Lord, I can't forgive your sins, but I have the power to end your suffering. I can make your death quick and painless or. . . . not. It's up to you."

I keep my eyes forward and my mouth shut. He's a liar and a murderer and I would sooner make a deal with the Devil before I would consider making one with Ryan Gregory.

"I forgot how brave you are," he mocks. "I hoped the beating you got at the wall would have knocked some sense into you, but apparently you haven't suffered enough. Maybe you are still that brave little boy trying to save his mommy except now you are trying to protect *my* future bride. Maybe I'm going about this the wrong way. Maybe I should have Emma brought here to trade places with you. I know how you love to save people, Declan. Tell me, would you sacrifice yourself for her? I can guarantee you, if she was in your shoes, she would have sung like a canary by now. She doesn't handle pain well at all."

My jaw starts to tic. He notices immediately that he's gotten under my skin and laughs.

"Oh, Declan, I hope you aren't a poker player. Those tells of yours give you away every time. I know that deep inside you want her. Tell me, Declan, all those times you two were alone in those little hospital rooms, why didn't you fuck her? Did you keep your filthy hands to yourself out of some misguided sense of nobility? Or are you just as much the weak little pussy you were all those years ago?"

Untie me and ask me that again, you fucking coward. Let's see how brave you are when it's a fair fight.

I never wanted to murder anyone so badly in my life. No longer willing to put up with my silence, Ryan grabs a handful of my hair and jerks my head back, leaving me no choice but to look up at him. He smiles.

"I have to give you credit, Declan. You may be too much of a pussy to fuck Emma, but it takes some brass balls to even think you can touch my property. Tell me, Declan, did you really think you were going to get away with this?"

He's baiting me with vague questions and I realize he doesn't know as much as he wants me to think he does. If he knew Emma had been in my bed he wouldn't be dicking around like this. I would already be dead and so would she. I know now for certain that Emma hadn't turned me in, that she had bravely kept our secret. I wonder what price she paid for her silence.

We glare at one another in silence for a few long moments before he screams, "You fucking spic, I asked you a goddamned question!"

I don't know what possesses me, but I spit in his face. I watch as the mixture of blood and bubbling saliva stains his crisp white dress shirt as it drips off his chin. I'm pretty pleased with myself for about four seconds until he throws me to the ground and kicks me in the ribs repeatedly with a ferocity only expected from the most dangerous felons.

On top of the beating I already received, it isn't long before he's able to extract a painful response from me. I'm breathless and gasping as he repeatedly kicks me with shoes that probably cost more than I made in the last five years. With my hands tied, I am helpless to protect myself as the blows continue, and by the time he's done, I'm close to blacking out.

As I lay there sputtering and retching, blood trickling from my mouth, Ryan drags me back to my knees by my hair. He leans in closely, almost intimately. "I could kill you right now, but I won't. The little time you have left, I want you to think about what I'm going to say. Do you understand me?"

I glare at him with loathing.

"Answer me!"

The punch to my face makes my eyes water and the room spin faster. I'm going to pass out if he keeps beating me, and the last thing I want is to be unconscious in his presence.

"Yeah, I hear you," I snarl.

He punches me again. "When you address your superiors, you answer, 'Yes, sir.' Do you understand me?" I say nothing. He hits me two more times before I finally spit out the loathsome words.

"I want you to spend every night of your remaining short, pathetic life knowing that Emma belongs to me. She is mine to do with as it pleases me and what pleases me the most is when I make her scream," he breathes. "I'll let you in on a little secret, just between me and you. Emma is one hell of a screamer. In fact, she screams and begs exactly the way I made your whore mother scream all those years ago." His words are slow and deliberate, a hateful sneer plastered on his face, his eyes glittering with superiority.

"*Spiritual law requires that nearly everything be cleansed with blood, and without the shedding of blood, there can be no forgiveness.* It's in *The New State Church Text.* Hebrews 9:22. As a founding member of the New State Church, I hold fast to my tenets of faith. For the sake of her spiritual redemption I will make Emma bleed to cleanse her of your filthy taint. The *Text* states the only way to remove tainted blood is to shed it. Lucky for me, I have just the knife for the job."

I have never been so horrified in my life. I had been helpless to save my mother all those years ago and now will be just as helpless to save Emma. My fear for her must show on my face, as Ryan begins to laugh. I'm close to begging him to please not hurt her, but I also know that if anything, that will only make things worse for her. My stomach sinks to my throbbing knees.

I must already be dead. This has to be hell as only the Devil himself can be this evil.

"So, Declan, these are the thoughts I want you to consider in your remaining hours. I want you to remember your time with Emma, with your precious family, and realize what a colossal failure you are. You weren't able to save any of them. You have failed every single person in your miserable life. When you are burning deep in the fiery pits of hell, I pray they torment you with visions of Emma here with me. Because of you, her torture will be just beginning."

I can no longer stay silent. When I speak, my hatred gives a cold, hard strength to my voice despite the fact I can barely breathe.

"There are six things that the Lord hates, seven that are an abomination to him: haughty eyes, a lying tongue, hands that shed innocent blood, a heart that devises wicked plans, feet that make haste to run to evil, a false witness that breathes out lies, and one that sows discord among brothers. Proverbs 6:17-19. Last I checked, *brother*, you've done them all. That's one hell of an achievement. Your parents must be so proud."

The burning rage in Ryan's eyes proves my snarky quip hit one hell of a nerve. Judging by the look he's giving me, if he had a knife, I'd be Swiss cheese right now. He's so flustered he has no idea what to say, so without a decent comeback, he resorts to violence. He throws me to the ground, my jaw cracking on the hard floor as another wave of shooting pain washes over me. He aims a few more brutal kicks to my ribs and abdomen before straightening his tie, smoothing his jacket and exiting the room.

As I lay on the floor gasping for air I'm surprised to still be alive. If they do let me out of here, if Ryan Gregory wants to torment me by keeping me alive a little longer, he's just made the biggest mistake of his life.

Because I will never stop coming for him until one of us is dead.

30

Emma

The next morning I wake feeling slightly better physically, but emotionally, I'm a disaster. I keep asking the staff when I can go home and no one gives me an answer; they all just nod and smile and say *not yet*. When I try to go for a walk around the floor the guard at my door won't let me out. A quick glance to the end of the hallway reveals two more heavily armed sentries flanking the elevator doors.

Ryan wasn't kidding. I'm on lock-down.

The TV in my room is on, set to the mandatory showing of the midday news. The past few days' broadcasts have been filled with footage of violence cropping up outside the city. Barbarous criminals and bloodthirsty illegals are again trying to break in through the wall, intent on thieving our hard-won earnings, raping the women, stealing the children and murdering the good citizens of our city while we sleep.

What is it going to take before these people finally stop trying to get into the city? Why do they hate us so much?

The news anchor assures his viewers that the checkpoint and watch officers are on top of the violence. Scenes of captured subversives being beaten within an inch of their lives fill the screen as he speaks.

God, these videos are hard to watch.

The Committee tells us that publicizing the punishment of subversive factions is an effective deterrent to future criminals. Ardent patriots should watch the footage with pride knowing that our government is working hard to keep us safe. Failure to watch the footage is considered unpatriotic and especially when out in public, we all watch as if our lives depend on it.

And depending on who's watching you, your survival just might.

A few minutes into the broadcast I feel sick from the unending screaming. I grab the remote and hit mute. It takes a few stabs at the button before I get it to work but not before I see and hear the horrifying footage of Declan being beaten. The flesh on his back is torn and blood courses from the wounds and pools at his belt. Every swing of the baton sends blood spraying in a pink mist across the officer's already splattered clothing. Declan's eyes are wild with pain and fear as he screams.

Oh, God, no. Please, no.

I quickly un-mute the broadcast just as the picture goes to a close up of Declan. The anchor states his previous convictions were for two counts of murder, assault of an officer, and other crimes against the state. The screen flashes to other news in the city, but I can't get the vision of Declan shackled and on his knees out of my head. The spray of blood as the metal protrusions on the end of the patrolman's baton tore free of his skin has me racing for the toilet. My stomach immediately expels what little I ate today, leaving me gasping and weak as I slump against the bowl.

I close my eyes and clearly picture Declan's heavily tattooed arms, the images and patterns oddly familiar but I can't place from where. The numbers branded deep on the inside of his left arm come as a shock. How had I not realized he was a marked man? Shouldn't I have sensed it, been afraid in his presence? What's wrong with me that even after seeing this, I'm still not afraid of him?

It all makes sense now. Why he didn't want to take me as a patient at the hospital. Why Dr. Andrews had to talk him into it. Why he stayed so distant, never once opening up to me about anything. He had been afraid I would turn him in.

My God, I spent the night with a murderer.

My heart is pounding. I can't stop thinking about the brand on his arm. I think about his hands, my mind remembering all the times they had been on my body. He healed me with his gentle touch, almost instinctively knowing how hard to press on a knotted muscle to make it release and how lightly to palpate a swollen cheekbone yet reliably check for fracture. How can he be both a vicious murderer and a thoughtful healer?

This doesn't make sense.

Declan risked his life helping me escape from the raid. He didn't try to rape me, beat me or force me to do anything. He had every opportunity to ruin me that night and he didn't. Sure, Declan is brooding and distant and has a fiery temper, but never once has he hurt me. If he's truly a dangerous person, why didn't he?

This doesn't make sense.

I wonder what happened in Declan's past that landed him in prison. Who did he kill? How did he spend time in prison and still get a job at the hospital? How did he qualify for ID to get through the crossings as well as a hospital ID that gave him access to the most restricted areas of the hospital?

No, there has to be a mistake. The man on TV being beaten bloody can't possibly be Declan. I must have gotten knocked in the head harder than I thought. I watch the rebroadcast a half hour later, getting out of bed and padding over to the TV to look more closely.

It's absolutely him.

With a critical eye, I realize the footage doesn't look like a riot, in fact, it looks like the usually backed-up checkpoint crossing next to the hospital. Why would an illegal try to scale a wall or start a riot next to a heavily guarded border crossing? It would be suicide.

Think Emma. All the pieces are there. Put them together with what you know in your heart.

The New State News is lying. And if they are lying about this one man, what else have they lied about?

I need to find someone who will tell me the truth. It has to be someone I trust and there's only one person I can think of who can give me what I need.

I just pray he's still alive.

31

Declan

I lie on the floor and continue to spit blood and bile until the guards come for me. They rummage through my pockets until they find my hospital ID. Needless to say, I no longer have a job after this, and without gainful employment, I'm no longer permitted to cross the checkpoint. I will never legally cross the border again.

I expect to be issued a white card, which restricts me to my side of the wall. I can live with that—plenty of people I know have them and do just fine. However they don't give me a white card. They give me a black one.

I swear under my breath as they hand me a death sentence neatly disguised as a form of identification. People with black cards don't live very long. I can no longer purchase or sell goods of any type, not even food. I'm no longer employable, not even on my side of the wall. Anyone caught aiding me risks being shot on sight.

They should just kill me now and put me out of my misery. The beatings have left me weak and in such pain I'm positive there's internal bleeding. I'm not even sure I'll be able to walk out of here. They sure as shit aren't going to offer to give me a lift home, not that I'd take them up on it if they did. The last thing I want them to know is where I live.

The guards enter in a tight group and peel me off the floor. They force me to sit in the chair and shackle my hands, palms down, to the table. The head patrolman comes in and reads my list of sins, issues the decree that says I'm thoroughly fucked and nods at the guard that grabs my damaged hand and yanks the cover from it.

When the next person that enters holds a glowing brand, I struggle against my bonds knowing what's about to happen. I feel my skin ripping under the tight manacles and I don't care—if I had enough time, I would chew my hands from my wrists if it would prevent being burned again. It takes three guards in even my weakened state before I'm held still enough for the guy to place the brand on the outside of my damaged left hand. I scream from the pain like only one other time in my life.

They unhook me from the table and toss a thick black strip of fabric at me and tell me to put it on. Being defaced with the mark of Cain is humiliating, but the fact they make you do it to yourself somehow makes it so much worse. I am seething as I clumsily tie it into place around my right forearm.

Fucking bastards.

When they finally let me go, I stagger through the checkpoint like a drunk at last call. I slowly careen back to my house and sit out on the balcony staring at the river in the distance. It's late, the hour when most people have already finished dinner and little kids are tucked safely into bed. There's no way I'm sleeping anytime soon, the shifting of broken ribs and my oozing tight and swollen back objecting to every breath I take. My roasted hand throbs like it's been slammed in a car door thirty times. My entire abdomen is turning black.

I wonder morbidly how long it takes to bleed out.

I pull the offending ID card from my pocket and stare at it. How can something so small, so insignificant, be the thing that will eventually kill me? I'm thankful that for once in my life I'm not hungry, the bone marrow dripping into my bloodstream making me too nauseated to even think about eating. I have next to no food in my house and very little cash, not that any amount of money can help me now. It's just a matter of time before I'm yet another nameless beggar on the street, another bloated, fly-infested corpse picked up among the rubble by state sanitation.

Despite knowing it's a mortal sin, I find myself thinking about pulling an Emma and taking a dive off the balcony. If death is life's way of saying you're fired and suicide the way of telling life you quit, I need to make my final decision soon before I get too weak to hand in my resignation.

32

Emma

I am released from the hospital the next day and sent home with pain medication I don't need and a live-in nurse I don't want. My rooms have been vacuumed and dusted and I'm certain thoroughly searched before my return. Nothing is missing, but maybe they don't want me to *think* they searched it. I wonder again if there are cameras in my room.

They've placed thick iron bars over the windows as well as across the doors of my balcony. I'm on the ninth floor, so I think it's some serious security overkill until I realize all my sharp knives are missing, too. I'm amazed they let me keep my sheets and shoelaces until I realize there's nowhere to hang myself from; even my shower curtain rod's been replaced with a pane of clear plastic bolted in place.

After a few days of good behavior the all-seeing "nurse" vacates, much to my relief. Despite still being a bashed-up mess, I grab a jacket and decide to go for a walk. The guards in the lobby look at me like I'm insane when I inform them I'm going out. They tell me that they are under strict orders that I am not to leave the building for any reason unless approved by both my father and Ryan.

My phone blessedly never rings, but eventually I get so bored I call Caitlin just to hear another voice. The call goes to voicemail and she doesn't bother to return my message.

I spend a lot of time thinking about Declan and wondering if he's still alive. Bits and pieces of overheard conversations from the studio float through my head, especially one particular dialogue discussing Declan's mysterious background. Of all the therapists, he was the only one without diplomas on his walls and he never discussed his past, even when specifically asked. Anna had broken up that discussion quickly, snidely remarking that if the two gossiping girls worked their triple pirouettes as much as they ran their mouths they wouldn't still be members of the corps.

Good God, do I miss her.

A few days later we are called back to the studio and, for the first time in my life, I don't want to go. If they think that new hardwood flooring and fresh paint will scrub the memories of what happened from our minds they are sorely mistaken. The room's pristine newness is just as awful as if they never cleaned the blood-soaked floorboards and splattered walls and told us to just dance over it.

The morning of our first company class, those of us that remain slip silently into the room. No one talks. The replacement company members look at us cheerily but we refuse to acknowledge them. The few that try to be friendly we growl at like wild animals and they scurry off with their tails between their legs. They may be fellow dancers, but we aren't dumb enough to trust them. We know they are here to spy.

We have an entirely new staff that's bright and excessively chipper and *so excited* about the all-new State Sanctioned Christmas Ballet that it roils my stomach. Among the new staff is Patrick, our assigned physical therapist. His cheerful smile and sunny disposition make me hate him immediately. He's a watcher if I ever saw one. He doesn't even try to hide it.

Our new class dance mistress, Olivia, takes us through a painfully silent barre. I'm still off-and-on dizzy and nauseated from the concussion, my bruises dark and angry and painfully obvious. I go through the motions, too weak to really care how I perform in front of all the new eyes that watch me with interest. Luckily my legs were left unscathed during Ryan's beatings, so even though my ribs and head are throbbing, years of repetitive muscle memory carry me through class. I would give anything to once again hear Jeremy's witty corrections and Anna's biting insults. I leave the studio even more depressed than before.

Michael is gone and no one knows where. The last time he was seen was being dragged into the interrogation center with the rest of us. One of the other male principals said his rooms in the dorms were cleared out without explanation the afternoon after the raid. We all believe he's dead but none of us can utter the words.

My new partner is the exact opposite of Michael. He's young and inexperienced and completely void of partnering skills as evidenced when he drops me while practicing one of our more basic lifts. I am so frustrated and pissed off I lunge for him, screaming and shoving him to the floor. The boy nearly pees himself while I scream at Olivia to find me someone capable by tomorrow or I quit. Judging by the shocked look on my fellow company members' faces, my elevation to company diva is now official.

I realize my bounce off the floor actually gives me the perfect excuse to get a pass to Sports Medicine and go look for some answers. I'd been forming a plan for quite some time to find out if Declan is still alive and the first place to start is his office.

I go to the department flanked by my own personal bodyguard I've nicknamed Shadowman and show my pass to the receptionist. She looks me up on the computer, blanches slightly, and then tells me I will be seeing Patrick.

"Oh, is Declan off?" I ask lightly.

"He doesn't work here anymore." She says this as if she's reading the words off of a card while staring intently at me. Her eyes flick to the armed guard and back to my face, silently begging me to drop the subject. She looks terrified. I go through with the appointment, wondering the entire time if *he doesn't work here anymore* really means *he's dead*.

By the time my unnecessary appointment is over, it's nearly dark outside. I'm positively itchy to find the answers to my many questions, and there's only one way I know how. I stop back at the dorms just long enough to leave my shadow in the lobby, grab a flashlight from my room and head for the stairs. Although I'm scared out of my mind, my need for answers surpasses my fear.

I work my way gingerly down the ladder and stop to gather my courage for the trek ahead. I remember most of the way through the tunnels with only a few mistakes, eventually popping up at the former metro entrance nearest Declan's apartment.

Finding his building is a lot harder than managing the tunnels as all the buildings look alike, but I eventually find the same crumbling building with the sketchy emergency staircase that looks even more dangerous in full sobriety. I fumble my way through pitch black rooms until I find the hallway with the chained door and padlocked entry. The lock is on the outside, so he must be out. At least I hope that's what it means. It's chilly and damp in the hallway and I sit down on the concrete and pull my hood over my hair. I look at my watch and decide that if he's not back by midnight, I'll leave.

I must have fallen asleep because I awake with a start, the cold blade of a knife at my throat.

"Who are you and what the fuck do you want?"

It's him. I put my hands up slowly. "Declan, it's me, Emma. Put the knife down."

It takes him a second to register this news before he yanks back my hood and stares at me. His eyes have an eerie flatness to them, like my words haven't registered. He continues to hold the knife firmly to my jugular.

"What the fuck are you doing here?" he growls as he finally removes the blade from my throat. "You need to leave. Now."

"I want to talk to you, please."

"No. Go home."

"I'm not a dog for you to command. I'm not going anywhere until you talk to me."

He sighs in frustration, knowing me well enough to understand I'll stay here until he agrees. He opens the door and motions for me to go in. He doesn't reset the chain once we're both inside, no doubt not expecting me to stay long.

He lights two small candles as I make myself at home on his sofa. He sits as far from me as possible on one of the metal kitchen chairs. The deep purple and blue-black bruises coloring his wan face are not lessened by either the distance or the dark. A large section of his jaw is black and terribly swollen.

"You said you came here to talk. Now talk." Even in the dim light he looks different. Paler. Thin to the point of being gaunt. His stomach growls audibly. He even looks hungry.

"Are you okay?"

He laughs bitterly. "Do I look okay?"

"No, you don't, Declan. You look like death. I know what happened at the wall and I know you no longer work at the hospital. I was afraid you were dead."

"Well, the reports of my demise have been greatly exaggerated, sweetheart, although it's pretty fucking imminent," he adds nastily as he points to the black band circling his arm.

Dear God, please tell me that's not what I think that is.

"So now that you know I'm alive, it's time for you to go. Please excuse me if I don't walk you home, I feel like shit."

He removes his jacket and lets it fall to the floor. He starts to shiver involuntarily and tries to hide it by running his hands through his hair. He winces as he closes his eyes momentarily and holds his breath, trying to hide his terrible pain.

"Declan, talk to me. What happened?"

He takes a small breath before exhaling a short ragged burst, the pain wracking his body making him gasp before breaking into a thick, mucousy cough. I kneel by his knee and place my hand on his thigh. He looks down at me sadly, placing his hand over mine, patting it gently. My eyes go wide when I see the large, weeping, red X burned into the back of his hand before he pulls it away.

"Please, just go," he whispers.

Now that I'm here, I can't leave. He looks so, so sick. What frightens me even more than the barking cough and the terrible bruising is that lifeless look in his eyes. Even though he's in severe physical pain, it's his look of bitter defeat that terrifies me. Of all of the brutal injuries, it's the emotional wounds he suffers from that I fear the most. It's not only the present he's suffering from, but a resurgence of whatever happened in his past that tortures him now.

And I'm afraid I'm too late to save him from himself.

33

Declan

I don't have the fucking energy for this.

I stand and limp my way over to the bathroom, closing the door on Emma's horrified face. I lean my forehead against the bathroom door, my legs trembling and threatening to buckle. I haven't eaten in days and my head and stomach are killing me. Now, Emma wants to play twenty questions and all I want at this moment is to fall asleep and never wake up.

That look in Emma's eyes is going to haunt me. She's worried about me. When you worry about someone it means you care, and the last thing Emma needs is to catch feelings for me. Even if I wasn't black carded, I'm hardly boyfriend material. I have to make her understand that caring for me is a mistake, and if she thinks she feels something for me she has to stop. Somehow, I have to make her believe I never want to see her again, when all I want at this moment is to hold her in my arms and have her lie to me that we're both going to be okay.

I splash cold water on my face and grimace when I look into the mirror. Even in the dark, I look like shit. The fatigue, weakness, brutal cough and chills are getting worse. I should be in a hospital, but that's not an option. My only choices right now are to either let

Mother Nature take her time killing me or help her along with a self-administered lead supplement to the brain.

I hear Emma moving around in the other room. What the hell is she doing out there? Before she finds something that will prompt more questions I exit the bathroom. The sad, sympathetic look on her face as she holds my Glock in one hand and my black card in the other means that ship has sailed.

"Declan, no. . . ."

I snatch the loaded weapon out of her hand. "Just go. Now."

I want to order her out but instead the words come out like I'm begging. My God, the way she's looking at me makes *me* want to cry and I can't cry in front of her. I just can't. I've been brought so low already that tears would be the equivalent of handing over my balls in a gift-wrapped box with a giant floofy bow. I turn my back on her and hope she gets the hint.

When she wraps her arms around my waist and gently presses herself against my back, I cry out in pain and rip myself from her grasp. The pressure of her body against the infected skin creates a burning, stabbing wave of agony; my unstable rib cage causing me to gasp and cough spasmodically. She takes my uninjured hand in hers, her grip surprisingly strong, as she steadies me when I start to sway. Even when I try to yank it away from her, she doesn't let go. Now facing me, she pulls me into a gentle hug, careful to keep her hands off my back. I finally give up and let myself relax into her arms, closing my eyes as I emit a ragged exhale.

I know that when I'm dead, Emma will be haunted by this moment. After you lose someone you always remember the last time you touched them, spoke to them, were near them. She's going to spend the rest of her life wondering what she could have done differently to prevent my inevitable outcome. The truth is there's nothing, but she's going to beat herself up over this, just like I did when my parents died. And as miserable as I feel, the urge to comfort her is overwhelming. I want so badly to kiss her but I know I can't. It would be wrong. It would be too fucking sad.

I want her to stay here with me so badly it makes my chest hurt. I take one of her tiny hands in mine and press her knuckles to my lips before placing her palm over my heart. I want her to know that I am grateful she's here, that I am thankful we met. I can't say these words so I hope she understands my gesture. As we stand there a single tear escapes my watery eyes and splashes onto the back of her hand.

I place my burned hand on the back of her neck and lean forward, the scent of her shampoo, of ripe summer strawberries, filling my nose. It's during this tender moment my stomach decides to tell the world it's hungry with a noisy growl.

Emma pulls away from me suddenly. "Wait! I have an energy bar in my jacket—My God, you must be starving."

She slaps her hand over her mouth, horrified at her seriously poor choice of words. I stare at her for a long second before bursting into laughter. I laugh so hard tears run down my cheeks and the blinding, stabbing pain of my ragged breaths quickly turn my moment of mirth into the hacking cough of developing pneumonia. She walks towards me, concern etched on her face, but I put my hand out to stop her, shaking my head to reassure her I'm okay.

I take my first bite of food in days and although it sits like a ball of lead in my stomach, I close my eyes in rapturous relief. My despair lifts and I smile at her. Despite everything, Emma is here. She came back for me and maybe, just maybe, there's a slim chance we may still make it out of here together.

I'm feverish and possibly delusional, but right now I am experiencing the most dangerous of emotions. Hope. I haven't felt hopeful in a very long time and I pray silently that this time it is not misplaced.

34

Emma

Declan continues to shiver despite it being quite temperate in the city for this time of year. After he finishes the tiny grain and nut bar, he wraps himself up in a few blankets and carefully lowers himself to the mattress before motioning for me to join him. He looks exhausted.

"Lie down, I'm worried you're going to fall over."

He doesn't argue with me, kicking off his boots and slowly sliding under the large pile of blankets. He's keeping his weight off his back so he's curled up on his side facing me. He's so pale and tired and all I want to do is cuddle up to him and comfort him as he sleeps in my arms, but I don't.

"So, aside from bringing you food tomorrow, what else do you need?"

"Emma, no, you can't get involved. I'll be alright, really."

"Really? You're going to be okay?" My voice is uncharacteristically sarcastic. "You are really hurt and sick and starving to death, Declan. Don't treat me like I'm stupid."

"Sorry," he mumbles. "You have enough problems, you don't need to add mine to yours."

"Shouldn't I be the one to decide that?" I add more gently. He peeks up at me with eyes so sad and lost he looks like an abandoned puppy that's been dropped miles from home with no idea how to return.

I kick off my shoes and slide under the covers, my face inches from his. I take his uninjured hand in mine and squeeze gently. His calloused thumb lightly caresses my knuckles as we stare into each other's eyes. I want him to kiss me so badly I ache, but I am too afraid to initiate anything more intimate than holding his hand. What if he doesn't feel the same way? I would feel so foolish if he turns me away.

"So, aside from food, what else do you need? You could use more candles. What else? Without being able to work, you are going to be pretty bored. Do you like to read? Can I bring you some books?"

He starts to object, but I gently place the index finger of my unoccupied hand on his lips, silencing him. He looks at me sleepily, understanding that I will not take no for an answer.

"I love to read, but none of that State propaganda bullshit. I can't take that right now."

"I've got some good stuff." I smile, thinking about my illegal collection.

Although I'm far from being a doctor, I know something is really wrong with Declan. He needs medical help, but with a black card, he would be turned away at the hospital, if not worse. I ask him if John knows what happened.

"I assume if you found out he knows, too," he adds wearily. "But he can't get involved. It's too dangerous. He has a wife. He runs the clinic here. And if he gets killed trying to save my sorry ass, I will never forgive myself. Plus, he has no idea where I live. You're the only person that knows about this place."

"I'm honored." I smile, squeezing his good hand and he smiles back. He closes his eyes, giving in to his exhaustion. "It's getting late. I really should go." I lean in and kiss him tenderly on the forehead. His eyelids flutter and the corner of his mouth turns up in a small smile.

"I'll be back tomorrow," I whisper gently as I reclaim my hand from his. Before I even have my coat on he's fast asleep.

35

Emma

I spend most of the night thinking. There has to be a way to keep him alive until I figure a way to get him out of the country. Only then will he be safe. By the time the sun rises, I have my plans in place. In the morning, I make a quick call from a pay phone in the National's lobby to the hospital ER. I catch a lucky break and find John will be on duty today.

I arrive early for class with the intention of prepping a new pair of toe shoes before we begin. A few of the new dancers are already here, stretching, talking and laughing together. I ignore them as I take a seat in the corner of the room and start ripping the shoes apart. I pull a small shiny knife out of my bag that missed the suicide sweep and begin to slit the stitching. I need to "slip" and cut myself to make my plan work. I pause for a second before sneaking a quick look to the side, and seeing no one near, I jam the blade into the fleshy part of my hand near my thumb. I yowl like a cat with its tail slammed in the door as I jerk the knife out of my palm and try to staunch the surge of blood with the edge of my sweatshirt.

Jesus Christ, that really hurt.

The wound bleeds steadily, but it's nothing a few stitches won't fix. I now have an excellent excuse to go to the ER and find John. I grab my bag, leaving the shoes forgotten on the floor as I quickly exit the building through an emergency exit with a broken alarm. Anna showed me this a while ago when she used to sneak out for an occasional cigarette. Once again, I'm thankful for Anna's vices and my excellent memory.

I get to the ER and sign in specifically requesting Dr. Andrews. No one is going to deny my choice of doctor just like I know they won't make me wait. It's not going to take long for my shadow to figure out I'm missing so I need to act fast. When John walks in and sees me sitting on the exam table with a towel wrapped around my hand, he looks at me first with surprise and then knowingly. He takes my injured hand gently in his and turns it over to examine the wound.

"You did a really good job on this. How'd it happen?"

"I was prepping a pair of toe shoes for class, and the knife I was using slipped." I look him straight in the eye with my voice unusually deadpan.

He nods, understanding perfectly.

"Let's go to the suture room and I will fix this up for you. Please, follow me."

"This isn't a slip of a knife, is it?" he accuses after the thick door shuts behind us.

"Declan needs your help," I whisper. "He's really sick and I don't know what to do."

"Where did you find him? Where is he? I've been searching for him for days." He seems both relieved and panicked at the same time.

"He is living in an abandoned apartment building near the river. He's been beaten half to death, black-carded, and he's starving. I can get him some food but I don't know what to do to make him feel better—"

John cuts me off mid-sentence. "You will do no such thing, do you hear me?" He has both of his hands on my shoulders as he looks me straight in the eyes. "Give me directions and I will take supplies to him."

"No." The force behind my single syllable surprises us both.

"You can't get—"

"What John? I can't get involved? News flash. I'm already involved. He saved my life a few weeks ago and now I need to help him."

"What? You feel some sense of duty to help him? You are going to get him *killed*, Emma, and more than likely yourself, too. Aiding a black-carded individual is a capital offense. You aren't skilled at sneaking around and it's only a matter of time before you get caught." He grabs my hand and starts to clean the blood from it.

"Screw you," I snap. "You can't tell me what to do. Last I checked, I know where he lives and you don't. He said he never told you where he was holed up because he didn't want to put you and your family at risk. He said you were too important to too many people to chance you getting hurt. He's willing to die to protect you."

I start to cry, but I keep spitting out my venomous words. "I'm not important to anyone. I would rather die helping him live for another week than live fifty years with the life that's planned for me. If you ever cared for anyone in your life, you should understand why I have to help him."

John continues to stare at me, his face unreadable.

"It was a mistake for me to come here," I mutter as I try to leave the room. He puts his hand on the door and blocks my exit.

"Sit down and let me suture that wound," he commands.

I glare at him as I debate what to do. Judging by his stern look, I realize I'm not leaving without him fixing my hand. I hop up on the exam table with an exasperated huff and glare at him. He takes my hand in his. "Why did you come here, Emma? What do you want from me?"

"I need medicine for him and you are the only person I know that can help."

"Does Declan know you're here? Did he ask you to do this?"

The ensuing silence between us is deafening. If I answer no, John is going to tell me that Declan would want me to stay out of things but his next question rattles me far more. "Do you love him, Emma?"

No. Yes. Maybe? Yes, I think so. Yes.

I look up at him with pleading eyes. He shakes his head like he's incredibly disappointed in me and closes his eyes. He takes a deep breath and lets it go slowly, opening eyes that now look exhausted and resigned. He smiles sadly. "I know the look of young love when I see it. I may be an old man now, but not old enough to have forgotten."

He works in silence for a while, taking a syringe and stabbing it into the flesh of my hand. Once my hand is numb, he sets to work sewing a seam of tiny, perfect sutures. "I can't tell you what to do and I certainly can't tell Declan what to do. He is the most stubborn man I have ever met. I'm sure you know that by now. I just want you to be careful. Both of you."

Our eyes meet over the neatly repaired flesh. "You did the right thing coming here and confiding in me. I will keep your secret, although I really wish you hadn't stabbed yourself to get here. Maybe next time fake bad menstrual cramps?"

He's trying to lighten the mood as he pulls out some bandage materials from a drawer and begins wrapping my hand. He's deep in thought for a few minutes, choosing his next words with care.

"Declan has done so much for our community over the years and there are few families he hasn't helped, often at great risk to himself. We aren't the type of people who forget our friends when they are in need. He knows that, but being the stubborn ox he is, he won't ask for help. I'm surprised he agreed to let you help."

"I didn't give him a choice." I grin.

John smiles back. "Please, Emma, tell me where he is. I need to examine him to know what he needs."

I nod and he sighs in relief. He jots a few quick notes as I give him my feeble attempts at directions. When he's finished he holds my bandaged hand gently between his.

"I will care for him, I swear this on my life, Emma. I would give my life for him. I have known him since he was a boy and I love him like a son. Protect yourself. Walk away from him, Emma. We both know this will only end badly."

I place my uninjured hand over his. "I want to help," I whisper. "I need to help."

He nods sadly as he lets go of my hand and pulls me into his arms for a fatherly hug. I can't remember the last time my father hugged me that was not part of a photo op and even then it was cold and emotionless. I could stay in John's arms for days, his warm and genuinely caring nature comforting. I realize sadly that if this is what it feels like to have a parent, then I've been an orphan my entire miserable life.

36

BY THE TIME I leave the hospital with a brown paper bag full of stolen supplies I'm shocked my shadow still hasn't found me. Not wanting to tempt fate, I sprint to the commerce section of town and start buying supplies. I'm hardly recognizable, wearing a dark hoodie and sunglasses and my hair pulled back tightly, but I still worry that, at any moment, I will be noticed and detained.

I pay by cash for the four small bags of groceries and supplies that take up more than half of my savings. Even with my generous allowance from my father and the small salary I receive from the company, I barely have enough to cover my purchases. I pack everything carefully in my bag with the medical supplies and head back to my apartment.

When I return to the dorm, I make sure to use the front entrance. Shadowman furiously demands to know where I've been and I flash my bandaged hand. I tell him there has been a long wait at the ER and now I'm tired and need rest. I must be getting better at the whole lying thing because he seems to believe me.

Sucker.

I head up to my rooms and pick out a few precious books to bring with me. The minutes pass painfully slow, each tick of the clock feeling like ten instead of one. When I finally get to Declan's I am incredibly proud of myself for getting there undetected with all my stuff. It takes three trips to get everything up the stairs and I knock gently at the door. "Declan, it's me. Open up."

I barely hear him answer that it's open. The room is pitch black with just a faint bit of moonlight entering through the balcony doors.

"Were you asleep? I'm sorry I woke you, but I come bearing gifts." I keep my voice cheerful, almost chirpy, as I unload everything onto the kitchen table.

I light a few new candles before pulling out a box of broth and some thin noodles. I start to make some soup, something light that will sit well on a stomach left empty for far too long. I read the directions printed on the side of the propane stove, but I still can't figure out how to light it. I hate to bother Declan who hasn't moved yet from where he's been resting. I want so badly to appear capable, but I'm at a complete loss on how to work this stupid stove. Declan's world is so foreign that I'm helpless to even make him a simple bowl of soup. I sigh in frustration as tears fill my eyes.

Don't cry, don't cry, don't cry repeats through my brain. I close my eyes for a minute to gain my composure, and scold myself for crying over something so stupid as not knowing how to turn on a stove. When I open them, Declan's standing next to me.

He looks like hell. He sways slightly, his hands shaking. I steal a quick glance at him as he coughs viciously into a towel spotted with blood. His skin has a sickly gray-blue cast and when he's overtaken by coughing, it turns a frightening shade of white. Dark circles under his eyes make them look like they've sunken into his skull, and his cheekbones are even more prominent than usual. His condition is deteriorating rapidly and I pray that my aid isn't coming too late.

I force him to sit down at the table while I pull out the rest of my purchases. I know he's prideful, so I try to make the piles look as small as possible and put things away quickly whenever I can. An oversized heavy sweatshirt of mine that I like to wear warming up in class rounds out the last of what I've brought.

He's shivering so hard his teeth chatter even though it really isn't that cold in the room. I place the back of my hand on his damp forehead and am shocked by the heat radiating from him. I ask if he wants to put on the sweatshirt but he shakes his head, instead opting to drape it over his shoulders. He winces from the light touch of the fleece on his back.

His hands shake so badly after the last bout of hacking I have to feed him. He's so weak he doesn't even try to resist, but dutifully opens his mouth so I can spoon the broth into him. After only a few bites he stops—he's too dizzy and nauseated to continue. The force of the coughing has tired him to the point I'm concerned he might pass out. I guide him back to bed and recover him gently with a few thick blankets, tucking them snugly yet gently around him. His entire body shakes with a deep rattling cough that I know from the sound alone is dangerous.

I rearrange him on the pillows to help him find a more comfortable position, but he decides after a few attempts to stay curled over on his right side. His forehead is beaded with sweat just from the simple effort of trying to get comfortable. I know he's been through a lot, but something just feels particularly wrong. He's feverish, but the deathly pallor of his skin and the hacking, rattling cough frighten me more. As much as I want to be alone with Declan, I need John to hurry up and get here. He'll know what to do.

"I brought some books," I say quietly, still trying to pretend that everything is completely normal. "Would you like me to read to you?"

He nods, too weak now to even speak. I grab a book from the small pile I unloaded on the kitchen table and snuggle under the covers next to him. I maneuver myself so that I can sit up and have Declan curled next to me, his head resting on my thigh. My unoccupied hand begins to gently stroke his dark, wild curls while I read. It's not until he lets out a contented sigh and closes his eyes that I even notice what I'm doing.

"If you really want to hear about it, the first thing you'll probably want to know is where I was born, and what my lousy childhood was like, and how my parents were occupied and all before they had me, and all that David Copperfield kind of crap, but I don't feel like going into it, if you want to know the truth."

Declan shocks me by quietly reciting the last few words with me from memory. I stop reading in surprise and stroke his pale cheek with my thumb. "You've read Salinger?"

He looks up at me like I'm daft. "I may be a criminal, but I'm a literate one." He smiles before he begins to cough again, the same look of intense pain again contorting his features. "This book is one of my favorites. Please, keep reading," he encourages between coughs.

I read for a long time, all the while soothing him with gentle caresses. He closes his eyes and snuggles against me, resting his palm against the inside of my knee. A few times I think he drifts off, and I stop reading only to have him stroke the inside of my thigh with his long fingers, his silent way of asking me to continue.

I'm not sure how long John stands there watching us, but when he clears his throat, Declan and I both damn near jump out of our skin. I feel like I've been caught in the middle of committing a terrible crime, which in reality, I guess I am. After all, I've aided a black-carded former criminal, stolen supplies from a hospital, am unmarried, unchaperoned and in bed with a man that's not my husband and I'm reading aloud to a convicted murderer from a subversive text.

And those are just the laws I broke today.

"Jesus, John, you damn near scared the piss out of me," Declan rasps. "Can't you knock like a normal person?"

I close the book and stand to greet John at the door. I keep my voice low so Declan can't hear my words. "I'm glad you are here. He's a lot worse since yesterday."

"I heard that," Declan growls weakly from across the room. "I've had the shit kicked out of me, I'm not deaf."

John frowns as he kneels down next to the mattress and places a gentle hand on Declan's forehead. "Son, you don't look so good."

He pulls out a small flashlight and checks Declan's pupils before pulling a stethoscope from his jacket pocket. John pulls at Declan's shirt but it sticks to his back, the small section he manages to lift exposing the torn skin and sickening deep navy and black bruising surrounding his torso. Declan lets out a yelp that makes both John and me jump.

I've already brought the bag of medical supplies to John's side and he starts pulling fluid out of various vials with a few large syringes. He sends me for a large bowl of water and a few clean washcloths and a towel.

"I'm bleeding internally, aren't I, Doc?"

I spin around and look between the two men in alarm. I know Declan is very, very sick, but this sounds really serious.

"Yeah, Declan, I think you were, but I believe it clotted on its own. If it was really serious, well, we would have known by now." He gently pats Declan's arm, but his expression is grim. "But you've developed a hell of a case of pneumonia. I'm glad I brought IV antibiotics because you are going to need them. I'll come back tomorrow and bring a few more bags of ringers from the clinic to help bolster you from the blood loss. I hope you aren't too attached to that shirt because I need to cut it off of you before I can address the infected wounds on your back. If you're squeamish, Emma, this may be the time for you to leave."

I stare at him with haughty disapproval. "I'm a ballet dancer. My feet bleed almost every day and I've helped my fellow company members deal with some of the nastiest toenail infections ever. Trust me, whatever is under that shirt isn't going to bother me."

"Okay, tough girl, but if you hurl, you're cleaning it up," John jokes.

John sets me to work blotting the shirt with water in an attempt to loosen the fabric glued to Declan's back. The dried blood and pus creates a horrific odor once it gets wet and I have to breathe through my mouth to keep from retching.

While I work, John pulls a few blood tubes and a fresh syringe from his pocket and motions for Declan to pull up his sleeve. The branded numbers are much harsher in person, whoever held the iron to him left it on long enough to create indents into his skin. I wince just looking at it, but I refuse to look away. When I look up, Declan is watching me, an odd look on his face as he witnesses my reaction. He says nothing.

After I loosen the shirt from his skin, John takes the bandage scissors and cuts away everything but the pieces that remain stuck. The devastation to the flesh makes me gag but I refuse to throw up. There's no surgery in the world capable of repairing this without significant scarring.

John curses under his breath before taking another vial of drugs from his pocket and pulling up a generous dose of morphine. "I've got to knock you out for this part, buddy. This is not going to be pleasant. Emma, at this point I have to ask you to leave. This I can guarantee is not something you want to see and it's already nearly 2 am. If you leave now, you can get home during the patrol shift change. It's the safest time for you to be out."

As much as I don't want to go, I know John's right. When I reach the door, I turn to take one final look at Declan. He looks so frail, the drugs kicking in and his eyes fluttering closed. I don't want to leave. I want to stay by his side, hold his hand and continue to soothe him with quiet words and gentle touches. But I know John's right, too. I spare him one last look before I close his door, etching his sleepy face in my memory.

I'm grumpy as I stumble my way home, debating turning back and demanding John let me stay. Then I realize that tomorrow is another day, tomorrow night another night. And as long as I remain vigilant and am super careful, there's no reason why I cannot return tomorrow.

37

Declan

I spend most of the next two weeks working to kick the virulent infection, spending most of my long, boring days asleep. My limbs are weak and heavy, and my joints are agony to move. When my back finally starts to heal, it itches so badly I'm close to going nuts from resisting the urge to scratch. The only thing keeping me going are my visits from Emma and John. As much as I am forever in John's debt, I have to admit, I enjoy the time I spend with Emma more.

In the beginning, I don't have the strength to converse so we spend the evenings with her reading to me as she gently plays with my hair. It reminds me of when I was little and my mom would read bedtime stories to me in her low, soothing voice, lulling me to sleep. As I start to feel better, I realize the way Emma reads to me is nothing like how my mother had. The way Emma reads the forbidden classics in her deep, soft voice, as she gently caresses me is starting to excite me in ways the authors, I'm sure, never intended. When my dick starts perking up the second Emma enters the apartment each night, I know I'm going to survive.

Emma never comes empty handed and as my health improves, she brings me things I never dreamed I would have again. I nearly cry when she arrives with fried chicken and mashed potatoes one night.

What can I say? I'm a cheap date.

We often talk well into the night and after a while, I worry our late night chats are exhausting her. After all, I can sleep during the day while she endures a full schedule of rehearsals. Some nights, when she looks especially wiped, she lets me take over reading aloud.

On these evenings, often within minutes, she falls asleep in my arms, looking like an angel that's fallen to Earth. These are the nights I quietly close the book and I spend the hours silently memorizing every detail of her face as she sleeps. I count the tiny freckles on her nose and trace the pale pink scar on her cheek with my fingertips. Her lips are full and look so soft, her lower lip jutting out in an adorable pout. I can't help but wonder what they taste like, and if they are as sweet and addictive as I imagine.

We develop an easy friendship in those weeks. I'm not happy unless I've got my hands on her, and I get the impression she feels the same. We find excuses to touch each other, even if it's gently in passing in the cramped confines of my apartment or snuggling as we read. Neither of us make a move to do anything more even though there've been more than enough opportunities. But any time I think to pull her to me and kiss her, I find myself frozen, unable to do the things with her that I'm able to do in my dreams.

My God, those dreams are enough to make me want to stay asleep forever.

The nights she doesn't come to me are maddening. I wonder where she is, if she's with Ryan, and worry nonstop about what he's doing to her. I live in constant fear that each night she's absent he's beating her within an inch of her life. These are the nights I can't get his sneering voice out of my head and when I do sleep, the violent nightmares of my youth return.

I never tell Emma about Ryan's hand in the beating. I'm going to carry that secret to my grave. There's no reason to burden her with that information and she sure as shit doesn't need any more reasons to hate him. I worry if she knows she might somehow slip and say something to Ryan that would give away our visits and get her killed. I wouldn't be able to live with myself if that were to happen.

Sometimes Emma returns the night after an absence with excuses of late running rehearsals, but usually the only thing that keeps her from me are her required performances with her asshole intended. I'm normally not a jealous man, but knowing she's out there with him makes me physically sick. The blend of worry and fear, of rage and disgust, and a jealousy that's slowly consuming me whole leaves me sleepless and jittery. I find myself counting the minutes until she can come to me again.

Sometimes she returns unscathed, but more times than not, there's some telltale cut or bruise or a gingerness to her movement that gives away her painful secrets. She always blows off my concern, being brave for me so I don't go off half-cocked and get myself killed trying to murder him. I hate that she does that for me, and hate myself even more for not being able to keep a leash on my emotions.

I want Emma with me day and night and I'm not happy unless I'm holding her. The sexual desire I have for her is growing daily, and if I don't do something soon, I'm going to blow a nut. My feelings for this woman are growing exponentially with every minute I spend with her. There's a weird tightness in my chest when I think about her that's not caused by pneumonia, but by something more virulent and more than likely fatal when I can no longer receive the nightly doses of my cure.

For we are Romeo and Juliet, Vronsky and Anna, Heathcliff and Catherine. We're destined to be the doomed lovers of a piece of literature yet to be written, the sort of tale where the reader knows from word one this story won't end with happily ever after. I look into Emma's sapphire eyes every time I want to kiss her and remember I'm with someone else's pledged bride, that she's got a wedding coming up, and I'm not the groom. Starting something with Emma now will only end in heartbreak and I don't know if what's left beating in my chest can handle losing another person that means the world to me.

By early November, I've finally gotten some of my strength back. I'm going crazy trapped within the walls of my confines, so I start taking long, slow walks after dark when I'm least likely to run into a patrol. I always make sure I'm back by 8 or 9 pm to make sure I don't miss any of my time with Emma. Taking John's advice, she usually leaves around two when the patrols are changing shifts and it's less likely for her to be intercepted.

Tonight's a rare night as Ryan's out of town for the weekend, so Emma isn't worried about missing an early morning summon. As we lounge together, our bodies wrapped around each other reading, we hear a loud rapping at the door. It's John. He's holding a large paper bag in his hand and he strides into the room wearing a long dark cloak and a white plastic skull mask over his face. I start to laugh. "Get up, you two. We're going out."

Emma looks at him like he's lost his last remaining marble, but I understand simply by looking at the crazy getup John's wearing. I must have lost track of the days since I began my self-induced sequestration. It's the weekend of the Remembrance Festival.

From inside the bag, John hands Emma two identical black cloaks, a wildly-colored long, full skirt and a frilly white blouse. There are two masks, one for each of us.

"Come on, hurry up and get changed! Marta's waiting for us at the square." John pushes Emma towards the bathroom while I change into black jeans and the thick, warm black sweater Emma just bought me along with my usual heavy black boots.

Not long after I don my heavy cape, Emma emerges from the bathroom looking positively stunning. The long skirt hangs seductively off her tiny hip bones, and the thick vibrantly-hued folds gently swish around her dainty ankles. She still has on her long sleeved black leotard from class earlier in the day and her fitted bolero-style sweater instead of the thin frilly top. The look suits her. I'm glad she's dressed sensibly, it's going to be chilly tonight.

Since when did I start worrying if a beautiful, scantily clad woman is cold?

I take the black fabric mask decorated with beads and sequins that she holds in her hands and use the attached ribbons to tie it in place behind her head. I remove the clip from her ponytail and let her thick blonde hair hang long and loose around her face.

By God, she's breathtaking.

"You look beautiful," I whisper while covering her shoulders with the cloak and pulling the hood over her glossy hair. I tie the strings around her neck and take her hand in mine.

38

Emma

The center of town is filled with people laughing and cavorting in a carnival-like atmosphere. Men and women dressed in costumes laugh and converse as they move from group to group in social greeting. The pungent, delicious smells of unusually spiced food hang in the air and make my mouth water. Musicians play festive, happy music on the village green where people of all ages dance and clap. I can't help but smile. Everyone looks so happy.

John stops every few feet to greet different people with a hug or a kiss on the cheek. Many of them speak freely to him in illegal languages that I have not heard in many, many years. I'm tempted to grab them, warn them that in a crowd of this size that their behavior isn't safe. Just one person speaking a forbidden tongue could be enough ammunition for a patrol to gun down an entire village. Yet not a single person here seems concerned.

John grabs two glasses from an elderly gentleman pouring drinks and hands one to me and Declan before taking a third for himself.

"*Salud!*" He lifts his glass and we all drink. The icy green beverage is brutally strong and burns as it goes down my throat and I cough hard. Once I get over the shock, it's delicious. I look over and Declan's laughing at me.

"What? Have you never had a Margarita before?"

"No, never. I've been bred to be more of a white wine spritzer girl," I answer playfully.

"Well, we are going to have to change that, won't we?" He grins devilishly, a naughty glint in his eyes I haven't seen before. A slight rosy tint to his cheeks where he's been kissed by the cool night air makes him look healthier than I've seen him in a long while. He looks younger tonight, more carefree and lighter than I've ever seen him.

Declan swaps our empty glasses for two full ones, reaches for my free hand, and leads me through town. He points out the small local shops and the grocery store where he's greeted by name and waved over by the proprietor. Senor Gonzales is a short, heavyset man with an infectious smile and a tenuous grasp on the English language. He drags us inside for a shot of celebratory tequila and rattles off something in rapid Spanish to which Declan responds easily. I had no idea Declan could fluently speak a forbidden language. I find it oddly exciting.

The old man hugs and kisses him on both cheeks, then wraps his chubby arms around me and hugs me tight. He loudly whispers in broken English, "He is very good man. You two make beautiful babies," he adds with a knowing look and a wink at Declan—who blushes.

I'm sure the look on my face is priceless, as both men laugh heartily at the blood rushing to my cheeks. They speak a few more words before we're off again. Declan reaches for me and I take his hand like it's the most natural thing in the world. We walk through crowds of revelers as Declan points out more places and I meet more of his friends. He introduces me by my first name, I assume he believes the mask and cloak are enough to protect my identity.

I take a look around and find a small group of young women

staring at me and I'm suddenly afraid. It would only take one finger pointed at us, one accusation, and Declan would be a dead man. Yet he doesn't seem concerned in the least. Despite everyone having heard Declan had been black carded, not a single person side steps him, many of his neighbors even offering help as they profess deep empathy for his plight.

I've never seen a community so caring, so together in thought and action. My side of the wall could learn a lot about good Christian behavior by watching these interactions. Christ knows the hypocrites at the First New State Church I attend can use some lessons.

At the end of the street stands the remains of what must have once been a huge, beautiful church. Most of the stained glass windows have long ago been shattered, but the few pieces of gemstone-vibrant glass that remain have a broken beauty that's impossible to describe. Inside the church, right before the altar, there's a large pine tree covered in little white ribbons that have been tied to the branches. The ribbons all have names on them.

Declan takes a pen and two ribbons and scribbles a name on each one. He gently kisses the writing and ties the two ribbons together and then ties them to the tree. He stops for a moment and solemnly crosses himself as he backs away from the altar. Declan apparently is a man of the Old Faith, something else about him I never expected.

He takes my hand and leads me to a pew where I sit. He genuflects as he follows me into the row, crossing himself before dropping to his knees and bowing his head reverently in prayer. He seems so at peace, so relaxed, the bitter anger he wears like a second skin lifted and exposing the vulnerable man within. He crosses himself again and sits back on the pew next to me looking down at his hands.

"This is a very special holiday for people in our community. As you can see by the destruction, we were hit very hard during the war. Not one family managed to escape losing someone. Children, wives, husbands. . . all gone within seconds. After the fighting stopped, the retaliation of the Committee was even worse. Many tried to run, but by then it was too late. They stole the children and put them in cages where they lingered for years before most died of a combination of disease and starvation. New mothers had their babies ripped from their arms and placed in infant detention centers. They required the sterilization of fertile women with Hispanic blood to make certain their line died out."

The look of shock on my face makes Declan stop and stare at me quizzically. "Is this the first time you're hearing about this?"

I shake my head. "No, I had heard about this but I never thought it was true. I always thought it was some sort of fake news. That's what my father called it."

"No, it's all true," he replies quickly, the fire in his heart lighting his eyes. "We call that time *la purga*. Our people tried to smuggle as many children as they could to safety but few made it. John and Marta had tried forever to have a baby, the two of them trying everything before finally giving up. They remember thinking it had been for the best she never conceived, as it would have killed them to lose a child after trying for so long.

"Talk about Karma being a bitch—pretty much the day after saying that, Marta got pregnant. Watching what was happening to their neighbor's children, they knew how dangerous it was to bring a half-Mexican baby into this fucked up nation. If they didn't send the baby away, at some point, he would be ripped from their arms and sent to live his short life in a cage somewhere. They knew it wasn't a question of *if*; it was a question of *when*.

"So, the two of them prayed over what to do for months, and eventually decided it was more important for the baby to stay alive than for them to be selfish and try to keep him. Their son was only a few hours old when they put him in a smuggler's arms and sobbed as he was carried away. To this day, they have no idea what happened to their boy."

I am so horrified I can't speak. I can't believe this really happened, but one look at Declan's glassy eyes tells me it's all true. I reach over and squeeze his hand that's cold as ice. He gives me a tight watery smile and squeezes my hand in return before taking a deep breath and continuing.

"This is the weekend when, every year, we honor those we've lost. Many of my heritage believe tonight is the one night the dead return to us, to check on those of us still living. We honor them by holding a festival in their honor. We want them to know they have not been forgotten."

I wait patiently as he pauses again to collect his thoughts. "The tree I believe is a local tradition. The Old Faith states that it is important to not only honor and remember the lost, but we must also let them go in peace, that it's not right to hold their spirit hostage in our hearts. So tonight, we celebrate and remember them. We write their names on the ribbons and tie them to the tree. Tomorrow, we come together and pray for their souls. After the service, we carry the tree out to the square and burn it. As the smoke rises, their spirits are released. It's our way of saying we will always love and remember them, but we give them up to be forever with God."

His voice is barely a whisper. A large lump forms in my throat as tears fill my eyes. "That's a beautiful tradition," I whisper before pausing for a second, thinking. "Declan?"

"Hmm?"

"I know he didn't fight for the same side, but I would really like to add my brother's name to the tree."

Declan sits unmoving in silence, and I worry I said the wrong thing. My brother fought against and killed people just like the ones that lived in this community. I realize too late that I have no right to ask to add his name for their prayers just because I miss him. Just as I'm getting ready to apologize for my insensitivity, he speaks.

"I think you should." He pauses for a second before continuing. "It doesn't matter which side of a fight a person's on, what matters is that you lost someone you love and you want to remember him. That's what this tradition honors, not which side a person died for."

He releases my hand and nods his encouragement. I walk over to the table where the ribbons are laid and select one. I write Adam's name on it and just as Declan had, kiss the ribbon before tying it to the tree.

Adam, I hope you have found peace.

I stand there for quite some time staring at the tree until I feel Declan's arms wrap around my waist. He gently kisses my cloaked shoulder before reaching for my hand.

"Come with me. There is so much more I want to share with you."

* * *

The party intensifies as the night goes on. People dance to the music in the village square, and although the style of dancing is not nearly the sexual free-for-all of the club, there's a sensuousness to the music that's highly arousing. Here on the square we see vans filled with patrolmen arrive on the far perimeter of the field, each man carrying a weapon almost as large as themselves. The illusion of safety I had been so comfortable in just minutes ago goes up in smoke.

I now fear every person, the masks and costumes no longer providing the level of safety I once believed. Many of the dancers in the square notice the troops' arrival at the same time and rush to the safety of the shadows. Those that defiantly remain no longer dance as close to one another, making sure to leave a space at least the size of the *Text* between them as required by the Protocols.

I feel Declan tense beside me. "Dance with me."

His voice is quiet but demanding, his words a hushed order as he takes my hand. An icy chill rips through me and I pull back, shaking my head. It's not safe. He refuses to take no for an answer and grips my hand more firmly, pulling us to the center of the deserted dance area. Declan takes me firmly in his arms, our gaze locked, our two bodies one as he leads me through unfamiliar steps. We stare into each other's eyes, aware only of each other and oblivious to the crowd forming protectively around us.

Together we connect in a cloaked swirl of arms, legs and skirt that feels as beautiful and graceful as I'm sure we look. A few times, pain flashes in Declan's eyes, a quick inhaled gasp telling me we should stop, this is too much for him, but he is a slave to the music just as I am his to command. We surrender ourselves to the dance, to the night, to each other.

When the song ends I am pressed tight against his length, his arms wrapped protectively around me. I feel every beat of his heart through his sweater, every exhale of warm breath on my cheek. I am lost in the obsidian depths of his eyes and I pray that I am never found. I want to spend the rest of my life looking into the eyes of the man that holds me tight. His lips descend towards mine as I tilt my chin up for his kiss.

The crowd roars in cheers, applause breaking our trance as we jump apart from one another. My cheeks are so hot I could fry bacon on them. Declan firmly takes my hand and we hasten for the shadows. We've drawn too much attention.

The rest of the night our hands never leave each other. With our fingers laced together, we walk down the street. When we eat, we feed each other bites of food we want the other to try. Where seating is limited, Declan picks me up and sets me down on his lap, his arms wrapped possessively around my waist. He props his chin on my shoulder, his warm breath tickling my ear. The night is so perfect, I wish it could go on forever. But all good things eventually must end.

As the party breaks before curfew, Gonzales flags us down as we pass his store. He motions for us to wait as he disappears inside, returning with a large cardboard box overflowing with food and thrusts it into Declan's resistant hands. There's a heated exchange of words in rapid-fire Spanish that I don't need to know a word of to understand. Some of the revelers turn to watch the exchange, that same sour-faced girl from before taking particular interest in what's going on.

I grab Declan's elbow and yank him into the shadows just as two patrolmen round the corner looking for the source of the noise. They ask Gonzales a bunch of questions as we press ourselves against the wall like we're trying to become one with the bricks. After a few minutes, the patrolmen grow bored, giving the old man a harsh slap that knocks him to his knees before striding away.

If it wasn't for my vice-like grip on his forearm, Declan would have lunged.

"No, Declan, don't," I hiss. "They'll kill you both."

The old man gets up on wobbly legs as two neighbors rush over to aid him. He catches our eye and gives us a glare and a shake of his wrist, the international sign for *get out of here* if I ever saw one. Declan mumbles a string of curses under his breath as he stalks off, not speaking a word to me the entire walk home. He's gone from one of his great moods to one of his darkest in less than a minute and I am helpless to rouse him from his thoughts.

When we get back to the apartment, he drops the box on the kitchen table and strides over to the balcony, looking out the glass door with a brooding scowl. I root through the items in the box, trying to get Declan to engage in conversation, but he won't even look at me. I find a sticky thermos in the bottom of the box and open it carefully, taking a tentative sniff.

"I don't think he wants our party to end yet," I laugh, as I take a sip of the eye-watering contents. "I think this is twice as strong as the margarita we had earlier. Might even be straight tequila. That or I just drank paint thinner."

I try unsuccessfully to lighten his mood. Declan takes the thermos from me and takes a drink.

"Yeah, pretty much straight tequila," he agrees as he takes another long pull before handing it back. He turns back to the deck doors and places his hands against the cracked glass, his head hanging as he stares at the floor. By now, it's nearly 2 am and it's time for me to leave. I start to gather my things.

"Please, don't go. Not yet."

He turns his pleading eyes to me. Declan grabs a few blankets and lays them out on the safest section of the balcony before taking the thermos and a bag of tortilla chips from the box and sits down outside.

"Join me. Please." He pats the space next to him and I sit beside him. He pulls me to his side and enfolds me in his cloak, my head settling cozily against his chest. He's so warm I want to check if his fever returned but I resist the motion knowing how he hates to be mothered. His arm wraps snugly around my waist. "I'm sorry."

"For what?"

"Everything." He sounds exasperated.

"Declan, what is going on in that foolish head of yours?"

He doesn't answer for a long time and I don't push him. I know whatever thoughts he's processing are hard for him. He again reminds me of a poorly socialized puppy who has to pull each new experience completely apart and put it back together a million times before deciding whether to resort to fight, flight or pee on the floor in fear.

"I want you to stay with me tonight," he finally chokes out as he stares into the darkness. "All night."

I pull away so I can look into his gleaming eyes. My heart stops for a few beats, my breath caught in my chest. I can't speak, but not in a bad way. I have wanted this moment for so long and now that it's here I don't know how to respond. I raise my hand to his cheek, and stroke his slight stubble with my thumb. Even though my lips say nothing, both my body and my eyes say yes.

39

Declan

Sometimes I am one incredibly stupid asshole.

I'm having probably the best night of my life. We drink and dance and party and then instead of taking Emma into my arms and kissing her passionately under the stars, I fuck it up by taking stupid, unnecessary risks that could have put everyone in danger. Pride goeth before a fall, someone once said. Well, my pride had been stomped so far into the ground that I really wouldn't be surprised if someone busted an ankle if they stumbled into it.

When Gonzales came out of nowhere with that big box of groceries, my pride deflated like a blow dart to a pool float. I wasn't raised to be a beggar and take handouts. My dad taught me that a real man provides for those he loves; he shelters, clothes, feeds and adores them. He protects his loved ones with his life and shields them with his body. And here I am, penniless, injured and unable to protect her. That box of food represents every possible thing I'm unable to do for Emma and makes me feel like a fucking two-bit chump.

What that old man did for me tonight is positively heroic. If anyone rats him out for giving me food, his head will be on the chopping block right next to mine. He knew the consequences for aiding me and yet he did it anyway. He even put name-brand Oreos in the box, and black market Oreos are really, really expensive.

Fucking Oreos. He easily could have sold the pack for twenty bucks or more and he *gave* them to me because he knows they're my favorite. Am I grateful? You bet your sweet ass I'm grateful. I want to *cry*, I'm so goddamn grateful. And how did I repay his kindness? By creating a scene that ended with him getting a bloody mouth courtesy of two Gestapo wanna-bes.

I'm in a tremendous snit the entire way home, and when we get back to my apartment, I don't even know where to begin to apologize for my behavior. I suck at expressing my feelings and I know I need to make amends for screwing up an otherwise perfect night. So, I start off by asking Emma to sit with me on the balcony.

It's chilly, so I grab some blankets off the bed and make a small nest for us to sit in. When she curls herself against my chest and I wrap her in my arms I know she's already forgiven me. By now we are so in tune to each other it's almost like we can hear each other's thoughts. And when I ask her to stay the night with me, I'm not trying to find a polite way to ask her if she wants to fuck. No, I'm not interested in a one-night fling. I'm not that kind of guy.

Well, that's not completely true.

Okay, sure, I've had more than my fair share of one night stands through the years, but Emma isn't the kind of girl you fuck and forget. I want more. I'm not sure exactly when it happened, but Emma changed something in me. I don't just want her, I crave her. I need her like a heroin addict needs a fix.

The rational side of me keeps repeating that this relationship is illogical, irrational and irresponsible and going to end with me swinging from a rope. Relationships like ours never end well in books unless they are fucking fairy tales, and my life sure as shit has never had a blue-bodied genie in it granting me wishes.

When Emma places her fingers gently on my face and turns me

towards her, I immediately know that all the things I will never be able to give her don't matter to her one bit. She has everything the daughter of a wealthy, powerful man could ever want except the one thing I can give to her in spades.

Love.

Emma's gaze is heavy-lidded, her eyes sliding between my wanting stare and my descending mouth. I close my eyes as our lips touch. Emma exhales softly into my mouth as my lips part ever so slightly, kissing her gently, my breath a whisper against hers. Her fingers press lightly to my cheek and then slide slowly behind my neck, gently tracing my hairline before entwining into the longer, unruly curls at the back of my head. I glide my tongue over her full lower lip, tasting the remains of salt, tequila and lime. She's more intoxicating than any beverage and I find myself getting drunk on her kisses.

Emma tentatively pokes her tongue just a few millimeters into my mouth, and I reward her bravery by opening mine a little more for her, inviting her to explore me at her leisure. We give and take from one another, our tongues dancing, our lips moving faster and more sure with each strangled breath. A low moan slips from between her lips, the sexiest sound I've ever heard in my life. Well, that is, until she pulls away slowly from me and whispers for me to take her to bed.

I stand and reach down to her, grasping her outstretched hands in mine. I take her in my arms again, kissing her fervently as she wraps her arms around my neck. I open the sliding glass door with my free hand before guiding her to my bed and lowering her to the mattress. It's all I can do to not moan out loud feeling her body rubbing against my raging erection.

I remove my cloak and kick off my boots and she does the same. Her skirt slides up her thigh showing an expanse of silky pale legs that are so beautiful I have to touch them. I place my hand above her delicate ankle and slowly run it up her smooth thigh. When I reach high enough for it to be decidedly improper, I remove my hand from her naked leg and place it on top of her clothing. I lie down next to her, taking her into my arms and resume our fervid kisses.

My fingers slide up her side and my hand travels over her ribs until it rests, flat and unassuming, over her breast. I kiss her with unchecked need, waiting for a cue that she's okay with this next level of intimacy. When she kisses me harder and rubs the full length of her body against mine, I know she's giving her consent.

Her breast is little more than a handful, but it's positively perfect in its shape and feel as I acquaint myself with her body. When I run my thumb over her nipple, she inhales sharply but then lets out a long sigh of contentment. I repeat my touch in slow gliding strokes, letting her enjoy the sensation. She responds by pressing her breast more firmly into my hand as I take her nipple between my finger and thumb and gently roll it between them. She moans in pure pleasure.

I am wild with lust. I want to peel her clothes from her and take that perfect breast in my mouth and suck it until she screams for more, but I know I have to take things slow. Emma has only had traumatic sexual experiences and the last thing I would ever want to do is frighten her. I plan to be painfully patient with her, to fully gain her trust before we go further.

I almost laugh aloud thinking about how painful patience can be in these situations. I'm currently sporting a hard-on the size of a battering ram and the blue balls heading my way are going to be hell on Earth. But no matter how painful things become down below, I'm not going to do anything to hurt her. Releasing her breast from my grasp and sliding my hand up to her face, I cup her cheek. She's so tiny my hand looks enormous against her pixie-like features. I press my finger to her lips, breaking our connection as I pull back just enough so I can look into her questioning eyes.

"Did I do something wrong?"

Oh, God, no. How could she possibly think that?

"No, no, sweetheart, you are absolutely perfect," I whisper, kissing the tip of her nose gently.

"Then why have you stopped?"

I pull her towards me and turn her around, cradling her with my body. My chest is flush against her spine, her sweet, sweet ass firm against my throbbing cock. How am I going to explain this to her?

"You know when you are reading a great book right before going to sleep and you know you can either continue reading although you are getting really tired and probably will miss important details, or you can wait for the next day, when you are fully rested and can completely enjoy the ending knowing you haven't missed a single important word?"

"Yes. . ." she answers quizzically.

I wrap my arms around her more firmly and brush my lips against the nape of her neck. "You, sweetheart, are the most amazing book I have ever laid my hands on. I don't want to risk missing out on a single syllable by rushing through the chapters." Continuing to gently kiss and nibble her smooth, long neck I whisper, "Sometimes, the greatest enjoyments in life come from taking your time and savoring every moment. I plan to relish every second I have with you."

* * *

Emma

Within minutes, Declan's fast asleep. I stay awake listening to his light, even breathing that's a far cry from the thick, rattling cough of just a few weeks ago. I know he's brave and stupidly stoic, pretending to be more healed than he is, and I'm ready to kick myself for not realizing sooner that tonight must have been exhausting for him. I feel guilty for keeping him awake so long.

I try to sleep, but my mind races like a toddler on a sugar high with the most awful thoughts. I've fallen in love with a man I can't have, a man that I think loves me, too. But he hates my family, and my parents would never in a million years allow us to marry. If our relationship doesn't scream *Romeo and Juliet*, nothing does, and if memory serves me correctly, that story didn't end well for anyone. Even though our story is non-fiction, life has a frightening tendency to imitate art. And if that's the case, there will be no happily ever after for us, either.

Knowing our future is bleak at best, I wonder how Declan really feels about me. I love to think he's smitten, but what if he's not? Does he keep me around because I bring him stuff? Am I just a toy to play with until he's executed?

Damn my father.

I shake my head to clear my thoughts. I refuse to let the distrust of men that he and Ryan have instilled in me cloud the one beautiful relationship in my life. Declan has done nothing to deserve my distrust. If anything, I'd be shocked if he wasn't at least a little concerned about *my* motives.

I must have finally fallen asleep because I wake a few hours later with the sun rising and Declan nuzzling the back of my neck. His warm breath and whisper-light kisses send a shiver of pleasure through me. I purr quietly as his hands move gently from around my waist and slowly explore my body.

"Hmm, I want to wake up like this every day."

He chuckles at my words as he continues peppering me with tender kisses. His groin presses into my backside and judging by the size of his erection, he feels the same way. We kiss and touch each other for hours, unaware of time and blissfully wrapped up in each other. Declan never once attempts to touch me any more intimately than he already has. As much as I want to have him ravage me, I can't form the words. The last thing I want is for him to think I'm wanton.

Good girls are pure in mind, body and spirit.

Yeah, but being bad feels absolutely *amazing*.

Declan pulls himself from my arms and asks me if I'm hungry. I nod and he gets up and starts to make breakfast. The food is simple, some thick spicy sausages, scrambled eggs and toast. I feel guilty for eating as much of Declan's precious food and feel overly full from the unaccustomed type and amount. I think about making myself sick until I realize that's simply not an option in this tiny apartment. Declan would hear and I don't want to get into that with him. He won't understand.

"Don't even think about it." Declan's voice is stern, his eyes peering at me with distrust. I wonder if he can read minds or if he's just picking up on how guilty I look. His face relaxes and his eyes soften.

"Why do you do it? You do realize it's only a matter of time before it kills you. Or is that what you're hoping for?"

He comes over to my chair and squats down in front of me, taking my hands in his before commanding me to look in his eyes. He sees my affirmative answer in every detail of my face and he sighs sadly. I'm so overcome with emotion I can't speak as tears well up in my eyes. I don't know how to tell him that if I can't have him, if I have to marry Ryan, if I have to stop dancing, I'd rather be dead. I'm terrified he's going to think I'm crazy, but I'm not crazy, I'm *desperate*. There's a big difference.

"I don't want to talk about this now," I manage to whisper, pulling my hands from his and standing.

Before I can go anywhere, he grabs my wrist and pulls me to him as he stands. He wraps those strong, hard arms around me and holds me tight. "I know I can't make you stop. I know you use it as a way to cope, but you're killing yourself in the process. I want to help you, Emma, but on this matter, you are the only one who can stop. If you can't live for yourself, then live for me. I need you." He kisses me gently on the cheek and lets me go just as my tears fall. I can't say anything, so I nod.

He gives me a small smile and turns to clear the table. I help him wash the dishes before cleaning myself as best as I can with the icy tap water from the bathroom sink. When I come out of the bathroom, Declan's lying atop the freshly made bed waiting for me. He's removed his shirt, his hair still damp from his earlier ablutions. In the harsh light of day, every scar on his alabaster skin stands out, yet whereas these scars would have been considered faults in a piece of art, on him, they simply accentuate his fierce beauty.

His loose drawstring sweatpants are riding dangerously low on his hips and I see the thin dark line of hair traveling from his navel to his nether regions below. I have a sudden urge to undress him fully, to look at him in all his masculine glory.

"Didn't they teach you in fancy rich person school that it's not polite to stare?" I can tell by his tone he's teasing and I blush.

"Come here," he commands, his eyes twinkling with mischief. "If you have time to stare, I can think of *much* more entertaining ways for us to spend our time."

40

AS NIGHT DESCENDS we once again don our cloaks and head back to the square. Tonight, there's no loud music or cheerful greetings, but a somber ambiance that feels almost holy. Along with the rest of the community, we file quietly into the church. I feel completely lost, not having been raised in a family that believes in God. It wasn't until we were required by law to attend the New State Church that we even went on the mandatory holidays.

The Old Faith service is not long at all, maybe an hour at most, and it's nothing like what I've experienced going to the First New State Church. The priest gives out bread and wine to those that want to participate, and most do. On our way here, Declan tried to explain the whole concept of the body and blood of Christ, but I still don't get it. When I tell him it sounds like some form of cannibalistic rite, he laughs and says if that's what I got out of it, he didn't explain it right. I ask him that maybe on our way home, he can try again, and he looks surprised when I say that. Because his faith is important to him, I want to learn about it, too. I don't think he realizes it, but I want to know everything about him.

When the service ends, we file silently out of the church. We are handed small previously used candles that we light from a large taper one of the altar boys holds and start our solemn procession to the square. The tree filled with ribbons is carried from the church and firmly staked in place in the middle of the field. We stand next to John and Marta as the priest comes out and gives another blessing in rapid Spanish. Marta, like many other men and women, is crying silent tears as John tries to comfort her. Declan's face is relaxed but stony, his eyes glazed and unfocused with deep thought.

When the priest sets the tree alight, the people around me blow out their candles. I watch as Declan bows his head and says his own silent prayer before gently extinguishing the flame with a short breath. He shakes himself out of his reverie and whispers that it's time for me to let Adam's spirit go.

As the tree burns, people start milling about, consoling each other, hugging one another and trying to calm those who sobbingly refuse to blow out their candles. Although I didn't understand a word of the ceremony in the square, I am deeply moved, not even realizing I'm crying until Declan brushes a tear from my cheek before leading me home in silence.

We again decide to enjoy one of the last temperate evenings of the season on the balcony as the bitter cold of winter will soon be here. Declan opens a beer for each of us and hands me one. We drink in silence, the reverence of the somber service still reflective in our communication. He has that broody look he sometimes gets, and I know when he's ready he will tell me what he's thinking. Part of me dreads what he's going to say, somehow knowing that whatever he's going to confide will change my perception of the world forever.

41

Declan

I sit on the balcony still wrapped in the thick protective layer of mothball-smelling wool that does nothing to shield my heart from what I'm getting ready to say. There's so much about me that Emma doesn't know and much of it's too dangerous for her to hear. But there's one story I need to tell her, with a few edits, of course, before we take whatever this thing is between us any further.

It's the story of how I became the man I am today.

I push the hood off of my face so I can see Emma without looking directly at her. Some stories you want to tell while looking your audience in the eye.

This is not one of those tales.

Unlike Emma, my childhood was great. I had parents that loved one another fiercely even though they came from two very different worlds. My dad was Irish and my mom Hispanic, which explains my pitch black hair and painfully white skin. My mom came here legally to go to medical school and she became a doctor. A trauma surgeon, actually, and a damn fine one. My dad was a blue-collar guy who worked in construction. He was pretty rough around the edges.

He loved good beer, cursed like a Russian sailor and worshiped my mother with every ounce of his being.

They met when one of his co-workers crushed his hand on a site. A cinder block had fallen from two stories above and landed on this poor sod and my dad, being a good guy and the fastest driver, rushed him to the hospital.

As fate would have it, my mom was the surgeon on call that day. She walks into the room, all business like, introduces herself and picks up the towel over my dad's buddy's smashed hand. My dad takes one look at the mangled limb and hits the floor. Hard. When he wakes up, my mom's standing over him. Whenever he told the story, he would say he thought he had died and gone to heaven, as there was an angel standing over him. Then with a waggle of his brows, he'd add that, better yet, she was an angel wearing a short skirt and no panties. That's when my mom would smack him playfully on the arm and blush, swearing that part was not true. He would always wink and insist it was.

I laugh out loud just thinking about them. Emma settles next to me, intent on devouring every word of my history. Her slight body is turned to face me although I'm not looking at her, either staring out into the dark or looking down at my untouched beer.

I was born before things got really fucked up in this country, well before the war. My folks and I had a great life. We lived in a big house on a nice street with neighbors who didn't give a shit about the color of our skin. We went to church every week and I went to school with all the other kids from the neighborhood. Even though I was of mixed blood, nobody cared. As far as anyone was concerned, I was just another kid on the block.

Things started getting weird as I got older. People became angrier. Meaner. More hateful. I blame a lot of this on a phenomenon called "social media." Social, my ass. When you say someone is social, you mean they are friendly. This was hardly friendly. When people were conversing behind a computer they acted differently. They felt there were no consequences and they started acting like a group of fools. Racism, sexism and a whole lot of other isms ran rampant as people started pointing fingers at entire cultures, races and different sexual orientations as the cause of all of our stupid first world problems. As a nation, we got nastier and nastier.

There were terrorist attacks all the time. Usually they were blamed on any number of brown-skinned people, like Hispanics, people from the Middle East and people with ancestors from Africa. In truth, the violence was almost never created by minorities but by unstable white men caught up in the new white nationalism movement.

The internet was full of racist chat rooms where these bastards traded bomb recipes and egged each other on to kill as many "illegals" as possible by opening fire in crowded places. Ninety-nine percent of the time the people killed were legal residents with the simple misfortune of having brown skin. There was no remorse for killing kids, either. In their minds, the children would only grow up to continue tainting the population so schools with high percentages of minorities also became popular targets.

For a long time the pervasive fear was focused against people of non-white skin and the typical "brown-people" religions. As that is a pretty predominant theme in the overall history of the world, no one really noticed that things were getting out of hand until it was too late. For the average white-skinned person, things were still alright. Closeted homosexuals, "well-behaved" women, and really light-skinned brown folks still lived somewhat normal lives.

When I was in my early teens there was a great move to start building walls around the country. The cuckoo far-right group that would eventually become the new regime said we didn't need any more people coming through our borders. They argued that the illegals were going to eventually steal our children, rape our women and murder the white men, and half the country suddenly fucking *believed* it.

As soon as the walls were erected then all the brown people *within* the country were under suspicion of being terrorists. The focus became rounding up these unfortunate souls and either deporting them or locking them up in filthy detention centers to rot. Children were ripped from their mothers and sent to group homes until they were old enough to work. Many children died in the "youth centers" as hygiene and medical care were scarce if not outright denied.

African-Americans had it really bad, too. The new White Nationalist platform couldn't decide if it hated Hispanics or Blacks more, so they targeted both. Police brutality against black people rose exponentially in both frequency and intensity, with black people dying for infractions that most white people would merely get a ticket for. In the South, a lot of states were doing their damndest to disenfranchise African-Americans. When the newly formed White Nationalist Party came into power, they tried and failed to repeal the Fifteenth Amendment by only the slimmest of margins. Many states were pissed about this, so they adopted some of the most bizarre voting restrictions you could ever imagine. A number of them withdrew from the Union and chaos erupted across an extremely divided nation.

As time went on, the rich got richer and the poor got poorer, leading to more crime and violence. If history has taught us nothing, it's that starving people are willing to do almost anything to eat. When dying from a bullet sounds better than a slow, miserable death from malnutrition, there's not much motivation for even the most law-abiding citizen to continue to walk the straight and narrow. Riots and looting became the norm, kidnappings and home invasions less usual but certainly more frequent. Cops resorted to shooting first and asking questions later, especially if the suspect wasn't a prime example of good ol' Aryian breeding.

Nobody knows for sure what was the final straw that led to the riots that fateful January day, or who planted the bombs that caused the Capitol to blow up like some sort of fucked up Fourth of July fireworks display, taking a joint session of Congress with it. The only survivors were those who weren't there, and I can give you three guesses who those people were, but you'll only need one. Yeah, the handful of survivors were all members of what would officially become the Committee.

The fall of the Republic was the last straw for the remaining sane Americans who banded together and came after the newly formed government. The ensuing civil war was a complete bloodbath that started and finished in three weeks. It's amazing how fast a war ends when one side has all the power, the money, the weapons and is more than happy to wipe out millions of people at a time. For months after the war ended, people were rounded up en masse and executed. If you ever said anything against the Supreme Archon, as he by now declared himself, someone showed up at your house and shot you in your driveway. The nation's population was halved within the first year of his rule.

We were no longer the world economic power we'd been up to only a few years before. After the war, the stock market crashed. The price of oil went through the roof, and nobody drove their cars anymore, because no one could afford fuel, so they all sat home and watched their TVs and were force-fed more fucking propaganda disguised as news. We lived in an endless circle of propaganda, fear, hate, crime and then back to a new rhetoric once each potentially "dangerous" group was wiped out.

The Supreme Court was packed with Committee-approved members who had free rein over the laws. Now that the brown-people menace was "under control," the Committee turned its focus on suppressing women. Almost overnight, abortion, women's reproductive rights and all forms of contraception became illegal. Then, women could no longer hold jobs unless it was something deemed wholly feminine, like domestic service or sewing. Next, women could no longer own computers or cell phones, drive cars or have private bank accounts.

So now minorities *and* women were under attack. They went after the LGBTQ community next. If you weren't a straight-laced-missionary-style-I-only-fuck-my spouse-who's-the-opposite-sex kind of person, you got taken in for "retraining." No one we knew that went in ever returned.

Anyone with half a brain could see we had become another Nazi regime. The Committee hijacked the media and pulled the plug on the First Amendment. Journalists who had overstepped their boundaries had been disappearing for years, their mangled bodies washing up on beaches all along the East Coast. Now, the Committee went a step further, cleansing the profession of anyone who refused to spin their bullshit garbage. Rachel Maddow and Katy Tur were probably the biggest names who refused to kowtow to the Committee, the two of them last seen being hauled out of MSNBC headquarters fighting the patrolmen with every last ounce of their strength. They've been presumed dead, no one having seen them in years, although there's been occasional rumors they are behind the outcropping of resistance newspapers that circulate from time to time. I like to think they are still alive raising hell somewhere. I always liked watching them on TV.

It was open season on journalists at that point. Thousands of men and women were slaughtered who did nothing more dangerous than raise a pen to write the truth. By the time the Committee was done "cleansing" the media, the only place you could get news was on FOX. No one was a bit surprised when a year later the channel was renamed *The New State Press*.

Now, there was no longer anything remotely resembling free speech. You paid for every goddamn word you produced.

We became a culture afraid of its own shadow. When fear permeates a culture they do stupid shit like build walls to keep the 'different' people away from them. Now it wasn't enough to have walls between us and Canada and Mexico, now we had walls around the major cities, too. Once those went up, the Committee started a campaign to get rid of the perceived remaining "menaces to their safety" that resided *within* the walls.

The Mandatory State ID Card system went into effect shortly after that, making it illegal to leave home without it. They started moving people around based on their ethnicity and, in short, the whiter you were the better you lived. My mom didn't qualify to stay within the city limits because of her Hispanic blood, and as a result of being her kid, neither did I. They told my dad if he wanted to divorce her and disown me he could stay; the look of hate and disgust he gave that patrolman as he handed over his drivers license and accepted his new restricted ID is one I'll never forget. We were given twenty-four hours to pack our shit and move to the slums where we lived with four other families in a rat-infested house that was the size of the basement of our former home.

The Committee was no longer interested in just cleansing our nation; now they wanted to rid the *world* of the brown menace. To say the least, that was not taken well by much of the rest of the planet, who despite what the *New State Press* tells us, is not remotely as white as they want us to believe. Our Allies told us to fuck off one by one, leaving our country alone, friendless and open to attack.

For years, foreign governments tried to get involved and stop the madness with no success. The United Nations hit us with sanctions. No one wanted to trade with us anymore after we put in place some really bizarre trade tariffs and rampant inflation jacked the prices of everyday items through the roof. A gallon of milk cost thirty-nine dollars, whereas a few months before, it was four. I remember that as clearly as if it happened yesterday. My mom had sent me to the store for milk and bread with a twenty-dollar bill and I came home, completely freaked out, without either.

The Supreme Archon closed the churches when he realized how many of them were trying to help those of us the government had already deemed unworthy. He created a new state-sanctioned "religion" with himself at the head, not surprisingly, making it one based on fear and hate. The new leaders of the "faith" heavily edited the Bible to suit their needs and justify their actions. The Purity Laws were enacted, with rewards for neighbors to turn one another in if they suspected someone of participating in 'moral indiscretions.' People disappeared at an alarming rate.

As the National Purification Movement gained ground, there were mass raids where thousands of people were rounded up for all sorts of reasons. There were no more trials as everyone was guilty, so there really was no point. Now they just shot you. Whole armies of Purity Police went on old social media sites and poured through the "evidence" people had unwittingly "confessed" over the years. If there was "proof," sometimes something as simple as a Tweet or a Facebook post, they found you guilty. Punishment was delivered quickly and severely. When they enacted the Brother's Keeper Act, if you suspected someone was breaking a Purity Law and you didn't turn them in and someone found out, they killed you, too.

I stop and take a long drink from my beer. Even though I haven't smoked in nearly a decade, I really wish I had a cigarette right now. This is the kind of truth that should only be told with a good ol' cancer stick hanging from your lips. I take a sideways glance at Emma and she's gone ghostly pale. I know this is a lot for her to take in all in one go, but if I don't finish this story now, I'll never find the strength to pick this back up. It's too hard to remember the past.

When they started taking the kids away from mixed race couples and placing them in work camps my parents decided it was time to run. My mom hadn't been allowed to work in the hospital for a few years at this point, but had wanted to stay to help the people in the ghetto where we lived. My dad was skilled with building traps and catching food, sneaking out a few times each week after curfew to hunt. He had managed to take apart a crossbow and sneak it into the ghetto with us, so sometimes we even had venison that we shared with as many people as we could.

My folks had been smart and taken out what little money we had before the banks emptied our accounts, but with inflation as bad as it was, we were now nearly broke. For so long they held onto their misplaced faith in the goodness of mankind, honestly believing that the wrongs were going to somehow right themselves. But things were only getting worse.

As naive as my folks may have been about things initially, they hadn't been stupid enough to not have a plan B. They had been quietly planning an escape to our cabin in the woods for years, and while we still could afford a car, had started stashing stuff there when we went out on weekends. Now that we had little more than the clothes on our backs, we had no choice but to walk.

It was an arduous, weeks-long hike out to the Shenandoah, the fear of being caught adding to our already significant misery of incessant hunger, blistered feet and exhausted muscles. But once we got there, we knew we had done the right thing. We felt safe for the first time in ages, the invisible weight of overwhelming stress finally lifting from our weary shoulders.

We had a good run in the cabin. My mom had a hell of a green thumb, so she planted a large vegetable garden with seeds she'd hoarded for just this possible scenario. My dad could usually snag some form of game for us to eat, teaching me to snare, track and hunt on our many outings together. I was never as good as he was, as, truth be told, I hated even the idea of taking the life of an innocent animal. Even when it meant the difference between having dinner or not, I always felt sick letting those arrows fly.

The day I killed my first deer was a bigger deal for my dad than it was for me. He sat me down and gave me the carved bone-handled knife his dad had given him after his first kill. His eyes had been a bit teary as he told me that I now had the skills to provide for my mom should anything ever happen to him. He had been so proud of me that day, his smile never leaving his lips as he regaled my mom with the tale of my perfect shot over and over until I begged him to stop.

We lived simply. We had no electricity, no TV, no phone, no hot water and we only had each other for company. A lot of families would have killed each other under the strain, but not us. We were happy, if not happier, than when we lived in the city.

By now, I knew I wanted to be a doctor, just like my mom. So, when I turned fourteen, my mom started training me. She had hidden all of her medical texts in the cabin, so I had plenty of books to learn from as well as her vast surgical experience. I spent every second of daylight memorizing everything I would need to know to be a great doctor, just like her. I secretly decided that once I got my license, I would practice under the name Dr. Declan Mendoza Byrne, honoring my mother and her heritage by inserting her maiden name into mine. I couldn't wait for the day I would surprise her with my diploma and show her how honored I was to be her son.

It was shortly after my fifteenth birthday when they found us. Patrols had pretty much cleared out the cities of every subversive they could find, so now I guess they had some free time to start tracking down those of us that ran.

That last day my dad had gone hunting. It was a beautiful early spring day, the first after a long, cold winter and I was inside studying when my mom told me to go out and catch some fish for dinner. This was the time of year we were the hungriest, when we had eaten through all of the vegetables from last summer and were subsisting solely on whatever my dad could track and kill.

Something in my gut told me to stay home, but at the same time, it was so nice out, I was itchy to get outside. I grabbed a fishing pole, kissed my mom and told her I'd be back with dinner in a few hours. I didn't go far, maybe a ten minute walk from the cabin. I was there about an hour when I heard my mom scream.

She was a really brave woman, so for her to scream, something major had happened. At first, I thought maybe a bear, or an early season snake had startled her. But she kept screaming and screaming.

I stop speaking to steady my nerves. I never told anyone except John this story and that was many, many years ago. I had cried like a fucking child when I told him and I don't want to do that in front of Emma.

Please God, don't let me cry in front of her.

I knew something was really wrong, and I ran as fast as I could. I burst out of the trees to find five heavily armed patrolmen standing around in a circle, their guns pointed at the ground. The sixth guard had my mom pinned to the dirt and was raping her. She screamed for me to run, but I couldn't leave her. I ran screaming towards the guards demanding they let her go. I was blinded by rage and fear and I wanted to save her so badly I simply just didn't think.

It took three guards less than a minute to knock me to the ground. I had the hunting knife my dad gave me attached to my belt and I took it and slashed at one of the guards, catching him in the arm. It was nothing more than a deep scratch, but he was enraged. He beat me within an inch of my life, but stopped before I lost consciousness. He pulled me to my knees, all the while saying the most God-awful things. . .

Oh, fuck. I'm not going to get through this.

I stop speaking for a second to compose myself. Emma places her hand lightly on my forearm and squeezes gently in support, but I can't even look at her. I take a deep steadying breath and blink back the tears that threaten to take over.

I don't know how long it went on, but they took turns with her. All of them. The one I had scratched with the knife took a second turn on "principle." When he was done he beat her so badly I thought she was dead. He took my knife and did the most disgusting things to her with it. They forced me to watch, every time I closed my eyes or turned away they beat me. I begged them to leave her alone, to hurt me instead, but all they did was laugh at my childish tears and pathetic pleas.

Even after all these years, I can still hear her screams. I can no longer remember the sound of her voice, but God in Heaven, I remember those screams like it was yesterday. She was dying slowly and painfully and they laughed while they made me watch her bleed out. I begged them to help her. I had no pride anymore. I would have done anything to save her, but my pleas fell on deaf ears.

They questioned me about who else lived with us. I lied and told them it was just the two of us. I prayed they would kill me and get out of there before my father got home. They ransacked our cabin and found pictures of us with my dad. They kept asking where my father was. I told them he was dead. They didn't believe me. I was a lousy liar back then. I didn't have the experience with it as a kid like you get when you're an adult.

My dad must have known something was off when he came back close to twilight. Maybe he heard the guards speaking, maybe he saw footprints. He managed to get arrows into two of them before they shot him. He was killed instantly.

By now, my mom was barely alive. I swear, knowing my dad was dead was what really killed her. As much as they loved me, they loved each other in a way I have never seen before or since. She gazed at me with tears in her eyes, whispered she loved me, and took her last breath within minutes of his.

A tear slides down my cheek and I bow my head in shame. My heart's breaking all over again. Over the past sixteen years, I've done everything I could to not think about that day and here I am willingly reliving this nightmare to the woman I'd been crazy enough to fall for. I take a deep ragged breath, the pain in my chest from trying to contain my tears ripping through me. I fight as hard as I can, but I can't hold them back any longer. It hurts as if someone's squeezing my heart in a vice.

Without a sound, Emma moves closer and tries to wrap her arms around me. I shrug her off. I don't want her to hold me. There's nothing she can do that will make me feel better and now, on top of everything, I feel like a fucking fool for crying. I stand up and throw the now empty bottle as hard as I can off the balcony. I turn towards the door and try to steady myself against the cracked glass, my head bowed in shame.

Emma stands behind me, placing her palm flat against my back and rubbing gentle soothing circles. It feels so good, but it starts waterworks that I'm powerless to stop.

"Come here," she whispers huskily as she turns me to face her. Before she takes me in her arms, I see her eyes are shining with tears, her cheeks as wet as if she'd been caught unprepared in a summer storm.

I fall into her arms, no longer self-conscious. I sob against her, finally allowing sixteen years of pent-up sorrow flow from my broken heart. I think of nothing except purging myself of the fear, the hate, the blame and self-loathing I carry because I had been unable to stop what happened all those years ago. Emma holds me tight and I cling to her the way a drowning man clings to the idea of life. I am probably squeezing the hell out of her, but I can't let go. My barely-healed ribs scream from my self-inflicted torture.

"*Shh*, it's okay, let it out. . ." she whispers as she holds me, her voice raw with emotion. When I finally feel like I can cry no more, I pull back from her and look into her red-rimmed eyes. I take my thumb and gently catch a tear as it slides down her cheek. She turns her head into my hand and brushes her lips against my palm.

I know in that minute I love her. It's stupid and dangerous and going to end badly for us both, but my God, I love her. I lower my lips to hers as I tangle my fingers in her hair. With stray tears falling from our eyes, we kiss each other tenderly and slowly. Our lips, hands, bodies and hearts are one as we explore one another. Our gentle kisses become more ardent, each breath more ragged. Unlike last night's cautious explorations, tonight we kiss each other with a fervid passion that leaves us breathless and gasping. We stagger over to the bed and fall upon it wrapped up in each other's arms.

Emma kisses me like she knows she has the power to heal me. With every touch of her sweet lips she takes away a little more of my pain. She clings to me fiercely, her chewed finger tips digging into my flesh. My heart pounds in my ears and I think of nothing aside from the curative effect of her lips. I pull her tighter to me, a gasp leaving my lips when I move too quickly and my ribs protest they are too injured to perform.

Pain be damned.

I rip at the ties of the cloak around my throat and then attack Emma's, relieving her of the extra material. My hands rove all over her perfect little body. I can't get enough of her. She reaches around and grabs my ass with her hands, pulling me towards her. I slide my hand under her shirt and take hold of her breast over her thin bra, the heat of her skin enough to make me wild. I pull the shirt over her head, straddling her tiny frame.

"My God, you are so fucking beautiful," I growl as she reaches for me, pulling the hem of my shirt out from my belted jeans. I oblige by yanking it over my head. My heart pounds as I lower myself to her and feel my bare chest contact hers. As much as I want to rip the rest of her clothes off, the voice of reason reminds me to take things slow.

I know taking our time is the right thing to do, but Holy Christ, do I want to strangle that voice in my head.

I kiss her lips hard, entangling my hands further into her hair and grabbing fistfuls to keep me from finding more intimate parts of her to touch. I don't want to rush things, but there are no words to describe the need I feel to be inside her.

Emma initiates the next move, unbuckling my belt and slipping it from the loops that hold up my too-loose jeans. I take this as a sign that she's ready for more and I untangle my hands from her hair. I place one hand on her breast and slide my swollen lips from hers. I kiss her neck, each brush of my lips traveling further down her body. My fingers slide under the thin lace of her bra and she inhales sharply as my fingers explore her velvety skin. I torture us both by going as slowly as I can, kissing her collarbone and sliding her bra straps from her shoulders before snaking my hand behind her back and unfastening the clasp. Still straddling her, I sit up so I can watch as I slide the thin satiny straps down her arms, revealing her breasts.

I'm ready to come in my pants just looking at her.

I thought she might be shy and try to cover herself, but she doesn't. Instead, she surprises me by taking my damaged hand in hers and untying the laces of the brace that covers the ruined skin and hideous brand. She looks me unblinkingly in the eyes while laying my uncovered hand upon her lips, kissing the grotesque scars without apprehension. She slides her tongue over the disfigured tissue, wasted muscle, and fried skin, kissing it so tenderly, I swear I feel sensation in the nerves destroyed over a decade ago. When she's done, she places my ruined hand on her breast and squeezes gently.

I want to tell her I love her. I love her because she risks her life every time she comes here. I love her because she's not ashamed or afraid of any part of me. She wholly accepts every inch of my battered body and mind, my horrible past, and the fact I am nowhere near good enough to deserve her. I love her deeply and completely for all of it.

But when I try to say the words they catch in my throat, my tongue unable to do the necessary gymnastics to take them from thought to word.

Instead, I lean down and take her puckered nipple in my mouth and gently touch my tongue to it. She tenses below me and then exhales long and slow as she arches her back, pressing herself deeper into my mouth. I lick and suck at her until she moans in pleasure, gently taking the tight bud between my teeth and tugging slightly. She gasps, but not in fear, rasping out my name as she digs her fingers into my shoulders.

I have never been more turned on in my entire fucking life.

As I focus my mouth on one breast, I caress and plump the other with my palm. She's wild from my touch and I know if I were to stroke between her legs she would be soaked. But before I can test my theory, she somehow works her way out from between my legs and flips me over onto my back. She grins devilishly as she pants, "My turn."

Jesus John F. Kennedy Christ. What the hell is she planning to do?

She kisses my lips deeply and passionately before trailing a path of kisses down the side of my neck. She takes the tender flesh and metal of my pierced nipple into her mouth after having played with it between her fingers, her other hand running over my chest and landing over my heart where it rests gently. I take that hand in mine and raise it to my lips and kiss her fingertips. I slip her index finger into my mouth, sucking and licking it suggestively before letting go. She slides her damp finger to my other nipple and pinches it hard. I close my eyes and gasp aloud, enjoying every stroke of her tongue as her lips suck harder. I reopen my eyes to find she's watching me as she toys with my body.

Little minx.

Still peering into my eyes and ministering my nipple with her exceptionally talented tongue, she slides her hand down my chest. Her tiny hand fits easily through the opening between my loose jeans and raging cock and she deftly takes me into her firm grasp and starts to stroke me. I close my eyes and moan out loud.

"Am I doing this right?" Emma asks between licks at my breast.

If I wasn't breathlessly enraptured by her touch, I would have laughed at her silly, silly question. I answer her by pulling her away from my chest and bringing her face to mine. I plant another possessive kiss on those perfect lips as she strokes me harder and faster. I moan against her, whispering her name over and over. Her fingers slide from around my cock to undo the button on my jeans.

Oh, holy fuck, if I don't put a stop to this now I'm going to do something I know I'll live to regret.

I groan aloud as I place my hand over hers. "Emma, no." My cock expels a particularly juicy drop of pre-cum just as I say the words, his way, I'm sure, of asking *what the ever-loving fuck, asshole?*

"It's okay, I want to." She moves her lips from mine before slowly working her way down my body. As soon as I realize where she's headed with that mouth, I place my hand on her chin and tilt her head up to look at me. As much as I want to have her lips wrapped around my cock I know letting her suck me off is an express, one-way ticket to out-of-control land. Logistically, I need to be naked for her to do what she wants and I know the second my cock's loose, I'm not going to want to stop until I've fucked her sixteen ways to Sunday.

My dick is crying to be buried inside of Emma's warm, wet mouth and as Christ is my witness, it takes the strength of a thousand men for me to stop her. I can't put myself in a position to lose control and I'm not willing to put Emma's life at risk. If things get out of hand and I take Emma's virginity, she will be in grave danger if anyone finds out. If that someone turns out to be Ryan, he will kill her for certain.

"I mean it Emma, no. We can't. . . ."

She looks crestfallen. "You don't want me to?"

I close my eyes, counting to ten before answering between

clenched teeth. "Seconds ago you had your hand on the best possible indicator of what I want and you're *still* asking me?"

I open my eyes to her puzzled expression. I pull her to me so her lips are a breath's width from mine, my body somehow now hovering over hers, caging her in. I'm sexually frustrated to the point I could implode, and the confused and disappointed look on her face is giving me serious second thoughts about letting her continue. The blood that should have been going to my brain has redirected itself southward and in a moment of weakness, I grind my cock against her pelvis as I whisper huskily in her ear between bruising kisses.

"You want to know what I want, Emma? I'll tell you, baby. I want to rip off your clothes, spread your legs and feast on that sweet, sweet nectar between your thighs. I want to worship your body with my fingers, and anoint it with my tongue. I want to hear all your sweet sounds of pleasure as I take you to a level of ecstasy you have never experienced before. I want to make you come over and over again, climaxing so hard you'll beg me to stop, swearing you'll die if you come even just once more. But I won't stop, sweetheart. No. I'll keep going until you come on my tongue just to prove how strong you really are."

Emma's breathing so hard now she's practically panting. Her cheeks are bright pink, her mouth open slightly, her tongue peeking out to hungrily swipe at her lower lip. She grinds her pelvis up into mine, giving a delectable little moan when she feels how hard I am for her. She bites her lower lip, her eyes glittering. "Then what?"

I drop kisses on her eyes, and nose, down her neck, giving little nips and nibbles between words that make her wiggle underneath me in the most delicious ways. "Then, I'll tangle my fists in your gorgeous, long hair and slide my cock into your sweet pussy, giving it to you slowly, inch by inch, making you beg for more. When I'm finally seated inside, I'll ride you slow and sweet, so I can hear you sigh and purr, then, when we can't take it anymore, harder and faster. I'll fling your legs over my shoulders and pound you so deep you feel every inch of me for days after we're done. I'll fuck you so good that when you orgasm around my cock, you'll scream my name so loud they'll hear you in China. And when I can't take the ecstasy any longer, I'll come inside you, filling you so full and riding you so good you come again. And when we're done, and we're both panting and breathless and dripping sweat, I'll start all over again from the beginning until we both pass out from exhaustion."

Emma closes her eyes and breathes a barely audible, "Yes, please..."

Christ going commando. What the fuck do I do now?

Those two little words shock me. I thought if she knew the depths of my passion, it would frighten her, but all I've managed to do is turn her on more. My cock is raging, my balls drawn up and ready to burst. I sigh sadly, knowing this fantasy will never become a reality. I take a hard swallow, and position myself to look into Emma's lust-filled eyes. I place my hand gently on her cheek, letting my thumb caress her soft skin.

"Emma, you asked me what I want, and *that's* what I want. But I can't. *We* can't. As much as I want you, you aren't mine to have. We are playing with fire, Emma, and I care about you too much to let you get burned."

I flop over onto my side facing her. She's silent for a while as she stares up at the ceiling, the gravity of the truth sinking in. Just as I'm going to ask if she's okay, she turns on her side and looks at me, her eyes huge and shining.

"I want you to be my first, Declan," she whispers as she laces her fingers through mine. "I want you to be my only."

Sweet Jesus on a jet ski, she is going to be the motherfucking death of me.

I close my eyes as her words slide into my heart like a knife. She wants me as much as I want, no, it's more than want, as much as I *need* her. We're playing a game of Russian roulette but with five of the six chambers containing bullets. As much as I want to claim her, to make her mine and have all our fantasies come true, it's simply not possible. We are from two different worlds, only together in this stolen season through the grace of God and a cruel twist of Fate. We are the bird and fish that fall in love but have nowhere to create a home.

During the past sixteen years, if I were to find the mystical genie in a bottle that's willing to grant me one wish, I would have had the same request every single time. But not today.

Today, I want something more than revenge.

I want to live every minute of the rest of my life with Emma.

42

I WAKE WITH Emma entangled in my arms, our fingers laced together, the first traces of day casting soft shadows over her sleeping form. I brush the pad of my thumb over her hand, savoring the feel of the taut skin and dainty bones. I commit to memory the sinewy muscle and delicate rope-like tendons. I marvel over the gentle rise and fall of her knuckles and cringe at the scabs and scars exposing nearly half a decade of desperation and self-harm.

I feel almost guilty studying her hands as she sleeps, something about the notation of every freckle, every scar, almost perverse in its scrutiny. Yet I find myself unable to stop. My study goes beyond a lesson of anatomy, of remembering Latin-based terminology and becoming one of art appreciation. I memorize the subtle color difference around the beds of her nails, and the change in texture between the satin smoothness of the back of her hand and the light calluses on her palms.

Even with their scars, scabs and bitten-down quicks, these hands are beautiful. Rodin could not have sculpted a hand more lovely. The hands Michelangelo painted on the Sistine Chapel? Nowhere near the complex beauty of the ones I scrutinize. The tale these hands tell is one that could never be properly put to words, even Shakespeare unable to give them justice in a sonnet.

I lift her hand to my mouth as I open her palm, a pale orchid blooming against the background of my larger scarred hand. I close my eyes and press my lips to the center tenderly, the way one would kiss the ring of a beloved Queen. This simple act of devotion is a wordless promise, my sacred vow, to protect, honor, and worship her for as long as she allows. This chaste moment is, by far, the most intimate of my life.

Emma purrs sleepily, my kiss waking her; a faint, sated smile playing at the corners of her mouth. Her hair is mussed, her lips puffy from last night's fevered kissing. Her eyes are glazed with sleep, her lids heavy as she leans in and presses her lips over my heart. She runs her hands through the dark hair on my chest as she works her lips one lingering kiss at a time towards mine.

There's no frenzied urgency to our explorations this morning, both of us content to slowly enjoy one another in the sunshine. We are warm and comfortable wrapped in a tangle of sheets and blankets, our expedition of one another somehow managing to be both lazy and detailed. Hours pass, our means of communication remaining nonverbal, the occasional sigh of contentment or quiet moan of pleasure the only soundtrack to our morning play.

For a long while, we lie staring into each other's eyes as our hands ghost over each other's half-dressed bodies. I caress her cheek, smoothing an errant hair behind her ear, before reverently tracing my fingers down her throat like one reading the Bible in braille.

Emma props herself up onto one elbow, her pretty, peach nipples hard and eager to be touched. My hands ache to stroke them, my mouth watering for another taste of their satin texture. As I reach for her she intercepts my hand and laces her fingers through mine. She studies the damage without comment, her face devoid of the horror and disgust most people can't help but express when faced with disfigurement.

"Will you tell me how it happened?"

I knew at some point she was going to ask and I really, really don't want to tell her. It's certainly not on my top ten list of favorite stories to share, especially not while in bed with a beautiful woman. It's a tale that doesn't paint me in the best light in a number of shameful ways. Despite trying not to, my body stiffens at her request. Emma senses my reluctance and turns my wrist over so my forearm's up and studies the deep brand on my arm before touching it gently. I shudder at the touch.

"Does it still hurt?"

"No. I think it's just some form of sensory pain memory. Some-times it burns, sometimes it itches, but that's just nerve damage." My tone is clinical. I can handle talking about physical pain and what I'd been through pretty casually. It's the emotional and mental stuff that shreds me.

"So, it is true. You did time in prison," Emma states matter-of-fac-tually, trying to get me to restart my story. I want to discuss these years with her as much as I want a fire-ant enema, but in all honesty, she deserves to know. Because it was those years that made me the monster I am today, and I want her to clearly see the sort of demon she's gotten herself into bed with. Literally.

I let out a long slow breath. "No, baby, I didn't go to prison. I went to hell."

I was a minor, just a few days over fifteen years-old. Nothing more than a terrified kid on the cusp of puberty. If I had been an adult I would have certainly gotten some form of horrific medieval-style death sentence but I was mucking everything up for them by being underage.

When I went before the tribunal, I was shocked to find I had been charged with everything they could think of, including the death of the two patrolmen my dad killed. It was clear the State planned to make an example of me. The piper wanted payment and I was the only one still alive who could pony up the dough.

Fathers shall not be put to death because of their children, nor shall children be put to death because of their fathers. Each one shall be put to death for his own sin. Deuteronomy 24:16. Well, that's how the text *should* read. However, they twisted the words up and that allowed them to charge me with everything. The law also read they couldn't kill me outright because I was well under the age of eighteen, so I was sentenced to stay in maximum security until I was twenty-one.

Six fucking years.

The prison guards took one look at me and laughed out loud. They told me I had better odds winning the lottery than making it out of there alive. Still recovering from the beating I took outside the cabin, I felt every bit the hot mess I appeared. I couldn't see out of one eye that was still swollen shut and I couldn't run because I'd been kicked so hard in the knee that it looked like I had a baseball shoved under the skin. I had numerous broken ribs. I was scrawny, just an innocent kid in a place that was going to eat me alive. I was scared shitless.

I always thought that prisons were places that try to better criminals, that the point of incarceration was to rehabilitate inmates into productive members of society. Boy, was I wrong. I walked into that prison as innocent as a week-old fawn. I learned how to be a criminal *in* prison.

The overcrowded facility was the most disgusting, filthy place I had ever seen and housed the most unrepentant and vicious felons imaginable. Many of these men would serve out the rest of their lives there, and after decades of living in that shithole, had become even more violent and deranged than when they'd arrived. With nothing to do to pass the time, they amused themselves by trying to maim and kill one another.

The guards? They didn't give a shit what happened as long as the attacks weren't against them. Most of them were lazy and stupid, too busy placing bets when inmates fought to be bothered to break them up. A lot of them were twisted fuckers too, and more than willing to turn a blind eye when one of their co-workers wanted some "alone-time" with an inmate. The warden did nothing to stop them; in all honesty, he was the worst sexual predator of them all.

Unable to defend myself, it was open season on me from the second I walked through the door. I went through the worst kinds of hell in there, getting the shit kicked out of me every day. After a few months I was close to starvation because my food was almost always stolen from me. The guards did nothing to help except keep me in practice of being in severe pain should I manage to make it a few days without an inmate getting a hold of me. At least inmates could only beat me with their fists. The guards had any number of fun tools at their disposal to aid in my "reeducation."

As if the days weren't bad enough, the nights were much, much worse. Every night I would try to find a dark corner, curl up into a ball and pray no one found me. The inmates did things to me in the dark that you could never in a million years imagine unless there's something really, really wrong with you. I lost my innocence to a gang of sick bastards within the first forty-eight hours. It only took two weeks before I was so mentally and physically damaged I tried to kill myself with repeated stabs to my jugular with a broken plastic spoon. I was that desperate for a way out.

That was when I caught the warden's eye, the fat fuck looking like someone rang the goddamn dinner bell when I was escorted into his office the next day. The guard laughed as he left the room with me having no clue what was so funny. I expected a lecture on the evils of suicide, and ended up with him busting a nut in my ass. I became his new toy during the day while at night, I was a plaything for the most feared inmates.

We rarely got showers or fresh clothes, the smell of too many unwashed bodies in too tight a place repulsive, to say the least. Disease ran rampant along with the lice and rats and eventually I got really sick. I laid delirious in my own filth for about a week before someone complained I was stinking up the place. I had to literally be dragged to the infirmary. I had been inside about six months at that point. That's when I met John for the first time.

I feel Emma's expression change against my chest. No, sweetheart, he wasn't an inmate. He was the prison's doctor.

I had already gone feral at this point, the beatings and sexual abuse fucking with my brain. John tried to take my pulse and I bit him. Hard. The guards came in and started beating me for doing that but John stopped them. I stayed in the infirmary for weeks. John only had very rudimentary medicines at his disposal, so he had his work cut out for him when it came to patching me back together. He worked his ass off to save me, not that I wanted him to. I repeatedly begged John to kill me. Don't fix me, just *end* me. Of course, he refused to listen and eventually I got better. After a while, he couldn't make any more excuses to keep me in the infirmary and I got sent back to general population. This vicious cycle was my life the first two years.

Between malnutrition, the beatings, abuse and a chronic lack of sleep, I was a late bloomer. I was at everyone's mercy until I finally grew up a little more, put on a few more inches and gained some weight. When I stopped looking like a kid the warden and the pedophiles lost interest in me as fresher, younger meat was incarcerated. They assigned me to work digging mass graves and repairing the crumbling border walls, and as I got stronger and put on some muscle, the smaller guys that liked to fuck with me got smart and backed off.

By the time I was eighteen there were only three or four guys that still dared to mess with me. Just to make things clear that I was done being everyone's punching bag, I started to retaliate against the inmates that had made my life hell. I planned my attacks, using the element of surprise to take them down one at a time. Even though I was ruthless, I didn't have it in me to do the sick things they had done to me. If a shrink had studied me at that point, it would have been tough to say how off-the-charts crazy I had become. I don't think I ever crossed the line to being a true sociopath. I think that in order for that to happen, the crazy has to be born into you. My kind of insanity was solely a result of my environment.

After I put a few guys in the infirmary, my reputation for being a hothead spread. I was nasty and vindictive, a real loose cannon. I only looked out for myself. If some poor dude was getting gang raped or beaten to a bloody pulp, well, I wasn't sticking my neck on the line for him because no one had done it for me. I sure as shit didn't want any of these sick career criminals as friends so I kept to myself. There were a few guys over the years thrown in jail for bullshit charges and we'd talk occasionally if I was in the mood. They knew not to approach me. Anytime someone came near me, I lashed out. I beat the shit out of a guy one time who, I found out later, only wanted to borrow my lighter.

The only exception to my rule was if there were kids involved. I couldn't save them from the warden or the guards, but I could at least keep the inmates off them. A few lifers that wanted to test me found out the hard way to not touch the kids when I beat the shit out of them and removed their offending fingers while they were unconscious.

I think that was at least part of the reason why the summer after I turned nineteen I was transferred to work on a section of the wall somewhere near the Mexican border. The steel factory they sent me to was hotter than hell twenty-four hours a day. Only the biggest, toughest guys went there as the work was grueling, and unfortunately for me, I was one of the smallest and youngest.

Things got ugly for me fast. I was back to getting the shit kicked out of me almost every day and many of these guys were armed with knives they made with stuff they stole from the factory. As the new guy, I hadn't had a chance to arm myself, so I was forced to defend myself solely with my wits and fists.

My reputation as being a cocky asshole preceded me and they were ready to knock me down a few pegs the second I arrived. When they saw I wasn't much more than a teenage punk they decided they were going to make me their bitch. They came after me in groups and cornered me after dark. They liked to give me choices of how they would hurt me on a particular night and I'll tell you right now, there were no good options.

They were getting bored with just beating the shit out of me and now they wanted parts of me that I made clear were off limits. They made promises that if I just gave in to them they would back off on the beatings. I told them nothing would change my mind and to just beat me and get it over with. They gave me a choice every night and I took the beating every single time. I knew it was just a matter of time before they stopped playing games and took from me what I refused to give. It was no longer a question of *if* but *when*.

I was only there a few weeks before one crazy bastard decided he had waited long enough. I fought this sick prick right on the factory floor as fiercely as I could, but I was in bad shape by then. Even if I had been healthy, I was doomed from the start. He was twice my size and had a knife. Everyone, including the guards, stopped to watch us. People placed bets loud enough for me to hear I was getting crushed in the odds. I knew there was no way I was winning this fight without playing dirty.

The guy I was up against was the size of the Incredible Hulk and if I wanted to have a shot at survival I needed a weapon. A row of three inch diameter steel rods had just been pulled out of the fire less than ten minutes before this fucker took a stab at me. Not thinking clearly and forgetting I had already removed my heat-resistant gloves, I reached over and grabbed one of the rods with my bare hand.

Yeah, not the smartest decision of my life.

I fell to the ground as the metal flash-fried my hand but not until after I shoved the pointy end of the rod through the other guy's eyeball. I achieved cult-like status after that. No one fucks with you when they think you're that crazy. Luckily for me, my fellow inmates didn't realize what I had done wasn't out of madness but stupidity. Nobody came near me after that.

I really fucked up my hand and the factory had no medical team, and sending a con to a public hospital was out of the question. We were lucky to get fed; they sure as shit weren't paying for medical care. Unable to work, I got sent back to the same crappy prison where I started. By the time transport got me back there, the burn was so badly infected they wanted to amputate my hand above the wrist. I went fucking ballistic, knowing full well I would never survive the rest of my sentence with one hand.

John happened to be there that day. He calmed me down and said if I promised to not bite him again he would try to save my hand. I was in the infirmary for months while he tried to piece what was left of it back together.

The pain from that hideous infected burn was the worst I'd ever known. Trust me, I've felt every possible form of torture before I was even old enough to legally drink, so I'm kind of an expert. As convicts, we weren't allowed pain meds so everything John did was beyond excruciating. He tried to smuggle in some Vicodin for me one time, and for his effort, he got a beating from the guards neither he or I will ever forget.

After what he tried to do for me we kind of became friends, but I think he thought of me more as a really messed up kid brother. I confided in him one day that I always wanted to be a doctor. I eventually told him about my parents and how I watched them die and I cried like a baby for the first time in years. I told him I wanted my life back.

John saw I still had a sliver of humanity in me and he was determined to save me. He somehow managed to get me permanently moved to be his assistant at the infirmary. He never told me what he did to make that happen, but he must have called in the mother of all favors. He's the only reason I'm still alive today.

John figured out the gaps in my education and started to train me. He taught me not only medicine, but brought me books to read to help pass the time. He talked to me about God and forgiveness and we debated Bible passages while we worked. Although not the type of reading material I loved, I was hard up for ways to pass the hours, so I read the Bible he smuggled in for me cover to cover several times. John had joked that if medicine didn't work out for me and I could handle the celibacy, I now had the skills to be a kick-ass renegade priest.

When my sentence was up, he brought me home to meet his wife and they asked me to move in with them. He was still looking out for me, even though I was a volatile piece of shit most of the time. I stole from him, got drunk regularly and did any and all drugs I could get my hands on. I brought home prostitutes and fucked them loudly in their house. Sometimes I took off for weeks at a time because I knew I couldn't be around people without getting in trouble. I got into a lot of fights.

Yet no matter how many times I broke their hearts, John and Marta never gave up on me. When I had my act together, John continued to train me at the clinic. When he let me do more than just simple sutures and wrap sprained limbs I behaved better. I began to take pride in my work, drank less, cut out most of the drugs and quit smoking.

When I was ready, John let me assist him in surgery. I took out my first appendix when I was twenty-three. Over time, I learned how to piece people back together after gunshot wounds and near-fatal beatings. I delivered babies and saved women bleeding out from backstreet abortions gone wrong. John taught me the harsh realities of medicine by making me help him bury the ones who didn't make it. Together we prayed for their souls.

We knew that if we could just get our hands on a bigger variety of better quality drugs we could save more people. There's only so much you can do with a broad spectrum antibiotic that expired two years ago and bags of IV fluids labeled *for veterinary use only.*

By now, I had gotten the job at the hospital because John stuck his neck out for me. I met Anna when she came to me for PT after one of her knee surgeries. She liked to tip me in weed so I knew she had connections. Eventually I broke down and asked her where she got it and she told me about the underground markets. I told her what we needed and she got me in touch with people who could smuggle it in. The tunnels by the old Union Station are some of the most dangerous in the area not just because of increased security, but also the huge number of criminals hiding out looking for an easy score. I was the only one working at the clinic with no kids or family, so I volunteered to be our one-man drug procurement team.

I started working and playing harder and I was having fun for the first time in well over a decade. It scared me. I had entire days where I didn't think about my parents' deaths or my time in prison. I almost forgot what real pain was and that scared me even more. I started getting inked because I wanted to remember my heritage, my parents, my family. I wanted to remember the pain, the loss, the trauma. It would be an unspeakable tragedy for me to forget everyone and everything I lost.

"Then I met you." I rub my hand against Emma's arm and take her hand in mine, placing it flat on the center of my chest. Although I still can't say it, not yet, she holds my heart in the palm of her hand. I know that someday soon I'll do the most frightening thing ever and tell her that I love her. Opening myself up and making myself vulnerable to another person is the second-most terrifying thing I can think of. The only thing more devastating would be if I were somehow to lose her.

43

Emma

I wake to the shrill ringing of what sounds like an air-raid siren before I realize it's my telephone. It takes a few seconds for me to realize I'm no longer in Declan's modest home, but back in my gilded cage.

I answer the summon with a sleepy and irritated "What?" I'm cranky, already feeling the effects of Declan withdrawal even though I only left him a few hours ago. Since that first weekend we spent together, I have done everything in my power to see him as often as I can. Sometimes it's only meeting up for a quick kiss but we've managed a few more nights together here and there when Ryan was out of town. So far, I don't think anyone's the wiser, but my anxiety of being found out heightens with each undetected return.

My crankiness only worsens when Ryan's bitchy social secretary informs me I'm being picked up for a multi-day visit to the Executive Mansion within the hour. I groan, knowing I don't have it in me to play my role for three straight days.

I pack only a small bag of toiletries and other essentials knowing all my clothes, or should I say costumes, will be delivered to the

Mansion. Tim, Ryan's long-time, dutiful driver, arrives with a bag containing my outfit for the day and a request for me to please change quickly. He always has a bit of an antsy quality to him, but today something's got him positively twitchy.

The suit I'm supposed to wear is a lovely shade of deep strawberry pink with wide navy lapels. It's very conservative in cut and has a cool, vintage couture feel. In the bag are matching pink and navy heels and a tiny box-like pink hat that I'm not sure how to wear; a pair of short white gloves finish the ensemble. The overall effect is modest, retro-chic, if a bit too subdued for my taste. My new stylist certainly has different taste than what Caitlin used to pick, but it fits well and is beautifully made. Tim takes one look at me in the suit and flashes a wide, laughing smile as he helps me adjust the hat. Apparently, he likes the look as every time he lays eyes on me, he grins like a fool.

The ride to the Mansion is interrupted only by picking up Ryan, who spends the rest of the ride on the phone in agitated conversation. He's wearing a dark navy suit with a tie that coordinates with my dress.

We match. How sweet.

Right before entering the gated drive, Ryan ends his call and acknowledges me. Judging by what I overheard, he isn't expecting the next few days to be easy. He's fidgety and tense, two words not usually associated with his usually unflappable demeanor. I hope whatever is on his mind occupies him enough to keep pummeling me into the floorboards a low priority.

"We have a very important few days ahead of us. I need you to be perfect, do you understand me?"

I nod, keeping my eyes lowered. "Yes, sir."

He curses under his breath, my response apparently not what he wanted. "As much as I like you submissive, cut that shit out for the next few days in front of our guests. I want you to be the fucking poster-child of dutiful, silent wives. Watch your manners. And if any of them try to lure information out of you, you tell me immediately. Do you understand?"

"Yes, of course, darling." I plaster a syrupy smile on my face as my eyes shoot daggers at him. He doesn't look at all pleased with that response either, but before he can retaliate, his phone buzzes. He takes his frustration out on the poor bastard that picked the absolute wrong moment to call him with what sounds like more bad news.

When our car pulls up in front of the stately white mansion I am impressed by the old charm of the building that somehow withstood most of the Capitol riots of years past. Once inside, I am immediately deposited into a side drawing room to wait for my performance to begin. I know I should sit quietly and read the copy of *The New State Text* that's been left on the table for me, but I'm too curious about the large historic home to not give myself a tour of the room.

The interior is decked out with enough gold leaf to feed Declan's entire community for the rest of their lives, the thick velvet drapes and over-sized furniture making the spacious rooms feel cramped. The gaudiness of the interior makes the building seem tired, much like an old woman clinging to youth by wearing too much makeup. I wish I could have seen it before the decorators turned the poor old building into a gilded whore; the grand dame must have been beautiful in her day.

I'm studying the brushstrokes on yet another portrait of an unattractive, unsmiling man when the door opens, catching me by surprise. A man about Declan's age strides into the room, a smile lighting his pretty blue eyes and triggering the deep dimples in his cheeks. He's tall and muscular with thick, dark blonde hair, his sun-kissed skin supple and smooth. His navy uniform is perfectly tailored, the left side of his jacket heavy with meritorious service medals. If the National Ideal were ever to have a physical embodiment, it would absolutely be him.

"Good morning, Miss Bellamy. I'm Apprentice Archon Alex Smith. I'm going to explain what is going to happen during your stay and what your role is in the festivities. May I get you some tea before we begin?"

He flashes his even white smile as his eyes study me. They appraise every detail, making me feel strangely naked under his scrutiny. He momentarily frowns as he checks out my suit before catching himself and replacing it with the same wide smile that no longer seems as sincere.

"No, thank you. I am just fine." There's a moment of awkward silence as he continues to stare. "Is something wrong? Am I not dressed appropriately?"

He turns fifty shades of red as he shakes his head, that toothy smile getting wider as his eyes look more troubled. "You look lovely, Miss Bellamy. I'm just surprised your stylist picked. . . ." He stops mid-sentence, clearing his throat as he reaches into his pocket and pulls out a roll of antacids. He pops three in his mouth and chews frantically. I wonder what he was going to say but I don't dare ask.

The rest of our time together is pleasant, and I'm surprised to find that after he relaxes a bit, I actually enjoy his company. He's witty and smart, a wealth of knowledge and quick to laugh. He even gives me a full tour of the public rooms of the building, pointing out exotic and rare antiques and telling me funny stories about the building's many important visitors. Despite our time together being rather delightful, I can't get over the odd start to our meeting. As much as I hate to think it, I conclude he's a watcher.

I chide myself for the uncharitable thought. Yes, he's very young to be of such high rank, but certainly not everyone gets where they are through nefarious means. After all, nepotism runs rampant among the uber-wealthy; a powerful father does wonders for a career in the Supreme Archon's lair. Of course, it is also possible he genuinely earned the position through hard work and ardent patriotism. I guess I'll never know for sure. It's not like I'm going to ask.

But regardless of how nice he seems, he's not my friend. So, I keep my tone light and my words reverent when I speak of my father and Ryan. I have no idea if he believes my lies, but I force out the words with a smile so when he reports to his superiors, it can at least be said I spouted the party line.

Before he leaves, he gives me another of his award-winning smiles. "I have thoroughly enjoyed my time with you today, Miss Bellamy. I hope we can spend more time together in the near future."

I have no idea what to say to that. Is he flirting with me or just being friendly? Is he trying to lure me into saying something unwise? He's waiting for my reply and I've got nothing to say that won't somehow bite me in the ass. I give him a tight grin and simply nod my head, for once following Ryan's command. In this situation, I have no doubt, the less I say the better.

44

Ryan

Is this fucking day ever going to end?

I'm exhausted and thoroughly annoyed, my day starting off badly and getting exponentially worse with each passing hour. It all started at 5 am when I got a call from Bellamy's bitch secretary saying he's had some sort of emergency and isn't able to meet the delegates arriving this morning. When I tried to call him, his phone went straight to voicemail.

Asshole.

He knows diplomacy is not my strong point. Just like the Supreme Archon, I am a no-nonsense say-it-as-I-see-it kind of guy, and these extortionist rice-eaters from hell all want to be handled with kid gloves. To top it all off, this is no social call. They're pissed. They want their money and they want it now, and I have nothing to give them. Today's sessions were less of a civilized summit and more like a gang of 1920's Chicago mobsters threatening to break my kneecaps with a baseball bat.

When our economy tanked years ago and they tried to collect on their loans, some genius thought that instead of cash, we should repay our massive debt with natural resources. Everyone thought it was a great idea. Oil, soybeans, pork and beef were in high demand in their country and we had plenty to share.

The problem with this plan didn't surface until a few years later when our cash crops stopped producing. Out of nowhere, we were hit with multiple years of horrific storms and all forms of new diseases and invasive pests that wiped out entire seasons of produce. Overseas scientists have stated it's due to global climate change and the after effects of nuking a few west coast cities that continued to refuse to submit to the Supreme Archon's command. Our own experts have vehemently claimed it's due to nothing we have done, and the Supreme Pontiff said it's retribution from an angry God displeased by a nation full of sinners. If that is indeed the case, things will turn around shortly after I take my seat on the throne and I weed out the remaining reasons for our continued punishment.

My agricultural advisers are saying this year will bring another poor harvest of soy and wheat and the virulent, antibiotic-resistant disease running rampant in the giant pig farms in the Carolinas has taken the lives of another half million porkers. So, in order to meet our quota, we will have to dip into the food supply ear-marked for our own population and these cocksuckers don't give a shit if we starve as long as they get their promised share. I know what they are trying to do. They are hoping a starving population will rise up and overthrow our government, leaving us easy picking for annexation.

Fuck them. Before I let them take even an acre of land, I'll nuke this fucking country until even the cockroaches beg for mercy.

Our country is failing and failing fast. China is ready to dismantle us one star and stripe at a time and turn us into another Russia. I refuse to see us become another nameless country whose only purpose is to feed the ever-growing wealth, power and population of their Imperialist Nation. No, that's not going to happen. Not on *my* watch.

They think they are so smart, but little do they know, I have a foolproof way to solve our soaring debt issue without paying back one fucking red cent.

Is it legal? No.

Moral? Hell, no.

But will it work?

Abso-fucking-lutely.

Once I'm the Supreme Archon, I will finally have enough power to point and wield that heavy sword alone. When I'm done, my people will not only look at me as a Supreme Leader, but as their Savior. But until the old man croaks, my hands are tied. I told my fellow Committee members they have just one job and that's to keep the Chinese off my back for just a while longer. That's all I ask and apparently they can't even do that.

Useless fucks are more trouble than they're worth. They better watch it, or they'll be the first ones I pink slip via car bomb when I'm sitting on the throne.

Because of their ineptitude, I spent eight hours today in a circle-jerk with these dumpling-eating assholes while they squeezed my nuts so hard I thought a diamond might shoot out of my ass. Don't they realize I have more important things to do with my time? Just last week, a group of unemployed factory workers blew up a warehouse at our largest food storage facility in Philadelphia. An entire shipment of corn, soy and wheat scheduled for export is currently rotting at the bottom of the Schuylkill river, feeding nothing but the two-headed fish that swim in that diseased cesspool.

Fucking Philadelphia. No matter how many times we bomb that city, the well-organized group that calls themselves *The BSB*, whatever the fuck that means, continues to be a massive pain in my ass. It just may be time to shut that shithole city down for good.

This terrorist group has no idea how much worse things are going to get after pulling this stunt. Thousands of American citizens are dying of complications from starvation every day, and the less we send overseas, the less we can keep to feed ourselves. They've cut off their nose to spite their face, and when their bellies are empty this winter, they are going to be unjustly pissed at *me* as they suffer the ramifications of *their* actions.

That means in a few months, my job is only going to get harder. Anyone who ever heard of the French Revolution knows starving people are historically the first to revolt. Even without offering them cake, a number of rebel groups have already called for my head on a spike. But unlike Marie Antoinette, I have a fuck ton of nukes to protect myself in my own little Versailles. For now, I'm safe but the old man needs to do us all a favor and drop dead. Soon.

It might be time to give him a push in the right direction.

I tie my bow tie for the fifteenth time and still can't get the damned thing straight. Emma enters the living room from her bedroom across the suite we're sharing, probably wondering why I'm uncharacteristically late. Now, despite being dog-ass tired, I have to put up with Little Miss Sunshine because her fucking father demanded her presence at tonight's formal reception. She spent the day touring the house and sipping tea while I was getting financially gang-raped for hours on end. Fucking woman has no idea how good she's got it.

My head is pounding. I pour myself a generous helping of scotch and down it like a shot. After two more, I feel a little better. When I look over, Emma's looking at me with the oddest expression.

"What the fuck do you want?"

"You look upset." She fiddles with the clasp on the thick diamond bracelet around her wrist. "Is there anything I can do to help?"

I'm shocked by her response. That's the last thing I expect her to say. I glare at her hatefully but I don't get her usual cowering response. Normally a solid withering look from me is enough to make her quake, but today it doesn't. She cocks her head to the side, eyeing me in my tuxedo. She walks right up to me and straightens my crooked tie so it sits perfectly. We stand there for a moment, silently appraising one another.

I know she's up to something—she's never this cordial. Without another word, I take her hand and weave it through my arm. It's time for us to make our entrance. I'll figure out what the sneaky bitch is up to later.

The Governor is already there when we enter. He's laughing, smiling and entertaining the delegates with Apprentice Smith at his side. Bellamy's flavor of the week stands beside him laughing at his joke, her navy blue sequined gown casting little prisms of light across the room. Her back is to me, but I don't have to see her face to know she's gorgeous. That old bastard is only seen with the most beautiful women while his feeble-minded wife sits at home getting wasted. I feel a fresh surge of hate for him as I glare at his daughter.

Bellamy and Smith are acting positively chummy in a way so unlike our failed attempts of civility. There's almost something fatherly in Bellamy's interactions with the young soldier, a warmth he's never shown to me. I don't even realize I've tightened my grip on Emma's arm until she squeaks in protest. Right now, I don't know if I hate Smith or Bellamy more.

Bellamy claps Smith on the shoulder, laughing at something he said as Smith turns to the delegates, adding something in Mandarin. The delegates roar with laughter. I had no idea Smith spoke their language. Unless you have a job as an official State translator, speaking foreign languages has been illegal for nearly a decade. We have one official language in this country and it is American. This kid's daring to break the law and Bellamy's allowing it. Tomorrow, I most certainly will address this.

Great. Just add that to my growing list of shit to do.

The laughter in the room subsides and the atmosphere cools considerably after Emma and I are announced. Bellamy's date wanders off in the direction of the restrooms as he saunters over and shakes my hand. Even though there's a smile on his face, his eyes blaze with anger.

Fuck him.

If he's pissed about the outcome of the meetings today, he should have been here. I remind myself to ask him where the fuck he had been that was so important he couldn't bother to show up and do his damn job.

Bellamy turns from me and kisses his daughter's cheek, leading her towards the delegates. She's charming and sweet and the men fucking *love* her. Bellamy gushes over her like he actually gives a shit, telling the men she's a gifted dancer, and he would love for them to come for another visit, as his *guests*, to watch her perform.

What. The. Fuck?

The delegates eat this shit up with a spoon while Emma blushes at the unexpected compliments and Smith ogles her like he's never seen a pair of tits before.

I'm going to have to keep an eye on him.

Bellamy turns to me with a look on his face that reads: *this is how you act when you owe money to someone you can't repay.*

I grab a drink off a passing tray and down it.

Yeah, that old bastard needs to hurry up and fucking die. I'm tired of playing nice.

45

Emma

The night starts off well enough despite Ryan being at least three drinks in before we even descend the stairs. The tension grows with every second he and my father share the room. Ryan's twitchy irritation is almost comical compared to my father's smooth charm. The two men stand at opposite ends of the room, their hostility evident to the men they should both be doing their best to entertain.

When Ryan wanders off to find another drink, Alex excuses himself from the delegates to stand next to me. "Miss Bellamy, you look beautiful tonight." His smile is broad and welcoming, but once again, there's something odd about the way he looks at me.

"Why, thank you Alex, you are very kind to say so. And I must add, you are looking quite handsome tonight, too."

He blushes as he swipes at an errant piece of hair that's flopped into his eyes. "Now you are being the kind one, Miss Bellamy -"

"Alex, please. Call me Emma. Miss Bellamy is too formal."

Ryan comes back with another drink in hand, his eyes already glazed and a bit unfocused. Before he reaches us, Alex excuses himself, obviously not wanting to be anywhere near Ryan, not that I blame him. The clasp on my bracelet comes apart again and I fiddle with it for a few seconds before Ryan elbows me and nods towards the door. I excuse myself and head to the hallway to find someone to repair it. My head's down as I continue to try to fix it myself so I don't see the woman walking my way until I nearly slam into her.

"Sugar, you really need to watch where you're goin'."

I look up in shock to find Caitlin dressed to perfection in a blue sequined gown, her hair up and her ears and neck dripping in diamonds. She has a funny little smirk on her face and a nasty glint in her eye.

"Caitlin? What are you doing here?"

"What? You think I'm not good enough to be here?"

I stare at her in bewilderment. "No, that's not what I said. Ryan told me you got another job but I don't understand. . ."

Caitlin laughs cruelly. "Yeah, honey, I got another job. It pays better, I get to go to all the important events and party with the rich and famous now. I even have my own stylist."

Okay. . . I'm still not putting the pieces together as to why she's *here*. "That's great, Caitlin." I keep my voice light to hopefully defuse some of her antagonized tone. "Who are you working for?"

Her lip curls up in a devious half-smile. "Your father."

Caitlin grabs me by the wrist and drags me away from the ballroom. I am beyond confused. Yes, my father paid her salary as my stylist, but now that I'm under Ryan's care, he provided me with a new one. So why is Caitlin still getting paid by. . . .

Oh. OOOOH.

My cheeks start to burn as I realize how Caitlin is earning her keep. "Please tell me this is a joke. Please tell me you aren't sleeping with my father."

She laughs without mirth. "I keep tellin' your daddy you aren't as dumb as you look. I had a feelin' you'd figure things out right quick once you saw me here."

The room starts to spin like I might faint. I stumble back a step as snippets of the last few months pop into my mind. "How long has this been going on?"

"Oh, it's been a while. A little over a year now, I suppose. Your daddy treats me real good, Emma. I have no intentions of lettin' him slip through my fingers."

I gape at her in shock before the building anger inside of me takes control. "But he's married," I somehow manage to both state and ask at the same time.

"So? Your mamma isn't takin' care of him, so I'm steppin' in to do it for her. If she wasn't a lush, if she understood him and his needs, he wouldn't need me in his life."

I have no idea what comes over me but I pull back my arm and slap her as hard as I can. The impact of my hand striking her cheek sounds like an explosion as she staggers back towards the wall with her hand against her face. My bracelet comes off when I hit her and when I reach for it where it lies on the floor, I see it's spotted with blood. I look at Caitlin and see she's bleeding, the broken clasp leaving a narrow slice in her cheek.

"You bitch," she hisses. "How fuckin' dare you." She strides towards me, her face contorted in rage. "He's already told me when the divorce goes through, he's gonna marry me. When I'm your new step-mamma, you're gonna wish you'd never been born."

I laugh bitterly. "Jesus Christ, Caitlin. You can't possibly be stupid enough to believe that. He's not going to marry you. If my father married every whore he screwed I'd have a hundred mothers by now."

Caitlin looks like she's two seconds away from lunging at me. I wrap my bracelet around my hand like a pair of brass knuckles, preparing to fight. Caitlin's a fair bit bigger than me, but I'm stronger and faster. If she lays a finger on me, I'll let her have it.

"Well, if that ain't the pot callin' the kettle names. Honey, if I'm a whore for what I'm doin' you best color yourself the same shade. Only difference I see is you've got a ring on your finger and I don't.

When you're married, Ryan's gonna provide for you, buy you all sorts of pretty dresses, all the jewels you want, and you'll never want for nothin'. How's that any different than what I'm doin'?"

"I'm nothing like you," I spit between clenched teeth. "You're nothing more than a two-bit opportunistic whore. I can't believe I was ever friends with you."

She laughs, a cruel sound I have never heard from her before. "We were never friends, Emma. My *job* was to make you pretty and tell your daddy what you were up to. In the beginning I felt bad for doin' it, but after a few months of listening to you whinin' and bitchin' about how hard your life is even I wanted to strangle you. I had a feelin' at some point you were gonna do somethin' stupid and sure enough, you did. Let me tell you, your Daddy was none too pleased when I gave him that ID card I found in your jeans."

I am speechless. The fake ID was in the pocket of my jeans that I threw in the incinerator. I know I burned it, just like Declan told me to.

Wait.

Had I been so sure it was still in the pocket that I didn't check? Shit. No, I didn't.

It had never dawned on me that Caitlin would go through my things looking for ways to hurt me. I had been such a fool. All this time, I never once suspected Caitlin. My stomach drops with a wave of nausea that almost consumes me.

"What I didn't understand was why he wanted me to stay quiet? It was his duty to turn you in but he didn't. You needed to be punished. That's why I snuck into your daddy's office and faxed a copy to Ryan. Someone needed to hold you accountable for your actions, and I knew he would."

She's so busy gloating she doesn't see the punch coming. I catch her square in the nose, the diamond bracelet adding extra oomph to the blow. Blood sprays everywhere as the bone cracks under my knuckles and the platinum prongs holding in the giant diamonds dig into her skin. She howls as she tries to staunch the blood and tears that flow between her fingers.

"You fucking cunt!" I scream as I shove her against the wall. Everything that happened in the past weeks, my fellow company members that paid the ultimate price, the beating I sustained, Declan's nearly fatal assault and banishment—fucking *everything,* is because of her.

"Do you have any idea what you've done? Of the people that are *dead* because of you?" The murderous rage that has taken over my brain begs me to keep beating her until she's no more than a stain on the carpet but somehow, I keep it at bay. I am shaking from head to toe, my index finger pointing angrily in her face.

"Stay the fuck away from me, you bitch. If you ever come near me again, so help me, I'll kill you."

I catch my reflection in the hall mirror and don't even recognize myself. I feel sick and horrified that when provoked, my first instinct is to lash out with my fists just like Ryan. I feel absolutely defeated. As long as women feel the need to use one another, to bring each other down to raise themselves up, our sex has no chance of ever overcoming the oppression that keeps us enslaved.

"I'll call a car for you, you are obviously in no condition to entertain. I'll be certain to send your regrets to my father."

"You just wait 'til I tell him what you've done. He'll hide your ass for this."

I had started to walk away but now I turn back. There's no energy in my words, only a deep sadness. I don't want to play this game, but right now, I have to make a choice. It's got to be either me or her, and for once in my life, I'm choosing to be selfish.

"You do that, Caitlin and see where it lands you. But if you squeal on me, I'll tell my father how you went behind his back to Ryan. I can tell you right now, he won't be pleased. Loyalty is a trait my father reveres above all others. Trust me, you don't want to know what happened to the last whore that double-crossed him. As far as I know, they still haven't found her body."

Caitlin blanches. "You're making that up. Also, there's no proof I did anything. Stop tryin' to scare me."

As much as she's got her bravado on, I can see she's terrified. I remain nonchalant and shrug my shoulders in ambivalence. "Caitlin, I can't make you do or not do anything, but I'm warning you, if you want a fight, I'll bring you a goddamn war."

"What the hell are you talkin' about?"

I have her scared and that's right where I need her. I sigh and give her a sad, condescending smile. "There are records of faxes that come in and out of every Committee member's office. It would only take me a few minutes to get what I need to show my father how untrustworthy you are."

I spin on my heel and walk away, Caitlin's frantic pleas for me to remain silent left unanswered. I hear her fall to the floor, still burbling out sobbing, terrified apologies as she realizes her critical error. I make my way back to the ballroom, pausing only to wipe the few drops of blood spatter on my arms on the ugly velvet curtains.

When I look up I see Alex staring at me with wide eyes that let on he heard everything. I have no idea what to do or say when he strides over and whispers, "Don't worry, your secret is safe with me. If she gives you any trouble, slugger, let me know, and I'll set her straight."

His now laughing face puts me at ease as he reaches for the blood smeared bracelet that I place in his hand. "I'll get this back to you shortly. I have a guy here that can fix this."

I breathe a sigh of relief. "Thank you, Alex. You're a Godsend, do you know that?"

He blanches, his smile disappearing and the laugh drying up in his throat. "My pleasure, Miss Bellamy. And should I call a car for Caitlin? She doesn't appear well."

I'm confused by this new formality, not sure what I said that upset him. "Yes, please. And for her sake, please, be discreet. I'm sure she's mortified enough as it is." He nods quickly and spins away from me. I'm fairly certain I hear him chuckling as he walks off.

My father gives me the oddest look as I re-enter the ballroom. "Did you see my companion while you were out there? She went to the bathroom and has been gone for a long time." He starts towards the door, obviously intent on looking for her.

I think fast, grabbing his arm and pulling him towards me conspiratorially. "Oh, Caitlin? Yes, she was in the ladies room. She has a terrible nosebleed that she can't seem to stop. She said not to worry, it happens all the time. I called a car to take her home, she's already gone."

He nods. For the first time ever, he believes my lie. My father pats me on the shoulder the way one would approvingly pat the family dog. "Good call. Thank you, Emma. Thank you for taking care of her."

Yeah, father, I took really good care of her.

I suppress a giggle. I know it's wrong, and later I'm going to again feel bad about what I've done, but right now, I bask in the sweetness of revenge and blackmail done well. I swipe a glass of champagne off a passing tray and take a large sip. Right now, I feel just a little bit stronger, a little more in charge of myself and maybe, just maybe, even a little more in control of my destiny.

46

THE REST OF MY VISIT is dull compared to the events of the first day. All of my dresses show too much skin for Ryan to even think about hitting me, and each night he gets so drunk he passes out before he can demand my attention to him in more personal ways.

I spend much of my time touring the building and the manicured grounds and reading everything I can get my hands on. Although illegal in any other part of the country, world newspapers are easy to come by in the Mansion. Like his drooling boss, Ryan is beyond paranoid about what's being written about him overseas, so every day, stacks of foreign periodicals arrive at the Mansion for an entire team to annotate. Once picked apart, the staffers leave the precious documents scattered about where they are easy for me to grab and commit to memory.

I'm fascinated at the freedom the outside press has to not only condemn our government, but to write negative stories about their own leadership, too. Until Declan told me, I never realized that most of the world not only tolerates but supports journalistic freedom. When he told me our own country had once been that way, I'd been even more amazed.

Nearly every foreign press paints a bleak picture of our country that's a far cry from what's in *The New State Press*. Leaders of over twenty different countries are demanding Ryan step down from being next in line, most of them demanding free elections and a return to democracy. Fat chance. I can tell them right now, even if God came down from Heaven and decreed the change, the Committee would never allow it. They enjoy their power too much to let even the Lord get in their way.

The worldwide press seems charmed by me, even if one of the European papers calls me "not much more than a wee child." There's apparently also some sort of irony concerning the pretty strawberry pink suit I wore. Apparently someone named Jackie wore one just like it many years ago when someone shot and killed her husband during a parade. I remind myself to ask Declan if he knows what they're talking about because I don't have a clue.

I can't wait to tell Declan everything about my trip. Brought up before the war, he knows so much more about the world than I do. Whenever I overhear something I don't understand, I ask him for clarification. He always answers me in a way that doesn't make me feel stupid, understanding they keep me, and women in general, uninformed for a reason. When I asked him what that reason was he said because we're a threat. I laughed out loud when he said that. How could anyone find women threatening? What were we going to do, knit someone to death?

It's after midnight by the time I reach Declan's apartment. I know he won't be expecting me and more than likely, I'm going to wake him up. But then I think of the ways I'll make it up to him, and I'm sure he won't mind one bit.

When I reach his apartment, I hear heated voices carrying loudly through the door. One of the voices belongs to a woman, her pleading tone readily discernible even if her words are not. Declan sounds angry, his voice clipped and harsh. He's pacing, as sometimes I can hear him better than others. He repeats the word *no*, his tone more vehement with each utterance.

The springs on the sofa creak as he sits heavily with a sigh. He sounds like he's giving in to whatever she's requesting. There's a dreadful silence from the other side of the door that terrifies me. If I walk away now, I will always wonder what was happening, and if I barge in and he has another woman in his arms, I will be shattered.

I can't take the silence any longer. The knob turns easily in my hand and the door swings open silently, surprising Declan and the heavily-tattooed woman next to him. She's gripping his hands tightly, her eyes looking pleadingly into his. He takes one look at my stunned face and jerks his hands out of the woman's grasp. I guess he realizes how bad this looks because he jumps up so quickly he stumbles, nearly flipping the coffee table in the process.

Something flashes in me that I have never felt before. I am hurt, angry and jealous. Very, very jealous.

"Who's she?" I spit.

The woman looks at me with bored disdain. "I guess that's my cue to go," she smirks. "Dec, just think about it, okay? I'll be in touch."

The woman pats me on the shoulder and pushes past me like I'm insignificant. I stare at Declan in disbelief. She'll be *in touch*? How do they know each other? Unlike me, she's so secure in her relationship with Declan she even has the audacity to use a nickname for him in front of me.

I feel like a complete and utter fool. I thought Declan and I had something special. I thought he cared for me. I thought he was falling in love with me every bit as much as I am with him. Tears spring to my eyes.

Do not cry, do not cry, do NOT cry repeats over and over in my head.

Declan grabs my arm when I try to run from the room, spinning me to face him. His eyes register my pain and I see the jumble of emotions competing for priority in his mind. In the shifting looks of guilt, fear, worry and sorrow, he ends up looking repentant.

That's great. He's remorseful. I just need to know for what.

He runs his fingers through his hair, tugging on the roots. Whatever I just walked in on he's now unable to explain except to say, "It's not how it looks."

When I finally speak my words are bitter and sarcastic. "Really? Tell me, *Dec*, how does this look to you?"

"Please, Emma, let me explain -"

"How could you do this, Declan? How?" My voice is pleading as I start to shake. As much as I don't want to cry, a tear slides down my face. He reaches forward to wipe it away with his thumb and I back away as if he slapped me.

"It's not what you think, please, you have to believe me."

His voice begs me to let him explain, but I don't want to hear what he's got to say. He's either going to lie or he's going to confess and I can't bear to hear either at this moment. Either way, his betrayal, especially on top of Caitlin's, will destroy me.

"Are you sleeping with her?"

"What? With Amy? No! Jesus Christ, Emma, please, please let me explain."

He places his hands on my biceps and looks deep into my eyes. He takes my hand and tries to lead me to the sofa, but I yank it away. I sit on the cold floor, pulling my coat protectively around me as there's no way in hell I'm going to sit on the same cushion that woman's ass just warmed. Declan sits on the edge of the coffee table, facing me, looking down at his hands. He stays silent for a long while, every moment confirming my worst fears.

"Emma, there is nothing going on between me and Amy. I swear it. Please, believe me."

"Give me one good reason why I should believe anything you say?"

I wait. He looks absolutely miserable, his eyes misting over as he carefully chooses what he's going to say next.

47

Declan

This is not how the truth was supposed to come out.

I knew at some point I was going to have to tell Emma everything, but I never dreamed it would happen like this. She isn't going to understand and she sure as shit isn't going to like it. She's going to hate me, and as much as I hate to admit it, she's got every right to.

"Emma, I'm not who you think I am."

She already knows way more about me than anyone else on the planet, other than John and Marta, of course. I'd been brutally honest about my childhood, my parents' murders and my time in prison. But that's where the truth ends and the lies of omission begin.

What I left out is that I'm an active officer in the resistance, recruited, trained and under the direct command of Anna and her wife, Amy. I volunteered to be part of the underground opposition the day I got out of prison. I had been brought into the fold by John.

I know that's a lot to digest and, right now, you better believe I'm sorry I didn't confess sooner. But I couldn't. I was under orders to keep my identity hidden and my mouth shut, and if I've learned anything in life, it's that when you disobey orders, people die. Even though I've known for a while that I could trust Emma with the cold, hard truth, I still couldn't bring myself to fess up. My loyalty to the cause prevented me from telling Emma who I really am.

Now, that decision will cost me the only woman I have ever loved.

Wait—I'm getting ahead of myself. Let me start at the beginning. The day Emma first came to the ER as a battered mess, John saw her as a rare opportunity to help our cause. As a doctor, he sees a lot of people that are in dire situations and desperately need help. He fixes them up, sure, but it's his careful questioning and fatherly kindness that gets people to trust him. He's got a sixth sense about these things, I swear. His job is recruiting new members to our cause and he just knew Emma would switch to our side as soon as she knew there was another team she could join.

That's when he asked me to get involved. I told John from the beginning I wanted nothing to do with his plan, but he twisted my arm so badly I thought it was going to break. He made me feel like a complete shit if I didn't agree to at least take her as a patient. I told him fine, but that's where my involvement *ends*. I told him I would help piece her back together but I was not going to do a damn thing to convince her to help us. I meant it.

Please, Emma, you have to believe me.

This wasn't the first time I've been given assignments like this. People think of resistance members as wearing all black and carrying guns and shooting bad guys and blowing things up. Yeah, sometimes we do that, but so much more of resistance fighting happens between the ears. It's John's freakish ability to decide who to trust, who to target, who may have information and be willing to spill it. It's Anna's ability to piece together hard won details and make plans. It's Amy's genius computer skills and dark web contacts that enable us to import the things we need as well as smuggle the most at-risk people out.

Then there's me. I'm the guy that puts those plans into action and makes shit happen.

Much of the time, my assignments require me to get information out of unwilling people. Most of the people I've targeted aren't monsters, just misinformed bigots with something I need. I've been well trained in the art of "persuasion" and combined with my knowledge of the human body, I can get even the most stalwart subjects to cough up their secrets pretty quickly. I only kill people when I have to, and even then, I do it as quickly and painlessly as they allow me.

I do what I have to because it's my job and although I act like it doesn't bother me, deep down inside, I hate being the muscle. I hate killing people. Trust me, I'm well aware of my sick hypocrisy, one minute dedicating my life to healing people and an hour later, slicing off some guy's fingers one knuckle at a time because he refuses to talk. It wasn't until I started on this path that I understood why most veterinarians I know are vegetarian.

My commanders don't give a shit how I get my information, and it didn't take me long to understand there are actually many ways to persuade someone to talk. I'm not a vain guy, but I'm not blind either. I know women find me attractive. I know if I say the right things, smile a certain way, I can have a certain effect on ladies that makes them not only drop their panties, but also their inhibitions and secrets.

If I have to get between the sheets and pretend to like someone, I do it. Most of the time my exploits in the sack are with loose-lipped wives of Directors and spouses of lower-level Committee members. I was surprised at how many rich bitches love the idea of secretly sticking it to their disinterested husbands by letting an ex-con fuck them. They never realized I was pumping them for information even as I was pumping them with my dick. As they had just as much to lose as I did by getting caught I never worried about them turning me in. Blackmail is a tremendous equalizer when used correctly.

As much as I didn't want to, I've fucked a few guys over the years, too. Often, the most fervent followers of the New State Church are the biggest hypocrites when it comes to homosexuality. There were a few high-up leaders in both the church and government that were pretty twisted in the sack and eager for a tight-lipped fuck buddy. After a while, guilty consciences or stupidity caused them to spill secrets, usually after, and even a few times while their dick was crammed down my throat.

Fucking dudes is most certainly not my idea of a good time, to put it mildly. It often brings back weeks' worth of flashbacks and nightmares from prison, but if me taking it up the ass from time to time will help us retake the country, I feel like in the long run, it's a small price for me to pay.

Turning Emma was one of only a handful of assignments over the course of ten years I refused. It was too dangerous. *She* was too dangerous. There were too many factors playing into flipping her that made taking her on more of a suicide mission than a recon assignment. One misstep and I was a dead man. And as reckless as I sometimes am, I'm not ready to die yet.

I only refuse assignments when I feel they are unnecessarily risky, and even then, I often find myself getting talked into them. I'll be the first to admit I'm still so consumed with the need for revenge that if someone said I had to drown a bag of kittens to get the world right, I would do it without blinking. I would hate myself forever and it would haunt me until my dying day, but yes, I would do it. I joined the resistance all those years ago not for noble reasons, but because I want a front row seat when we finally bring these murdering bastards to their knees. I have a short list of people I want to take down with my own damaged hands and Ryan Gregory tops that list.

From the first day Emma came into my life, both Anna and Amy thought I was nuts for refusing to take her on as my mark. They know how deep my hate runs for Ryan, and they exploited every avenue trying to talk me into this assignment. Leave it to Amy to point out what would be better revenge on Ryan than taking Emma's precious virginity? Even if he never found out it was me, how ironic would it be for Ryan Gregory to end up saddled with one of my sloppy seconds? At the time, I had laughed, thinking that actually sounded pretty good.

Yeah, I know. I'm a real prick, and I'm not proud of any of this. I said it before and I'll say it again. I'm not a good person.

But still, my answer had been *no*.

The more I got to know Emma, the happier I was I turned my commanders down. Emma was not my typical mark. She was frail and young and so emotionally damaged she made *me* look like the poster-child for mental health. Most people going through what Emma has would have become bitter and hateful, yet no matter what's happened, she still looks for the good in people. From the first minute I spent with her, she looked for the good in *me*.

Every time we were together, Emma scratched away a little more of the wall I erected between us and it fucking terrified me. I really thought I'd go the next four lifetimes without letting anyone past my emotional boundaries, yet here was sweet, innocent Emma easily knocking down the walls I spent decades building.

I couldn't let her succeed. I just couldn't let her in, and it's not because I'm hard or I hate people. It's because I'm fucking terrified of losing yet another person I love. I don't have the strength to go through that again. I would rather die.

I did my best to piece Emma back together as quickly as possible. I was starting to feel again and I couldn't let that happen. The day I walked in and found her asleep in my treatment room woke something in me that I thought would never be resurrected. Emma looked so pure, so innocent, that for the first time in nearly two decades I wanted to *protect* someone. It suddenly didn't matter anymore that no one had been there to protect me.

That day, Emma brought me to my knees. Despite everything I had done to prevent it, I somehow had fallen under her spell, and I had to stop this before things went any further. Having feelings for another person makes you weak and the weak are always the first to get picked off. I've worked too hard and come too far to let that happen.

I had to let her go.

Cutting her loose was the hardest thing I'd ever done in my life. The day I discharged Emma from my care I wanted nothing more than to kiss her just once before never seeing her again, but I knew I couldn't. I knew she would become my personal heroin, one taste of her lips and I would be hooked for life. That was the look she saw on my face that afternoon. Despite my efforts to protect myself, it was too late. She had made me weak. I fled that room like my ass was on fire knowing I had to forget her.

But, goddamn it, Emma just wouldn't fucking disappear.

Do you wanna know something crazy? Emma was the first client of mine to ever send me a thank you note. She wrapped her hand-written missive around an opening night ticket for the ballet she was starring in, a ticket that I could have sold for a small fortune. I sat in my room and stared at that fucking ticket for days deciding what to do. I could have sold that ticket and had enough money to eat well for a year. But what did I do? I borrowed a suit and for the first time in my life, I went to the ballet.

From the second the curtain rose and Emma flitted across the stage I couldn't tear my eyes off of her. She looked so beautiful, every movement so graceful and awe-inspiring I actually had to remind myself to breathe. My heart was thumping in my chest and my hands itched to touch her. I was infatuated, and when it was over, I damn near wanted to cry. I didn't want it to ever end. If I could have afforded it, I would have gone every goddamned night just to gawk at her on the stage like a lovesick teen.

I was a miserable prick the entire next week. Every time the door opened at work, I prayed it was her coming to say hi. But she never stopped by to ask me what I thought of her performance, just as I never stopped by the studio to tell her how much I enjoyed watching her. As much as it hurt to not see her, I knew the best thing for us both was to keep my distance.

But fate had other plans for us and that cosmic bitch kept throwing us back together. The night at Union Station. The early morning at the hospital. Her risking everything to come find me and risking even more to get John involved.

The first time I kissed Emma I knew I was done for. When her lips touched mine I felt an electricity between us I never felt before. I didn't want Emma. I *needed* Emma. Every time I taste her skin, every time my fingers tangle in her hair, I lose another piece of myself to her. I want to make love to her, to worship her with my body, to bury myself inside of her and never let her go. I am so desperately in love with her I ache when she isn't with me. For weeks I've wanted to admit those three little words that would destroy me if she doesn't say them back.

Now I'm too late.

I take Emma's hand in mine and she looks at me warily. I rub my hand over my eyes roughly, trying to summon the courage I'm gonna need to get through this.

I take a deep breath and tell her everything, and I mean *everything*.

The night at the rave had all been a set up but not by me. I swear to God and all that is holy, I knew *nothing* about it until well after the fact. Anna had been beyond pissed at me for refusing to take Emma as my new pet project so she took her on instead. She eventually got enough information out of Emma to know she was desperate for a way out. She went to resistance leadership and told them if we helped Emma escape, she knew she would help us any way she could. They agreed.

As is always our way, we never tell the people we're extracting what's happening just in case things go sideways. The less they know the safer they are. Marcus and Brian's job that evening had been to distract, drug and get Emma to the port where a boat would be waiting. We always drug our evacuees to prevent possible last minute issues, like suddenly getting cold feet. As bizarre as that sounds, that happens a lot more often than you'd think.

Anna was coordinating with a few other members who were bringing evacuees as well as managing the shipment of medical supplies that was being delivered. Procuring the drugs was the *only* reason I was there that night. When the guy didn't show, I figured I was off duty for the evening. When I saw the beautiful girl in the short black wig I was drawn to her in a way I've never felt before. Ever.

"I swear on all things Holy, Emma, I had no idea it was you. I was drunk and high and I saw a beautiful woman with a rockin' body and I wanted you. Once I had you in my arms, you made me so weak, I could barely breathe, nonetheless think."

My first clue that Anna had planned to get Emma out that night was when I found the fake ID. That stupid, simple card that caused so much fucking trouble would have allowed Emma to be transported across the river to our extraction point. It damn near broke my heart when I had to drag her back through the tunnels to her dorm. I hated having to return her to the life she just told me she would rather die than live.

My confession pours out of me. Things I never thought in a million years I would confess fall from my mouth. I tell her Ryan was one of the patrolmen that raped my mother and murdered my father; how he made sure a scrawny kid served time in one of the most dangerous prisons out of spite over a cut that didn't even require stitches. I tell her he was the one who beat me within an inch of my life and ordered me to be branded like an animal.

I tell her I'm not going to stop hunting him until I kill him.

Emma doesn't move a muscle the entire time I speak. She sits, staring at me with those impossibly huge blue eyes. She doesn't even blink. I'm breaking her heart and yet I don't stop talking until I confess all of my sins. I'm so disgusted with myself I can't even look at her. I feel a searing pain in my chest as my heart shatters into a thousand jagged fragments.

She's going to leave me.

We sit in silence for a long while. Emma pulls her hand from mine and absently picks at a cuticle on her thumb making it bleed. When I try to stop her from mutilating herself by gently placing her hand on mine, she hauls off and slaps me as hard as she can. I don't even flinch. I deserve everything she gives me and a whole lot more.

"So this was all a scam," she says quietly. "You, Anna, John—you were all in this together."

"No. It wasn't supposed to be like this."

"And what exactly does that mean?" Her face is a mixed mask of confusion, anger, and fear. I have wounded her deeply.

"I'm sorry," I say with quiet defeat. "I am so, so sorry, Emma. I never meant to hurt you."

She lets out a short exasperated laugh before her face contorts into an ugly sneer. "Really? You didn't mean to hurt me? Fuck you, Declan. You said it yourself, I was an asset. You were more interested in revenge than what happened to me. This is nothing more than a game to you, isn't it? You *used* me. You don't give a shit about me, do you?"

She stands up to leave. I want to jump up and grab her and try to explain, but she's right. I did use her. I don't deserve to keep her just because I fell in love with her. I'm going to lose her and that is going to kill me. My love for her is going to destroy me.

She stands with her back to me, pausing motionless for a long minute before turning back to me. "I just need to know. . . Why are you telling me the truth now?"

Her eyes are full of unshed tears. Dear God, please, let her hit me, beat me, kill me, but please don't let those tears fall. . . . and they do.

My voice comes out thick and needy. "Because I fell in love with you, Emma. I love you so much that sometimes it's hard to breathe. I love that you are so good and kind and all the things that are right in this rotten, miserable world. I love that you make me think and feel and see there is still beauty in life, in living, in hoping and dreaming for a better future. You make me want to be a better man, a good man. I swear Emma, if you please, please give me another chance, I will never, ever lie to you again. I swear on my life."

I drop to my knees in front of her. I don't say a word, just kneel silently at her feet and look up at her, imploring her, begging her for forgiveness. She stares at me, tears coursing down her cheeks. "How do I know you aren't lying now?"

"There's nothing I can say or do to erase the mistakes I've made and make you trust me again. That's a decision you have to make for yourself."

She sinks down to her knees across from me and places her hand over my heart. I close my eyes and feel the tremble of her broken heart through her palm. Right now, I would gladly stop my own if it would take away even an ounce of her pain.

My breath is coming fast and shallow. I am so, so afraid I've ruined everything. For the first time in my life, I am willingly on my knees and completely emotionally naked. There are no more secrets. I place my scarred hand on top of her perfect one that hovers over my heart. I fold her fingers in mine, and press them to my lips. My other hand reaches forward, brushing the tears from her cheeks with my thumb. My chest aches like it's been crushed in a vise as fresh tears form in her eyes. Emma starts to cry harder and she lets me take her into my arms. I hold her to me, gently stroking her hair. Her body shakes in my arms as I whisper to her over and over the only words my constricted throat can still form.

I'm sorry.

When she finally pulls away from me I'm so afraid. It feels like goodbye. Her voice quivers as she wipes runaway tears from her cheeks. "Say it again, Declan."

"I'm sorry," I choke out. "God, Emma, I am so, so sorry."

She looks at me blankly for a moment before attempting a watery smile. "Not that," she whispers. "Tell me again that you love me."

48

Emma

Even though I forgive him, I'm wrecked by Declan's confession. I know the old saying that all's fair in love and war and right now, I'm calling bullshit. The choices Declan made, the danger he put me in—none of it was fair. Even after he developed feelings for me and knew he could trust me, he still made impossible decisions for us both without consulting me. He's constantly weighing the needs of the resistance, his need for revenge and his need for me with some sort of scale that only makes sense to him. He needs to trust me enough to include me in all of our decisions and I make it crystal clear that I expect that from here on.

I think a lot about his confession, especially in the ways he referred to himself. What destroys me is how Declan believes what they told him in prison. He's been brainwashed to think he's a horrible person and I refuse to believe that's true. Yes, he has a vicious temper, major trust issues and a suicidal-level need for revenge. I'm not completely love-blind and unable to see these are some pretty major character flaws, but he's far from the villain he's convinced he's become.

I don't know how to make him understand that he's the most amazing man I have ever known. He's been through hell and still manages to not let that make him a demon. They physically and mentally broke him, yet he still left prison wanting to dedicate his life to healing others. And through all of this, he still somehow found the strength to fall in love with the daughter of one of his greatest enemies. A person capable of that type of dedication, personal growth and overwhelming love could, in my opinion, never be evil.

We love each other in a twisted, dangerous time in a way that defies all logic. Not forgiving him was never an option. I love him too much to live without him.

Now that Declan is almost completely healed, he restarts his clandestine operations in the tunnels. Sometimes he smuggles in drugs for the clinic, other times he carries critical messages out to other resistance groups. He's never gone more than a day or two, but I worry incessantly about him while he's away. I better understand now what he goes through when I have my mandatory visits with Ryan.

The closer we get, the harder it is to not take things further sexually. I'm adamant that I'm not going to marry Ryan, so I argue that staying a virgin is not a necessity. But Declan refuses to discuss it, just repeatedly saying that's a risk he's not willing to take. I enjoy teasing him, trying to get him to crack and give in to desire, but no matter how hard I make him, he's adamant our pants stay on.

Declan comes clean to his commanding officers, telling them we've fallen in love and that he's told me who he really is. He gets in a ton of trouble but he tells me he doesn't care. With a shy smile and a kiss, he tells me I'm worth it.

A few days after his announcement, Declan finds out he's being reassigned. The highest levels of the resistance decide it's too unsafe for us to stay here, and they offer us a way out. In return, I will do everything in my power to get foreign powers invested in our cause and hopefully secure money, humanitarian aid and weapons. My testimony to the UN and NATO will be crucial, as will imploring the Chinese Imperial Powers' top leaders to take mercy on our starving nation.

Declan's been charged with my protection, not that he needs to be ordered to care for me. He's become overprotective since we've gotten the word we will be sent abroad, determined that nothing will get in the way of what more than likely is our one and only chance to make it out of the country together.

Time flies by as we wait impatiently for more details. My days are filled with ballet and every night I can, I spend with Declan. A week before Christmas, Declan receives word that the last transport until spring will leave our port on New Year's Eve and we are expected to be on it. It's only a few weeks away and whenever I think about it, I shiver with gleeful anticipation.

That night, I lay in bed under a thick pile of blankets in Declan's arms, tracing the intricate knots of his Celtic tattoos with lazy strokes of my fingers. Although the room's freezing, I'm content in the warmth of his arms wrapped around me, my back pressed against his chest. He gently kisses my bare shoulder, occasionally giving a gentle nibble, when he whispers softly into my ear, "Will you marry me?"

At first I think I heard him wrong. His warm breath tickles my ear making me giggle. "What did you say?"

He holds me tighter, a few seconds passing before he whispers, "Marry me."

He's so still he feels like he's stopped breathing. I turn to face him, the surprise evident on my face. He smiles as he takes my hands in his, staring deeply into my eyes.

"One more time?" He knows I'm teasing. The most beautiful words in the English language were just spoken to me by the most incredibly brave, loving and handsome man I've ever met. I want to hear him say those words just one more time. He caresses my blushing cheek with his fingertips, as he brings his lips within inches of mine.

"Emma, my love, will you marry me?"

Tears spring to my eyes as my face breaks into a giant smile. I kiss him with every ounce of love in my heart before pulling back and whispering, "Yes, Declan. Yes. I will marry you."

* * *

Declan has only one request. He wants to be married in the Old Faith, just like his parents had, before we leave the country. Of course, anything pertaining to the Old Faith is considered treasonous since Church and State united and our marriage won't be legal in the eyes of either entity, not that either of us care. Having grown up in the Old Faith, Declan feels the need to have our union blessed by the God he believes in, and I can understand that, but how he continues to have faith in a Savior that certainly seems to have turned his back on him boggles my mind. I keep that thought to myself, realizing that just because I don't understand his beliefs doesn't mean I would ever deny his right to them.

We decide to get married on Christmas Eve.

It's impossible for me to act normally as the time nears. I'm smiling all the time, and I can't help it. People are starting to notice that something's changed and I try to tone down my excitement and happiness, but it's hopeless. I have one last evening with Ryan scheduled before his vacation and even that's unable to dampen my spirits. I say what I need to and do what I must to get through the night unscathed. I do not want his marks on my skin on my wedding night.

The day of our wedding dawns bright and sunny, if much colder than I would have liked. Declan tells me it's bad luck to see the bride before the wedding, so I sleep in the dorm for my last night as an unmarried woman. The day drags on, and I can barely contain my excitement when it's finally dark enough for me to head into the tunnels.

I follow Declan's directions to John and Marta's house, where Marta immediately sets to work helping me touch up my hair and makeup. John is nowhere to be found and Marta finally lets on with a giggle that he's helping Declan get ready. She confesses he looked very, very nervous when he stopped by that morning asking John for a favor. In fact, he was so nervous, he refused to eat. She laughs when she jokes she thinks he might be dying. Declan has never before refused her cooking.

Marta claps her hands together and leans over me, whispering, "I have a surprise for you."

She jogs up the stairs and comes back down carrying a beautiful white gown. It's old and very plain and made of heavy satin. The dress is unadorned with a simple tank style top and a narrow princess waist. The back is cut low with the only embellishment a long row of tiny satin buttons that run from waist to hem.

"It's beautiful." It's exactly the style of dress I would have picked if I'd been given a choice. "Wherever did you get it?"

"It's the gown I wore many years ago when John and I married. I always prayed to have a daughter who would wear this on her wedding day." She smiles, her eyes brimming with tears.

"Today, God has answered my prayer."

I jump from the chair and hug her tight. This sweet, sweet woman is more of a mother to me in the few hours I've spent with her than in all of the years I lived with my biological mother. She confesses how she made a phone call to the costumer at the dance company to get my measurements, posing as someone making a costume for me for an upcoming performance.

"I told her if she gave me the wrong measurements to make me look bad, I would tell everyone where I got them and she would be out of a job," she giggles.

I'm surprised at her deviousness, but get a good laugh from her story. Even in doing something as simple as altering a wedding gown,

Marta is taking risks in her own life just to make Declan and me happy. Sometimes I think she can't possibly be real, that she's actually an angel in disguise.

When it's finally time, Marta helps me into the dress and secures the top three buttons. She put in a hidden zipper knowing that with Declan's damaged hand, the tiny buttons would be difficult for him. Her kindness and forethought touch me more than words can say.

The dress fits perfectly. As I reach for my coat, she smacks my hand away and pulls out a second surprise. It's a floor-length white hooded cape made of thick wool on top with pelts from God only knows how many small furry creatures sewn together to make up the luxuriously soft, warm lining.

"I borrowed this from another family. I told them John and I were going to a wedding and she offered this for the bride for good luck." She reaches up to place the cape on my shoulders while I tie the strings around my neck. "You look beautiful," she whispers as she lifts the hood and places it gently over my hair.

I can't stop the tears forming in my eyes as I reach over and squeeze her hand. "Thank you so much, Marta. I can never repay you."

She waves her hand dismissively. "I should be the one thanking you."

I look at her quizzically as she pauses, choosing her words carefully.

"When I first met Declan, he was so broken. What they did to him in prison was enough to kill a strong man and yet he was not much more than a boy. John and I prayed so hard for him, prayed that we made the right decision to bring him into our home. It was not an easy road. John repaired the worst of the bodily damage Declan suffered, but his soul was beyond our ability to mend."

She pauses a moment to smooth a stray lock of my hair back under the hood. "Yet no matter how badly he behaved, we couldn't turn him away. He had been tortured for so long, he no longer knew what it felt like to love or to be loved, and John and I had love to spare. But no matter what we said or did, he wouldn't let us fully into his heart. Not until he met you."

A small, sad smile forms on her lips. I'm barely breathing as I listen, my heart thumping loudly in my ears. "He loves you, Emma. He loves you so, so much. I don't know how you did it, but he somehow remembered how to love and he loves you as fiercely as those he hates. Many people would find that frightening, but obviously, not you."

She stops to wipe the tears from her cheeks before she takes me in her warm embrace. "Love him, Emma. Love him with every fiber of your heart and soul. Only you can make him whole again. You are so strong, mi hija. As proud as I am to call Declan my son, I am just as proud to call you my daughter."

Her tears fall freely now as she leans back and kisses me on both cheeks. That's the moment, John walks into the room, dressed in the same black suit and dark gray coat he wore to the ballet so many months ago. Marta walks over and kisses John gently on the lips. She gently pats his arm and explains, "I was just welcoming Emma to our family."

John helps Marta into her tattered brown coat as she takes a deep breath to steady her voice. "I also told her by this time next year I expect a grand baby," she quips, turning back to me with a wink.

49

Declan

For being thirty degrees in the church it sure is hot in here.

I'm sweating like I'm sitting in a front row seat in Hell. I feel sick. I need air. I need a drink.

I need Emma.

I stick my finger behind the tie John forced me to wear and try to loosen it. It feels like a fucking noose and I somehow succeed in only making it tighter. How's that even possible?

Sounds like you've got cold feet, asshole. Still time to run if you want to punk out.

Shut the fuck up, of course, I'm not changing my mind. Maybe I'm getting sick. Shit, I hope I'm not getting sick. I run my fingers through my hair and tug at the roots, a comforting, although I'm well aware, strange thing I do when I'm uncomfortable.

Wait. Sweaty, hot, heart racing, huge lump in throat—This is what it feels like to be nervous. It's been nearly a decade since I'd had an attack of the nerves and I laugh out loud. Every fucking horrible thing that could happen to a person has happened to me, and yet the first time since I got out of prison my brain chooses to lose its shit is on my wedding day. How exactly is that normal?

Of course it's normal, fuck face. Because if she doesn't show up, you'll feel worse than if she ripped your heart out with her teeth.

Seriously? Is everyone's voice in their head as big an asshole as mine?

John spent up until the last ten minutes with me and I had been fine. Abso-fucking-lutely fine. So what's happening that I'm freaking out now? I spent the past sixteen years of my life alone and apparently today's the day I develop separation anxiety like some sort of inbred Labrador retriever.

Congratulations, ass-wipe. You've been pussy whipped.

Just as I'm getting ready to punch myself in the face to shut up that evil, smart-ass voice, the priest walks in and tells me my bride has arrived. I'm so relieved I nearly kiss the man, even though I know that's frowned upon in his particular line of work. I take another deep breath and attempt to smooth my wrecked hair before following the priest out to the altar. I stand next to him and await my bride to make the long walk up the aisle.

The doors to the back of the church open revealing Emma, *my Emma*, on John's arm. He's giving her away. He's giving her, with his blessing, *to me*. My heart's pounding and I break into probably the most foolish toothy grin to ever embarrass a groom and I don't care one bit. I'm so damn happy my heart just might explode.

Emma looks gorgeous. Absolutely gorgeous. I knew about Marta's surprises for her, but I had no idea that the borrowed garments would make her look like an angel. *My* angel. It takes everything I have to hold myself together. I want to laugh and cry and scream to the world that Emma Bellamy is mine. *All mine.* Where these caveman-like possessive thoughts are coming from I don't know, but I like them. I like them *a lot*. I love that after the next hour, Emma will forever be mine just as I will always be hers.

John and Emma stop just a few feet from me and I feel like a dumb kid on his first date. I don't know what to do or say so I just stare at her with this stupid smile. Her normally pale cheeks are touched pink by the cold, or maybe she's blushing. *My blushing bride.* It's all too perfect. If this is all just a dream, someone just kill me now. If this is all some sick bastard's cruel joke I will never recover.

John turns to Emma and kisses her on the cheek. She hugs him tight before he turns to me. He straightens my tie, shaking his head laughingly at my messy hair. He pulls me into a bear hug that nearly knocks all the air from my lungs. When we pull away from each other we both have tears in our eyes. When he speaks, his voice cracks, the emotion of the moment overwhelming him. "I'm so proud of you, son."

Aw, fuck, now I'm gonna cry. I can't say it with my voice, but my eyes are clear. I nod.

Thanks, Dad. Thank you for everything.

I turn to Emma and place my hand on her cheek. I feel her sigh as my fingers brush her wind-chilled skin. My heart slows. My pulse returns to normal. She restores me.

I slip my fingers under the hood and gently lower it to her shoulders. I stare into her eyes, when suddenly her smile deteriorates into a thoughtful frown.

No. Oh, God, please, no. Don't let her change her mind now.

"Before we start, Declan, can I ask you a question?"

I nod because I can't speak. What could she possibly have to ask that's so important she's holding up the ceremony?

"I can't believe I never asked you this before, but what's your last name?" She grins and then laughs, a sound so precious I bet it makes the angels weep with envy.

I nearly melt into the floor with relief. "Does it matter?"

"No, it doesn't. I just want to know the name I will be taking and someday passing on to our children." She's mercilessly teasing me in front of John and Marta, the priest, God, and who the hell knows what saints and it's the most perfect moment of my life yet.

"Your last name, after today, is and forever will be Byrne," I whisper into her ear, even spelling it for her. She smells so damned good I can't help but lean in and gently place my lips against the shell of her ear.

"Byrne," she whispers back. "That's unusual. It fits you. I like it," she teases, remembering perfectly the conversation we had all those months ago.

"I'm glad you approve." I gently kiss her ear again, this time almost imperceptibly touching the tip of my tongue to her perfect skin. She shudders in pleasure as she reaches for my hand and squeezes. I pull back a few inches and we smile at each other like only two people that are completely and hopelessly mad for each other can.

We somehow manage to sober ourselves for the service. Emma's unfamiliar with the Old Faith service and I see she's horrified to find out she was supposed to bring a ring for me. Right as I see she's starting to panic, Marta takes Emma's hand and deposits a plain gold band into her palm. Emma sighs in relief, sliding the ring onto my finger as she repeats the sacred vows. I do the same to her with an identical but much smaller band. She's stunned that somehow I managed to even get the size right.

What can I say? I'm full of surprises.

When we are finally pronounced husband and wife, I pull her into a passionate, lingering kiss before the priest can say *you may kiss your bride.* She melts in my arms and kisses me back with every ounce of love in her heart. If it wasn't for John clearing his throat twenty or thirty times I just may have stayed there all night making out with my beautiful, beautiful wife.

When we separate, Emma's breathless and her cheeks are an adorable dark pink. We thank the priest who then graciously thanks us for giving him the opportunity to share our happy occasion. It hadn't occurred to me until now that probably ninety percent of his job over the years was administering to the sick and the dead, not to blessing marriages and welcoming children into the faith. We leave the church arm in arm and when we open the door, we're cheered by nearly a hundred people who clap, hoot and chant for us to kiss. I don't know how they found out, but I strongly suspect it was Marta who couldn't keep the secret.

Honestly, I am so freaking happy right now I don't care if she took out a billboard and posted the news. As long and hard as I tried to keep the community at arms' length, these incredible people still managed to become family. They've been there for me since day one and never abandoned me, even when I was at my worst. My family would never turn Emma and me in. They would die first.

In front of everyone, I take Emma in my arms and kiss her with every ounce of passion I have. I feel her knees buckle, but I hold her steady in my arms. I swear on this moment, on my *life*, I will never, ever, let her fall.

50

WE ARE CONGRATULATED, hugged and kissed by at least a hundred people in five different languages. There are probably twenty dinners' worth of rice thrown in the air as I take Emma's hand in mine and run through the cheering crowd and into the darkened streets towards home.

When we're clear of the crowd, I take Emma into my arms and kiss her until we both gasp for air. Drunk on her kisses, I hadn't realized it had started to flurry until I see the flakes shining like diamonds in her hair. I pull the hood over her, shielding her from the falling snow. Protecting her is now my job, and it's a responsibility I will never take lightly.

Laughing like two giddy school children, we run hand in hand back to our apartment. When we reach the locked door, I instruct her to close her eyes as I scoop her into my arms and carry her across the threshold. She's as light as a feather.

John and I spent the entire day decorating for this special night. I watch Emma's face as she takes in the hours of work that I knew would make this night perfect. John cut branches of pine and fir and the two of us carried them up the four flights of stairs. We decorated the room with garlands of holly and ivy, bringing in the smell of the outdoors and of holidays long past. We brought nearly fifty candles that we lit right before we left for the ceremony and not-so-jokingly prayed wouldn't burn the building down before we returned.

The tiny table is set with a threadbare tablecloth, chipped china and borrowed silver, where I will serve my wife our first meal together, courtesy of the heavy picnic basket lovingly put together by Marta. Bless her, she even baked and decorated a tiny cake for us to feed to one another before I carry my love to our blanket and fur laden bed where I will make love to my wife for the first time.

"It's perfect," she whispers, her voice catching in her throat. "Absolutely perfect."

She turns and kisses me again, pulling me into her arms. I'm torn between taking her to bed right then and there and to hell with dinner, but something stops me.

No, we're going to do this right.

I disentangle myself from her and remove her cloak. The propane heater that John procured from somewhere "on loan" warms the room. Something in the way John said that made me think the "loan" may be a bit of a fib, but I honestly didn't care enough to ask. Just the thought of it being warm enough to make love to my new wife without hiding under thirty pounds of blankets is probably the greatest gift one man can give another in these trying times.

I lead Emma over to the table and pour her a glass of deep red wine. There's Peruvian chicken, rice and roasted vegetables that I left on low heat on the camp stove to keep warm and thankfully hadn't burned. I raise my glass to Emma, but suddenly, I have no words.

"Forever," I choke as I touch my glass to hers.

"Forever," she whispers as she smiles her beautiful, perfect smile.

I absently play with my wedding band that feels foreign on my damaged hand. Our rings are a gift from John and Marta; they gave us theirs with heartfelt wishes that the simple bands will bring us many years of love together like they have shared. I told Emma how I measured her ring finger one night as she slept with a piece of twine, marking the exact diameter to be certain the ring would fit. She laughs but I can tell she's impressed with my ingenuity.

We sit on the ancient sofa and cut into the tiny cake after we finish dinner. We feed each other bites of the delectable confection, laughing as we lick the caramel sweetness off each other's lips and fingers. Full from a wonderful dinner and our heads lightly buzzing from the wine, we continue to kiss like two horny teenagers until I can take it no longer and carry my bride to bed. We stand next to our familiar mattress and hold each other, kissing one another tenderly as if it's the first time we've ever touched.

I'm flushed from the wine and the unaccustomed warmth of the room. I strip off my borrowed shirt, allowing the air to cool my over-heated skin. Emma steps forward when the shirt hits the floor, her fingertips gently grazing my chest, the glint in her eyes demanding I kiss her again.

As we suck each other's tongues and lips into our mouths, her hand slips to my pierced nipple, where she tortures me with a feather-light caress. I want her to take it into her warm, wet mouth and suck it, but our wedding night is not the time for that type of request. Tonight will only be about my wife's pleasure. I will ask nothing of her. Only when she offers and is fully willing and ready, will I gladly relieve her of her virginity.

I slip wordlessly behind her and slide her long golden hair over her shoulder, giving me access to the back of her dress. I kiss the back of her neck slowly, gently sucking her flesh into my mouth as she quietly moans my name. I don't care if I leave behind my mark. In fact, I want the world to see that she's mine.

My progression is painfully slow, watching for any hint she's uncomfortable as I graze my teeth down her spine. Emma purrs against me, arching her back and pressing her perfect round ass against my swollen cock.

Holy fuck. I had every intention of taking this slow, but how in the hell are you supposed to do that when the woman you have been waiting for your entire life pulls a move like that?

Emma slips her hand behind the small of her back and massages my cock through my pants. I close my eyes and moan in rapture. I want to take things slow, but if she keeps this up, I'm going to have some sort of penile aneurysm if I don't come soon.

Not to mention, I still have no clue how the hell to get Emma out of this dress without an instruction manual. I drop to my knees and start to unbutton the 6,000 minescule fucking buttons on this dress with shaking hands. I have to get Emma out of this gown before I ruin it by ripping it off of her. If I hand the remains of the heirloom dress back to Marta in a brown paper lunch bag with nothing more than an apology and a sheepish grin Marta will kill me for sure.

I take a deep breath to steady myself. No, I'm going to hold it together if it takes me all night. Emma giggles when I swear that someday I'm going to find the motherfucker that designed this dress and kill him.

"Oh you think this is funny?" I growl as she laughs. Before she can utter a syllable, I spin her to face me and lift the front of the skirt, sliding my hand over her damp lace panties. My other hand plants firmly on her ass, pressing her into my roving fingers.

"Look at me," I demand as my fingers slide under the lace and between her folds. My plan to tease and torture her with my fingers shits the bed as Emma widens her stance, a wicked grin daring me to fuck her with my fingers and to hell with the dress.

I'm clinging to the final shred of my self control, the feel of Emma's slick folds against my fingertips making me insane. I groan, spinning her around to face the fucking buttons again. "I'm not touching you again until I get this goddamn dress off of you."

She sputters out a hearty laugh, nearly losing her balance. I'm probably thirty seconds from having a goddamn stroke and she's *laughing.* I bite down on my lower lip in concentration as I again focus on the buttons.

"Baby?"

"Hmm?"

"There's a zipper under those buttons. They're decorative, they aren't meant to be undone."

Motherfucker. She tells me this *now.* Sure as shit, I flip over a fold of fabric I had been too lust-blind to notice and there's the zipper. Emma's still laughing when I peel the dress from her and toss her gently onto the bed in nothing but her pale blue panties, thigh-high stockings and heels. I look ravenously down upon her as she looks up at me seductively from under lowered lashes. She rises to her knees and grabs my belt, pulling me towards her. Her eyes never leave mine as she undresses me completely, leaving my hard cock defenseless against her waiting lips.

I try to back away. I don't want her to do this. I know this is Ryan's preferred method of humiliating her and I don't want her to think that is what I want. I want this to be all about her, but when she grabs me in her tiny palm that's suddenly as strong as a vice grip, I realize not only am I no longer in charge of this party, I never was to begin with. She literally leads me by the cock to within millimeters of her moist lips and pretty pink tongue, her eyes never once wavering from mine. She's so intent on what she's going to do next I'm almost a little afraid of her.

I stand naked and vulnerable in her warm, firm grasp, not breathing, not moving, but staring into the mischievous blue eyes of the woman, of my *wife,* who has me completely at her mercy. For the first time in my life, I willingly give someone sexual power over me. When she takes me in her mouth I nearly blow my load instantly. Her mouth is every bit as warm and wet as I had dreamed, her tongue licking and stroking my shaft in the most decadent ways. She places one hand on my ass and urges me deeper into her mouth while her other hand fondles my balls. She's watching me carefully as she pleasures me, taking as much enjoyment of my lust-filled moans and guttural words of encouragement as I am of her oral ministrations.

I feel my boys tighten, my core contracting with the desire to explode in her mouth. I know she would deny me nothing, that she wants nothing more than to please me. I have to admit, that's absolutely the most arousing sentiment any woman has ever conveyed to me with her lips wrapped around my dick. But I don't want my first time coming with her to be like this.

I back up a step, releasing myself from her mouth and gently push her so she falls backwards on the mattress with a gentle thump. Her hands land aside her face, her hair loose and wild spread over the pillow. I don't even recognize my own voice, it's that raspy with lust and want.

"Emma, you are so fucking beautiful."

Dropping to my knees I straddle her body and lower myself to her, feeling her breasts tickle my chest as I kiss and suck the tender flesh of her neck into my mouth. I leave a trail of kisses in my wake as I work my lips down her body, taking her breasts in my mouth, sucking and licking hungrily as she gasps and moans in pleasure.

Her pulse quickens as I slide further down, hooking my fingers into those lovely lace panties and sliding them from her before spreading her thighs with my knees. The perfume of her arousal makes me positively high as I slip my tongue between her folds. I feel every muscle, every twitch, every breath as I lap her creamy wetness into my mouth. She arches her back and moans deeply, the sounds of her pleasure going straight to my dick. When she starts whispering my name in her lust-filled voice and begs me for more I push my tongue deeper and harder inside her crease and she cries out in ecstasy.

I have always been a talker in bed. It's always been a huge turn on of mine so I guess, in turn, I like to pass the pleasure on. I tell my wife she's sweeter than anything I've ever tasted. I moan that she has me harder than I have ever been in my life. I confess that this is the most turned on I have ever been. *Ever.* There's so much more I want to say, but I don't feel that our wedding night is the time for me to start getting down and dirty with her.

That will have to wait until tomorrow.

She's wet and wanting and I am so, so hard my balls ache painfully with their ferocious need for release. I want nothing more than to pound into her until we beg each other for mercy. I have always like my sex rough and wild and somewhere on the spectrum between out of control and complete insanity but as much as I want that tonight, I can't do that to her.

This is her first time.

It's our wedding night.

I have to calm the fuck down.

As I continue to lick her, I slide my fingers to her dripping entrance and gently run them through her short, pale blonde curls. She tenses slightly and then exhales, preparing herself. I take my time. No matter how well I prepare her or how slowly I take things, our first time together will hurt her. It cuts me to the bone knowing that she will forever associate our wedding night with even the mere thought that I brought her discomfort.

Well, I'm just going to have to make the pleasure so extreme she won't remember the pain.

I slowly advance my finger into her, feeling her undeniable warmth and wetness. Her walls squeeze tight around my finger and I moan aloud just thinking about how glorious it's going to feel to bury my cock inside of her.

I take her clit into my mouth and lick and suck on it until she begins to buck her hips into my hand. Her fingers entwined in my hair hold my head in place as I rhythmically pump my finger in and out. The way she moans my name makes my dick jump, reminding me to not forget about him, but my mouth is too greedy to share. I curl my finger against her walls and find the spot that makes her nearly levitate off the mattress. I pick up the pace and lick and suck until her first orgasm rolls through her, shattering her inhibitions. She cries out repeated pleas or prayers to God, I'm not sure which.

"Baby, you flatter me, but I'm your husband not your Lord," I growl against her as she continues to thrash against my hand. I take this moment to slide a second finger into her, feeling her contractions wrap my fingers in warm, wet velvet as my fingertips bump dangerously against her virgin barrier.

The taste of her on my tongue, the smell of her arousal and her slippery goodness on my fingers is too much to bear. I slide back up her quivering body, peppering her with kisses and tiny bites. I press my lips to hers and we kiss like two people drowning, stealing their last gasps of oxygen from one another. She closes her eyes, tilts her head backwards and pants into my mouth.

"I want you, Declan. I want you inside me, please."

Those are the words I've been dreaming of for months and I'm not going to deny either of us a second longer. I position myself to her and slowly press inside. She gasps as I enter her, her eyes widening at the unfamiliar sensation. I instruct her to look into my eyes and no matter what, to not look away. I want to watch her every expression as I destroy that last wall between us.

We entrench ourselves in each other, our hands grasping, our breaths rapid, our hearts racing as I thrust into her. She cries out, clawing my scarred back with her nails. I don't care if in her passion she draws my blood, as in that last motion, I have done the same to her. I take from her what she has freely and lovingly offered and I will forever treasure the gift she's given me.

She's breathing hard from the exquisite mixture of pleasure, passion and pain, a single tear leaking from her eye. "I'm sorry," I whisper as I lean forward and lick the tear from her cheek.

"Don't be," she whispers huskily as she tilts her pelvic bones to take me further inside, dictating the ebb and flow of my body within her tide. She begins to relax when I place my tongue to her nipple and lick her until she loses herself in pleasure. I want to come so badly I swear I can hear my unborn children screaming in my balls.

As my fingers circle over her clit she moans my name, begging for me to make her come again. I pulse myself between her legs, stimulating her with my fingers as I push into her until I can go no further. She takes every inch of me and continues to rock harder against me, begging for more with eyes that never leave mine.

"Emma, baby, you feel so fucking good." I feel myself beginning to lose control.

"Come for me, Declan. Please, please come for me." She arches her back, grinding herself against me. She's so tight and slick that I forget all my previous sweet sentiments. My hands move to her hips and I hold her in place as I pump into her in long, hard strokes.

We are lost in the moment, victims to our mutual need for orgasm. I lean forward and lace my fingers through hers, placing our hands on either side of her face. I kiss her mouth hard enough to bruise her sweet, tender lips as her orgasm crests, her body milking my dick and demanding my release. I pump faster and harder into her and she slides her legs around my waist and locks them around the small of my back, pinning me to her. She whispers huskily for me to let go, to come in her, to fill her until I have nothing left.

I don't know if it's her deep, lusty voice, her tight virgin walls or the fact I've waited so long for this moment, but I'm ready to explode. I growl out a warning for her to be careful what she wishes for as she continues to beg me to ride her harder, faster, deeper. I had such grand intentions to be tender and gentle for her first time, but that romance-novel bullshit is obviously not what she wants. No, she's pushing us to our limits, our sweating bodies smashing together, our voices mingling in a rapturous duet of lust-crazed ecstasy. She rips her hands from mine and pulls my face to hers. We kiss passionately, violently. The pressure builds inside of my body, taking control and making me a slave to its most primitive needs.

I come with an intensity that I never knew was possible. I scream out her name as wave after wave of pure, unadulterated ecstasy sweeps over me. My heart is pounding erratically, my breath ragged, my voice hoarse from crying out in pleasure and pain. I'm gasping and panting as sweat drips down my brow and between my shoulders.

It takes me a few dizzying minutes to catch my breath before I slide from between her legs and lay next to her, our heads sharing the same pillow. I place her hand over my heart and then place my hand over hers.

"This belongs to you now, Emma," I whisper roughly, gently rubbing her hand over my wildly beating heart. "Know that I live for you. I would die for you. Be gentle with my heart, my love, as it no longer belongs to me. I have given it, in its entirety, to you."

I raise her hand to my lips and kiss it gently. She places her hand behind my shoulders and pulls me towards her, her lips again pressing to mine. I kiss and nibble them gently as I run my fingertips lightly over her face and neck as she shimmies closer, pressing the full length of her body against mine and draping her leg languidly over my hip.

My heart is still beating way too fast and I need it to slow considerably before I even think about starting round two. The last thing I want is to make Emma a widow on our wedding night.

I need to start doing more cardio.

I heard far off church bells chiming faintly in the distance. It's midnight. Emma kisses me passionately before pushing me onto my back and straddling me with a naughty glint in her eye as she takes my cock in her hand and strokes it hard from base to tip. "Merry Christmas, my love. Are you ready for your present?"

I smile.

Oh, Santa, I must have been a very, very good boy this year.

51

Emma

We make love all night long and by the time the sun rises we are exhausted. We fall asleep entwined with one another and the sheets and blankets that smell of satiated arousal and mingled sweat. I awake a few hours later to the sound of sizzling bacon and realize I'm ravenous.

I take a long, languorous stretch and savor the delicious soreness in my body from last night's exertions. The joints in my neck, spine and hips pop and creak, my muscles pulling and releasing with luxurious release. I look up and startle to find Declan standing over me, completely and unapologetically naked, with a spatula in his hand. Once again, he's hard as a rock.

I burst out laughing.

"What's so funny, wife?" He tosses the spatula in the sink and launches himself playfully on top of me. He pins my back to the mattress and presses his mouth possessively to mine.

"You," I tease as I take hold of his hips and slide my hands over the toned muscles of his ass. "Are you trying to damage the goods by cooking naked? Bacon grease to the balls sounds pretty painful." I reach between his legs and take him into my hand. He moans almost painfully and I wonder if I'm being too rough.

"I'm going to burn breakfast," he half-heartedly admonishes as he tries to disengage himself from my grip.

"Let it burn," I whisper seductively as I squeeze harder. He moans again, but manages to pry himself away from me to shut the gas off before coming back to bed. With his hair tousled and a devilish gleam in his eyes, he looks ten years younger. I'm suddenly very hungry, but not for bacon and eggs.

He advances slowly, stalking me one predatory step at a time. I shudder in anticipation. He laughs as he pounces on top of me, and I shriek in surprise, laughing as his lips find mine.

I knew last night he had been holding back. I felt the tension burning in him as he paced himself carefully and took things slowly. I appreciate his concern, but I will always want Declan as he is—raw, untamed and more than a little out of control. Last night, no matter how much I begged for him to let go I could feel something holding him back.

There's *nothing* holding him back today.

Many people use the words *make love, have sex* and *fuck* interchangeably, but not Declan. In his mind, these are three very separate acts, not to ever be confused. Lovemaking is tender, slow and sensual with a gradual build up and long, smooth strokes. It's a fierce yet gentle sexuality that makes you shudder and moan. It's an intimacy of connection, of accepting and giving pleasure on equal terms, an act that, at its pinnacle, you feel as one with your lover in mind, body and spirit.

Fucking is feral, wild and borderline violent and it both frightens and excites me just to think about it. It's an erotic connection that tends to be more selfish and greedy, almost like the feel-good scratching of an itch with a fingernail until it bleeds. Fucking is insistent and commanding, the type of coupling where demands are made and limits pushed in search of that next mind-blowing release.

Having sex is not even on the spectrum, a lesser act where one can't bother to either make love or fuck. It's passionately indifferent, an activity that doesn't care enough to fully invest itself and ends in a mediocre orgasm, at best. Declan is one of those rare men that would rather abstain than have sex. He's only capable of making love or fucking as is true of all genuinely passionate lovers.

He takes my nipple between his teeth and bites down lightly, his eyes watching my face intently. I try to look away, my cheeks flaming with embarrassment. It's one thing to be bold in the dark with a little help from a glass or two of wine. Here, stone cold sober in the bright winter sunshine is a whole new world. I reach for the sheet to cover my nakedness and Declan stops me by lacing his fingers through mine.

"Are you embarrassed?" Declan places his hand against my cheek, turning me to look at him. Now I'm embarrassed about *being* embarrassed. If I get any redder, I'm going to burst a blood vessel.

"Oh, sweetheart," he laughs as he rolls off of me and onto his side. He places his hand to my cheek and rests his forehead on mine. "You have *nothing* to be embarrassed about." He gently caresses my cheek with his thumb. "I wish there was a way for me to show you how perfect you are, that there's some way you can see yourself the way I see you."

"This is all so new, so strange."

"New doesn't mean wrong, does it?"

I shake my head. He presses his lips to mine and pulls away with a small lick to the underside of the tip of my nose. I laugh.

"I know you've been taught a lot of crazy shit regarding sexuality by that fucked-up church you go to, so listen up, baby, and let me set the record straight. Being naked is not shameful. Enjoying each other's bodies is not evil or wrong. Sex should never be boring, or a chore, and it's more than just for making babies. It's supposed to be fun, exciting, and raw and feel just a little bit dangerous, or depending on your mood, maybe a lot. Physical love is how you show someone how you feel instead of relying on words that are all too often inadequate. Does any of this make sense?"

"Yes, I guess so." I feel the burning color fade from my cheeks as I relax.

He reaches forward, kissing me gently, pulling my body to his. When he speaks, his voice is a throaty whisper. "You are so fucking beautiful, Emma. I know you don't believe me, I see it in your eyes. I hope if I keep saying it, if you keep seeing how you affect me, you'll start to believe it for yourself."

His voice becomes deeper, softer, a gentle rumble, as he removes his lips from mine and trails a string of kisses to my throat. He gently pushes my shoulder into the pillows, shifting me onto my back, as he works his lips down my body, savoring each taste of my skin. He takes such enjoyment from me physically, an enjoyment I have difficulty understanding.

I've been at war with my body for nearly two decades, always pushing it to its limits, starving it, torturing it, hating it, often denying it the most basic necessities. I've held this vessel of bone, muscle and blood in such contempt, such disgust, that I didn't care I'd been murdering it with deliberate calculation.

Declan sees me in such a different light from how I see myself. He's always calling me perfect and beautiful, words that mean nothing to me because I feel they aren't true. I'm not beautiful, my reflection in the mirror giving me years' worth of feedback that I am anything but lovely. Yet Declan reveres me with lust-filled gazes, hungry lips and greedy hands. He worships my body with his own, like I'm his own private goddess to idolize and serve. Last night, when we were coupled in the throes of passion, he made me feel beautiful and worthy for the first time in my life.

It's harder to remember those sensations in the light of day when all my faults are so painfully on display. I think back to the harsh words of prior dance masters, stylists, my father, Ryan and my own brain that find issues with every inch of my being. Declan has never once said a word about my deficits and I wonder why. Maybe he's just being polite. Then again, I never mention his scars or burns. But those I think somehow are different—they are as much a part of him as his beautiful dark chocolate eyes and his full, soft lips. Could it be that he sees my flaws the same way?

My conflicted mind is brought back to the present by Declan's tongue toying with my breasts as he tortures my hardened nipples with feather-light flicks. His eyes are on mine, and when I gaze into those brilliant, dark orbs, his ravenous stare makes my belly flutter and warmth flood my sex.

My train of thought derails when Declan takes hold of my hips and his lips slide down my body. I spread my thighs for him and he rewards me with a growled, "Good girl," and a languorous lick between my folds.

I drink in every detail of him with my eyes. He's right, it's *much* more rewarding to make love in the daylight. He must feel my gaze as his eyes flick up and lock with mine as he works his way up my body, his mouth finding mine and kissing me hard. He momentarily, rapturously closes his eyes when his cock enters me in one long smooth thrust. Tilting his head back, lips parted and glossy, he moans my name. My God, is he gorgeous like this.

When he's buried inside of me, I feel again like I did last night, beautiful and loved, cherished and needed. We clutch one another in euphoric embrace, inseparable, as we have become one flesh, one body, one being. We come together this time, our bodies exploding simultaneously.

I marvel at the beauty of the human body, that when coupled with another, can release such feelings of bliss. Declan's sheen of satiation, the heavy-lidded look of having had yet another Earth-shattering orgasm, is a privilege to behold. As much as I am quick to find fault with my body, I have to give credit where it's due. The fact that even in the unforgiving light of day my body can evoke that look on my husband's face means everything to me.

In my mind, I hear a tiny, whispered voice I've never heard before. It urges me to accept Declan's truth as my own. The voice is driven away quickly by the stronger, more pervasive reality I've lived with so long, but regardless, I feel a spark of hope. The fact this voice even exists, not to mention is brave enough to finally speak, is new, but doesn't frighten me. Maybe, just maybe, this is the first step in mending the estranged relationship between my body and brain.

And for the first time in my life, I think there just may be a chance for them to reconcile.

52

THE WEEK BETWEEN Christmas and New Year's Eve is a blur. Except for when I have to tear myself away to perform, I'm never outside of Declan's line of sight or his embrace for more than a few minutes at a time.

I have never been happier in my life.

I can't help but wonder if people notice a difference in me. I wonder if people can tell I'm no longer a virgin. My newly found happiness has to be noticeable. I laugh more. I feel lighter.

I feel whole.

With only two days remaining until we're out of here, I am giddy with excitement. Declan and I are finally going to have the sort of relationship I have dreamed about, the things I want for us simple and acceptable throughout the rest of the world, just not here. I want to be able to walk down the street holding my husband's hand. I want Declan to no longer be a hunted man, always only one step ahead of being murdered. I want him to finally have a chance to pursue his passion for medicine. I want to dance on the stage for as long as my body allows, or until we decide to start a family, whichever comes first. I don't want to be rich or famous. I just want the right to quietly live my life with the man I love and I don't think that is too much to ask.

But before we can fade into obscurity, we have to do what we've promised. Declan's cohorts are taking an enormous risk to help us escape, and in return, we will make the world see how bad things have become for the American people. I have to find some way to make these foreign powers want to get involved.

Somehow, together, I know we will succeed. Declan has helped me find an inner strength I never knew I possessed. I feel bolder both mentally and physically when he's by my side. He's a tonic to my soul, infusing me with a hope for the future I've never experienced before.

I'm sore and exhausted from hours of lovemaking and lack of sleep and yet there's a spring to my step and a glint in my eye. I stop by the dorms on my way to the theater for a matinee performance to gather a few new pairs of pointe shoes. Last night, I broke the vamp in my last pair, rendering them useless. I somehow managed to muddle my way through the end without falling on my face, but today the arch of my foot is sore, not that I really care. I'm too happy to focus on what, in the grand scheme of things, is little more than an annoying ache.

I'm running late, so I sprint up the stairs two at a time, flinging open the stairwell door with a bang. I twirl joyously into the hall, my arms thrown wide, eyes closed, and my face tilted upward. Giddy laughter burbles from my throat that I'm too ecstatic to contain.

Two more days!

"Well, I'm glad to see someone's in a good mood."

The angry voice stops me dead in my tracks. I freeze in shock, swallowing hard.

This can't be happening. No. Not now.

I open my eyes and my worst fear is confirmed.

"Ryan! What are you doing here?" My mouth is suddenly painfully dry. "I wasn't expecting you back for a few more days."

"Where have you been?"

My mind goes blank. The patrolmen that guard the main entrance would of course have told him I was in residence. After last night's performance, I came back to the dorm through the main entrance and then immediately left as usual to go to Declan's using the tunnel that ran below the building. According to the guards, I've been in the building this whole time.

This is so not good.

"Ryan, please, I have a performance in an hour. Can we talk after? I'm running very late."

I try to keep my voice even but even I hear the tremble in my words. Ryan grabs my upper arm and throws me against the wall, caging me in with his arms. There's an odd smile on his face and a strange look in his eyes, and for the first time since I've known him, there's not even a hint of alcohol on his breath.

He leans in, studying me closely, his eyes narrow and suspicious. I try to cringe away, but there's nowhere for me to go. His cologne mingles with the odor of stale sweat and semen that rises from my body. I'm terrified he can smell Declan on my body.

He places a hand gently around my throat in warning. "I don't believe you are addressing me with the respect I am due, Emma. Do you need a reminder of how to behave?" His fingers tighten slightly, that sneering smile getting nastier by the second.

I shake my head, words failing me completely. His fingers tighten further. "Now listen closely, Emma. You know how I detest repeating myself. You are coming with me. Now. You have fifteen minutes to get yourself presentable. Duty calls."

I stare at him in uncomprehending shock. "I don't understand."

Ryan lets go of my neck and backs up a step, his smile widening. "Haven't you heard?"

My stomach drops like I'm hurtling down an elevator with a snapped cable. Time comes to a stop, my breath catching in my throat. His icy eyes darken, a deep sinister gleam lighting his face in a malevolent way.

"The Supreme Archon is dead."

53

I SIT IN TEARFUL SILENCE in the black limo that takes Ryan and me to the Executive Mansion. My father is already there presiding over the funeral arrangements, handling all the trivial details that I'm sure he feels are beneath him. Now that Ryan holds the highest office in our land, my father is just like the rest of us—another slave to the Supreme Archon's ego.

The modest long-sleeve black dress, floppy black hat and sunglasses are unable to hide my inconsolable grief as tears run down my cheeks. Once I'm in my new "home," I am trapped. There's no way I will ever be able to sneak out of there with the countless patrolmen, soldiers and watchers that lurk behind every corner. The Mansion is now my cage where I will remain at Ryan's pleasure for as long as he allows me to live.

Now that Ryan is the supreme power of our land, he can do whatever he wants. After all, he's above the law. Untouchable. And just like our deceased Supreme Archon, morality will not dictate his actions. He once famously claimed he could stand in the middle of the street and randomly shoot people while snorting blow off a dead hooker and still not lose the adoration of the people. And unless Ryan does something colossally unwise, his blind sycophants will feel likewise. So it's no stretch of the imagination that even though we are unwed, he can bed me any time he chooses with or without my consent.

And when he finds out I'm no longer a virgin?

The tortures he will invent to punish me are beyond even the capability of my overactive imagination.

I haven't stopped sobbing since we got in the limo that's delivering me to my own personal Hell. Anyone who sees me would think I was heartbroken over the Supreme Archon's death, but that's not why I'm inconsolable. I am mourning the beloved husband I leave behind and the life together we will never have.

My plain gold wedding band now sits on my right hand, as I must wear Ryan's hateful engagement ring on the correct finger or risk his fury. I refuse to abandon the ring that symbolizes the love and commitment to the man I married, to the man I will forever love with every fiber of my being. Continuing to wear the band Declan gave me is a small act of defiance, but one I didn't think twice about. I want to wear his ring as a visible symbol of our vows and I found a way to do it. I know I will frequently be on television, and I want Declan to see I have not, and never will, forget him. Even if I never see him again, never hear his deep, lusty voice or feel his hands and mouth on my body, he will always be a part of me. I will never stop seeking a way back into my husband's arms, even if it kills me.

I'm surprised at these ambitious and very dangerous thoughts. Am I actually strong enough to attempt an escape on my own?

All these years, I was taught to believe that, as a woman, I am inherently flawed and terribly weak. But now I know that's bullshit. I am not weak, stupid or immoral. I am fully competent, able to make my own decisions and follow my own moral compass. I am empathetic, passionate and capable of great love.

I think of Anna's acumen and intelligence and Marta's compassion and benevolence; both women steadfast in their integrity and incorruptibility. Sure, it's a rare woman who's as physically strong as a man, but mentally and emotionally, what if we are actually the stronger sex?

I stare hatefully at Ryan behind my dark sunglasses as I wipe the last of my tears from my cheeks. I am not his child to discipline, nor his slave to command. Just as he's ascending to a new level, I will elevate alongside him.

As Consort to the Supreme Archon, I will be the American equivalent of a Queen. Anyone who has ever played chess knows that the Queen is the most powerful piece in the game. Although the game itself revolves around the King, the Queen is the only piece that can go anywhere. She's the only piece without limits. If women aren't inherently capable, the Queen would never have been made the most dangerous piece on the board. Frankly, I'm shocked I never realized this until now.

My tears dry and my grief lifts. If Anna were in my shoes, she wouldn't despair. No. She'd be thinking and scheming twice as hard to find a way out. I can't let myself go down the rabbit hole of despondency. As long as I follow Thomas Dylan's advice, there's still a chance, no matter how small, that things may still work out for Declan and me.

I sit up straighter, pulling my shoulders back, as Ryan sits smug and oblivious to the forming of my new resolve. If he thinks I will go gentle into that good night, he's got another thing coming.

Because before my light dies, I have an awful lot of raging left to do.

54

Declan

I haven't seen my wife in ten days and I'm ready to lose my fucking mind.

John came to me the first moment he could to tell me the Supreme Archon was dead. The New State Press reports there will be thirty days of mourning before the grand investiture of the new Supreme Archon. Thirty days from then will be what the administration's calling the grandest wedding the country has ever seen.

Ryan and Emma's wedding.

Now that the old man is dead there's nothing to stop Ryan from doing whatever the hell he wants. He and Emma are living in the Mansion together and there's no one to stop him from hurting her. If he rapes her and finds out she's not a virgin he will kill her. Every second she is with him is another moment she's in mortal danger.

I have to get her out of there.

John begs me to not do anything stupid, but the truth is I can't get within a hundred yards of the Mansion without a sniper putting a bullet in my brain. I have no weapons, no army, no nothing. It will take the force of the troops that landed in Normandy to break her out, and I have no well-armed allies to give me aid.

I don't eat, I can't sleep and I have zero ability to concentrate on anything, so I pray. I get on my knees and I pray for hours. I beg God to please, please, bring her back to me. Two days later, John returns to tell me he saw TV footage of Emma. She's still at the Mansion, an unwilling participant in the extravaganza that's the old man's funeral. She's stuck there for as long as they deem her necessary to the pageantry. He doesn't say what we're both thinking.

I may never get her back.

No. I refuse to believe that. We've come too far and I love her too much to give up. I refuse to become despondent and mourn her while she is still very much alive. I'm going to get her back and we are going to get away, somewhere far from this Godforsaken country. I'll get my medical license and open a practice in some picturesque little European village and Emma will continue to dance for as long as she damn well wants. I'll make love to her every day and we will have half a dozen babies and together we will raise them in a home full of love and laughter in a little house by the sea.

I know that is probably the hokiest sentiment to ever run through my addled brain, but I want this so badly I can fucking taste the salty ocean air. I want my wife back and I'm willing to die trying to make that happen.

Every night I troll the tunnels trying to find resistance members willing to help. I stay out for days on end and so far all I've found are a handful of half-starved black cards and one highly inept mugger. I'm exhausted, starving and ready to drop. I'm so wiped I curl up in a ball and pass out in a corner of what once was the metro stop in Rosslyn. I haven't seen anyone in a few days, and I feel safe enough getting a little shut eye before I fall over. I wake some time later with the sharp edge of a knife against my throat.

"Hey, handsome. Miss me?"

I must have been out cold because it takes me a second to register the blade, the sultry Russian accent, and to remember where the hell I am. "Anna?"

"The one and only," she laughs as she removes the blade from my neck. "I almost slit your throat before I see it is you. You look like shit."

"Where the fuck have you been? I've been looking for you for months."

She shrugs her shoulders. "Well, you suck at looking. Aside from few weeks in Philly, I've been here whole time. I need to lay low, yes? Now, come with me. This place is not safe."

We creep noiselessly out of the tunnels and through the remains of the area that once had been a hotbed of government and private business. Sticking to the shadows, we are particularly careful as our close proximity to the Pentagon means there's twice as many patrols on the ground. We slide into the remains of one of the many collapsed underground parking garages, shimmying through a narrow opening until we come to an oddly placed door amid the rubble.

When we get inside, Anna introduces me to a few other guys before leading me into a dimly lit kitchen and pouring herself a large cup of coffee. I swear, as long as I've known her, she's never been anywhere without a huge cup of coffee, a giant glass of wine or a shot of vodka in her hand. I'm pretty sure I've never seen her eat.

"What's your poison?"

"Coffee. Black." She pulls out an unlabeled bottle and pours at least three shots worth of something into a beer stein-sized mug before topping it off with something freakishly akin to tar. It tastes fucking divine. She motions for me to sit as she rifles through the fridge, pulling out boxes and sniffing at them questioningly before handing me a small carton of greasy congealed takeout and a fork.

Boozy coffee and week-old lo-mein. Dinner of Champions.

I don't complain. I'm ravenous.

"Let us talk business, yes?" Anna gives up on her coffee and instead takes long swigs out of the unlabeled bottle. "So, what are you doing this far from home? Were you thinking of being the little wife's one man rescue? I tell you right now, if you think you do that and survive you are having deluge." I nearly choke on a noodle laughing at her wrong choice of word.

Wait, how does she know we got married?

Yeah, that's Anna for you. Somehow, this bitch knows everything and by everything I mean just that. *Everything.* I glare at her as she smiles triumphantly, proud that once again she's one step ahead of me. I guess that's why she's the boss and not me, not that I care. I don't want to be the boss.

No, Anna isn't going to make this easy. She plans to turn this moment into some form of after-school special teaching moment. "I wasn't going to sit at home and wait for help to come knocking on my door."

She leans forward, placing her elbows on her knees and gives me a mocking incredulous look. "What? You think trolling tunnels is great way to make new friends? Maybe people you meet help you rescue Princess Buttercup? What, you no longer bad enough to take down whole Committee yourself?"

Anna takes another long drink from the bottle, appraising the building fury she sees in my face. Then she smiles that self-assured smirk that always makes me wish she was a man so I can punch her in the face.

"So, big, bad, Declan finally sees he is mere mortal like rest of us," she teases. "Maybe he need help after all, yes?"

"Fuck you, Anna," I spit. I may be grateful for the food and the whatever-the-hell I'm drinking but I'm not in the mood for her bull-shit. "You gonna help me or not?"

She smiles devilishly, her eyes gleaming in the low light of the one working fluorescent bulb.

"Anything for you, baby," she teases. She leans back and makes herself comfortable and starts to talk business. She has a plan.

Oh, thank Christ, she has a plan.

It isn't rocket science, but it's solid enough that it *could* work. Some of it's dependent on if we've read our marks right and at least a quarter of its success will rely on simple dumb luck. I hang out with Anna for a few days more, meeting new members of her team and sharpening our plan. We are running out of time and we have only one chance of this working.

I refuse to fail.

55

Emma

This stomach virus is going to be the death of me.

The past few days I've had my head stuck in the toilet bowl and for once, it isn't because I'm sticking my fingers down my throat. It's the strangest thing. The violent nausea comes in waves and just when I think maybe I should go see a doctor, it subsides. I chalk it up to nerves.

Thanks to my father's promise to the Chinese delegates, I'm still slated to dance in *Swan Lake*. Ryan is more than happy to delay our wedding until the end of the March, but he insists I live in the Executive Mansion with him where he can keep close watch over me. I've been moved to one of the many extra bedrooms and driven to and from rehearsal every day. I'm supplied with my own security detail, and in place of one shadow I now have a dozen. I am always under armed guard for "safety reasons" and when that isn't feasible, I am under the watchful eye of some high-level staffer. One night, I wake up wanting a snack and find the door to my suite locked from the outside.

They are taking no chances. There is no way to escape.

I spend more and more time chaperoned by Alex after he's named my official staff liaison. He's friendly and funny and always has a compliment for me no matter how last minute my attempts to get myself together. On one of my sicker days he even holds my hair for me while I puke into a plastic bag in the car.

Now that is going the extra mile.

No matter how lousy I feel, I drag myself to rehearsal every day. This is going to be my last performance, my swan song, in more ways than one. Time is running out. I'm staring out the limo window when Alex clears his throat loudly.

I turn and smile. "Sorry, did you say something?"

"I offered you a penny for your thoughts."

"My thoughts are only worth a penny?"

He laughs. "Seriously, I was wondering what you were thinking."

"Nothing important," I shrug. I can't tell him the truth—that I'm mourning the loss of my husband and unable to find a way to escape the giant mess I'm in. I'm not dumb enough to think Alex will keep my secrets. No matter how nice Alex is, he's still a member of the Committee.

"Are you nervous about marrying Ryan?"

I don't have to utter a word, my body language says it all. I stop breathing, my muscles tensing, my eyes widening in fear. I don't know how to respond so I stick to the party line. "What was blessed by Our Dear Departed Supreme Archon is His will and will be done."

Alex looks at me sharply. "You didn't answer my question."

I look at him closely, wondering what he's trying to say, wondering about his motives, wondering if he will report my words verbatim to Ryan when he sees him next.

"Emma, I wish you would confide in me. I won't tell them what you say, I swear. I'm just worried about you."

He seems so sincere, so honest, that I wonder if I'm missing an opportunity that's been magically dropped in my lap. Would he help me escape if I asked? I want to trust him, everything about him screaming for me to give him a chance, but I'm just not sure. Making a mistake could easily be the difference between life and death.

I smile and let out a small staged sigh. "You got me. I am nervous about the wedding. It's just all happening so fast." He nods in acceptance of my reply but doesn't seem to believe what I've said. This question had obviously been a test and it will only be a matter of time before I find out if I answered correctly.

* * *

Three weeks later, I'm still puking on nearly a daily basis. I'm dizzy and exhausted, often needing to take a break halfway through the long days of rehearsal to lie down in my dressing room. Yesterday, I was so wiped out I spent the entire day in bed. Even with all the rest, I can still barely keep my eyes open this morning.

On our way to the National, Alex requests the soundproof divider put up between us and the driver. He looks deadly serious. I'm horribly nauseated and I'm positively green as I slide into the car across from him. He frowns.

"You look horrible."

"Thanks, Alex. Every girl loves to hear that first thing in the morning," I croak. My throat is sore from a night of steady vomiting.

"You need to see a doctor."

"No, I'm okay, really -" Right as I try to convince us both I'm not going to die, my mouth fills with warm, thin saliva. Another bout of violent retching is imminent.

"Please, pull over, I'm going to be sick," I gag as I realize I've forgotten a plastic bag. Alex barely gets the command to the driver and me out onto the grassy shoulder of the road before I throw up again. He holds back my hair, handing me the water bottle he plucks from my bag so I can rinse the bile from my mouth.

"Emma, are you pregnant?" he whispers urgently into my ear.

Christ Almighty. Am I pregnant?

The blood drains from my face. I hadn't even thought about the *possibility* I could be pregnant, but in that split second I know. I'm pregnant. My shock wears off just long enough to realize my glass face has given me away.

"Mother of Christ," he whispers as he rakes his hand across his eyes as he looks around, terrified we may have been overheard. "Please tell me it's Ryan's."

I stare at him like a deer in headlights.

"*Jesus H. Christ, Emma.*" He looks like he might be the next one to puke.

"Please, please, don't tell Ryan."

He shakes his head. "You know he can have you stoned for this."

I must look like I'm going to faint because he grabs my arm to steady me. Alex is one of those guys that always seems fairly unflappable, but right now he's beyond flustered.

"I swear, I won't tell Ryan but *when*—not *if*—but *when* you get found out, you better not say I knew. He hates me. If he finds out I knew and didn't tell him immediately, he'll kill me for certain."

"I swear, Alex. On my life, no matter what happens, I won't say a word." I sigh in relief as Alex helps me back into the car.

He smiles a small pinched smile. "Congratulations?" he adds with raised eyebrows and a shrug of his shoulders as he tries to lighten the mood. Neither of us laugh.

If I had thought I was in trouble before, things just got immeasurably worse. I look down and find that I've been absently rubbing my still flat belly that at some point soon will give away my secret.

56

Alex

I have every intention of keeping my word. There's no way I'm telling anyone, *especially* Ryan, that Emma's pregnant. When he finds out he's going to kill her. I doubt she will even make it to the stadium to get stoned, he'll do it himself. He's that kind of guy.

I swore to protect her, but this mess is far beyond my ability to sweep under the rug. All this time I thought my biggest concern was keeping her safe from Ryan's violent, drunken mood swings. I should have been more worried about keeping her safe from herself.

Honestly, I have no idea how Emma's going to get out of this. I'm sure there's got to be some doctor out there willing to do an illegal abortion but even if I found a doctor willing to risk his life, would Emma go through with it? The way her hand flew to her belly makes me think she wants to keep this baby, not that I can think of a single way that's even remotely feasible.

And who the hell is the father?

That's one question I'm simply too afraid to ask.

Even if it turns out she's not pregnant, it's pretty clear that sweet, pink-cheeked, wholesome-looking Emma is no longer a virgin. I don't know Ryan well, but one thing I do know is he will kill her right on their marital mattress if she doesn't bleed for him on their wedding night.

Oh, you stupid, stupid girl.

I'm not going to lie. I like Emma. I like her a lot. She's kind and beautiful and incredibly intelligent aside from her blinding lack of common sense. She deserves so much more than what she has coming to her in the upcoming years, if she lives that long. I'm old enough to remember the good old days when people could love who they chose no matter of sex, race and economic factors. Emma deserves to be with the one she loves just like every other freaking human in this country.

It's times like these when I'm horrified at what this country has become. How quickly we went from a respected Republic to this freakish offshoot of totalitarianism is still beyond my comprehension. I've always been an avid student of history and even I missed the signs of where we were headed. If it weren't for concern for the safety of my family I would get the fuck out if I could. Aside from my mom and my siblings, there's been no reason for me to stay for nearly five years.

I feel terrible for Emma and the predicament she's in. I want to protect her, but choosing that route would mean severe consequences for many people should I be found out. There's no doubt in my mind that helping her constitutes multiple acts of treason, but if I don't aid her, who will? I wonder if the man that fathered her child has any way of helping, if there's any hope her Prince Charming will come riding along on a white horse and whisk her out of harm's way.

I wonder if his horse is big enough for me to hitch a ride and gallop off into the sunset with them.

I have no idea who fathered this child, and honestly, I don't care. One thing I'm sure of is Emma wouldn't have risked everything to have sex with some random guy. No, whoever fathered this child is someone she loves very, very much. In the grand scheme of things, it doesn't matter who he is. Whoever the guy is that Emma fell for, took her virginity and got her with child still has one last thing to do.

He's going to get her killed.

57

Emma

The day of Ryan's investiture dawns bright and sunny even though it's one of the coldest days of the year, so far. The wind whips the flags outside the Mansion, rattling the ropes that shackle them to their poles.

I'm actually hungry this morning, which is a surprise. Up until a few days ago I was still arguing with Alex about needing to see a doctor for my severe morning sickness. I finally got tired of listening to him and told him if he could find a doctor he feels he can trust with this life and death secret then, by all means, tell him to come on over. He shut up after that.

Before Ryan's investiture my father's taking his Oath of Command and officially becoming an Archon. Apparently, Alex and my father are working well together as my father put him up for promotion, bumping his rank to Lieutenant Archon. On the other side of the spectrum, Ryan and my father are more at odds than ever. Every afternoon they sequester themselves into the Supreme Archon's office and Ryan curses and yells at the top of his lungs, while my father's voice can barely be heard replying in low, venomous tones.

After spending what feels like a lifetime getting my hair and makeup done, I'm presented with a pale blue and metallic silver shift dress to be worn under a thin white and silver wool coat and another pair of impossibly high stilettos. I'm given strands of pearls to wear around my neck and a pair of pearl earrings. My hair's pulled back into a sleek chignon and the whole ensemble topped off with a tiny veiled hat. Unless they staple it to my scalp, it's never going to survive the forty-plus mile-per-hour winds. I'm going to freeze to death in this outfit, not that anyone cares.

Ryan looks amazing in his new white wool dress uniform, his wide chest adorned with a variety of colorful medals and thick coils of looping gold braid draped gracefully over his left shoulder. The full effect of him in his precisely tailored uniform makes him appear even more intimidating, the haughty look in those pale, cold eyes making me shiver.

Alex salutes him and I reverently bow my head a few degrees. After the ceremony, I'm going to have to follow protocol precisely to avoid his retribution. As he isn't the Supreme Archon yet, I'll be damned if I'm going to scrape and bow to him any earlier than I must.

The televised ceremony is scheduled for 11 am with a lengthy military parade to follow. A record-setting crowd is expected in attendance and security's going to be extremely tight. I heard bits and pieces of conversations of the excessive cost of today's events and the freakish amount of security being hired. I keep praying that someone will kill Ryan and end this nightmare before it begins. It would only take one well-aimed bullet. Really, how hard could that be?

It would be next to impossible.

Ryan and I have our own car to the ceremony and for once in his life he actually looks pleased. After all, why shouldn't he? All of his dreams are coming true. Ryan catches me staring at him and returns my glare with a vicious sneer. Although I wonder what the hell could be going through his head, unless I'm certain it's going to be a bullet, I'm not opening myself up to ask.

The well-rehearsed ceremony held on the stairs of the defunct Supreme Court building goes off without a hitch. I do my duty, holding the *Text* for both my father and Ryan to swear on, as, of course, my mother is too wasted, I mean, *ill*, to attend. By the time Ryan finishes his lengthy speech, I'm close to frozen. The wind is whipping and snow has started to fall. By the time the parade begins, I can't stop my teeth from chattering.

When the events end we're herded back into waiting cars that blessedly have the heat blasting. I'm deep in thought when Ryan surprises me.

"You did well today."

"Thank you, Sir." I swivel my head from the window to look him in the eye.

"I've been impressed with your recent behavior. I think you are finally learning how to act like a proper wife to a world leader."

Yes, because I'm playing to your overstuffed ego, you dumb prick. Oh, and for the record? I still fucking hate you. I'm just trying to keep you from splattering my brains on the pavement during your next temper tantrum.

No, I better not say that. "Thank you sir," I manage to choke out as I lower my eyes to my hands so they don't give away my lie. "Your approval means a great deal to me."

"As your reward, tonight, after the ball, I've decided to honor you by allowing you to start your wifely duties."

My head snaps up and I can't help staring at him with obvious revulsion. My father warned me that now Ryan is officially the Supreme Archon, he can do whatever he wants without consequences. Apparently what he wants is to fuck me. Tonight.

"B-but we aren't married yet," I stammer. "It's against the law."

His eyes light up with an evil glare. "You are forgetting, Emma dear, that as of now, I am above the law."

The second we arrive back at the Mansion, I flee to my rooms, summoning Alex about a half hour later. I don't have a choice anymore. I beg him to help me as I don't know what to do. And judging by the look on his face, neither does he.

58

Declan

I watch the swearing in ceremonies on John and Marta's tiny television, as they, in turn, watch me. They tell me not to, both of them in agreement this is a bad idea. Fuck, I *know* it's a bad idea. It's going to be torture to watch her with Ryan but I have to see her. I miss her so much I physically hurt. I swear to John and Marta I won't freak out, or get pissed off and do something stupid. They also know that's an oath I'm incapable of keeping.

At first glance, Emma looks so beautiful standing out there in the whipping wind, tendrils of her hair blown loose and dancing around her frost-tipped cheeks. People around the world watching will see exactly what her stylists and the administration want them to see: a pretty, pink-cheeked, smiling and dutiful fiancee.

But as her husband, as someone who loves her more than life, what I see makes me furious. She's doing her damnedest to hide it, but she looks like she's close to frozen. For fuck's sake, her teeth are chattering, she's so cold. She's flanked by high-ranking men all wearing warm wool suits, heavy dress uniforms and fur-lined gloves, yet she's expected to brave the elements in the business equivalent of a bikini. She looks pale, thin and very, very tired. She smiles at all the right times and she's playing her part well, but I see the sadness in her eyes. She looks like the light that once was within her has burned out.

59

Alex

Ryan wastes no time and within an hour, there's already a team in motion moving Emma's things into his suite. The poor girl nearly faints right there in the hall.

What the fuck am I going to do?

I get Emma a glass of water and tell her to lie down. I promise her I'll be back shortly. I have an idea, but it's going to be risky for her as well as for me. Especially for me.

I head over to my rooms in the executive apartments next door and go through my shoebox of over the counter medications. I pull out a box of diphenhydramine and some prescription alprazolam and crush the pills up into a fine powder using the heel of my dress shoe. I pray I've made enough to knock out a good sized man yet not kill him when mixed with the copious amounts of alcohol I plan to ply him with.

Is it a good plan?

Hell, no. But it's the best I'm going to come up with on a few hours' notice.

60

Emma

I'm not sure what Alex put in his drink, but I'm more than a little afraid right now that Ryan's dead.

For the most part, the ball had gone off without a hitch. Ryan and I danced and smiled, putting on a great show for the cameras and our guests. As usual, Ryan drank way too much, and as the night lumbered on his facade of control cracked. My father pulled Ryan aside several times demanding that he lay off the booze, but it never failed that less than five minutes later, Alex found a way to get another glass of scotch into Ryan's hand.

I was painfully well chaperoned throughout the evening's festivities, and every possible exit was heavily guarded. With no way for me to slip out, I could only pray that whatever plan Alex came up with would work. He hadn't let on what his plan was, but I assumed by the way he'd been eagerly attending to Ryan's beverage needs, at some point, he planned to slip something in his drink.

By the last half hour of the ball, Alex looked twitchier than someone afflicted with Tourette's. Ryan was very, very drunk and my father positively livid. He tried multiple times to find some way of getting

Ryan out of the ballroom without making a scene, all to no avail. My father finally resorted to grabbing me by the arm and steering me out onto the dance floor. He whispered for me to get Ryan out of here. Now. He said he didn't care how I got his ass upstairs, but he wanted it done fast.

Once again, dear old dad was willing to sacrifice me to make his wishes happen. Bastard.

Without any other option, I performed my duty. I headed towards Ryan, a very insincere smile plastered on my face, just as Alex handed him another drink. Alex gave me a nearly imperceptible nod, my cue that he'd done his part. I stayed downstairs with Ryan another fifteen minutes waiting for Alex's cocktail to kick in before whispering in Ryan's ear that I was ready to head upstairs.

Ryan smiled suggestively at me, sneeringly making all sorts of inappropriate comments that made the people within earshot cringe and look at me pityingly. By now, Ryan could hardly stand. When Alex and I finally got him to the residence, Ryan was incoherent and passed out the second his head hit the pillow.

My father stalked upstairs a few minutes later after completing some damage control, the three of us now standing here silently, staring at our Supreme Archon in varying degrees of disgust. I'm not sure which of us hopes more that he never wakes up.

As if finally coming to his senses, my father grabs Alex's arm and drags him off without a word or a second glance, leaving me alone with the incredibly intoxicated world leader. I hadn't been in the newly refurbished private rooms that Ryan and I now share, so while he's asleep I give myself a tour. The decor is cold and dark, much like his penthouse had been. Gone are the gaudy gilt mirrors, heavy velvet curtains and oversize furniture. The private residence had gone from excessive tacky glitz to dark, cold and uncomfortable.

Gotta give the designers credit. They certainly know how to personify the surroundings to the Supreme Assholes that live here.

There's an office off the side of the living room that catches my eye. I slip off my painful heels before walking into the room and sitting behind the desk, resting my forearms on the polished wood. I open the drawers and rifle through papers as much out of boredom as interest. When I open the center drawer of his desk I gasp. There, once again in a place of honor, right at his fingertips, is the knife Ryan held to my throat all those months ago.

Horrified, I slam the drawer shut, but something about the knife compels me to take another look. I don't even want to touch it, but there's something familiar about it and not just in the I-was-previously-threatened-with-it kind of way. Gently lifting the weapon by its ends, I touch it the same way someone would pick up a dirty tissue. I place it on the edge of the desk, looking at the scrolled roping carvings and intricate knots expertly chiseled into the hilt.

I can't believe what I'm seeing. I close my eyes, praying that when I open them, things won't look the same, but when I do, I'm horrified.

I know exactly where I have not only seen, but touched and even tasted these patterns before. All the hours I spent tracing these exact designs with my fingertips are so ingrained in my muscle memory I could draw them blindfolded in my sleep. Over time I've learned the meanings of every one of the symbols. There is no mistake; this is the same intricate Celtic knot-work tattooed on my husband's arms.

This is Declan's knife. After all these years, Ryan kept it as a fucking souvenir.

I pick up the weapon and yank it from the leather scabbard, feeling the balanced weight in my hand. I trace the carved patterns over and over again with my finger, just the same way I used to do to the ones inked on my husband's arms.

I don't know how long I sit there running my fingers over the designs lost in thoughts of sorrow. Holding the knife that once belonged to Declan, to his father, and his father before him makes me miss him even more. The history of the Byrne men is embedded in this heirloom, the tragic tale of a cursed family trapped within the carvings. This is the last known possession of his family and it belongs with my husband. It doesn't belong in a drawer as the sinister trophy of a cruel and dishonorable man.

I hear movement in the other room and I quickly re-sheath the knife and slide it back into the drawer. I swipe the fallen tears from my cheeks seconds before my father enters the office. He motions for me to follow him.

I stand slowly, my hand caressing the closed drawer just a second longer. In the oddest way, I feel the knife call to me, imploring me to take it with me. After all, am I not a Byrne, too? At that moment I don't know how, but I just know this blade has more work yet to do.

"Hurry up, Emma. I don't have all goddamn night," my father calls from the other room.

A sinister smile forms on my lips as I rise.

Yes, this knife certainly has more work to do.

61

RYAN DOESN'T WAKE UP for nearly twenty-four hours.

Almost the second Ryan rouses, my father's in his bedroom, his voice stern and impassive as he lays down the law. An hour later, a memo's sent out to residence and staff members stating that for the next two weeks, Ryan will be traveling on urgent business. Less than an hour after that, a limo picks up a scowling and reluctant Ryan and takes him to a discreet rehab facility somewhere far away.

With Ryan out of the Mansion, I'm safe for another two weeks. We're in the last days before the opening of *Swan Lake* and I rehearse daily, often eight to ten hours of runthroughs, lighting checks and last moment blocking changes. The last two fittings of my costumes require a fair number of alterations as my body changes to accommodate the life growing within me. My costumer smiles, stating that my upcoming marriage must suit me as I'm putting on weight and look stronger and healthier than ever before.

Oh, if she only knew.

Although my stage of pregnancy is still too early to show, I already feel the difference in my body. I'm trying to eat more regularly and healthier and I've stopped forcing myself to throw up. I am trying so hard to be the good mother I always wanted and that my baby deserves.

As promised, the delegation from China returns the Wednesday before opening night. As Ryan's Second-in-Command, it's left to my father to entertain them, and he does it with grace and dignity. When I am available, I also join in the social aspects of the festivities and together, my father and I charm them. Quite surprisingly, I even enjoy my interactions with the delegates who treat me with a level of kindness and courtesy I could easily become accustomed to.

On Thursday evening we put together an informal party with dinner and dancing that my father presides over the way a true Supreme Archon should. He's witty, entertaining, complimentary, fully sober and sane. The fact that this trip couldn't possibly be more different from the one from a few months ago is lost to no one.

I watch my father closely as he addresses the delegates. He's friendly to the point of joviality, respectful, and a truly gracious host. One of the delegates even goes so far as to mention this has been the best visit they've had since the "last decent" President was in office. Despite the fact the delegate has made a huge faux pas by discussing the times before the war, my father does not correct him. He overlooks the error completely and takes the statement as the compliment it's intended.

I have no idea what my father's up to, but he most certainly has some sort of plan in motion. With him, every word, gesture and thought has a meaning and all are part of some master plan. With Ryan out of the picture and unable to ruin my father's carefully laid schemes, I have no doubt that whatever he's up to is going to work.

62

THE NEXT MORNING I'm afforded the luxury of sleeping in as tonight's opening night. I lounge sleepily in my comfortable bed, my hand gently caressing my belly as I wish good morning to my baby. I finally drag myself out from under the covers and pad around my rooms looking for a way to occupy myself. I spend the day relaxing, reading and puttering around the residence, conserving my energy for the night ahead. When my nerves start kicking-in during the early afternoon, I occupy my mind and idle hands by prepping my toe shoes for the weekend's performances, yet another of my calming rituals. I pull out my stash of supplies and set to work.

As I slit through the stitching on my third pair of pointe shoes, the handle of my cheap knife breaks, barely missing my palm in the process. I swear out loud as this is not a good omen for tonight while looking around my room for something sharp. I find nothing. As time gallops closer to my wedding day, anything dangerous has mysteriously disappeared from my rooms. My father is taking no chances.

I know there's one place I'll find what I need. As much as the knife in Ryan's desk creeps me out, I'm short on time. Just as I finish sewing the ribbons onto my last pair of shoes, a knock on the door announces the arrival of my car. Not wanting to be late, I shove everything in front of me into my dance bag in one sweeping motion. I'm glad I had enough time to finish so I can relax a bit at the theater. Tonight's going to be a big night, and I'm going to need every bit of energy to get through it.

63

SINCE ITS FIRST performance in 1877, there have probably been a million different versions of *Swan Lake*. A favorite of audiences worldwide, directors and choreographers around the world have continued to draw crowds with the promise of a new twist that will make their version the best ever. Personally, I have always believed the classics should remain unaltered, but as a dancer, you don't get to make those decisions. You dance what you are told to dance.

Damn, if that's not the story of my life.

The National is not a company eager to reinvent the wheel, so we're doing most of Petipa's original choreography in a series of four acts in which I dance the roles of both the white and black swan. It's an exhausting ballet, both physically and mentally and I am relieved the severe nausea that plagued me for weeks abated. I'm still not one-hundred percent, but have regained most of my strength.

My costumes are gorgeous albeit heavy. The designers made certain they are the most beautiful, elaborate and most expensive ever created. Once my thick makeup and feather headpiece are carefully pinned in place I transform into Odette, the cursed Swan Queen. I take one last look in my dressing room mirror, checking again that all the pieces of my black swan costume are ready for my quick change between acts two and three. We are thirty minutes to curtain, time to head up for a final stretch before we begin.

I know I dance a brilliant white swan even before the curtain falls for intermission. Although not usual, I am told to go out for bows before heading back down to my dressing room to change for act three. I sprint to my dressing room, knowing I have little time remaining to do the elaborate change of makeup and costume that usually takes the entire intermission. I have already unpinned the feathered headpiece and have my tutu partially off when I burst into my private dressing room. Before I even sense I'm not alone, I'm grabbed roughly by the arm and dragged inside. A hand clamps hard over my mouth while someone else slams and locks the door behind us.

"Do not scream. It's me."

What the fuck? Anna?

She spins me around and faces me, her emerald eyes glittering. She's clad in my black swan costume, her makeup thick and her hair dyed to perfectly match mine. Except for her sparkling green eyes and being a few inches taller, we would be nearly impossible to tell apart even within the confines of the cramped room.

"Get dressed, we're getting you out," an eerily familiar voice says. The creepy blonde guy from Union Station stands at the dressing room door, a rifle in his hands and the limp body of Shadowman lying in a pool of blood at his feet.

"You remember Brian, yes?" Anna hands me a pile of all black clothing. I nod. "Good. Go with him. Do what he tells you. No questions. Understand?"

"Yes." I should say no. Right now I'm beyond confused but I do as I'm told. I strip off my costume and put on the belted thick black leggings, t-shirt and heavy cotton hoodie. I lace up the ankle high black boots tight as I have a feeling there's a lot of running ahead of me. Suddenly I stop as a terrifying thought occurs to me.

"Anna, how are you going to get out? At some point, someone's going to realize you aren't me." I feel my happiness deflating.

"Don't worry about me, I'll be fine. I am like bad penny. I always turn up." She's brushing me off. I don't know what she's planning but I don't want her to die for me and I tell her that.

"Who says I am going to die?" She pulls Declan's knife out of my bag she obviously already searched and attaches the scabbard to my belt.

Things have suddenly gotten very real. Judging by the looks passing between Brian and Anna, more will happen tonight than just my rescue. Anna hands me a towel covered in makeup remover to get the glowing white foundation off of my face before hugging me fiercely. The third act is ready to begin and they are calling places.

"If you have a girl, you better name the crotch goblin for me," she hisses in my ear before leaning in and kissing me fiercely on the mouth. She's wearing the same dark purple lip stain we had both worn at the club. I lick my lips that taste of dark chocolate, currants and red wine, the flavors that will forever remind me of Anna. I look at her in amazement, getting ready to ask her how she knew, but she beats me to the punchline.

"Emma, darling, you not learn by now that I know everything?" She gives me one last wide smile and a wink before darting out of the room.

64

BRIAN DRAGS ME down the hall after checking there's no one to intercept us. We exit through the fire door in the back where Marcus awaits us with two more dead guards at his feet. We run fast, making certain to stay in the shadows before ducking into an abandoned Metro entrance. Two more armed men join us, reporting the tunnels are clear and we are safe to proceed. I have a million questions and no time to ask them. After a few minutes, we hear an explosion followed by an Earth-shaking rumble.

"God damn, she did it." The note of awe in Marcus' voice frightens me. I want to ask him what she did but I'm too afraid to speak.

We stop a few times to catch our breath. I have no idea where we're headed and in all truth, as long as it's away from my father and Ryan, I don't care. I'm terrified to ask where Declan is. I know the resistance is strict about not having members with spouses and children involved in dangerous missions. Yet knowing my stubborn husband, I find it hard to believe he wouldn't find some way to be involved.

"We're close. The extraction team's not far from here," Brian tells me, eerily reading my mind. "Ready to see your husband?" He grins.

"Yes," I breathe. I'm nearly giddy, finally knowing for certain he's alive.

"Don't worry, no one told him you're pregnant. Anna threatened us with a slow and painful death if we let it slip. She said he needs to hear that from you."

They laugh quietly as they pick up their heavy weapons and we jog down the long dark tunnel. By the time we make it to the doorway that leads up a flight of crumbling concrete stairs, I have a serious stitch in my side and I'm soaked with sweat. We burst out of the service stairwell and cut through a deserted neighborhood until we reach an old highway sound barrier. A couple people emerge from the shadows and set up two tall ladders. We climb wordlessly, cresting the top before people on the other side see us and erect ladders on the other side for us to climb down.

No sooner than my feet hit the ground I sense Declan is near. I don't know how, or where, but I just know he's here. A heavily armed man wearing all black walks towards me. At first his steps seem unsure, almost afraid but, with every step he takes, his pace quickens. He removes the large rifle slung across his shoulder and hands it quickly off to another black-clad man before breaking into a run.

I race to him and launch myself into his arms. The fresh, summery smell of relief overpowers the noxious fumes of fear of the past few months as we cling to one another. The other people cease to exist for us as Declan kisses me soundly, whispering repeated prayers of thanksgiving to the God he's crediting for delivering me safely into his arms.

"You gotta go, Declan. You don't have time for this right now." Marcus slaps Declan fraternally on the back as my husband kisses me one last time before reluctantly pulling away. He calls out heart-felt thanks to everyone, grabs his rifle and takes my hand in his. Within minutes, we're speeding away from the city that, with any luck, we will never call home again.

65

Declan

It worked. Mother of Christ, thank you, thank you, thank you. Anna's plan actually fucking worked.

Anna, in true genius form, had managed to kill a shit-load of birds with one stone. Except in this case it wasn't birds but a number of high ranking Archons and officers and the C4 bomb planted in the Supreme Archon's private box proved considerably more effective than a rock.

Like I said before, a lot of this plan depended on nothing more than dumb luck. First, we had to get into the old Kennedy Center undetected and plant the bomb. Anna then had to get in unnoticed, get into costume, get Emma out and then go on stage and dance until right before the end of the third act when she detonated the bomb and ran for her life. Only time will tell if she made it out, but like a true Russian she was prepared for everything, even carrying a cyanide capsule just in case she got caught.

We don't know for sure who was sitting in the box at the time of detonation, but we believe it's Ryan, Bellamy, a few other inconsequential Archons and the key players of the Chinese delegation. That number of casualties is more than good enough for me. We were going more for quality than quantity.

I feel bad for the Chinese guys when Emma tells me they all seemed decent enough when she met them before. They all hated Gregory with a passion, which makes them okay in that 'the enemy of my enemy is my friend' kind of logic. I had initially been concerned about killing them, not for any humanitarian reason, but because I feared the Chinese government siding with the administration and retaliating against us.

Anna had given me the strangest look, one of immense pride and yet full of mocking disdain as she patted me on the cheek and told me not to worry. Apparently Amy had hacked into Ryan's private server and found some shit he planned that made our few dead bodies look like the work of incompetent toddlers. Within a few minutes of the blast, Amy electronically sent Ryan's files to every major world leader. Neither would let on what they found, but apparently his plans are so heinous, if the blast doesn't kill him, some Chinese assassin will.

I thought I would have been chomping at the bit to know if Gregory and Bellamy succumbed in the blast, but I honestly don't give two shits about them right now. I am so damned happy to have my wife back safe, sound and in one piece that I could float to the moon. Everything else that goes right tonight is just gravy.

We're headed to a little town in rural Virginia called Bluemont with one of the last remaining unmonitored airstrips. Because the roads are terrible, it takes us several hours to make it to the deserted farm where we hide the car and walk the remaining miles to the safe house. It's the middle of the night and pitch black except for the half moon and stars that pierce the sky and light our way.

I hold Emma's hand as we walk and if it wasn't for the seriously fucked up circumstances that cause us to be here, our moonlit hike might even have been kind of romantic. I feel a burning need to have my hands on her at all times, no doubt residual fear that she will be ripped away from me again. The entire time we drove here, Emma had been pressed against my side, my arm wrapped around her. We probably looked more like a young couple going on a date than the two revolutionaries fleeing the scene of a crime that we actually are.

We finally make it to the small log cabin located well off the road on the side of a steep cliff. It's maintained by the same farmer who takes care of the airstrip, a cantankerous Gulf War vet that's been working with us pretty much since day one. I'd never met him before, but I was warned that he's a nasty son-of-a-bitch that's not quite right in the head and quick to pull the trigger. When he surprises us on the cabin's porch with an assault rifle large enough to make mine look like a kid's toy, I really think there's a good chance he's going to blow our brains out before I can utter the safe word.

"What the fuck you doin' out here, asshole?" he drawls in a thick West Virginia accent, the rifle pointed at my heart. He's missing so many teeth he spits when he talks and it sounds like he's saying *athhole*.

"We're here to meet the *crop duster* that's coming in tomorrow." I feel more than a bit foolish saying the safe word for a wide variety of reasons.

"Ya don't say," he grumbles, sounding sincerely annoyed that I passed his test. He looks like I just pissed on his parade.

"I picked you up on the trail cam an' didn't know who you was. Neither of you look old enough to be who I was expectin'." He turns his back and shuffles into the cabin. "Well? You comin' in or not?" he rasps, motioning us to walk behind him.

He tells us his name's Ralph and he owns the cabin we're going to overnight in. Once we get inside and he gets a good look at us, if I thought he'd been hostile before, well, I was sorely mistaken. He's as twitchy and agitated as a hibernating bear woken up getting a murder hornet enema.

"What the ever loving fuck are *you* doing here?" He points an accusing finger at Emma. "Whole motherfuckin' world out lookin' for you, and *you*," he emphasizes, turning and poking at me with one gnarled finger, "There's a bounty out for you. A big one."

Emma and I stand stock still, unsure of where this is going and I wonder again if Ralph is as trustworthy as everyone thinks. I've learned over the years that even the most ardent patriots think twice when they are starving and Emma and I have made it too far to have our heads served to the remaining Archons John-the-Baptist-style now. Before I can decide whether to shoot the old man or not, he breaks into a wide gummy smile.

"Atta boy!" He howls with laughter and claps me on the back like I'm a beloved golden retriever that just caught his first Frisbee. He goes over to the fridge, pulls out three bottles of beer and opens them with his teeth.

Well, if that doesn't at least partially explain his dental issues.

According to Ralph, the New State Press is reporting that Emma was kidnapped by domestic terrorists and there's a $500,000 reward for her safe return. There's a million dollar award for anyone who brings me in, dead or alive. I find it pretty telling that the administration is more concerned with finding me than getting Emma back.

After the blast, the former Kennedy Center collapsed. There are only a handful of survivors and most of them aren't expected to live. I was involved in procuring the bomb and from what little I know of explosives, this sounds like a crap ton of damage for the tiny bit of C4 we received. We never intended for the building to fall, we only wanted to take out the people in and closest to the Supreme Archon's box.

Something's not right.

Ralph mentions that the Supreme Archon is in critical condition with severe burns and some form of head trauma. I ask if there's been any mention of Anna and he says there's been none. Emma asks about her father, careful to call him Archon Bellamy and not remind Ralph of her relation.

"There's been no mention of him bein' there when it happened."
Emma and I look at each other in surprise.

After Ralph finishes his beer he takes the one Emma hasn't touched and starts drinking it. He gives us some instructions on the place, including telling Emma to 'not flush no tampons and shit like dat down the toilet, as we's here on septic,' that makes her turn purple with embarrassment. He tells me if I cum stain his sheets I better leave a fifty on the dresser so he can get new ones.

Holy shit, this guy's a piece of work. I hope I'm even half as lively as him at that age.

He claps me on the back and winks suggestively at Emma. "Now don't fuck too loud. I wanna get some sleep tonight an' don't need you two screamers keepin' me up remindin' me what I ain't getting no more."

He heads towards the door and stops for a second. "I live about a half mile that-away. If y'all need somethin' ya better wait til 'morrow. At night I shoot first and ask questions later. I don't wanna put no extra holes in ya by accident. Hear me?"

We try to conceal our grins, telling him we understand and thanking him for his hospitality. The second he leaves, we burst out laughing.

This has been one weird fucking night.

66

Emma

It's chilly in the cabin, so Declan decides to light a fire for us after Ralph promises no one lives close enough to see the rising smoke. I'm in desperate need of a shower; between the ballet and running like a fugitive, I'm sticky and uncomfortable and certain I reek to high hell. Declan smiles devilishly and tells me to go heat up the water and he'll join me in a few minutes.

I let the water run in the stone walk-in shower until it's close to scalding before stepping under its steaming spray. I breathe deeply, trying to relax my knotted, adrenaline-fueled muscles. I stretch my overworked body, loving the calming sensations of muscles lengthening and joints releasing under the hot water.

Lost in the bliss of cascading water, I startle when a pair of arms wrap around my waist and Declan presses his naked body against my backside. He pushes aside my dripping hair and kisses my neck, nibbling and sucking the skin into his mouth. His hands reach up and caress my breasts, his cock hard and impatient as it presses against my ass.

"I missed you so much, Emma," he breathes. My husband keeps one hand on my breast, alternating between plumping and petting it in his calloused palm and teasing the nipple with gentle, rolling pinches and feather-light flicks of his fingertips. His other hand slides down the center of my body, cupping my sex in his palm before letting his fingers slide between my folds. When he teases my clit, I can't help but whimper with growing need, a sound that makes him chuckle darkly.

I press back against him, trapping his cock between our writhing bodies. He inhales sharply, swearing under his breath before pressing against me harder. I reach between us, grabbing his cock and firmly stroking it from base to tip. He hisses in mingled surprise and pleasure.

He whispers beautiful, filthy words in my ear as his hands worship every inch of my body. When he knows I can take his teasing no longer, he sinks his dick into me from behind in one hard, smooth thrust. I gasp and moan as he tortures me with long, slow strokes of his cock, his deep sexy voice dirtily narrating our pleasure and driving me insane with desire.

I beg him to let go, to come in me hard, and he emits a wicked laugh. He continues to taunt me until the combination of his voice and touch are too much for me to hold back. My core clamps around his girth and now it's his turn to let out a long, ragged moan as he tenses behind me, his body preparing to claim mine.

I take his one hand and press it to my breast, his branded hand I place over my belly. He grips me tight as he finally gives in and pumps furiously into me, lost in an overwhelming need to satiate us both. His teeth bite and suck at my skin, leaving the proof of his passion blooming on my neck. His rapturous cries are somewhere between a scream and a moan that excite me beyond measure. I beg him for more, demanding he thrust harder and faster until he explodes within me, bringing me to ecstasy within seconds of his violent release.

We gasp together, both searching for breathable air in the foggy confines of the room. Declan pants against my neck as the heady glow of our orgasms dim, our hearts frantically searching for normal rhythm before they burst from over-exertion. His voice is thick and raspy as he groans out random curses between the sweetest words of praise and love.

Declan's hands roam my body, caressing here, pressing there, stroking and cajoling, teasing every last ounce of sensation out of my spent body. I shiver with delight as his hands explore my swollen breasts and hardened belly, finally resting on the ever-so-slight swell of our baby within.

Suddenly, they stop.

Declan's breath, hot and winded just seconds ago, ceases altogether. He turns me to face him, his eyes wide, his face pale despite the humid air and violent orgasm he has yet to recover from. He's oblivious to everything as he presses two fingertips to my lips to silence me when I begin to speak.

As he lowers to his knees, his eyes drink in every changed detail of my body as his fingers trace gently from my mouth to my throat, under my collarbones, and over my swollen breasts. He spreads his hands over my ribs, the motion only stopping to linger lightly on my belly. He closes his eyes momentarily, his lips moving rapidly, almost soundlessly.

"You're pregnant."

I know exactly what's going through his brain; he wants this baby to be his so badly but he's terrified to ask. I've been locked in the same house with Ryan for months and my husband has no idea what may or may not have happened. He looks away, trying to hide the mix of fear, anger and sadness in his eyes that breaks my heart, but his hands remain splayed over my small bump.

In that moment, the strength of his love for me leaves me breathless—for I know that even if I were to tell him the child is Ryan's, he wouldn't forsake me. As hard as it would be for him, he would raise the child of his greatest enemy as if it were his own because his love for me is that strong.

I rest my palm lovingly against his cheek before turning his head and forcing him to look into my eyes. His expression is one of grief, his eyes glassy with tears as he fears the worst.

I place my other hand over his and give it a squeeze. "Sweetheart, without a doubt, the baby's yours."

He looks positively stunned as my words slowly penetrate his mind. I'm ready to repeat them again when, finally, his face breaks into the most exuberant, beautiful smile to ever grace a man's face. Euphoria lights his eyes as pride colors his cheeks. He laughs, tilting his head back as he stands, taking me in his arms and hugging me tight.

"We're having a baby," he whispers over and over as he alternates between laughter and tears of joy. He takes a step back and cups my face in his palms, his eyes red-rimmed from crying but glowing with more love than should be humanly possible for one person to emit.

He smiles more broadly as he raises his hand to swipe away my own happy tears. He takes me in his arms, both of us still laughing and crying as we passionately kiss until the water heater gives up and starts spewing icy water. We spend the rest of the night naked in front of the flickering fire, the room warm enough to make love, slowly and tenderly, on the cliche animal-hide rug.

When exhaustion overtakes us, Declan musters the last of his energy to pick up my sated body and carry me to bed. He lays me under the thick quilts and kisses me sweetly before joining me under the crisp bleached sheets. He cradles my head against his chest, his arms protectively wrapped around me before kissing me one last time on the top of my head. Within seconds, we both fall blissfully and soundly asleep.

I feel like I've been asleep for mere minutes when I hear pounding at the door. The sun is just coming up and I vaguely remember Ralph telling us the pilot will come to our cabin to hang out for the day before we leave the following night under the protective cloak of darkness. Declan's sound asleep, so I throw on his shirt and answer the door, my hair askew, my body fragrant with the wild lovemaking my husband and I enjoyed mere hours ago.

I wait for the coded knock and when it comes, I open the door. I take one look at the tall figure before me and think I must still be asleep—this has to be a dream. Standing in front of me is a ghost.

"Hiya, sister," the tall, handsome man grins, leaning his lithe, muscular frame into the doorway.

That's the last thing I remember before I pass out.

67

Declan

I'm not sure how I managed to sleep through the pounding on the door, but when I hear a strange male voice repeating my wife's name, I wake up fast. I burst into the living room with only a damp towel tied around my waist to find Emma wearing nothing but my t-shirt passed out in another man's arms.

I don't stop to ask questions. I've had more than enough of other men touching my wife, thank you very much. This SOB is going to learn a lesson in respect he's not soon to forget. The fact I have no idea who this guy is or why he's here is secondary on my list of concerns right now. Luckily for all of us, he picks up on my murderous intention and begins to spill his guts the second I lunge for him.

Turns out this guy's our pilot.

On top of that, our pilot turns out to be Emma's *brother*.

Yeah, the brother we thought was dead all this time.

From how she described him from her childhood, if he were to pull a Lazarus I never would have pictured the guy in front of me to be the same dude. From her description, I would have expected a scrawny, pasty-faced mouse of a guy, but the man holding up my wife is none of those. He's tan, with dark brown hair and light gray eyes and looks frighteningly like what I expect his father had when he had been the same age.

Adam's at least six inches taller than me and built like a brick shithouse. He has a Smith and Wesson holstered on his right hip, a Glock strapped under his left arm and a big-ass knife sheathed in the top of his hiking boot. He eyes me suspiciously, looking as unsure of me as I am of him. In a fair fight, I would have my hands full with this guy, something about him making me realize he's been trained to take shit from no one.

Once Emma comes around and we all figure out who everyone is, the tension in the room starts to ease. Emma hugs her brother, sometimes clinging to him as she sobs, sometimes angrily beating his chest with her fists as she yells. She wants to know where he's been, why he left her and most importantly, why he never came back. She's as close to hysterical as my brave, sweet wife has ever been in her life and when she passes out for a second time, I take charge of the situation. This sort of stress isn't good for her or the baby.

I carry her back to the bedroom and hold her as she wakes. She sobs fresh tears in my arms, mumbling questions I can't make out and more than likely, wouldn't know how to answer, anway. The stress of the past few months coupled with pregnancy hormones, yesterday's dangerous escape and our exuberant reunion has left her exhausted and wildly emotional. The shock of having her dead brother suddenly show up was just the final push that would shove pretty much anyone over the edge.

Once she cries herself to sleep, I gently extricate myself from her arms. I pull on my jeans and head back out to the living room where Adam sits at the kitchen table, drinking a beer and staring off into the dying fire. He looks guiltier than fuck.

Well, Adam, where the hell have you been?

I throw a few more pieces of wood on the fire before grabbing myself a beer and sitting down across the table from him. I suck a long drag out of my brew while debating what to do next. I chicken out on speaking first, opting instead to merely cock a questioning eyebrow in his general direction.

We talk for a long while. Well, *he* talks for a long while and I listen. It's a hell of a story, one he will have to repeat to his sister as it's not mine to tell. I tell you one thing, though—as crazy as much of it is, I believe every word.

He wants to know my deal and I fill him in on the Cliffs Notes version of the story that's Emma and me. I tell him that no matter what, his job is to make sure, come hell or high water, he gets her out of the country and somewhere safe. I tell him I'm expendable, but my wife and my baby are not.

I hadn't realized Emma was standing behind me as I fill in her brother on what I believe should be his priorities. He gives me the 'heads up' by flicking his eyes to the doorway behind me where Emma stands, glaring angrily at the back of my head.

I sigh. I've been back with my pregnant wife less than twelve hours and I've already managed to make her mad. I take a deep breath, shaking my head and gulp down another deep swallow of my beer as my brother-in-law looks at me pityingly.

Fuck the woman scorned.

Hell hath no fury like a pissed off pregnant woman.

68

Emma

These fucking men. Things are going to change around here fast or I'm going to kill them both.

Now that the worst of the shock has passed and it appears these two buffoons aren't going to go caveman again, I want answers. Declan sets about making breakfast for us, informing me as he places a heaping plate of scrambled eggs with cheese and toast in front of me that Q and A time has to wait until after I clean my plate.

If looks could kill he'd be dead ten times over. Out of spite, I push the plate away only to have him shove it right back with a growled command to start eating, that he isn't going to sit idly by and watch his baby starve. After staring hatefully at him for another second, I shove a fork full of egg into my mouth. I shoot him a look that says this argument isn't over, but I eat every last bite as Declan sits next to me and gloats. He kisses me on the top of my head before grabbing a blanket from the sofa that he throws on over his bare shoulders and carries his loaded-up plate to the front porch. When the front door clicks shut I look up at my brother with red-rimmed eyes, cuing him to start talking.

Adam gets up and throws another log on the fire, stoking the flames for a moment before sitting down in front of the hearth. He motions for me to join him, wrapping a blanket around my shoulders when he erroneously believes my shivering is from being cold and not the deep sense of dread I can't help but feel. As much as I want to know everything, I have a terrible suspicion that what he's going to say is going to be the hardest thing I've ever had to hear.

He sits across from me and takes my hands in his. They are so large, so strong, the hands of a man, not of the boy I had once known.

"I don't know if you ever picked up on it, Emma—you were so young—but our father has always hated me."

He goes on, his voice steady and confident, not a bit self-pitying but gut-wrenchingly honest. Even as a child I knew what he was saying was true—that my father loathed his only son. It wasn't hard to miss—the cruel, cutting remarks along with heavy-handed blows were practically a daily occurrence in our household.

"I tried so hard to be a good kid, but no matter what I did, I couldn't make him love me."

Growing up, none of us were immune from my father's temper, but Adam absolutely suffered the most. My father viciously singled him out, regularly stomping into his room after coming home angry from work and thrashing him with a belt for some imagined infraction. I remember begging my brother to try to be better, as I was too young to understand that what my father was doing was abuse, pure and simple. Adam could have found the cure for cancer and my father would have still beaten him.

It wasn't until long after my brother left the house for good that I realized the problem wasn't Adam. The problem was my father.

My mother wasn't much better. She could barely glance at Adam without looking like she was going to cry.

Although my parents didn't treat me much better, there was something different in how they treated him. Harsher. Crueler. Every blow from my father, every time my mother walked into a room to find him only to spin on her heel and flee, stomped his heart into the carpet that much further.

Yet their treatment of him didn't make him bitter or angry. It made him kinder. Gentler. He looked out for me and cared for me, comforting me when I cried and even taking blame for my childish mistakes so I wouldn't get punished. He was selfless and thoughtful, and probably the sweetest boy that ever lived.

As Adam grew up, he looked more and more like a carbon copy of my father. Same exact dark hair, olive skin and strong jaw, but with beautiful soft, gray eyes. We don't look like we should be siblings, each of us nearly identical to a different parent. What I didn't know until today is—

"I'm only your half-brother."

The story he spills next is unthinkable in its horror, a family torn apart by my father's predilection to fully embrace each of the Seven Deadly Sins in their entirety. Adam's mother, one of our father's many mistresses over the years, died in childbirth, leaving behind a son wholly unwanted by his father. When word of the lengths he went to in order to hush the scandal hit the news, everyone, including him, thought his career was over.

His advisors had been adamant—If he wanted to ever have a future in politics, he must not only step up and claim his bastard, he must publicly repent his sins. In order to repair his tarnished reputation, he now had to prove to the nation that he was a changed man. Over the next few years, our father presented himself as the archetypal chastened sinner, but in truth, nothing about his behavior changed except to better hide his salacious activities.

It took years for the scandal to be forgotten, and during that time, Edward James Bellamy was passed over for promotions. His prospects in politics plummeted. He told anyone who would listen how he was the victim of a liberal smear campaign, never once holding himself responsible for the position he now found himself in. Instead, he blamed my brother whose only crime had been the misfortune of not dying alongside his forsaken mother.

I can do little but gape in shock at the tale Adam tells of the horrors that happened in that gaudy, evil mansion prior to my reckoning. My brother explains that he was not the only victim of my father's hate and ambition—that my mother suffered tenfold what he had over the years. He doesn't tell me specifics, and honestly, I don't know that I could handle them right now.

I feel terrible for all the years I held my mother in contempt for not being a doting parent when under the circumstances there was no way she could have been. The look on Adam's face tells me that she had felt no choice but to lose herself in a haze of pills and alcohol. I wonder if I had experienced the same level of abuse at Ryan's hands, would I have been doomed to share her fate?

When I was born eight years later, my father sent Adam off to a military boarding school across the country, only coming home for major holidays and occasional summers. He was never asked if he wanted a career in the armed forces—it was a given that he would follow in my father's footsteps. Blessedly, the only way my brother emulated him was in his ability as an excellent soldier.

After graduating at the top of his class at Annapolis, it wasn't long before his brilliance was rewarded. For years he dreamed of becoming a fighter pilot, and his hard work paid off and his dream came true. He figured now his father would have to at least respect him. Right?

Wrong.

Even as a highly decorated Navy pilot, my father never once recognized his achievements. The only reason I knew about his many commendations was in my required daily reading of *The New State Press*.

"I had a job and I did it well, but unlike most of my fellow soldiers, I had a problem with the direction our country was heading. Then there was the war. The things we were ordered to do in the name of New Nationalism—they destroyed me. I wasn't the only one. I think many of us had at least some degree of moral issue with what we were told to do, not that any of us ever discussed it. Well, at least not when we were sober. When we were on leave, the amount of drugs and alcohol we took to cope with what we were forced to do was staggering. When we were so wasted we could barely stand, we often let things slip that would have been safest left unsaid."

That's where Adam made his biggest mistake. With the last name of Bellamy, his every word and deed were watched, notated, and reported. It was those alcohol-fueled confessions coupled with an overabundance of conscience that would eventually be his undoing.

When on leave one weekend, he came upon his own men gang-raping a young Hispanic girl that was no older than sixteen years-old. The soldiers were all drunk and horny, and when they saw Adam, their superior officer, they didn't back off and run. No. They offered him the next "turn" with the traumatized child.

He looks so sad as he continues his story, his disappointment in his crew, the men he considered his friends, his *brothers*, evident in the deep pain hazing his eyes. He ordered his men off the girl and told her to run, his crew beyond pissed that Adam spoiled their fun.

"My second-in-command, a guy I had always considered a friend, tried to calm me down. He swore the obviously non-consenting girl had begged for it. I honestly don't know what happened, Emma. It was like I blacked out. The next thing I know, his blood's all over my hands and he's lying on the ground. He wasn't breathing. I freaked out and ran back to the barracks and threw myself on the mercy of my commanding officer."

Luckily, the guy he beat to a pulp didn't die, but over the next few days, rumors about Adam's lack of fitness to command ran rampant. Some cadet he never heard of swore under oath that Adam forced him into homosexual relations. During the ensuing investigation, a few men under Adam's direct command reported he had shown sympathy to the rebel cause on multiple occasions.

"I was doomed. Subversion, Homosexuality and Treason, the trifecta that leads straight to the firing squad. There would be no trial. There needed to be no proof. I was going to be found guilty with no chance to prove my innocence."

Adam's commanding officer knew the only thing my brother was truly guilty of was having a huge heart. He even went so far as to call our father, who was the Governor by now, and begged him to intervene. But the last thing our father wanted was another scandal, especially now that his career was on an upswing. He told Adam's CO to do whatever it took to make the problem disappear, but I could tell by the look on my brother's face that what my father had actually said was to make *him* disappear. Permanently.

My brother looks out the window, a strange, far-away expression on his face.

"*As flies to wanton boys are we to the Gods. They kill us for our sport,*" he whispers with a sigh. He's silent for a moment, lost in thought. I imagine he's pondering the unfairness of life, of having a father as cruelly disinterested in his welfare as wicked children who pluck the wings from insects for fun. The line from *King Lear* fits his sad story as if it had been written explicitly for him.

Until this moment, I never saw the similarities of our lives to tales from the past—the truths of stories written so long ago as frighteningly valid today as when they were written. Adam had warned me when I was just a child to protect the written past, and at the time, I took his words literally. But he really meant so much more—that I need to hold these truths in my heart, to live my life as he has, seeking what's good and right even when the rest of the world around us has been blinded by hate.

I reach forward, placing my hand on his forearm and give him a sad smile. *"When we are born, we cry that we are come to this great stage of fools."*

He turns to me, startled, before giving me a twisted, wry smile. "In all of Shakespeare's works, I always thought you were the most like Lear's youngest. *Fairest Cordelia, that art most rich, being poor; Most choice, forsaken; and most loved, despised.* So young and sweet, and truthful to a fault, your fatal flaw being you are too moral, too honest. It's destined to be your doom, just like it was mine."

"Do you really think we are doomed?"

He grimaces. "I think we are *the natural fools of fortune.*"

He pats my hand as I look at him quizzically. I want to ask him what he means, but he brushes off my questioning look, shaking his head and sighing heavily before continuing.

"I was a dead man walking. Needless to say, I couldn't stick around, so I packed a bag and ran. Desertion is probably the worst sin an active duty soldier can commit, but the way I saw it, I was dead either way. At least this way, I stood a shot of survival. The only reason I'm alive today is because my CO stuck his neck on the line to warn me. I owe him my life."

While passing a newsstand a few days later, Adam was shocked to find out he was dead. According to *The New State Press*, his plane had been shot down by rebels while performing a routine recon mission. Obviously, his body was never found. After a few months of aimless wandering and being close to death from starvation, he was taken in by a settlement of stragglers outside of Baltimore that turned out to be a resistance cell. He offered them his services the second they confided in him who they were.

"In their eyes, I was the perfect recruit. Single, no attachments, and presumed dead. I had a skill set they desperately needed and reliable strategic information I was willing to impart. They welcomed me with open arms. I never asked them for anything except that at some point, I wanted them to help me get my sister out if she ever was in serious danger. So, here I am."

He squeezes my hands, letting me know he's done.

It's so much to take in, so horrible a story, that I'm at a complete loss for words. The look of sorrow that lines his face proves how heavily his part in the regime still weighs on his broad shoulders. I want to tell him to not be so hard on himself, that he saw the truth and atoned for his mistakes, but I can't find the words that will make him believe me. In truth, I hold myself equally responsible for all the years I believed what I had been taught and have yet to find a way to absolve myself. I can't help but feel that somehow, I should have known better than to believe the lies I'd been spoon-fed since birth.

I wonder how many people are out there that feel like us but keep their regret bottled well within their minds and hearts? It's so much easier to turn a blind eye to one's mistakes than to find the strength to admit your errors. It's even harder to attempt to rectify them and make amends with those you have hurt. If it has taken us this long to see the error of our ways, how many decades will it take to reopen the minds of an entire brainwashed country?

A single tear rolls down Adam's cheek and he brushes it away quickly. I launch myself into his arms and hold him tight, losing myself in the comfort of the embrace I never dreamed I'd be blessed to feel again.

I think back to my eighth birthday, and how I wished on those burning candles for an escape. I remember my childish tears when I woke the next morning without a set of sprouted wings or even a simple map to a magical, peace-filled island. That was the day I stopped believing in wishes on stars and lucky four-leaf clovers, of the glittery dust of fairies and the existence of pots of gold at the rainbow's end. I stopped believing in miracles, thinking that if my prayer had gone unanswered, yet again, that I must be deeply unworthy and undeserving of even something as simple as having a birthday wish come true.

Looking back, I realize I never set a timeline or a due-by date for my miracle to occur. Children don't tend to think of the logistics of wishes, their heartfelt dreams revolving more on strong feelings and naivete. In the history of wishes on candles, precious few of significance have ever borne fruit, even fewer coming true in a timely manner.

I realize now that the wings of our magical transport were never meant to be feathered and the destination not a tropical fairyland. My youthful wish did not come true because it had been the wrong time. For *the stars above us govern our conditions,* and only Fate knows the date and time of our deliverance.

69

Declan

Adam decides to catch a few hours' shut eye on the sunny porch and I wander back into the cabin to find Emma staring into the dying embers, deep in her thoughts. I throw a few more logs on the fire before plopping down on the floor behind her, wrapping my arms around her waist.

"You okay?" I place my lips against her ear and give her a gentle kiss. She nods unconvincingly. She looks like every ounce of energy has been sapped from her body. "You look like you need a nap."

Emma doesn't move or respond. I stand and extend my hands to her. She grasps my fingers allowing me to lift her from the floor. I pick her up in my arms and carry her to the bed, placing her under the sheets and covering her.

"Sleep," I whisper. "You need some time to process things." She nods.

I turn to leave the room, but she stops me. "Declan, please, stay with me. I don't want to be alone."

She looks so sad and lost in the large bed my heart breaks. I slip off my jeans and get under the covers, trying to convey to my dick that it most certainly is not time to wake up and play. I pull my wife to me and she snuggles into my embrace. A few silent tears drip onto my chest and I tell her that things are going to be okay, to just rest. Her breathing slows and it isn't long before she's sound asleep in my arms.

70

I WAKE UP HOURS LATER, the sun already nearly set. I'm disoriented as if something suddenly woke me from a deep sleep. I hear it again, a loud frantic banging on the door. I pull on my jeans and grab my rifle just as the door flies open, nearly knocking the weapon out of my hands.

"You gotta go. Now," Ralph gasps. He'd obviously been running way too far and fast for a man of his years. "Adam's already gone ahead to get the plane ready. There's patrolmen on the property. I picked 'em up on the trail cams. If you run, you can still make it."

Shit.

I run into the bedroom where Emma's already pulling on her pants, fastening the buckle on her leather belt, my father's knife attached firmly to her hip.

Where the hell did she get that?

As she stomps her feet into her boots I grab my jacket and throw it on over my bare chest, motioning for Emma to leave my shirt on. I know we don't have a second to waste when we hear the sounds of dogs in the near distance. I sling the rifle over my shoulder while listening intently to the directions Ralph gives us to find the runway in the rapidly darkening woods.

We set off fast. The woods echo, making it impossible to know how close the patrolmen are. Ralph stays at the cabin, hoping to buy us some additional time. Although we both know that's a really bad idea, he insists this will give us our best shot at escape.

The terrain is steep and rocky, every step an opportunity for disaster. Something as stupid as a twisted ankle would get us killed right now. We can't afford a second of lost time. The patrolmen are gaining on us. We now hear voices among the barks and howls of the hounds that have picked up our scent. We hear gunshots and Emma shrieks, turning her head back to me, her eyes wide and terrified. We both know what those shots mean.

Ralph is dead.

"Go!" I hiss at her as we find our first landmark, an old rusted gate where we make a hard right to follow the stream to the field below. Recent heavy rains make the terrain treacherous and deep and we slide and stumble our way down the forty degree pitch. I hear them getting closer and I look back up the mountain. To my horror, I realize that once they crest the ridge, they will have a clear shot at us and they sound like they're less than a hundred yards behind. I keep myself directly behind Emma, shielding her with my body. I'm fully prepared to protect her with my life.

We make it almost halfway down the slope when the first shots ring out. There's a second of searing pain as I stumble to my knees, but I get up and force myself to run.

They're right behind us now. I see the red laser dot of a scope as it targets Emma's back. I sprint the few steps towards her, pushing her away as a second bullet rips into me. The momentum spins me and I fall hard. Emma shuffles to a sliding stop and turns to find me writhing on the ground.

"Declan!" she screams, as she runs the few short steps to me. "Please, please get up!" she sobs, grabbing my arm, dragging me to my feet. She wraps her arm around my waist, supporting me. I know she feels the blood coursing down my bare skin when her look of fear turns to one of terror.

I knew the first shot wasn't fatal. I'm not so sure about the second.

"Emma, please, go on without me."

"No." Her voice is hard and determined. "I'm not leaving you behind."

I'm slowing her down and we're going to get caught. I feel them closing in on us, the labored breathing of the dogs straining against their leashes almost palpable against my cooling skin. I'm losing too much blood. Without some form of divine intervention, I'm not going to make it.

"Please, Emma, think of the baby. Leave me," I beg her again between gasps for breath. It's getting harder and harder to breathe, my lungs feeling like they're working in fits and starts. No matter how I plead, she refuses to listen. We stagger around another bend in the trail that momentarily shields us from the patrol's hungry weapons. Seventy-five yards ahead of us a figure looms into sight and we both gasp in fright at the man running towards us with his weapon drawn. It takes a few seconds for Emma to recognize it's Adam.

"Adam, he's been shot. Help me," Emma calls out to him, her voice choking with fear.

Adam continues to climb the steep slope towards us, sliding in the deep mud. "Emma, my orders are to get you out of here. *You* have to come with me now."

"No." Her voice is determined. "I'm not leaving without him. He's hurt, he needs help and if they find him they will kill him. They won't shoot me. They can't. Father wants me back alive for some reason. Don't argue with me and just fucking help him!"

My body is quickly shutting down and I won't be conscious much longer. I want to tell her to save herself, that it doesn't matter, I will soon be dead. I whisper to her I love her, but my voice is barely audible even to myself.

Then, I feel something about her change. She's made some choice, some decision. She's scaring me with this new, cool bravery she has pulled over herself like a thick cloak. Emma grabs my jacket and pulls me tight to her, kissing me fiercely. She slides her arms under my jacket where my chest is slick with blood.

I taste her lips one last time, knowing this is farewell. She whispers that she loves me, to keep fighting, to stay alive and come back for her, for our baby. Before I can do or say anything else, she tears her lips from mine and pushes me down the side of the mountain as hard as she can. I sprawl down the slick slope, too weak to do anything but let gravity take me as an unwilling victim. Adam nearly topples over when I crash into him. He sees I'm failing fast. He gives Emma one last imploring look before she turns away and starts running back up the mountain.

71

Emma

I know what I have to do.

My job is to buy them enough time to get to the plane. Declan's life is hanging by a thread and if I fail at my task, he will die. Tears cloud my vision before falling in torrents from my eyes.

We were so close.

I see the tiny red lights of rifle sights bouncing off the trees and rocks, and I know the patrolmen have me within their range. I say a quick prayer for Declan, for Adam, for my baby and for the success of my admittedly hair-brained scheme. When I'm less than a hundred feet from my pursuers, I dive to my knees on the cold muddy slope, the dead leaves rustling like so many discarded swan feathers under my knees. I take the knife from its scabbard and hold the blade to my neck, piercing the skin just enough to start a steady trickle of blood.

I pray that by now Adam and Declan have reached the plane. I don't know how long I'll be able to hold the patrolmen off. When the patrolmen get within fifty feet, one turns on a high powered light, blinding me.

"It's her!"

Okay, Emma, it's showtime. Let's see how brave you really are.

My voice comes out cold and steady with a deadly edge tinging each word. "Stop right where you are. If you come one step closer, I swear to Christ, I'll slit my throat."

For good measure, I pull the blade another inch across my flesh, causing the blood to flow faster. As my eyes adjust to the blinding light, I look down at my damp, shivering body. I thought the clamminess that stuck my soaked shirt to my skin had been sweat, but to my horror, I see that I'm covered in Declan's blood.

Oh, God, no. Please, please Lord, do not let him die.

The troops are upon me. One patrolman tries to slip past me to follow Adam and Declan despite my warning. He slides noisily on the mucky leaves alerting me to his presence.

"Asshole, do I look like I'm fucking kidding to you?" He looks at me in surprise, backing up quickly to join the others. "If one more of you tries to get past me, I swear to God, I'll slit my throat from ear to ear."

I'm oddly calm, my voice deep and hard. I detach from the moment, from the heartache, the pain, the anger and sadness. I feel that strange sensation again, like I'm watching a movie of my own life. I don't feel like me. In fact, the only feeling I have is the unwavering understanding I'm doing the right thing.

I wonder if everyone feels this way before they're going to die?

The patrolmen stop, their weapons trained on my chest, their dogs snarling and snapping at my face. We stand at an impasse for what seems like forever as I mentally beg Adam to get that plane in the air. It seems like an eternity, but I finally detect the engines starting to strain as the plane begins to bump down the grassy runway. I close my eyes and say a quick prayer of thanks. They're going to get away. A few seconds later, I see the lights on the plane as it climbs slowly into the air. I bought them the time they needed. Adam and Declan are safe.

The head patrolman is livid that I outsmarted him. He can't believe that I helped the two men that matter most in my life escape by sacrificing myself.

He knows nothing about love.

"Some friends," he sneers. "They actually left without you."

I'm suddenly outraged, my feeling of detachment gone in the blink of an eye. My mind and body reunite, jolting me securely back into reality. I don't have the luxury of allowing myself to fall apart right now.

"They will come back for me," I spit furiously. "And when they do, you are all dead men." I smile at him, the grin on my lips a sharp contrast to the daggers in my eyes. I feel myself calming further, my heart rate slowing, my breath steadying.

I am no longer afraid. I no longer wish to die. I'm going to fight and claw, and do whatever and say whatever's necessary to survive and I'm not going to quit until I find my way back into my husband's arms.

I remember, in what seems like a lifetime ago, Declan once said that love only makes you weak.

No, my love—no, that's not true.

I wish I could have said one last thing to my beloved before our time ran out.

My darling, love hasn't made me weak. It's love, your love, that has made me strong.

With that final thought, I look up into the sky at the plane now far off in the distance. I pull the bloody blade from my throat and drop it in the grass. The patrolmen quickly surround me, their weapons aimed at my breaking heart.

I stare them down as if I'm the one in control, as if I'm the one that holds all the power, as I all but dare them to take me into custody. There is not a trace of weakness in me as I audaciously tip up my chin and look down at them through mutinous, undaunted eyes. I raise my hands in the air as I surrender myself, the gesture not one of bitter defeat, but of brazen defiance.

To Be Continued...

ACKNOWLEDGEMENTS

AS A DEBUT NOVELIST, I went into this project with a head full of ideas, a heart full of emotion and little clue how to pull it all together. There have been so many drafts of this novel I lost count over a year ago, but with the help of the following uber-patient souls, I finally have in my hands something I never dreamed I'd be able to create.

First off, I must thank my mentor, my editor and dear friend David Hazard, who took me under his wing and made this manuscript so much more than I could have dreamed. Your unwavering belief in my story and in my ability to write well enough to pull off such a massive undertaking was often the only reason I kept going, especially when things got rough. I couldn't have done this without you.

Another enormous thank you to my dear friend, Linda Vacaro Treese, for encouraging me when I first called her and said, "So, I've written something and I need you to read it and let me know if it's crap. . . or not." Your support during those early weeks was immeasurably important, and I treasure your input every bit as much as our friendship.

To my darling beta readers, many who have read multiple versions and given me fabulous feedback, you helped me more than you can imagine. You all have very specific talents and backgrounds where your expertise was immeasurable in creating a well-rounded emotionally and factually correct novel. Many thanks to Nichole Aiken and Alexandra Ranieri-Deniken for their psychological insights, to Scott Judd for my frequent and often odd medical questions, and to Wendy Zajack Lipshultz for her sociological input. Alyssa Moody, Kira Smith, Kim Rodriguez, Lisa Johnson and Victoria Lincoln-Davis, your input, ideas and encouragement are phenomenal, and I'm so glad you are all part of my team.

Lastly, but most certainly not least, many, many thanks to my beloved husband for his unwavering love and support. I absolutely could not have done this without you.

ABOUT THE AUTHOR

THE IDEA FOR The Governor's Daughter came to me in a nightmare.

In September 2018, after watching the media coverage for the Senate confirmation hearings for Brett Kavanaugh, I was in a terribly dark place—I couldn't eat, couldn't sleep, couldn't do anything but chew my nails and watch TV in horror. As Dr. Christine Blasy Ford's testimony was picked apart by a prosecutor and a panel of very white and very powerful men, I grew more and more agitated with each of their ridiculous questions, disbelieving comments, and thinly-veiled accusations.

Of course, we all know now how this would end. Despite everyone agreeing that she was an exceptionally credible witness, the vote to confirm mostly went along party lines and Dr. Ford's moving testimony was disregarded.

I was furious. In my opinion, justice was not done, the bad guy won, and Dr. Ford was victimized. Again.

The experience also brought back traumatic memories of a time, decades ago, when I came forward with my own truth and was harshly silenced. As long-suppressed images and words from that time resurfaced, I realized the pain I thought I'd long ago put to bed had actually gone nowhere. The demons of my past were back and demanding to be dealt with, even though the last thing I wanted was to reopen old wounds. I fought against revisiting my trauma, but my mind wouldn't obey.

I've always had sort of a hard-on for justice, and it doesn't take a PhD in Psychology to figure where that tendency comes from. The day I came forward with my painful truth only to be warned what would happen to me with the accusations I brought had shocked me to my core. I was the victim, and I was being treated like the guilty party. Ever since the moment I gave in to those terrifying warnings, I have regretted my decision to let them silence me.

I swore to myself that I would never allow anyone to silence my truth again.

As most people do, I've grown braver with age. I am far from the terrified and easily manipulated young woman who was told to shut her mouth and get on with her life. If I was the person then who I am now, you better believe that part of my story would have a very different outcome.

But this was not the only issue troubling me during those Senate hearings. The press was filled with pictures of children in cages and stories of separated families. Margaret Atwood's *The Handmaid's Tale* was back on the bestseller's list as people likened our reality to the oppressive world depicted in her masterful fiction. Funding for Planned Parenthood was in jeopardy and there were grave concerns that Roe vs. Wade would be overturned. Voter suppression was just beginning to become an issue, the more damning evidence of its pervasiveness not to be revealed until after the 2018 midterm election. The President's rabid need for an unnecessary wall between the U.S.

and Mexico was all over the news, as was the devastation left in the wake of Hurricane Florence. Just like after past disasters, the hardest hit lived in the poorest economic areas where help always appears both too little and too late.

For weeks, I couldn't stop thinking about truth, justice, and freedom, and how the definitions of these have always been different for people depending on their race, gender and sexual orientation even within our own "evolved" nation. I began to envision what our future would look like if we failed to get ourselves back on the right track.

In truth, it took little imagination. All I had to do was watch the news each night and imagine the worst case scenario.

Then one night my subconscious put all the pieces together and I had the most terrifying dream. *The Governor's Daughter* was born.

I worried as the manuscript came together. I stressed over what people would think about the story, about me, about these characters that I love more and more every day. I worried my storytelling wouldn't do them justice, that I'm not a good enough writer, or have a vivid enough imagination. I fretted over the fact over 70 million people are going to have issues with my book based on my politics, alone.

I worried *I* wasn't enough. Despite my adamant proclamation to never again allow myself to be silenced, I found myself wanting to crawl into bed and hide under the covers.

With the help of my amazingly supportive husband, my genius writing coach and my most perspicacious friends, I realized I was once again letting fear dictate my life. My woulda, coulda, shouldas were reproducing with my insecurities and creating an entire infestation of biting baby doubts. My inner critic was setting my manuscript on fire and dancing around it, while the judge inside of me was demanding I abort this project immediately and go back to reporting and ghostwriting where I belonged.

Then I realized—If I scrapped this project, I'd once again be hiding my truth.

I had sworn to myself I would never do that again.

So, yeah, here we are.

My dear reader, I thank you for taking the chance on a debut novelist. I thank you even more for braving the darkness and seeing my beloved characters through their journey. Most of all, if you can find your own truth in these pages and maybe find yourself standing a little taller, a little braver, in the end, I will know I have indeed completed what I set out to do.

—Maria Ereni Dampman